PENGUIN BOOKS

THINGS I WANTED TO SAY
(BUT NEVER DID)

Monica Murphy is a *New York Times, USA Today* and international bestselling author. Her books have been translated into almost a dozen languages and have sold over two million copies worldwide. Both a traditionally published and independently published author, she writes young adult and new adult romance, as well as contemporary romance and women's fiction. She's also known as *USA Today* bestselling author Karen Erickson.

ALSO BY MONICA MURPHY

Coming Soon

Playing Hard to Get

Lancaster Prep

Things I Wanted To Say (but
never did)
A Million Kisses in Your
Lifetime
Promises We Meant to Keep

Wedded Bliss

The Reluctant Bride
The Ruthless Groom
The Reckless Union

College Years

The Freshman
The Sophomore
The Junior
The Senior

Dating Series

Save The Date
Fake Date

Holidate

Hate to Date You
Rate A Date
Wedding Date
Blind Date

The Callahans

Close to Me
Falling For Her
Addicted To Him
Meant To Be
Fighting For You
Making Her Mine
A Callahan Wedding

Forever Yours Series

You Promised Me
Forever
Thinking About You
Nothing Without You

Damaged Hearts Series

Her Defiant Heart
His Wasted Heart
Damaged Hearts

Friends Series

Just Friends
More Than Friends
Forever

The Never Duet

Never Tear Us Apart
Never Let You Go

The Rules Series

Fair Game
In The Dark
Slow Play
Safe Bet

The Fowler Sisters Series

Owning Violet
Stealing Rose
Taming Lily

Reverie Series

His Reverie
Her Destiny

Billionaire Bachelors Club Series

Crave
Torn
Savor
Intoxicated

One Week Girlfriend Series

One Week Girlfriend
Second Chance Boyfriend
Three Broken Promises
Drew + Fable Forever
Four Years Later
Five Days Until You
A Drew + Fable Christmas

Standalone YA Titles

Daring The Bad Boy
Saving It
Pretty Dead Girls

THINGS I WANTED TO SAY
(BUT NEVER DID)

MONICA MURPHY

PENGUIN BOOKS

PENGUIN BOOKS

UK | USA | Canada | Ireland | Australia
India | New Zealand | South Africa

Penguin Books is part of the Penguin Random House group of companies
whose addresses can be found at global.penguinrandomhouse.com

Penguin
Random House
UK

First published in the United States of America by Monica Murphy 2021
First published in Great Britain by Penguin Books 2023

007

Cover design by Hang Le
Photography by Kevin Roldan
Edited by Rebecca, Fairest Reviews Editing Services
Proofread by Sarah, All Encompassing Books
Printed and bound in Great Britain by Clays Ltd, Elcograf S.p.A.

The authorized representative in the EEA is Penguin Random House Ireland,
Morrison Chambers, 32 Nassau Street, Dublin DO2 YH68

A CIP catalogue record for this book is available from the British Library

ISBN: 978–1–405–95741–0

www.greenpenguin.co.uk

Penguin Random House is committed to a
sustainable future for our business, our readers
and our planet. This book is made from Forest
Stewardship Council® certified paper.

PLAYLIST

"Champagne Coast" - Blood Orange
"Rebel (If I lie)" - Eli Rose
"Monster" - Shawn Mendes & Justin Bieber
"that way" - Tate McRae
"Bitter" - FLETCHER, Kito
"Streets" - Doja Cat
"Daddy Issues" - The Neighbourhood
"Miss Summer" - ODIE
"sex money feelings die" - Lykke Li

Find the rest of the **Things I Wanted To Say** playlist here:
https://spoti.fi/3x0pqf9

PROLOGUE

The past

I REMEMBER the first time I saw him.

He didn't notice me, which was what I preferred. That way, I could stare at him unabashedly, fascinated with the bone structure of his face, the way he moved, how he never smiled.

Why didn't he smile?

We were much younger then. Innocent? I don't think you could ever use that word to describe either of us. We'd seen and done too much, that by the time we met again, we were too far gone to stop it. Stop us.

And the darkness.

I accompanied my parents to a party in Manhattan. My mother didn't want to bring me. Jonas, my stepfather, insisted.

Let her see how the one percent really lives, he said with a chuckle.

Mother scowled. She likes to think she is part of the one percent, when Jonas says he merely works for them.

The building we walked into was on the Upper East Side, with friendly doormen and stern security everywhere. The lobby was constructed of glass and marble. Sleek and gleaming. I must've looked like a country bumpkin, my head tilted back and staring at the soaring ceiling, dazzled by the twinkling lights above us.

"Come on," Mother said irritably, her fingers clamped so tight around my upper arm, she pinched my skin.

The elevator ride was smooth. Quick. We arrived on the penthouse level, and the moment the doors slid open, it was as if we were stepping into another world. No one greeted us when we entered the penthouse. No one was actually *inside* the apartment either.

Everything was white. The furniture. The walls. Massive paintings hanging everywhere the only pops of color. Most of them were abstract. I stopped in front of one of them, tilting my head to the side, trying to figure out what it could be. Mother practically dragged me away from it, muttering under her breath that they shouldn't have such vulgar art on display in front of children, and Jonas only laughed, asking what kid could figure out what that was?

That was when it hit me—the painting was a close-up view of a vagina.

I could hear noises coming from somewhere though. As we drew deeper into the apartment, they grew louder, until a wall of windows appeared, beautiful people milling about, clustered in small groups. Talking, talking, talking. Drinking, drinking, drinking.

I was starstruck. Dazzled. This was the sort of thing I lived for. Mother marrying Jonas Weatherstone was life-changing. He made big money. Real money. Mother worked at Jonas' real estate company, and they fell in love. He left his wife for Mother. Their divorce was difficult but eventually Jonas and Mother were married. I liked living with Jonas. He was kind to me. Our apartment was big, though nothing like this one.

This one was unlike anything I'd ever seen.

As we stepped out onto the terrace, the skyscrapers loomed. They looked close enough to touch. The city lights glittered and twinkled, but I didn't notice. I was too busy stealing sips from discarded champagne glasses, the bubbly liquid tickling my throat and making me feel funny. I savored the funny feeling. It made my brain fuzzy, helped me forget all of my problems. Like my parents. My stepbrother.

All of it.

He spotted me sneaking drinks and quietly approached. I set the glass down, pretending to look at something else. We were the only two kids at this party. I was fourteen. I guessed he was about the same.

Summer before high school and I felt very grown-up. I had boobs and they were bigger than my friends'. I'd discovered that touching myself in a particular place while in bed at night sent me spiraling, and I chased that feeling as much as I could. Yates kept trying to get me alone when our parents were at work. One time, he slipped his hand down my pants, trying to touch me there, but I slapped him away.

He's disgusting. He's my brother.

Stepbrother, but still.

Despite my being disgusted, Yates's dogged pursuit of me also left me feeling wanted. And there's power in knowing that someone wants you. Sitting at this party in a strapless black dress, sipping champagne, also made me feel older. Having the attention of this boy, this very beautiful, intense boy, also had me curious.

Who is he? What does he want from me?

"You want your own glass?" the boy asks, pointing at the discarded glasses on the table beside me. I'd sipped every one of them dry.

I glance up to find him watching me. He's wearing black pants and a white button down, the sleeves rolled up and showing off his forearms. His hair is golden brown, almost but not quite dirty blond, and his face is stunning. Arrogant.

Perfect.

I rise to my feet and stand in front of him, reveling in the appreciation flaring in his ice blue eyes. "Yes, please."

I follow him to the bar. He speaks to the bartender and slips him a fifty-dollar bill while I stand there, duly impressed. He hands me the glass, and takes a can of beer, slipping it in his front pocket.

"You don't like champagne?" I ask him as I glance around, clutching the stem of the glass between pinched fingers. No one's paying any attention to us, so I take a sip.

Delicious.

"No," he says. "Besides, the cheap stuff gives me a headache."

I don't know the difference, so I take his word as gospel.

I also take what I can get, so I'm not about to turn down this free and very full glass of bubbly.

I follow him inside, the hushed quiet sending a shiver through me. Or maybe that's the air conditioning that's on full blast, I don't know. We walk deeper into the house, until we're in a dark hallway, where all the bedroom doors are closed.

"My father's in one of those rooms, fucking your mother," he says casually, right as I'm sipping from my glass.

I practically spit it all over his face. I gape at him, blinking. "What did you just say?"

His expression doesn't change a bit. "You heard me."

"My mother is *married*."

"So is my dad. Like that matters." He shrugs, then pulls the can of beer out of his pocket. He cracks it open, then slurps up the foam before taking a huge drink.

"She wouldn't do that." When he says nothing, I feel the need to clarify. "Fuck your father."

It feels very grown-up, saying that word to this boy while drinking champagne. I take another sip, letting the bubbles linger on my tongue.

"Well, she is. Your mom's a slut." He drains the beer can, then crushes it between his fingers, tossing it onto the ground so it lands in a loud clatter.

I'm suddenly furious. Mother and I don't always get along, but he doesn't even *know* her. "You can't say that."

"Oh yeah? Well, I just did." He cocks his head, his gaze narrowed. So much anger there. And he's so young. I get angry sometimes, but nothing like this. "Are you a slut too? Like your mom?"

"Fuck you," I spit at him, flinging the champagne in his face.

He winces, slowly wiping his face off with his hand. I stand there, breathing hard, knowing I should go, but I'm too fascinated, watching this unfold.

Watching him.

It's like it's not even happening to me. And I've never done anything like that before in my life. Who am I? When did I get so brave? Or stupid?

"You're a bitch," he hisses. "Just like your mom."

"You're an asshole," I return, about to turn on my heel and walk away from him, but he grabs me.

Stops me.

His fingers sink into my flesh, his grip extra tight on my upper arm and I struggle against his hold, trying to get rid of him. "Let me go."

"No." He smirks, and I idly realize he's the devil hiding behind an angel baby's face. He shoves me against the wall and I fall against it like a rag doll, nearly sliding to the floor. He grabs hold of me before I land, yanking me up, and presses his body against mine. He towers over me, at least six feet tall, but he's lean. Skinny. Yates is broader. Meatier. But he's sixteen. Older.

This boy is just that.

Still a boy.

"What are you doing?" I ask as I struggle against him. Doing so makes me feel him and I'm intrigued. He's hard everywhere. Solid. Stronger than he looks.

"I think you like it." The smirk is still there and when he presses his lower body against me, I can feel something else.

He's got a hard-on.

I go completely still, unable to move.

"Your mom sucks my dad off at least twice a week," he whispers. "She meets him in his office. They call it lunch."

I gape at him. I have no idea what he's talking about. I mean, I know what he's referring to, but there's no way she does that.

No. Way.

"You have dick sucking lips," he tells me, and I almost bloom under the compliment, before I tell myself I'm sick and messed up, and he meant it as an insult.

"Shut up," I whisper, and he smiles.

"Want to suck mine?"

"Absolutely not." I tilt my chin, sounding like a haughty princess.

What would it be like, sucking a boy's dick? Girls do it. All the time. I found a magazine in Yates's room once, and snuck it back into mine. Photos of naked girls. Couples caught in mid-position. His penis inside her vagina. His mouth on her nipples. His penis inside her mouth as she stares up at him, doe-eyed and with her fingers between her legs.

I think of that now and heady warmth unfurls deep within me, making me weak.

Or maybe that's the champagne.

"You might like it," he says with the faintest smile. His teeth are perfectly straight. I bet when he really smiles, he's beautiful.

Pretty sure he doesn't smile much though.

"I won't," I tell him firmly.

"Ever done it before?"

I furiously shake my head.

"Let me be your first."

"No." I shove at his shoulders, but he doesn't budge.

"Come on. Your mom is my dad's whore. You could be mine too." He inclines his head toward the closed doors in the darkened hallway. "Like I said, they're in one of those rooms right now. I bet your mom is on her knees for him." He sneers. "I bet she swallows every drop of my dad's cum. You could do the same for me."

"Fuck you." His words are infuriating but also the faintest bit tantalizing. I've never thought of cum and swallowing and dicks in my mouth while talking to a boy. No one has ever spoken to me like this before.

No one.

He laughs. "No, fuck *you*. Your family is fucked up."

"Uh, I think it's your family that's fucked up," I tell him, thrusting my hips against his to get him off me.

It doesn't help at all. Just reminds me that he's hard. And I can't help but think that he's hard for me.

I have friends who've had sex already. Lana did it with David in the gym during our eighth-grade graduation dance. She told us later she walked funny for a week, his dick was so big. I had a hard time believing her, but said nothing.

Now I'm curious. This boy's dick seems large, not that I have much to compare it to. I want to see it.

Touch it.

"Let me go," I say through clenched teeth, struggling a little. I think he likes it. I sort of like it too. His strength. How I'm too weak to break free. What does this say about me? I'm sick. Twisted. Weird.

I've always had what I call 'the darkness.' I've never met someone who acts like he has it too.

He leans in close, his mouth mere inches from mine, and I can feel his breath. It's warm, and smells faintly of beer. "Make me."

Going on pure instinct, I part my lips, readying to scream, and he knows it.

So he kisses me instead.

It's harsh, a shock to the system, and I go completely still. His lips mash against mine, lacking skill, though I'm not particularly skilled either. But I know it can be better than this. Softer than this.

I purse my lips around his lower one, tugging on it. He slows. Relaxes. The kiss turns languid. His tongue darts out, surprising me. I part my lips, and his tongue touches mine.

My first grown-up kiss is with a boy who calls my mother a whore. Who said I could be his whore. I should shove him away. Bite his tongue in half. Knee him in the balls.

I don't do any of that. Instead, I let him kiss me, and God help me, I enjoy it. Warmth spreads through my veins, warming me from the inside out, and I cling to him. His hands are on my waist. I clutch the front of his shirt. His erection jerks against me, and that secret spot I've recently discovered tingles.

This is what Yates wants from me. The disgusting pervert. I will never give this to him, because we're family, and that's gross.

But the more this mystery boy kisses me, the more I'm willing to consider giving him whatever he wants.

We kiss for so long I don't know how we're able to breathe. Finally, *finally*, he ends it first and I open my eyes, staring at his parted, swollen lips. Slowly I lift my gaze to find him watching me.

He reaches for the hem of my skirt, his fingers shooting beneath it to touch the inside of my thigh and I bite my lower lip. "Are you wet?"

"What are you talking about?" I know, but he's so freaking young. Like me. We know sex is happening. We have access to all the porn on the internet, but still.

He talks to me like an adult. The boys I know won't even touch my boobs, and this guy is going straight to the spot between my legs.

"Like you don't know." He sounds disgusted, and I'm about to say something, a protest. An insult.

But he kisses me again, making me forget. This one is better. I guess I taught him well. It's slow and soft, the drag of his tongue against mine making me ache. He explores my mouth thoroughly, testing me, and I let him. I explore too. Our mouths are open, our tongues teasing, licking at each other, and my entire body tingles with anticipation. Somehow I touch him, my hand on the front of his pants, and he thrusts against my palm, letting me feel how hard he is.

I throb between my thighs and I want to touch myself.

No.

I want *him* to touch *me*.

"I don't even know you," I whisper against his lips.

He pulls away with an evil smile. "Liar."

"I don't." I'm confused. Why would he think I'm lying about that?

"You're at my house. My father is one of the richest men in the entire fucking world. 'Oh, I don't even know you.'" He's mocking me, his voice high-pitched. He sounds ridiculous.

Anger fills me. After what just happened, he makes fun of me? I don't care how good of a kisser he turned into, he's an asshole.

"Get away from me." I shove him off of me and this time, he staggers backward, letting me go. I stalk off, nearly tripping over the discarded champagne glass. I must've dropped it when we struggled earlier.

I don't even remember that happening.

He calls after me, but I ignore him, running as fast as I can on shaky legs. I push my way out of the house, back onto the terrace, searching for my mother. My stepfather, who's basically like a father to me. But they're both nowhere in sight.

I hear the boy. He says my name, though I never told him what it was. Panicked, I glance around, scared he's going to grab me, bracing myself when I feel a hand clamp around my shoulder but...

I turn around to find it's my mother.

"Summer! What are you doing? You look petrified."

Relief floods me. She's not locked away in a room fucking another man; she's out here. With me. At the party.

"Mother." I throw myself at her, hugging her waist tight and she laughs, sounding surprised. We've been fighting nonstop since eighth grade ended. All of my friends are going to high school at Lancaster Prep, and that's where I want to go too. I'm desperate to go there.

Jonas says no. He wants me going to St. Anthony's like he did. In the city. It's a good school and all, but I'll be lonely. My friends will be having fun in boarding school and I'll be stuck here.

Alone. With Yates, who'll be a junior. Our parents travel together all the time, leaving us alone, and Yates will be relentless. He'll wear me down, until finally I'll give in to him.

"Honey, what's wrong? You're shaking." She runs her hand up and down my back, soothing me, and I'm struck with the fear that this is the last time she'll do this. Believe me sweet and innocent. It's like a piece of me was stolen tonight, and that boy claimed it with his lips and tongue and wandering hands.

I try to laugh and pull away from her, desperate to play it off. "I'm fine. Really. I just thought—I'd lost you."

"Your cheeks are extra pink." She frowns, cupping my face. "You haven't been drinking, have you?"

I try my best to look innocent. "*No*, Mom. God. Of course not."

"Good." That was way too easy. I can't believe she took my word for it. "Stay away from the champagne. I know how much you like to sneak sips."

My cheeks heat even more.

Now it's her turn to glance around, and I study her. Really study her.

Her cheeks are flushed too. Her hair is a mess in the back, like she needs to run a brush through it. One of her earrings is missing. And the dress she's wearing, it's all crooked and rumpled. Like she needs to readjust it.

Oh no.

She looks like how I feel. Though I didn't have sex with that boy, I did let him kiss me, and I sort of lost myself for a moment.

Mother looks like she lost herself for at least a half hour. Maybe longer.

"Where were you?" I ask, my tone accusing.

"I've been out here the entire time." Her gaze meets mine once more, her freshly glossed lips curled into a frown. "Where were you?"

"Right here. The whole time." I glance over my shoulder to find the boy standing there, watching us. A man stands behind him, the older version of the boy. He's extremely handsome, with an air about him that says he owns everything. The boy is watching me.

The man is watching my mother.

The boy raises his brows, tilting his head in my direction. I turn away from him, not wanting to see the smug satisfaction on his stupidly handsome face. He knows I figured it out. He already had figured it out.

And damn him, he was right.

ONE

SUMMER

SENIOR YEAR

I WALK the hallowed halls of Lancaster Prep, my head ducked down, studying my feet as I place one in front of the other. Again and again and again. My shiny new penny loafers pinch my feet and the wool of my green and navy plaid skirt is itchy against my thighs. I remember wanting to come here so badly the summer before my freshman year, and how angry I was that my parents wouldn't pay the tremendous amount of money it cost to go to Lancaster.

Now I'm here, for one year only. My final year in high school. It's late August, and while the air is cool, thanks to the ocean breeze outside, it's stifling in this old building with the beautiful wood paneling and the horribly outdated cooling system. Do they even have central heat and air in this place?

Probably not.

"Come on," Mother says through her teeth, snapping her fingers at her waist to get me to walk beside her.

I hurry my steps, keeping pace with her, lifting my head to see other students pass by us with curious expressions on their faces, their gazes taking in the familiar Lancaster uniform that I'm wearing.

A new girl. A transfer. I'm sure they'll be curious. I'm sure they'll Google my name, and find out my family scandal.

I came out mostly unscathed. Mother made sure of that. She wasn't about to let my future crumble. She knows people, and she used that power to ensure that I would be protected.

That's why I'm here, at Lancaster Prep. The most elite boarding school on the east coast. Founded by one of the richest, oldest families in the country. The Lancasters go way back, to the time of the Vanderbilts, the Astors and the Rockefellers. Their money is so old, most don't know exactly where it originally came from.

Like me. I've heard maybe shipping? Oil? Bought up all available land on the east coast and then sold it over the years. I don't know. I don't really care. I just know they're filthy rich.

And for years, my mother, my prim and proper mother, was having a raging affair with Augustus Lancaster the fifth.

"Here we are," Mother singsongs, and I can hear the slight tremble in her voice. She's nervous for me, and I stand taller, wanting to prove to her that I'm not scared. "The admissions office."

She opens the door and I enter first, smiling at the older woman sitting behind the high wooden counter. She rises slowly to her feet, clad in a navy skirt suit, the jacket barely able to come around her ample bustline.

"Good morning!" The woman smiles at my mother before her gaze lands on me. "You must be Summer Savage," she says with an overly friendly smile.

"I'm her mother, Janine Weatherstone." She always holds out her hand in a way that makes it seem like she's a queen greeting her loyal subjects. I can tell this doesn't impress the woman whatsoever, but she takes her hand anyway, weakly shaking the tips of her fingers.

"Lovely to meet you. We're so glad to have Summer here for her senior year." The woman's expression grows solemn. "Such a tragedy, what happened. I'm sorry for your loss."

Mother glares. That is the last thing she wants to talk about, especially with a stranger. "Thank you," she says crisply. "Is Mr. Matthews available?"

The woman stands up straight. "Of course! I thought you'd want Summer's schedule so she can get going. First period has already started, I'm afraid." She casts me a look of judgment. Like it's my fault I'm late.

I can't help it that it took Mother forever to pack her things and leave the hotel room, complaining the entire time that she didn't get enough sleep. I, on the other hand, have been up since six, too anxious to sleep.

"Yes, please give us her schedule," Mother demands. "And we need to talk to Mr. Matthews first before she goes to class. I'm sure he'll write her an excuse."

"Of course." The woman—she must be the headmaster's secretary—hands over a pale pink slip to me. Mother snatches it out of her grip, glancing over my list of classes, and I stand there, anxiously awaiting a glimpse.

"She wasn't put in honors English," Mother says, shoving the schedule in my direction, her irritation clear.

Disappointment fills me as I scan the list. Senior English. World Religions. Math. Advanced French. There's a free period listed right after lunch, and American Government is my last class. "I'm okay with this schedule," I tell Mother, but her lips thin and she shakes her head.

"You're an excellent writer, Summer. Always scribbling in those journals of yours," Mother says. Her voice is low, but I see the way the secretary perks up.

My cheeks color and I shrug. "It's nothing. Please don't change the schedule. I'll be fine."

"Let's have you go into Headmaster Matthews' office and you can wait for him in there," the woman says, waving toward a partially open door behind her. "He's on campus right now but I'll let him know you're waiting. He'll be right in."

I follow Mother into the cramped office, the both of us settling into the chairs facing the giant, ornate desk as the secretary shuts the door with a quiet click. The moment Mother knows we're alone, she turns on me, her scowl obvious.

"What do you mean, you don't want honors English?" she hisses.

"I don't want to cause any trouble." I've become a mere shadow of myself since the accident happened, not wanting to draw attention. "It's enough already, don't you think? That you were able to pull some strings to get me in here."

"It's the least I could do, considering how long I've known Augie," Mother mutters, referring to her former lover.

The one who ended up divorcing his wife, thanks to my mother's years-long affair with her husband. It was a huge scandal. One splashed all over the internet and tabloids. It broke my stepfather's heart. And then it enraged him.

It was not a pleasant experience.

The door suddenly creaks open and in walks a handsome older man. Headmaster Matthews, I assume. He smiles at us, his dark eyes crinkling in the corners, his grin wide, showing off dazzling white teeth. He shuts the door and moves so he's standing behind his desk as some sort of barrier, and holds his hand out to Mother first.

"Mrs. Weatherstone, an absolute pleasure to meet you," he says, his voice smooth, his expression pleasant.

She rises to her feet and gives his hand a quick shake. "Thank you for meeting with us, Mr. Matthews."

They both settle in their chairs, smiling at each other and I blink at the two of them. It's almost as if they've forgotten all about me.

"This is Summer," Mother says, indicating me with a tilt of her head.

"Summer, we are so glad to have you here, attending our prestigious school," Mr. Matthews says, his voice warm and sincere. "I've personally looked over your transcripts, and I'm most impressed with your classes. And your grades."

"Thank you." I'm a good student. A little out of control in my earlier years and a little boy crazy, but I've always got good grades.

"You had some trouble early on though," he continues, his gaze meeting mine. "I assume you've straightened up since then?"

I stiffen my spine, nodding. "Yes, sir."

"She's not enrolled in honors English," Mother says, and I glare at her. She ignores me. "Summer is an excellent writer. She was on the newspaper staff at her previous school. She's won awards for her writing. It's exceptional."

"Ah, I'm afraid getting into the senior honors English class here at Lancaster is a privilege, not a right. The students in Mr. Figueroa's class have worked hard the last three years. He handpicks them at the end of their junior year, and there's only twenty in the class." Mr. Matthews rests his forearms on top of his desk, his hands clasped. "I'm afraid I can't just enroll Summer without his consent."

"Maybe you could talk to him." Mother's voice is lilting. Pleasant.

His smile never falters. "I'm afraid not."

"Maybe you could extend a favor my way." Her voice becomes a little sterner.

"It's Figueroa's class, not mine."

Her smile is gone. "Maybe I can reach out to Mr. Lancaster and see what he could do for me."

I want to die. This is so embarrassing. I don't care about the honors English class. I don't want to stand out. I definitely don't want to make a scene. Me walking into a classroom of twenty students who've risen up the ranks for the last three years would be a nightmare. They'd automatically hate me.

Matthews' lips quiver the slightest bit and his gaze dims. "I'll make it happen."

"See that you do." Her smile returns and Mother takes a deep breath, glancing over at me. "Will this alter her schedule dramatically?"

"No. No, it shouldn't." He finally frowns as he turns toward the computer on his desk. He starts tapping away at the keyboard, the screen angled just enough toward us that I see my information brought up on the screen.

My transcripts. Notes from previous teachers and my counselor throughout the years. Administration notes take up the most of it.

Summer is disruptive in class. Lashes out for no reason.

Was caught vaping in the bathroom. Two-day suspension.

Caught having sex in the gymnasium. Five-day suspension.

Detained and searched. Found with her mother's Xanax prescription in her backpack. Two-day suspension.

And that was all by the end of sophomore year.

My stepfather—God rest his soul—put the hammer down after the Xanax incident. He threatened to put me in military school for the remainder of my high school years. I cried and begged, pleaded with him on my knees not to make me go. They enrolled me. It was going to happen.

And then my mother's affair with Lancaster became public, and he forgot all about me. He focused on my mother instead.

We moved out. Found a smaller apartment. The media was so focused on my family, I retreated into myself. Stopped causing trouble at school and focused solely on my schoolwork. Lost all of my friends. Mother worked Jonas over. And over. And over.

Until we moved back into his house in the spring. Yates soon returned, home from college, and he was so glad to see me. He lit candles in his room and forced me to meet him that night. Put his hand over my mouth and his hand in my pants before he—

"Ah, we'll have to switch a couple of your classes," Mr. Matthews says, disrupting my thoughts, "but that shouldn't be a problem."

He taps a few more keys, angling the screen more toward himself, as if he just realized that we could read everything about me. Mother keeps up the pretense, but I see the tightening of her lips, the clouds in her eyes.

Those old memories aren't pleasant. I wasn't happy—far from it. No one was listening to me. I only found absolute peace when I got away from Yates and it was just Mom and me. Living with him, having to deal with him all the time, his persistence eventually wore me down. More times than I could count.

And it was...horrible.

Knowing that I was about to spend my entire summer with him, the summer before my senior year, pushed me to my limits. I did something that's almost...scary.

But it got me away from him.

Forever.

"I just sent your new schedule to the printer. Vivian will have it ready for you. Good luck today, Summer," Headmaster Matthews says, his shrewd gaze landing on me.

You're going to need it.

I can hear the unspoken words there, hovering in the room. Oblivious to it all and pleased with getting her way, Mother stands and I rise too, fighting the nerves swimming in my stomach.

"Thank you for understanding our needs," Mother says. "We're so grateful."

"Of course. Anything for a—*friend* of Mr. Lancaster's," he says.

I catch the emphasis the headmaster made. So does Mother. She marches out of his tiny office with her head held high, snatching the newly printed schedule from Vivian's fingers without so much as a thank you as we pass by her. Vivian mutters something under her breath, and I pretend like I didn't hear it, though I did.

"Whore," is what she whispered.

The word follows my mother everywhere she goes, and she's an expert at ignoring people. I don't know how she does it. I remember the boy I met. The son of the man she had the affair with, and how he called me a whore too. Those memories linger in the forefront of my mind, especially when I'm in bed late at night. I remember how he made me feel. His cruel words, his brutal kiss.

I've been chasing after that feeling ever since.

TWO
SUMMER

I ENTER the honors English class early, since I already missed most of first period, and go to the desk where a giant, dark-haired man is sitting, chatting with a couple of students. The girls are pretty, their uniforms immaculate, their hair a matching golden blonde, long and parted in the middle. They're carefree in the way they toss their heads back and laugh at something the teacher said, and I envy just how comfortable they are. They're so confident, so sure of themselves, and I understand why. They've been here for three years; they've put in the time, and now they're on top. The seniors. Ready to rule the school.

And here I am, barging into their class thanks to my overbearing mother, as if I belong here. I don't.

And I know it.

When they all turn to look at me, their expressions full of disdain, I shrink back from them, handing over my schedule to Mr. Figueroa with shaky fingers.

"Hi. I'm in this class," I say.

He glances over the schedule, his dark brows drawing together. "I'm afraid there must be some mistake."

I say nothing. Just glance around the classroom, pretending I don't know what just happened in the headmaster's office.

Figueroa picks up the phone on his desk and dials a three-number extension. "Hey. Yes, I have a—" he looks over my schedule, "—Summer Savage here, claiming she's in Senior Honors?"

He goes quiet, listening to whatever Headmaster Matthews is telling him and I want to disappear into myself. The girls are obviously listening, their gazes cutting to me, and one of them leans over to whisper to the other, her hand cupped around the other girl's ear so I can't hear them.

They don't bother trying to hide they're talking about me. I suppose I shouldn't be surprised.

"I see." His voice is low. A little cold. "All right then. Thank you." He hangs up the phone and looks at me, his expression impassive as he hands me back my schedule. "You can go ahead and sit down, Miss Savage. Class will begin in a few minutes."

I do as he says, sitting in the very front, on the farthest side of the classroom. I pull out a fresh notebook and a pen, taking the cap off with my teeth before I open the notebook, smoothing my hand down the blank page. I'm filled with the urge to write in my journal, but it's buried deep in my backpack and I don't want to pull it out, only to have to put it away.

My journal carries all of my thoughts. My feelings. Notes and doodles. Scraps of paper I wanted to save. A receipt from the time my friends and I went to that new coffee shop, right before

I moved. A concert ticket stub when I went to see Harry Styles. A note from Yates, threatening me. A rumpled, stained with champagne cocktail napkin taken from that party, the night I kissed that terrible boy. It was a dark navy blue, with a giant white L in the dead center.

For Lancaster.

Sometimes I like to flip through my journal, running my fingers over the bits of paper, rereading my entries. Some are hard to read, like the night of the fire. My interactions with my step-brother. The argument with my stepfather. My falling out with my friends.

Others make me smile. Still others make me yearn for the old times, when I was still young and innocent and believed there were good people in the world.

Now I'm not so sure if any even exist.

Students slowly trickle into the classroom, every single one of them looking at me with confusion in their eyes. They expect to know every single person in this class, so I understand why I trip them up.

"Okay, are we all here? I think so." Figueroa stands and goes to the white board, writing Romeo and Juliet in blue ink. "Welcome to senior honors English. It is truly an honor to be here." He smiles. The class chuckles. He points at the board with his capped marker. "This was your summer reading assignment. I hope you're all fully prepared for the assignments I'm about to make."

He sends me a doubtful look and I smile in return, writing Romeo and Juliet on the first line of my page. This is too easy. I read this book my sophomore year. I'll need a refresher, but I'm not worried.

"I'm sure you've all noticed we have a new student in here with us. Please say hello to Summer." His gaze never leaves mine as he speaks, and I look away first, uncomfortable with his scrutiny.

A few people offer murmured hellos, but not too many. I'm sure they hate that I'm in here with them. In their eyes, I'm sure they believe I don't belong here.

The door suddenly bursts open and a boy strides in, his head turned as he yells to someone in the hall. The door slams shut behind him, and everything within me comes alive. I sit up straight. My skin prickles. My heart races. My breath stalls in my throat, and sweat beads along my hairline.

I know who it is. I told myself he wouldn't be here, but I was wrong.

He is.

Whit Lancaster. The boy who kissed me. Who wanted to fuck me and called me a whore when we were barely teenagers. He's taller than I remember. Well over six feet, and his shoulders look so broad, clad in the requisite navy uniform jacket. His arrogance is palpable. He saunters into the classroom as if he owns the place, and technically, he does.

After all, it's his family name on the sign.

I stare, caught up in his magnificent face. It's better than I remember. He's heartbreakingly beautiful. Piercing blue eyes, sharp cheekbones, aquiline nose, angled jawline. His mouth is lush, his lips a deep pink and he bares his teeth in a smile for our teacher that is hopelessly fake.

"Whit. So happy you could make it," Figueroa says dryly.

Girls giggle. Whit scowls.

"Sorry." He doesn't sound sorry at all. His voice is deeper compared to the last time I heard him speak. "Something came up."

He doesn't even look at me and I sit there, folding into myself so my shoulders are hunched, and I drop my head. I don't want him to see me. Recognize me.

That would be a disaster. He hates me.

With everything he's got.

Why did I think he was a year ahead of me in school? How could I screw that up so badly? I don't know how I came to that conclusion, but once the idea formed in my mind, it stuck.

My mistake—a big one, too.

After our encounter that night, when I asked my mother who the man was and she told me his name, I Googled him. One of the top images that appeared was of the Lancasters, all five of them. The father, tall, proud and handsome. The mother, thin, arrogant and cold. The two beautiful girls, with matching smiles, stood in the front wearing matching dresses. Whittaker Augustus Lancaster stood next to his father, taller than him. His expression one of barely contained anger, so strong I could practically feel it. The more I studied the photo, the more curious I became.

What kind of family were they? They look picture perfect, but I know now pictures lie. At fourteen, I didn't believe Whit when he told me my mother was having an affair with his father. I couldn't even wrap my head around the idea. I loved my stepdad as if he were my own father, and I believed my mother felt the same way.

I found out later that I was wrong.

The scandal was revealed quickly. Midway through my sophomore year in high school, the Lancaster divorce was announced to the world, thanks to a scandalous photo of Augustus Lancaster in a compromising situation.

With my mother.

My elegant, never ruffled, always put together mother. Caught exiting a seedy hotel downtown with giant sunglasses covering her beautiful face, wearing only a loosely belted Celine trench coat and hand in hand with Augustus, the wind catching the coat's hem just so and revealing her long, bare legs.

All the way up to her hip bone. No panties in sight.

The press went wild. She was naked under that coat, they implied, and I assumed they were correct.

So did everyone else.

Nothing else was going on in the world at the time, so it turned into a national scandal. One the Lancaster family never fully recovered from. Our family didn't necessarily recover from it either.

As the oldest of three and the only boy, Whit is heir to the family fortune. Well, one of the heirs of the many Lancaster families' fortune. But his father is the oldest son of the oldest son of the oldest son...

It goes on and on for generations. They are old money—as old as it can get in this country. Lancaster Prep has been here for over one hundred and twenty years, and every single Lancaster has attended this school before they went on to college and bigger, greater things.

My mother's affair with Augustus changed their lives forever. Whit's mother, Sylvia, of the Rhode Island Whittakers— another very wealthy family, though not as established as the Lancasters—received a healthy sum in the divorce settlement. Neither of the Lancasters are allowed to discuss the terms of their divorce, or why exactly they divorced in the first place. There's a gag order in place. But everyone knows why their marriage ended.

Because of my mother.

While we have money, we're considered downright poor compared to the Lancasters, and money makes a person, or family, untouchable in certain circles. Meaning my mother was left for the wolves—the paparazzi, the society pages—and they tore her apart. Her carcass was ripped to shreds, scattered all over New York City. People whispered. Celebrity rags and blogs screamed her name in glee, running that photo of her exposed hip bone again and again and again. 20/20 on ABC ran a two-hour special on the affair and the devastating after-math of it all once the fire happened.

I always tend to push the fire out of my mind. Our family scandal ended in tragedy, while the Lancasters were left rela-tively unscathed. Money protects you. Insulates you. Those who win in the game of life, always win when they have the most money.

Unfair, but whoever said life was fair? I've also learned that the hard way.

Look at the Lancasters. Despite the affair and the scandal it brought with it, they emerged as golden as ever. Photos of the entire family together still pop up occasionally. The ever-modern family who can still get along while divorced. They do it for the kids, all the articles have said.

While Mother and I are left tarnished and scarred. Broken and barred from the society that used to accept us—specifically her and Jonas—with open arms.

A thought suddenly hits me: are the Lancaster sisters here as well?

They'd have to be.

Sylvie and Carolina are gorgeous. One of them is a dancer, I can't remember which one. But carrying on the Lancaster name rests squarely on Whit's shoulders.

My head still ducked, I watch as Whit walks in front of the rows of desks, settling into one in a row the farthest from mine, on the other side of the room. His expression is like stone, his lips formed into what looks like a pout as he glares at the teacher standing before us.

I swore Whit was older than me. At the time during our first and only encounter, he most definitely acted like he was older. He was so jaded, as if he'd seen and done everything already, and he wasn't impressed.

He's wearing that same look now. He hasn't changed much in three years. He seems completely bored with life.

I'm just grateful he didn't notice me.

I stay frozen in my chair as Figueroa continues his lecture, droning on about the relationship of two lovesick teenagers who sacrifice everything—including their lives—for what they believe is love.

"Was it love, though?" Figueroa asks at one point. "They're younger than you all are now. Historians figure Juliet was barely fourteen. We can assume Romeo was older, so sixteen, seventeen at most. By eighteen, he should've been married and even a father."

"Fuck that," one of the boys mutters, making everyone laugh.

"Indeed," Figueroa says, scowling at the boy, who only smiles at him in return. "But that's how it was then. How it's been for hundreds of years. Only during recent modern times have we as a society accepted that people get married for the first time at an older age. More and more people are becoming parents at a later age as well. You should thank your parents for that."

"I'm not thanking my parents for shit."

This is from Whit.

"Mr. Lancaster, I always appreciate your colorful commentary throughout my lectures. Witty and entertaining, as usual." The snideness in Mr. Figueroa's tone is telling. Someone doesn't appreciate the namesake in his classroom.

But I suppose there's not a damn thing he can do about it.

There's more talk of Romeo and Juliet, and I take copious notes, keeping my gaze on my notebook for pretty much the entirety of class. I don't want to draw anyone's attention. Not the teacher's—who resents me for being pushed upon him when he has no clue what I'm like or how my grades are—or the students, who've worked hard and earned their spot while I just walked into this class like it's mine to take.

I wonder if that's the case for Whit as well. Does he just get whatever he wants, thanks to his last name? Or is he actually smart? Does he do well in school? Or does he act like an asshole and put in zero effort? He doesn't have to abide by the school's strict rules, not like the rest of us.

The bell rings and I hurriedly gather my things, sling my backpack over my shoulder and exit the room without a backward glance. I have my schedule clutched in my hand and I scan it, noting I have math next.

My least favorite subject.

The wide hall is flooded with students, all of us making our way to our classrooms, everyone looking the same in their uniforms. I went to a private school in Manhattan, though we didn't have to wear uniforms. I'm unused to the itchy wool skirt, the stifling button-up shirt. And the jacket?

I hate it. I'm actually sweating right now.

My gaze drops to the other girls' skirts as I walk past them. Some of them are extra short, and I assume they're rolling them at the waist. I can't help but notice they all have beautiful hair. Vivid color on their mouths, dramatic makeup on their eyes. Brightly painted nails. A way of standing out from the crowd.

My long brown hair is pulled back into a simple ponytail. No paint on my nails or my face. A little bit of mascara on my lashes is the only effort I put into my look this morning, and I feel downright plain compared to these girls.

Maybe that's a good thing. I don't want to stand out. I don't want anyone to notice me. If I'd known Whit was in attendance, I would've never wanted to come here. For all my internet sleuthing regarding the Lancasters, that I never figured out he was still enrolled at Lancaster Prep is a rookie mistake. I should've known better.

I should've known period.

While the internet was full of talk about my mother's affair with Augustus, and there are plenty of books and numerous online articles about previous Lancaster generations, there's not a ton of information about the current generation. Maybe it's out of respect for their privacy, because of their age. And Whit doesn't put himself out there. He has a cousin—Brooks Lancaster—who's an influencer on Instagram. He has his own YouTube channel and is huge on TikTok. He's the one with all the fame.

Maybe Whit prefers staying out of the limelight.

I enter my math class and settle at the back of the classroom, deciding that will be my seat of choice for the rest of the day. I don't know why I sat in the front in English. Out of defiance? Figueroa frustrated me. Considering we're seniors in an honors English class, Romeo and Juliet is a trite reading assignment.

But I'm not going to complain. I'm actually grateful, considering I've already read the book. At least I don't have to catch up on anything.

An older woman enters the classroom and she shuts the door with a loud boom, turning the lock. She makes her way to the front with brisk efficiency, turning to face us with a brittle smile.

"Welcome to Math III. If you don't know who I am, my name is Miss Falk. As in, don't Falk with me." She smiles.

No one laughs. Guess they're taking her words to heart.

Passing out a syllabus, she talks about what she expects from us. She doles out our textbooks and a single sheet of homework, claiming she wants to assess our abilities, and I glance it over, frowning at the questions.

"Is there a problem?" Miss Falk asks, pausing right next to my desk.

I glance up to find her contemplating me, curiosity in her gaze. "No ma'am." I shake my head.

"Good. Welcome to Lancaster, Miss Savage."

She moves on.

A few people turn in their seats to openly study me and I smile wanly at them before ducking my head. I hate the attention. I don't want them to figure out who I am. I've always hated that I'm stuck with my father's last name. A man I barely know. A man who doesn't give a shit about me, and never really has. I wanted to be a Weatherstone like my mother, like my stepfather Jonas. Even my stepbrother Yates.

Yates Weatherstone is a mouthful. Literally and figuratively.

My stomach roils at the thought.

I go to French class, and it's a small, enthusiastic group. The teacher is young, asking all of us to call her Amelie and she talks in animated French. She's actually from France, and there are mostly girls in the class, which helps me relax. I introduce myself in French to everyone and they smile and nod in response, their faces friendly.

The first friendly faces I've seen all day.

Once it's lunch, I go to the dining hall, impressed with the food selection. I put together a salad at the salad bar, then make my way through the many crowded tables, hating that I know no one. A couple of girls from my French class spot me and wave me over, and I sit with them, silently eating my salad as they chat around me.

"Oh God, there's Whit," one of them says, resting her hand over her chest. "He's *so* gorgeous. Swear to God he got better looking over the summer. He's *so* tan."

No way can I turn and look at him. If he saw my face, I'm sure he'd recognize me. Of course he would. The media kept my face out of the news, but he knows exactly who I am. Just like I know who he is.

"He's sadistic," says the other girl. Her name is Jane, and she is far from plain. She looks like a model with her perfect features and long, lanky body. "I hear he likes to hurt girls when he ah, fucks them."

"What in the world are you talking about?" asks the other one. I stare at her, trying to remember her name, but I can't.

There have been too many new things today to remember them all, including names.

Jane leans in close, her voice dropping. "Farah had a thing with him last year. Nothing serious, but they'd mess around. Hook up. He was very demanding, she said. Every time he kissed her, he'd put his hand on her throat. Like he was trying to hold her down. She said sometimes his fingers would tighten, as if he were trying to actually—*choke* her."

The other girl gasps. I say nothing, though of course what she says sparks my imagination. It doesn't scare me. Nor does it shock me.

I can imagine him enjoying that. He was brutal when he was fourteen. Where could his imagination go now?

"That's disgusting," the girl whose name I can't remember declares with a sneer.

Jane grins and flips her wavy blonde hair over her shoulder. "I think it's kind of hot."

I watch her. How she snaps her bright pink gum—she's not eating anything at lunch—and her prissy mannerisms. This girl couldn't handle Whit Lancaster. He'd destroy her with a touch. A glance.

"He's so hot, I suppose I could ignore his idiosyncrasies." The girl—I just remembered her name, it's Caitlyn—laughs, her focus turning to me. "Have you met Whit yet?"

I slowly shake my head, but otherwise remain quiet. I'm neither confirming nor denying anything verbally.

"His family owns the school. He's untouchable," she says.

"Are you liking Lancaster so far?" Jane asks, tucking her hair behind her ear, snapping her gum.

"It's a lot to take in," I answer truthfully before I take a bite of my salad.

"Are you staying in the dorms? Or are you a day student?" This is from Caitlyn.

"Dorms," I answer, dropping my gaze. Thanks to Mother knowing Augustus Lancaster, I was able to get a single dorm at the last minute, which I'm sure is unheard of. Meaning I don't have to share my room with anyone else. I've heard those are rare.

Again, I'm getting special favors, thanks to my mother's connection to the Lancasters. Which is kind of messed up, but whatever. I have to take advantage of it where I can.

"Where did you go to school before?" asks Jane, sipping from her water bottle. Her eyes gleam as she studies me, and I'm sure she's trying to figure me out.

I don't trust her. Something about her sets me on edge. But, of course, I don't trust anyone. Not anymore.

Once you've been burned so many times, it's hard to let down your guard.

"Billington in Manhattan," I answer with a faint smile.

They both look impressed.

It's one of the best private schools in Manhattan. Jonas was on the school board when Yates attended there. That is how Yates was able to get away with so much—they looked the other way, thanks to Jonas' generous donations and position on the board.

I did the world a favor when I took care of Yates. Not that I get any thanks for it.

Not that anyone knows exactly what I did.

We make small talk for the rest of lunch, the spot between my shoulder blades growing warmer and warmer as the hour winds down. As if someone was watching me. I don't dare look back.

Too afraid if I do, I'll be staring into Whit Lancaster's cold, assessing eyes.

THREE

SUMMER

AFTER LUNCH I HAVE A BREAK, though it's actually a study hall period. I go to the library and find a spot in the back of the cavernous building, settling in at a small, unoccupied table. I pull out my math assignment, working through it hurriedly, distracted by the beautiful architecture. It's old, with soaring ceilings and gothic windows made of gorgeous stained-glass. Something you'd see out of a movie about witches and warlocks.

I receive a text notification and I check it to see it's from Mother.

Are you settling in?

I don't bother answering yet. Not that she cares. She's already on her way back home, to the apartment she inherited upon Jonas' death. No more fifth floor walkups for her. She'll be taken care of for the rest of her life. If I'm lucky, she'll leave a little bit for me when she dies.

Knowing how much she enjoys spending money, I probably won't be so lucky.

There are other people in the library, and they talk in hushed tones, their heads bent close together, gossiping and smiling and laughing. Seeing them makes me long for my friends at my old school. I miss them. But when the scandal broke out about Yates and me, just before the fire happened, I couldn't show my face there ever again. Everyone knew what he was doing to me.

And not a single damn person did one thing to stop it.

Shoving my anger back down, I focus once again on my math homework, oblivious to the sound of footsteps until a soft, female voice says hello.

I nearly jump out of my skin, my head jerking up to find a girl standing by my table.

She smiles shyly, her long, dark blonde hair flowing far past her shoulders. Almost to her waist. Her face is pale, her eyes a haunted blue, and she smiles with rosebud lips, vividly red compared to the snow white of her skin. "You're new."

I can't help but smile in return. "I am."

"May I sit with you?"

I wave my hand at the three open chairs at my table. "Be my guest."

She settles into the chair closest to mine, dropping her backpack on the table with a loud thump. I watch as she digs through the contents, pulling out a history textbook and letting it land on the table with an echoing slap. Somewhere in the distance, I can hear a faint, "Shush!" that I'm sure came from the front desk.

"She hates noise," the girl tells me with a faint smile.

"Who?"

"The librarian. Miss Taylor. She's as old as this building." The girl laughs and I can't help but join in. It's an infectious sound and I immediately feel at ease with her. Far more at ease than with the other two at lunch. "Notice how there are a bunch of spinster teachers who work here? I think this is where virgin educators go to die."

She laughs even harder. She reminds me of an angel, but she definitely has a devious mind.

I warm up to this girl even more.

"You like it here?" she asks me.

"It's nice," I say with a shrug, glancing at my math paper yet again. I have one more problem to solve, and then I'm done.

She leans in close, her voice a harsh whisper. "It's easy."

I raise a brow. "You think?"

"I *know*." She glances back, as if making sure no one's around, before she returns her attention to me. "I'm a junior. You're a senior?"

I nod, wondering how she knows. "I am."

"Went to Billington?" She whistles low when my eyebrows shoot up. "That place is fancy."

"And this place isn't?" My voice is dry, my heart racing.

How does she know where I went to school?

She shrugs. "It's nothing."

Her words are so dismissive. Obviously, Lancaster Prep doesn't impress her.

"Have you always gone here?" I ask her. That's the only explanation as to why she doesn't see the beauty of this place. The old buildings, the gothic chapel with the spire that rises high into the sky. The lush green grounds, the forest behind the campus, and the ocean just beyond, crashing against the shore.

It's like a dream.

"My whole entire life." She rolls her eyes. Blows out an exaggerated breath. "That's what it feels like, at least."

"How do you know so much about me?" I ask, curious. But not put off. She has a way about her that's nonthreatening.

"I have my ways. And access," she says mysteriously. "I know your name is Summer Savage. Cool name by the way. Very—primal. You're from Manhattan. You were enrolled at the last minute, even though Lancaster was far past the enrollment drop dead due date."

It's the way she says drop dead. As if she relishes the words.

"A single dormitory was assigned to you. Rather impossible, considering the enrollment situation, so you must know someone higher up. Dear old Augustus, maybe? Plus, I hear you made an appearance in honors English this morning, which I'm sure infuriated many. All those girls work so hard to be in Figueroa's class, desperate to get close to him. He's messed around with a few, though you never heard that from me. So yes, you definitely know someone." She smiles, her light blue eyes sparkling. "Friends in high places take you far."

Recognition dawns and I sit up straight, hating the dread slithering down my spine. This girl should hate me. She probably already does.

"My name is Sylvie, by the way. Sylvie Lancaster." The moment she takes a good look at my face, she throws her head back and laughs. So loudly, I hear Miss Taylor shush her again. "We've never met before, yet I feel like I know everything about you."

"Same," I admit, my voice hoarse. Talking to her is like fraternizing with the enemy.

Dangerous.

"Oh, don't look so shocked. I don't care about what your mother did with my father." She waves a hand, effectively dismissing all the lurid stories about our parents. "Our mother was hellbent on making our father's life as miserable as she could throughout their marriage. This was his only way out."

"You really believe that?" I ask her incredulously. It's as if it doesn't matter to her, whereas her brother treated me like a common prostitute when we were just kids. Barely teenagers.

I think of what the girls said about him, and how he likes to choke girls when he kisses them. Despite the depravity, I'm intrigued. I wouldn't mind knowing what it felt like, to have Whit's large, warm hand closing around my throat, pinning me to a wall as he tormented me with his mouth?

God, I'm sick. Seriously.

"I lived with them my entire life. A witness to the disaster they called marriage. Yes, I believe that," she says solemnly. "My older brother thinks your mother is the devil incarnate, and he puts all the blame on her. Our baby sister believes our father is the one who wrecked everything, and used to battle with him on the daily over the frail condition of mother dearest before she found her way out."

"And what do *you* think?" I ask.

"They're all responsible for their actions, are they not? They're adults. Was anyone thinking of the children? No. But when do any of them think of the children?" She doesn't give me a chance to answer. "They're all selfish. Wrapped up in their own little worlds. Why do you think there's a boarding school with our family name on it? So they can shove us all out here and forget we exist."

Sylvie explains all of this in such a logical manner that it makes complete sense. I'm sure she's right. When do they ever think of the children?

Never. My parents neglected me and Yates when it mattered the most. Why else was he so brazen in how he pursued me? He knew he'd get away with it.

Well, I showed him.

"Does your brother know I'm here?" I ask her, hoping my voice sounds casual.

"No. Yes? I'm not sure. We haven't discussed you, and your name has never passed his lips to me. Though Whit and I don't talk much. He finds me a nuisance," she says. She doesn't sound the least bit offended.

"How did you find out so much information about me?"

"I hacked into the school's files." She grins while I gape at her. "It's an archaic system. My grandma could hack into it, and she's been dead for two years."

I can't help but start to laugh. "Does anyone know you hack into the school's computer system?"

"Only a select few. You being one of them now." Her smile is small, her eyes sparkling. "You ever have a grade issue in class, let me know. I can fix it for you." She snaps her fingers.

"I get good grades," I reassure her.

"Now." She smiles, her expression never faltering, while my smile slowly fades.

I'm sure she's seen my entire file from Billington and read over every little detail greedily, soaking up all of those suspensions with barely repressed glee. Drugs and backtalk and sex on campus. I was a nightmare. The first two years of high school were difficult. I was acting out. It was a cry for help. I wanted attention, whether it was good or bad.

But no one listened. Worse, they were ready to send me far, far away, to military school, as if that would fix me.

I suppose getting away from Yates would've fixed everything, but I didn't want to do it like that. One of the last nights we were all together as a family, long after everyone went to bed, he held me close afterward and told me how much he would miss me once I was gone. I realized then he believed I didn't want to leave because we would be kept apart.

And that wasn't the case. Not even close.

At least, that wasn't the case for me.

"You seem like someone with a lot of secrets," Sylvie says, interrupting my thoughts.

I blink her into focus, to find she's watching me with narrowed eyes. "I'm an open book," I lie.

She says nothing. She doesn't have to.

Because she doesn't believe me. She shouldn't. I have all sorts of secrets.

And every single one of them is awful.

I HURRY into American Government just before the final bell rings, sending an apologetic look toward the teacher sitting behind his desk. I lingered too long in the library, enjoying my conversation with Sylvie, feeling guilty the entire time because of my connection with her brother. I never brought it up. She never brought him up. Only that one time.

And I preferred it that way.

The classroom is full, every desk occupied, save for a couple in the very back of the room. I scurry toward them, not paying attention to where I'm going when I trip over a backpack directly in my path, sending myself sprawling to the ground.

It feels like the entire classroom witnesses my fall from grace and erupts into laughter.

I lie there for a moment, my cheek resting against the cool floor, knees throbbing from my hard landing. Cool air brushes against the back of my thighs and I realize my skirt flipped up, exposing my black booty shorts that I am so damn grateful I wore instead of just my underwear.

The teacher rushes forward. I can hear his squeaky footsteps on the floor. "Are you all right?" he asks me.

My audience has calmed some, but I still hear laughter. Furious whispering, all of them talking about me. A boy asks straight out, "Who the fuck is she?"

I gather myself up quickly, rising to my knees, smoothing my hair out of my face. I hear someone suck in mouthfuls of air, as if in shock, and when I glance to my left, I realize I'm literally face to face with the fallen angel of my dreams.

The devil of my nightmares.

Whit Lancaster. Who's staring at me as if he's seen a ghost.

Gripping my backpack strap tightly, I stand, averting my head and sitting in the closest empty chair.

Directly behind Whit.

Fuck.

The teacher sends everyone a stern look, effectively shutting them up before he starts speaking, but I have no clue what he's saying. I can't hear anything thanks to the rapid beat of my heart. It roars in my ears, through my blood, and I try to hold my breath. Until I can't take it anymore and exhale in a stream of mint, thanks to the gum I chewed in the library.

God, I hope he doesn't notice.

I glance down at the floor in front of me, grimacing. I tripped over Whit's goddamn backpack. Of course I did. I sit there as if in a trance, my entire body shaking, my knees stinging from the fall. I stare at my desk, scared to lift my head, afraid I'll find him watching me. When I finally dare to glance up...

I'm looking at the back of his head.

As another shaky breath leaves me, I pull out my binder and notebook, along with my favorite mechanical pencil, my hands still shaking. Fully prepared to take notes, though the teacher is leaning against the front of his desk, his arms crossed as he talks about himself and what he expects from us this year.

He passes out a syllabus and my heart threatens to fly out of my body. Whit will have to turn around to pass me the syllabus. I wait, my hands clammy, my legs knocking together, and when my row starts passing the copies of the syllabus back, I watch as the small stack reaches Whit.

But he doesn't give me my copy. He holds on to both, his shoulders straight, his attention directed at the teacher. Irritation fills me, and I have the urge to poke him in the back with my pencil and demand the syllabus.

Instead, my hand shoots up in the air.

"Yes?" the teacher acknowledges me with kind eyes.

I'm sure he feels bad for my earlier fall.

"I didn't receive a syllabus."

He frowns. "Well, that's strange. I counted them out." Grabbing an extra from his desk, he approaches me and hands over the single sheet of paper.

"Thank you," I tell him.

The teacher drones for the rest of the period, but I'm not listening. I can't concentrate on anything else but the fact that Whit is sitting directly in front of me, purposely ignoring me, thank God. I can smell him. Warm and spicy and inherently male. I study his hair. It's a dark blond, almost brown but not quite.

Short, neatly trimmed, and a little longish on top. It looks soft. I'm sure if I ran my fingers through it, the strands would cling.

Finally the bell rings, signaling the end of the class—the end of the day. I sit there, immobilized as everyone around me gathers their things and practically runs out of the classroom. There are practices happening for all of the fall sports. They made an announcement over lunch. I'm trying to wait out Whit, so I can leave after he does, but he's slow too.

As in, he slowly turns around to face me.

"What the fuck are you doing here?" His voice is low, his eyes sharp.

"I go here," I say breathlessly.

"The fuck you do," he retorts, leaning away from me. As if he gets any closer, I might give him the plague.

I hate him. I do. But I'm drawn to him, too. The pull is there, tugging me closer to him, and I wonder if he feels it too.

"I'm enrolled," I say, grabbing my backpack and putting away my stuff. "Whether you like it or not."

He glares.

I do too.

He finally speaks first.

"Nice fall earlier. Landing on your knees like that must've hurt." He smirks. "Though I'm sure you're used to being on your knees."

His insult cuts me like a knife, slicing me open. "Fuck you," I say, rising to my feet.

Whit stands as well, blocking my path. He's far more formidable than he was over three years ago. Taller. Wider. Stronger. But I refuse to let him scare me.

"I'm sure you'd love it if I fucked you," he says, his voice low and taunting. I don't know how the teacher doesn't hear, but the man must be oblivious. "You're a cheap whore, just like your mother."

I dodge around him at the last second and make my escape, never looking back. I can hear his laughter follow me, all the way down the hall, and it's not until I completely exit the building that I realize it's just in my head. My thoughts.

Filled with his laughter. Reminding me that yes, I am my mother's daughter.

Nothing but a cheap whore.

FOUR

SUMMER

THE FIRST TWO weeks of school are much the same. Learning my schedule, trying to get a feel for my teachers and what they want from us, homework every night, though it isn't too hard. They always ease us into it at the beginning of the term. It's the same at every school. I've not really made any friends yet. Rumors went around that Whit tripped me on purpose on the first day of school, which left them with all sorts of questions. Plus, people witnessed our nasty little discussion after class ended that Monday, and slowly but surely, I've become a pariah at school.

No one will talk to me. They're all wearing a Lancaster muzzle. I haven't seen Sylvie since that first day in the library, so I can't even count on her friendship. It's as if I've become a ghost and no one sees me.

I should've known this would happen. The moment I realized Whit was on campus, I knew my chance at having a semi-normal senior year was through. He realized the second day of school that I was in the honors English class with him, but I refused to look back at him. He'd glared in my direction the moment he strode into class, always late, with that nonchalant *I don't give a fuck* attitude for Figueroa.

I'm sure the entire staff at this school hates his guts.

His poisonous words about me ate at my reputation, slowly but surely. Bit by bit. To the point that people literally sneered when they walked past me in the halls. The very girls I hung out with at lunch on my first day now pretend they don't see me. Or they shoulder check me in the dormitory, like Caitlyn did a few days ago.

It's as if he's trying to drive me out of here, but I refuse to leave. At lunch, he sits in the dining hall or outside, always surrounded by girls. Always accompanied by the same three boys. Chad, Elliot and Spencer, who are seniors like us, from prominent families, but ones not as prominent as Whit's. I'm surprised the devil has friends, but I suppose you get to be the devil by having a persuasive personality, and oodles of charm.

Sounds like something my mother would say.

I don't tell her what's going on. I definitely don't tell her about Whit and what he's doing. She thinks school is going well and I'm managing. If I told her there was a struggle with Whit, she'd contact his father. And then there would be hell to pay.

For me.

So I remain quiet. I moved to the next row over in American Government, so I no longer sit directly behind him. I've taken to spending my lunches in the library. I get all of my home-work done in there, since I have study hall directly after. At night, I grab some food from the dining hall and take it to my room, keeping to myself. I take a shower. Read or watch something on Netflix or whatever. My days are the same. Boring.

Lonely.

If I pretend I don't exist, then I don't. By the end of the second week of school, it seems as if Whit has also forgotten about me, which fills me with a quiet sense of relief.

But not too much relief. I don't completely trust him. He might have a plan secretly in place.

Having him so close though, leaves me curious. I watch him sometimes at lunch, when I'm there for those few moments in the dining hall. How he talks to the girls, and how they fawn all over him as if he's a celebrity. My ears strain in the classes I share with him and when a teacher calls upon him, he always gives the correct answer. He's smart.

He's also dangerous.

Everyone sucks up to him. When your family name and crest is the one on the school, I suppose that comes with the territory. Teachers and staff. Every single student. The only ones who don't seem impressed with his status are his three friends, though they treat him with a quiet reverence that lets him know he's in charge. Girls flirt with him—him and his three closest friends especially—in such a desperate manner, it's pitiful. They're pathetic.

I treat him much the same way he treats me—I refuse to talk to him. He called me a whore. Nothing's changed. He hates me.

I hate him.

I'm watching him now. It's the last period of the day. Friday. He's one seat ahead and to my left, right in my line of vision.

He taps his pencil against the edge of his desk in a steady rhythm that's annoying. I glare.

He doesn't even look in my direction.

His hair tumbles over his forehead, his lips curled into the faintest smile. There's no happiness in that face, though. It's all harsh lines and dark shadows. But oh, it is such a beautiful face, too. Cold and hard, like the statues in the gardens on campus.

The teacher puts on a video and turns off the lights, the only illumination coming from the large screen TV on the wall. It's a current events clip, talking about the state of the world and our woeful future, and I immediately tune it out.

I'm depressed enough.

The moment Mr. Stein leaves our classroom, the mood shifts. Phones are whipped out. People start talking. I doodle on an empty page of my notebook, tilting my head so my hair falls forward, covering my face. I don't want anyone to see me. I write my name in big bubble letters. Draw flowers around it. Then I write Whit's name.

And surround it with little devil faces, their horns long and extra sharp.

"Is that how you really think of me?"

A gasp escapes me when I hear his familiar deep voice and I slam my notebook shut, lifting my head to find Whit sitting right next to me. He'd somehow slipped into the empty desk behind him and slid it over silently to mine. How did I not notice?

"You think I'm the devil?" he prods when I still haven't said anything.

I turn away from him, wishing he'd leave me alone.

Wishing he'd keep talking to me.

"I suppose I have made your life a living hell," he says casually, as if we're making light conversation.

Still nothing but silence from me.

"I thought you'd be a crying mess by now, since I turned everyone against you," he continues. "You're stronger than I thought."

Slowly I face him once more, our gazes meeting, his sucking me in. Even in the dim light, I can see that glitter of light blue, his hungry eyes seeming to eat me up. I part my lips, but no sound comes out.

Besides, what would I say?

"But I guess you don't really care who likes you or not, huh?" His lips curve into the barest smile. "As long as you get what you want, you win in the end."

I have no idea what he's talking about.

"This isn't a game," I say, my voice low.

He lifts a brow. "She speaks."

I glare.

"You're wrong, Savage. Life is a game, and pretty much everyone that's in this room is a loser." He pauses for the barest moment. "With the exception of me."

His arrogance is astounding.

"Only because you have money," I remind him.

"And power. I have so much fucking power, it practically drips off of me." He leans in close, and I shift back, wanting to get away from him. "They're all scared of me. They'll do what I say, no questions asked."

"Like when you tell them to ignore me?"

He grins. "Yes. Sheep, all of them."

"And you're the sheepherder?"

"I'm the asshole who owns the land the sheep graze upon. One wrong move and I can slaughter them all." He studies me for a moment and I remain silent, willing myself not to speak. I can't give anything away. Not words, not emotions. "How did your mother convince my father to let you attend here at such a late notice?"

I have no idea, is what I want to tell him.

I remain quiet instead.

"Does she have something on him? Or did she drop to her knees like usual and suck his cock for your tuition?"

I don't even flinch at his words, not when I know he's looking for a reaction. I can tell from the way his gaze roams over me, from the top of my head downward. Lingering on my eyes. My lips. Waiting for a tell.

I refuse to give him one.

"I can strike a bargain with you. Make your life here much easier," he says, his voice pitched even lower and oh so persuasive.

"What are the terms?" I keep my voice cool. Calm.

His mouth curves upward. "Suck my dick and let me come on your tits for a week straight and I'll take the lock off everyone."

God, he's a pig. He wants to come on my tits?

An image comes to me, completely unbidden. Me on my knees before Whit. My lips wrapped around his impressive cock. I know it's big. It *has* to be. I doubt a Lancaster would have a small penis, and I remember its shape beneath my hand that one time I touched him. I'm topless, no bra, my tits out, just the way he likes it. I stroke him, let him fuck my mouth so deep I feel the head bump the back of my throat and right when he's close to tipping over that edge, a feral groan falls from his lips and he pulls out, spraying semen all over my chest so that it drips off my nipples.

He'd wipe his cum off my skin with gentle, lightly shaking fingers, the aftereffects of his orgasm still lingering. He'd drag them across my lips and make me suck them and I'd swallow his cum down without protest. I can see it all unfold, as plain as day, and I realize my fantasies are a little twisted, especially when you consider my previous sexual experience.

"Let me come on your face and I'll take care of everything in five sessions," he offers.

For the briefest second I'm tempted, but I immediately push the delicious image out of my thoughts. What the hell is wrong with me? "No."

"Three days. And I get to come on your tits," he counteroffers.

I stare at him, unable to find my voice.

"I'll make it two and you'll let me finger you right now in class." His grin is so wide, I swear his white teeth are blinding me even in the darkness.

"Absolutely not." I try not to squirm in my seat at the idea of Whit's long fingers under my skirt. Beneath my panties. In between my legs, stroking my wet, tingling flesh—

"You're thinking about it." His knowing voice interrupts my thoughts.

"No, I'm really not."

We stare at each other, my gaze dropping to his throat. I see his pulse point, how it rapidly beats, and I'm oddly reassured that I affect him just as much as he affects me.

"Your funeral," he finally says, his tone dismissive. "I'll get them all to turn on you."

"Haven't you already?" I don't know how I'm able to keep my voice so even, when inside, I'm quaking at having him so close. Threatening me with sexual blackmail. I should be offended. Why am I not offended?

Because you're attracted to him. Despite everything he's done and said, you like the idea of being with him. You crave what he can give you.

"You're right," he says. "I have. I thought you'd cave. A couple of blow jobs and everyone would love you? That's a deal, if you ask me. I know it's not easy being the new girl here, especially when a Lancaster hates you."

"Not all Lancasters hate me," I drawl, referring to Sylvie.

Whit's cheeks immediately turn red, his mouth tightening with barely suppressed rage. "If you're referring to my father, then you're a bigger whore than I thought."

He says those last words so loudly, heads swivel in our direction. He grabs his backpack and rises to his feet, exiting the classroom without another word.

I watch him go, ragged breaths escaping me. I can feel everyone's eyes on me, their curiosity, their hurried whispers. They heard him. How could they not? Their king called me a whore, and now I'll pay the price. Even more than I'm already paying.

He made it seem like I'm messing around with his father, when I haven't even met the man. He's more a myth. A fictional character who played a part in my life without ever having truly met me.

Now Whit assumes I've slept with his father to ensure my spot here at Lancaster Prep. Does he really believe I'd stoop so low as to sleep with the man who had a years-long affair with my own mother? I can't wrap my head around that line of thinking.

When it comes to Whit, there are lots of things I can't wrap my head around.

FIVE

SUMMER

"GET the fuck out of my way," a boy snarls at me just before he shoves me aside. My shoulder collides with the wall, making me wince, but he doesn't even bother looking in my direction. He just keeps walking, high fiving another boy as he approaches him. They glance over their shoulders at me and laugh before they walk away.

This is my life. The last three weeks, I've been completely ostracized. I have turned into everyone's punching bag at Lancaster Prep, and while I've just been taking it the entire time, the rude comments, the whispers as I walk past them, the glares, the dirty looks. It's all getting to be too much, and I am this close to exploding.

At first, it was much of the same. They ignored me. Pretended I didn't exist. Even the teaching staff started to catch on to what the students were doing. If we had a group project, they wouldn't include me in it. When a teacher would call my name, one of them would talk over me, as if I didn't exist.

I wasn't even worth existing in Whit's eyes, so therefore I wasn't worth it in everyone else's eyes too.

After a while, teachers stopped calling on me altogether.

Only this last week has it taken a semi-violent turn. And every time something happens, each time someone makes physical contact with me, I eventually see them with Whit, as if they need his approval for a job well done.

It's sickening. He's the biggest bully in this school, yet he doesn't have to lift a finger. He just gets everyone else to do his bidding and treat me like absolute shit.

Lunch has just started and I'm making my way into the dining hall. There are no sympathetic glances or whispered hellos from any other female in this room. They all view me as the enemy. The underclassmen are petrified to be associated with me for fear they'll be treated poorly too. I have no allies here. Not even Sylvie, who's disappeared completely. I haven't seen her on campus in the past six weeks since the first day of school.

I make my way to the line, contemplating the premade sandwiches in the cooler. I should grab one. I can eat half now and save the rest for my dinner later. That way, I don't have to leave my room for the rest of the night.

Pitiful, but true. My room is my only reprieve. It's where I spend most of my time, minus when I sneak out in the early evening and jog along the trails that lead to the ocean. Administration has already warned the females not to be out there after five. The sun goes down earlier and earlier, the woods that surround the beach are dark, and they don't want anything to happen to us.

I defy that rule. I'm treated so terribly during school hours, that time is my only refuge, and I'm not letting them take it away from me. It's the only moment when I feel truly at peace, with my AirPods in listening to music, getting lost to the rhythm of my feet pounding on the ground. I never understood the runner's high until recently. Now I feel like I'm chasing after it every chance I get.

I grab a sandwich, a small bag of chips and a Smart Water, and stand in line. Conversation is happening all around me, yet no one speaks directly to me.

"I hear she meets up with the guys after lights out," a girl whispers to her cluster of friends who are standing behind me.

"Which guys?"

"Whit. Elliot. Spencer and Chad," the girl says. "She sneaks them into her room."

"Right, because she has a single room, no roomie to deal with."

"Whit's the one with the suite. I hear they all meet in his room," someone else says.

They're talking about me.

"Whatever. All I know is, they take turns fucking her. Or she's getting fucked by one while giving another a BJ. Like it's one giant orgy, straight out of porn. Ew." They all laugh uncomfortably. "So disgusting."

Anger spirals in my gut, but I tap it down. They can say whatever they want. I know it's not true.

"I heard she sucks off Whit's dad all the time, too. That's how she's paying for her tuition," one of the other girls says.

"Gross! He's an old man."

"Like mother, like daughter."

I take a step forward, swallowing my words. The cashier is taking forever, making small talk with everyone, a giant smile on her face. Can't she just do her job and keep the line moving?

"Oooh, maybe they share her. Maybe they have a threesome with Whit's father," another one of the girls squeals, right before they all start laughing.

I can't take it any longer.

Turning around, I glare at them. They knew I was standing there all along, that's why they said everything in the first place, but they didn't expect me to react. Usually I never do. This is the first time I'm publicly standing up for myself.

Their laughter slowly dies and they stare at me in return, waiting.

"You're all disgusting," I say.

"At least I'm not fucking someone's daddy to keep myself enrolled," one of them taunts. She's young. Beautiful. Mean as a snake. One of Whit's hangers-on.

"At least I'm not slobbering all over Whit Lancaster's dick, desperate to get a taste," I toss back at her.

"You're a bitch," she snaps.

"And you're a heartless cunt who wears too much makeup," I toss back at her.

She gasps. So do her friends. A shadow suddenly looms over us, and I swallow hard, dropping my head to see shiny black shoes standing right next to my scratched-up loafers.

"Miss Savage," Headmaster Matthews says. "Come with me to my office, please."

I gape at him, then point at the girls. "But what about them?"

"What about them?" he repeats, his brows shooting up.

"They started it. They were bad mouthing me, I'm just trying to defend myself..." My voice fades and I snap my lips shut. My argument is pointless.

No one listens to me. No one cares.

"We don't handle our issues with name-calling at this school, especially such crude insults like what I just heard you say." He steps closer, his fingers closing around my upper arm. "And I did hear you say it. So come with me, please."

"What about my lunch?" I ask weakly. I set the items back haphazardly on a nearby shelf.

"Guess you'll be skipping it today," he says gleefully as he steers me around and leads me out of the dining hall.

I hear the girls burst into laughter as I walk away. We exit the building, and I glance to my right to find Whit standing with his minions, his gaze only for me as he watches me walk with the headmaster to his office like a criminal being led to the death chamber.

Such bullshit.

Once we're in Matthews' office, he closes and locks the door, then leans against the front of his desk. I'm sitting in the chair directly in front of him, and he's so close, I can feel his pant legs brush against my knees. I try to recoil back but it's no use.

He's in my personal bubble, and there's no way I can avoid him.

"Why did you call Miss Atherton a cunt?"

The word falls from his lips so easily, I'm taken aback for a moment. "She called me a bitch."

"So that makes it okay." His tone is maddeningly even.

"She was saying horrible things about me. They all were."

He lifts a brow. "Such as?"

I refuse to repeat the stories. It's bad enough, what he might've overheard. "Accusing me of doing—vulgar things with some of the boys on campus."

"Are you doing vulgar things with some of the boys on campus?" he asks, crossing his arms in front of him.

I'm struck silent by his accusatory tone. He doesn't believe me.

"Of course not. Everyone hates me."

"Yet they're all talking about you, so I assume *some* of them like you. Most likely the boys." When I lift my head to glare at him, I find he's already studying me, his gaze dropping to the hem of my skirt where it lays across the tops of my thighs. Reaching out, I tug on it, trying to cover as much skin as possible, and I don't even roll the waistband up. "I've seen this sort of thing happen before, Miss Savage. A girl ostracized by her peers. Rumors begin to fly. Most of them exaggerated, but always with a grain of truth in there somewhere." He leans forward, drawing uncomfortably closer, and I recoil back.

"The boys hate me too," I whisper. "They all do."

He studies me, his gaze wandering, taking me in. I stare back, not cowering under his scrutiny. I have nothing to hide. I'm not in the wrong here. My only crime is calling a cunt a cunt.

She deserved it.

"If we find any boys in your dorm room, you'll be expelled," he says, his words deadly serious. "There will be no entertaining the opposite sex in your room after lights out."

He says it as if I've already done it.

"What if I were a lesbian? Then would it be okay?" I retort.

His mouth sets into a firm line, lips disappearing almost completely. "You're not a lesbian."

"You shouldn't assume anything," I say, my voice quiet.

He straightens up, still glaring at me, his hands now resting on his hips. "You're getting detention."

"For what?"

"Insulting Miss Atherton. Calling someone a cunt goes against school rules," he says, going around his desk to settle into his chair.

I breathe a sigh of relief, relaxing now that he's not so close. "How many days of detention?"

"Three. Today. As well as Monday and Tuesday of next week. Oh, and you're barred from tonight's football game," he says as he pulls a pink pad out of a desk drawer and starts scratching his pen across it.

Big deal. I hate football. And who would I sit and watch the game with? No one likes me. I have no friends.

He hands me the detention slip. "You can go."

I grab my backpack off the floor and rise to my feet, ready to make my escape.

"Miss Savage?"

Pausing, I glance over my shoulder at Headmaster Matthews.

"I'd watch that mouth if I were you. It's bound to get you in trouble again."

I leave his office without a word, my head held high, my stomach grumbling. I hurry to the dining hall, slipping inside just as the bell rings and I find another sandwich—not my preferred choice but it'll do—and grab a bag of chips, a Smart Water and a Coke, before I go to the register to pay.

"Food line is closed," the cashier says firmly.

"Not you too," I say, my voice trembling. I glance around at the mostly empty dining hall, praying no one is watching me quietly fall apart.

Because I'm this close to collapsing onto the floor in a crying heap.

"Fine," she says irritably, scanning my items and giving me the total. I pay her in cash, tell her to keep the change before I turn and hurry out of there, bumping straight into a firm, hot wall where an exit is supposed to be.

"Summer Savage, where are you going?" Firm hands grip my upper arms and I jerk my head up to find Elliot McIntosh grinning at me. One of Whit's friends.

I'm sure he's heard all the stories. Believes they're all true. Thinks he can have his way with me and I'll just meekly comply.

"Let me go," I murmur, clutching my food and drinks close to my chest. I should've put them in my backpack before I left, but I was in too much of a hurry.

"Whatcha got there?" he asks, tilting his head to check out what I'm holding in my hands. "A late lunch, huh? You want to share? Head back to your dorm and hang out for a while?"

"Get away from me." I jerk out of his hold and keep walking, heading straight for the library. Elliot keeps up with me, his long legs making it easy to gain on my lead and I try my best not to look at him.

"Calm down, babe. You're in such a hurry." He laughs. I sneak a glance. He's dark haired and dark eyed, olive skin and full lips. As handsome as Whit, but in a different way.

Though my body doesn't quake just being in his presence. There's the monumental difference.

"Don't you have a class to go to?" I toss at him as I turn left. The library looms in the distance.

"I'd skip it for you." He reaches out, snagging my arm and making me come to a stop. "Let's spend a little time together. Get to know each other."

"I can't. I have class." As if that's the only reason I don't want to spend time with him.

His smile is easy. "No, you don't. You have study hall. So do I. Let's hang out in the library. I know a quiet spot in the stacks, where no one will interrupt us."

I try to pull out of his hold, but his fingers tighten on my arm. "No."

"Oh, come on." He steps closer, so close his body brushes against mine. "I know you give it up to Whit. He says fucking you is the experience of a lifetime. Just give me a little taste."

My mind goes white hot with rage at his words, and without thought, I lift my knee, aiming straight for Elliot's balls.

I make direct contact.

"Fucking whore!" he bellows, letting go of me so he can cover his junk with his hands as he falls to the ground.

I break out into a run, still holding on to my food and drinks, the double doors of the library drawing closer and closer. I can feel the tears running down my cheeks, wetting my skin and I didn't even realize I was crying.

I can't take it any longer. I can't. The taunts. The meanness. The violence. The pain. The lies. Whit is telling people we're having sex?

God, he wishes. The arrogant prick.

I hate him. I hate all of them.

How they won't give me a chance. How the teachers and staff stand by and let it happen. They see what's going on; they're just afraid to go against their fearless leader.

And he's not a fearless leader. He's a seventeen-year-old kid who acts like a vampire. Meaning he's supposedly seen and done it all, over a million lifetimes, and now he's bored stiff.

I can't fucking stand him.

What's the hardest part about all of this?

When they ignore me. Like I don't exist. I've dealt with that sort of behavior my entire life. You'd think I'd become used to it by now. But I'm not.

Doubt I ever will be.

One of the doors swings open, and there stands Whit, a closed-lip smile on his face, his gaze trained on me and no one else. It's as if he's been waiting to greet me the entire time. His gaze shifts to his friend, who's still doubled over in pain and writhing on the ground behind me and I come to a stop, panting hard, the tears still flowing.

"Did you hurt Elliot?" he asks me incredulously.

"Kicked him in the balls," I say with relish, hoping he'll think I could do the same thing to him. I stand a little taller, can feel the tears drying on my cheeks. It's as if I willed them to stop, and they heeded my call.

"And I hear you called Lacy Atherton a cunt?" He raises his brows.

"She is one." I lift my chin, hating that I'm still juggling my lunch and dinner in my arms. I feel stupid.

Vulnerable.

"You're not wrong," he says. "It's just no one ever calls her out for being one."

"Well, I did." I glare.

He stares.

"Stop telling people we're fucking," I throw at him.

Surprise flickers in his gaze for only a moment before his expression evens out. "I never talk about you."

"Liar," I hiss.

"Who told you I said that?"

"Your ball-less friend." I indicate Elliot with a tilt of my head.

Whit's mouth kicks up on one side. "He's the liar."

"Sure." I don't believe Whit. He's the asshole who's convinced everyone to turn on me. He has all the power on this campus, and they bow to him. Even adults. Especially the adults. They're probably terrified they'll lose their jobs if they defy him.

"You don't believe me?" Whit asks.

I shake my head.

"You're smarter than I thought," he murmurs, so low I almost didn't hear him.

But I did. I heard and he must think I'm absolutely stupid to fall for anything he says.

I've had enough of this. I just want some peace. I have an hour until American Government, and that class is absolute torture, considering Whit's in it. I don't know why I'm wasting oxygen on a prick who's hellbent on destroying me.

I'm over it.

"Let me in," I tell him as I stomp forward, doing my best to push past him.

He stops me with a hand on my hip, his touching searing me to the bone. I go completely still, concentrating only on that tiny spot where his fingers rest upon me. Even through the heavy wool of my skirt, the cotton of my shirt tucked beneath, I can feel him. Like a brand, hot and everlasting, as if he just permanently scarred me. Gooseflesh rises, my breathing shifts. Changes.

That dull, familiar ache settles low in my belly.

Lower.

We're standing so close. Like we're a couple prepared to go out onto the dance floor and sway to a romantic song together. I've never seen him in the library at this time of day before, and it's a shock to the system.

His touch is also a shock to my system.

I keep my head bent, staring at his belt buckle. The front of his navy uniform trousers. I'm suddenly tempted to reach out and settle my hand over him. Feel the slow swell of his erection as it grows for me, until he's rock hard. I know he wants me. I can practically feel it vibrating off of him, flowing into me.

I don't do it, though. I can't touch him. I despise him.

I do.

Instead, I stand there and wait.

"You've got secrets, Savage. I can feel them crawling all over your skin. Just dying to get out," he murmurs, his head bent, his mouth at my temple. "When are you going to share them with me?"

"Never," I whisper harshly. "I'd rather die."

He chuckles, and with his other hand, he touches my face. Draws his index finger down my cheek. Traces my jaw. Feather-light. Almost as if it didn't happen. A shiver sweeps over me, oh so obvious to him, and I hate the shame that swamps me at my inability to control my body when he's near. "I think you'd like it if I wrapped my hands around your throat and choked the life out of you. Knowing I was the last face you ever saw."

His words should instill paralyzing fear inside of me. But they don't. Desire swamps me in spite of my anger, and I throw out the first thing that comes to me. "I hear you like to do that. Choke girls."

The moment the words leave me, I despise myself for saying it. I don't want him to think he lives in my head, my thoughts, my dreams, my nightmares, because he does. He haunts me everywhere I go. The Lancaster name is all over this godforsaken campus, and he is the only Lancaster I'm truly interested in. The reminders of him are everywhere. I can't escape them.

And I can't stand it.

"Where did you hear that?" He sounds amused.

I close my eyes. Suck in a breath when his hand rests gently against my throat. Like a threat.

A promise.

"F-first day of school. Caitlyn and Jane told me at lunch." The stutter is a weakness and I remind myself I need to be strong.

A chuckle escapes him and he steps even closer to me, pulling me into the library with him so we're tucked into a dark alcove near the entrance. The door he'd been holding open with his body slams with a loud bang and I hear Miss Taylor shush us from the front desk.

"They're cunts who wish I'd put my hands on them," he says, still sounding amused. "So you were gossiping about me?"

"They were gossiping," I correct.

"And you had nothing to say."

"I know nothing about you."

His fingers tighten on my neck, applying the slightest pressure. "Little liar. You know some things."

"Like what?"

"The taste of my lips. The texture of my tongue. The length of my dick."

I'm trembling. He's right. I know all of those things. "That was over three years ago."

"You remember."

"Of course I do." I hesitate for only a moment. "You called me a whore. As usual."

"So the nickname has stuck. At least I'm consistent." His grip gentles and he streaks his fingers along my skin, down toward the collar of my shirt. "My pretty little whore. You're even more beautiful than I remember."

I want to preen under his compliment, but I tell myself to stop. It's still an insult, dressed-up in nicer words. "I was only fourteen."

"So young. So innocent. Drinking champagne and tongue kissing a boy you didn't even know. Wearing a dress with your tits practically falling out of it. If you were innocent then, I'm sure you've been completely corrupted by now," he taunts.

I dare to glance up at him to find he's grinning at me. If he only knew how accurate his words are. "Let me go."

"I like seeing you have a backbone, Savage." He squeezes my neck again, tighter this time, making the air in my throat clog up. "Keep it up."

He releases his hold on me and walks away without a backward glance, his steps hurried as he exits the library. I remain in the alcove, swallowing hard, desperate to calm my breathing, my racing heart. I hate how much I just enjoyed our interaction.

His fingers on my skin, the gentle threat beneath them. I wanted the pain. I was leaning into his palm, silently begging for it.

I hate myself for wanting it.

For wanting him.

SIX

WHIT

AFTER I LEAVE THE LIBRARY, I go to Elliot—who's still curled up in a ball on the ground, clutching his junk like a pussy—and kick him lightly in the back. "Get up, motherfucker."

He staggers to his feet, his face wracked with pain. I didn't think little Summer Savage had it in her, but she took Elliot down, and that is no easy feat. He's my friend. Loyal to the end, but he's also a giant prick with a big fucking mouth.

Meaning he's weak. And I can't have weak people in my circle.

He's on his way out.

"That little bitch kicked me in the balls," Elliot mutters incredulously, shaking his head before he spits on the ground.

"Don't call her that," I say, my voice purposely even. I'm this close to unleashing all over him.

"Call her what? A bitch? That's what she is. Didn't even hesitate either. Just kneed me right in the nut sack. Hurt like a motherfucker."

"You deserved it." I take a step closer. See the sweat dotting his forehead. She did a number on him. "You said something to her."

He frowns, trying to remember. "What? I said lots of things to her."

"Something you had no business saying."

Fear flickers in his gaze and then it's gone, replaced by irritation. "What, that you fucked her? We all know you want to—"

I grip him by the throat with both hands, my fingers pressing tightly. I can feel the fragile bones beneath my palms give slightly and I realize it would be so easy to end this guy. He scratches at my hands with his fingers, struggling so hard and wasting much needed energy. Idiot. "You told her I said we were fucking. We're not...yet."

He stares at me, his eyes bulging, and I realize he can't speak. This gives me so much satisfaction, I can't help but grin. "Don't ever speak to Summer Savage again, do you hear me? If I see you so much as look in her direction, I'll slice your balls off and feed them to you."

Elliot nods as best he can, which is difficult considering I'm squeezing the life out of him with my bare hands. His face is red, sweat covers his skin and I release him before it drips onto my fingers.

Disgusting.

He expels a large, gasping breath, bending over and resting his hands on his knees as he coughs, so deep his lungs rattle. I watch him with disdain, my lips forming into a sneer I couldn't rid myself of even if I tried.

I hate weak people. I've known Elliot a long time, but when a pretty little whore who buys her way onto this campus can befell him with one slender knee, I know he won't remain my friend for much longer.

She's stronger than him, that much is clear.

"She's not a bitch," I tell him as he heaves, his body bent so he can't look at me. He probably doesn't want to either. The coward. "You're the little bitch who can't handle her."

I walk away from him without a backward glance, heading toward the chapel. No one is in there this time of day, and I need some solace.

Some peace.

My thoughts are riotous. Filled with Summer. What else is new? I hate that she's all I think about. I'm a man obsessed. One would think I'd get used to the feeling, considering I've been obsessed with her since I was fourteen. Yet my thoughts of her haven't waned over the years whatsoever. She's always been there, lingering in the back of my mind, haunting me at the strangest times, or when I least expect it.

Seeing her in American Government the first day of school, witnessing her trip and fall directly in front of my desk, shocked the shit out of me. No one prepared me for her arrival. Not even my hacker little sister Sylvie, and that wench knows everything that happens on this campus. Did I go to her and call her out over it?

No.

Weakness, I refuse to show it.

Once I realized Summer was going to pretend I didn't exist, I turned everyone against her. Yet no one broke her. She strode across campus, down the halls, into the dining hall, the library, the gardens, as if she owned this place. Her head held high, her nose in the air like a queen. Above it all.

Well, I eventually took her down.

She downplays her beauty, which I don't understand. Every other girl tries her damnedest to make herself look unique. Hair, makeup, nails, jewelry, it's always flashy. I get why. The uniform is limiting, and they want to stand out.

Summer does nothing to accentuate what she has, yet she stands out—at least to me. No makeup. Her glossy brown hair pulled into a simple ponytail, those long, wavy strands streaming down her back. Makes me want to grab it in my fist and tug. Her skin pale, her cheeks pink, her mouth...

Her mouth is the stuff of fantasies. Full, bitable lips, especially the bottom one. I'd love to sink my teeth into her flesh and tug. Witness those lips wrapped tightly around my cock.

That's what I want more than anything. To witness little Summer Savage kneeling before me, working my dick with her perfect lips, letting me come all over her luscious tits. Her face. She's almost eighteen and jaded as fuck. I'm sure she's given plenty of blow jobs. What's a couple more with me? I would've called off the sheep and her torment would've been over.

Easy as that.

Yet she refused me, and no one refuses me. I saw the way her pupils dilated when I offered to finger her at that very moment, yet she still turned me down. I'd been so angry when she mentioned not all Lancasters hated her; I'd become positively enraged.

And called her a whore loud enough for everyone to hear.

It's what she deserved. How else could I break her? I asked people to apply even more pressure. Get mean, I told them. Play dirty. Hunt her.

Hurt her.

Fuck her and her pious behavior. She believes she's above it all, when no one is. They all bow to me.

Eventually, she will too.

SEVEN

SUMMER

I SKIPPED AMERICAN GOVERNMENT.

I couldn't stand the thought of facing Whit after our conversation in the library. I hate that he's tainted my safe space. The one building I haven't found him in yet. He's ruined it. I have nowhere else to go to escape him.

He took the library away from me with just his presence.

I retreated to my dorm room and ate my late lunch. Instead of saving half the sandwich for later, I downed it all. Including the chips, and the Coke. It was like I was starving after that interaction with Whit, with Elliot, all of it. The fight with the girls in line. Listening to Matthews drone on, the word cunt falling from his lips so easily—twice—had taken its toll. Even the bitchy cashier in the lunch line almost sent me into an emotional breakdown.

Impressing Whit with my precise aim wasn't part of the plan. Yet somehow, his compliment felt good. His words made me stronger, despite the cruelty behind them. He still wants to break me. I know he does. He wants me to do his bidding, and every bit of that is sexual.

Would it be so awful, to become Whit Lancaster's sexual plaything? Probably. I'd guess he was into humiliation and all sorts of weird, far too worldly things that no teenager should know about. What happened to him that he's become so damaged?

I have no clue.

Hiding away in my dorm room wasn't smart though. It made it that much harder for me to leave and go to detention. I check the pink slip and see that it's being held in one of the classrooms upstairs in the main building, so I make my way there, trudging up the stairs with what feels like leaden feet. No school I've ever been at holds detention on a Friday afternoon. Billington had Saturday school, which was awful. I'd done my fair share of time there in the past, and hated every second of it.

I suppose a sixty-minute detention on a beautiful Friday afternoon won't be so bad.

I walk through the open classroom door to find a smattering of other students already inside. One of them is hunched over their desk, his head resting on his backpack like it's a pillow as he tries to nap. A few are doing homework. Others are staring morosely at the man sitting behind the desk with a faint smile on his face.

Headmaster Matthews.

Why is he wasting his time with monitoring detention?

A girl sits in the very last row, near an open window, her long, pale blonde hair gently lifting with the breeze from outside.

It's Sylvie Lancaster.

"Summer Savage, you almost got marked late. That would've cost you another three days of detention," Matthews says with glee.

I say nothing in response. Just make my way toward the empty desk next to Sylvie's, fully prepared to settle in when Matthews warns, "Don't sit next to each other please. And no talking."

I take the next desk in that row and sit, glad I brought my back-pack so it looks like I just came from class.

Matthews will see that absence in American Government and I'll eventually get in trouble. It'll mean more detention and I hate that, but it's too late now.

We all watch as the headmaster stands and heads for the door. He's about to close it when someone bursts through, pushing the door and our headmaster aside so he can walk in.

It's Elliot. The moment our eyes connect, he smiles.

"You're late," Matthews snaps.

"Sorry, sir. Had to come clear across campus. Plus, I'm missing practice."

Elliot is a football player. Of course.

"Are you playing tonight?"

"Yes, sir."

Sylvie sighs loudly. I glance over at her to see her yawn, holding a delicate hand in front of her mouth. That was also loud.

"Don't be late again," Matthews tells him before he returns to his desk. "Just to run over the rules, detention is officially over at four o'clock. For now, your time belongs to me. There will be no talking, no looking at your phone—I will confiscate it if I see it—and no sleeping. That means you, Garza."

Matthews slaps the edge of his desk, and Garza sits straight up, brought out of his nap and looking around in confusion.

Someone giggles. I think it's Sylvie.

"I suggest you work on homework. Maybe get ahead on those class reading assignments. If I catch you doing anything else, I have a fun little topic for a five-hundred-word essay that'll be due by midnight tonight." Matthews grins. I wonder if he gets off on torturing students. "Do we understand?"

God, what a condescending jerk.

We nod. A few of us murmur yes.

"I want to hear you say it. Do you understand?" he repeats.

"Yes, sir," we all say in unison.

"Good." He nods.

I bend to my left and unzip my backpack to pull out my math textbook when a folded piece of paper lands on top of it. Barely glancing up, I see Sylvie flash me the quickest smile before she resumes scribbling in her open notebook.

Grabbing my textbook and notebook, I set them on the desk, the note safely tucked beneath the front cover. I grab a pencil and then open the book to my latest math assignment before opening the notebook to a clean piece of paper.

Very, very carefully, I unfold the note Sylvie passed me.

How are you holding up at our lovely institution?

Anger simmers low in my belly. She has to know how awful it's been for me, especially lately. It's so obvious. And the ring-leader of all this mess is her asshole of a brother. I don't hesitate in sharing my feelings with her. She's not a friend. She's an enemy.

Terrible. Your brother is an asshole. Don't bother being nice. I'm sure you hate me too.

I fold the paper back up, watching Matthews the entire time. He's on his phone, his index finger scrolling, scrolling, scrolling and I assume he's on social media.

Dick.

As inconspicuously as I possibly can be, I drop the note back-ward. It flutters with the breeze, I can see it as I turn my head slightly to the left, zig-zagging in the air before it lands on the ground. Sylvie steals her foot forward, stepping on it as she drags the paper toward her desk.

I do not want to write that stupid essay Matthews referred to. If we get caught, I'm going to be pissed. Especially since commu-nicating with Sylvie is a complete waste of my time.

Figures that the one person who seemed interesting, who also seemed interested in me, is related to the biggest asshole on this campus.

Minutes tick past—we can hear the clock that hangs on the wall ticking, it's that quiet in the classroom—and I grow sleepy. Working on math doesn't help the situation. I tap my pencil on top of the notebook again and again, picking up speed until Matthews lifts his head and glares.

"Stop it," he says mildly.

I drop my head, my gaze snagging on the folded piece of paper that is somehow beneath my shoe. Making a show of it, I slam my book shut and lean over to shove it into my backpack. I pull *Romeo and Juliet* out, stashing the note in the middle of the book before I set it on my desk. Matthews watches me the entire time, annoyance on his face, and I crack the book open and pretend to read.

His gaze remains on me far longer than necessary until finally I glance up to find he's returned his attention to his phone. Slowly, I open the note, tucking it into my notebook, and read Sylvie's response.

I have no idea what's going on. I'm sure you probably don't believe me, but I've been sick and off campus for the last month. That's why I haven't seen you. I only just returned today, and got in trouble in World History for talking back to the teacher. That's why I'm in detention. So stupid. I don't have the same power as Whit, but I do have some power. Maybe I can help you, but you have to tell me what happened.

I want to believe her, but it's hard. What does she mean, she's been sick? I believe she's been off campus. I haven't seen her at all, so that makes sense. But sick? Does she have an illness? A disease? A drug addiction?

What do I say to her? I'm hot for your brother, but he treats me like shit and has ostracized me on this campus? Yet, for whatever reason, every time we talk, I'm tempted to lean in and kiss his mouth just to see if he tastes as good as I remember?

Pressing my lips together, I concentrate on the words she just wrote, reading them over again. I start to write, not wanting to get into too much detail, just in case someone—Matthews—catches us passing notes and we get in trouble.

Let's talk after detention. I can tell you what happened then.

I fold the note, then hold my left arm down straight, the paper pinched between my fingers. I let it fall at the same exact time a familiar voice yells out, "Headmaster Matthews!"

Dread fills me, my stomach churning, my sandwich threatening to come back up. It's Elliot. I glance over at him to find him watching me, a smirk on his face, his eyes dancing. He's ready to get me back for what I did to him earlier.

"Yes, Elliot?" Matthews asks.

"Sylvie and Summer are passing—"

Sylvie erupts into violent coughing. It's loud. Bone rattling. I turn to her in concern to find her hunched over her desk, her hands covering her mouth, her entire body shaking. I slide out of my seat and go to her, resting my hand on her back. I can feel her trembling, the coughing continuous and Matthews rises from his seat, making his way over to us.

"Are you all right, Sylvie?" he asks, his voice gentle.

"She doesn't sound all right," I tell him, fear racing through my blood. She wasn't lying. She sounds terrible, so she must be getting over something. She's so small, so thin, I don't know why she isn't passing out from the exertion the coughing is taking.

"I—I am." She wheezes. "I'm f-fine," she gasps out.

"Let's get you to the nurse's office," Matthews says, glancing around the classroom. "I'll be right back."

"You can't leave, Mr. Matthews," Sylvie says. Her voice is scratchy, the words like air. No substance. "I-I can walk there by m-myself."

She starts coughing again. I glance around the room, noting the expressions on everyone's faces. Most of them seem completely unaffected, as if they've witnessed this sort of thing before, and they're bored.

"Absolutely not. Someone needs to accompany you." His gaze lands on me. "Will you walk her, Summer?"

I can't even believe he's going to let me. Elliot was fully prepared to rat us out, and now Matthews is letting us leave. "Yes, sir."

"Drop her off and come right back. That should take you no longer than fifteen minutes. Understood?" He sends me a look.

I nod.

Sylvie gathers her things and I wait for her, concern making me want to tell her to stop. I'll help her, though she suddenly seems perfectly capable. Matthews heads back to his desk, sitting down, his gaze zeroing in on the boy who was about to snitch on our note passing. "Did you have something to say, Elliot?"

"Never mind," he mutters, sulking. "Doesn't matter."

We leave the classroom, Elliot's gaze never leaving us, a scowl on his handsome face. He's mad. I can tell, but I don't care.

Clearly neither does Sylvie.

The moment we walk down the flight of stairs and head for the exit, Sylvie breathes deep, flashing me a smile.

"That hurt like hell, but it was worth it to get out of there," she says.

I push open the door and we walk through it, the breeze and waning sunshine greeting us. "Did you just cough like that as a diversion?"

"I had to. Elliot was going to tell Matthews what we were doing," she says, as if her coughing fit was the logical choice.

"Sounded painful."

"It was awful. But again, worth it." She steers me to the right, toward the administration building. "Got me out of detention at least. Sorry that you have to go back."

"I'd rather get a break than stay there the whole time. I was getting sleepy."

"It's the most boring thing in the world. Sucks that Matthews sits there and plays on his phone the entire time. It's like he does it on purpose," she says.

"I'm sure he does." I hesitate. "Does he always supervise detention?"

"Yeah. I think it gives him a thrill, torturing us."

"I had the same thought."

Sylvie comes to a stop just outside the admin building, reaching out to touch my arm and causing me to stop too. "Is Whit making your life a living hell on campus?"

I nod. Her kind eyes and low tone could almost make me start to cry if I don't watch it.

She blows out a breath, gazing toward the chapel. "He loves nothing more than torturing a girl he's interested in. He's done it before. He's like that boy in first grade who chases you and hits you, but he actually really likes you."

"He's not interested in me. Not like that," I say firmly, the lies falling easily from my lips. He might dislike me, but he's definitely interested in me. "He hates me for what my mother did with your father."

"His hatred is aimed in the wrong direction. He should be mad at our dad."

"He's also mad at me."

"Whit is loyal to a fault. That includes being loyal to our mother, even though she's a snake, always lying in wait and coiled to strike," Sylvie says bitterly.

I'm taken aback by her tone, her words. I've never heard anyone say anything bad about Sylvia Lancaster before. All details shared about the Lancaster divorce painted Augustus as a man who couldn't keep it in his pants—ever—and his wife is the patron saint of the family.

"I don't understand why Elliot was so ready to tell on us," Sylvie continues as we get closer to the building. "He's a friend of Whit's. Meaning he shouldn't be so quick to get me in trouble."

I explain to her what happened earlier. How Elliot grabbed me, and I kneed him in the balls to get free. I don't go into detail about my encounter with her brother, or the things we said to each other.

That incident doesn't matter.

"Oh my God, that is so awesome," Sylvie says with relish once I'm finished explaining. "He fell onto the ground? Really?"

The wind picks up, whipping across us, and I glance up to see clouds rolling in the sky, black and foreboding. "He dropped like a sack of potatoes."

We both start laughing and it feels so good, so light. The lightest moment I've had since arriving here. Until Sylvie's laugh turns into a cough and she covers her mouth, her chest heaving with exertion.

"We can't laugh," I tell her, smoothing my hand down her arm. "Come on. It's getting cold out here. Let's get you to the nurse's office."

"I'll tell my brother to call off his dogs," she says as we enter the building. "He's not playing fair. Though he never does, so this shouldn't surprise me."

I say nothing. She can ask him to call off his supposed dogs, but I don't believe it'll happen. He won't be happy until I'm gone from this campus. And even then, my leaving still probably wouldn't satisfy him.

Once I make sure Sylvie is under the nurse's care, I hurriedly make my way back to the detention classroom, practically sprinting. No way do I want to get more detentions because I took longer than I should've. I breeze into the room, nodding in Matthews' direction when he lifts his gaze to me. He says nothing.

Neither do I.

Guess I passed that test.

I resume preparing for an essay for Romeo and Juliet, making notes. Writing and rewriting my introduction sentence. It occupies my time for the rest of the period, and I'm startled when

Matthews announces, "You're dismissed. Have a nice weekend."

Everyone quickly gathers their things. Matthews walks over to the window and shuts it, cutting off the cold wind blowing through. "No wonder she caught a cough," I hear him say.

Huh. Maybe he's not so bad. Still don't trust him though.

I'm about to head out of the classroom when I realize Elliot is right there, glaring at me. He falls into step beside me, keeping pace as I hurry down the hall. Run down the stairs.

He never says a word, which is creepy. I'd rather he give me a bunch of shit.

"Go away," I tell him once we're outside. No one else is around. The sun is completely gone, masked by the ominous black clouds in the sky, and thunder rolls in the near distance.

"No one's around to save you now," he says with a big grin.

"I don't need to be saved. I'll just knee you in the balls again," I retort.

He takes a step back. "Why are you like this?"

"Like what?"

"Such a bitch."

I turn and start walking, the wind pressing against me, making it a struggle. I hate this guy. I don't know why I've suddenly become a target, but he makes me uneasy. And he's right.

There's no one around to save me.

I make my way toward the dorms, picking up my pace. I can hear Elliot behind me, screaming obscenities, the words lost in the impending storm. Water droplets hit me, one after the other, and I realize it's raining.

I begin to run.

Within minutes, I'm inside the girls' dormitory, the door tightly shut. I turn and face the window, watching as Elliot approaches. My newfound jogging habit has made me faster, but I'm panting heavily, my heart racing triple time.

He marches right up to the window and bangs on the door, making me jump. He grins, the wind blowing his dark hair across his forehead, his jacket flapping open. I take a step back, my mouth dry as he runs his finger across his throat and then points at me.

Just before he turns and walks away.

EIGHT

SUMMER

THE STORM DOESN'T last long. It dumps rain for approximately thirty minutes, just enough to stir up the football field and make it nice and muddy for tonight's game. I sit at my window in my dorm room and watch it fall, homesick.

But I have no home to return to. Not really. Even if I begged my mother to let me come back, I wouldn't feel comfortable in that apartment. Not with all the memories there. The family photos. The little shrine she made for Jonas and Yates. She sent me a photo of it last week, and I found it so odd that she'd do such a thing. Photos of each of them on a small table. Candles burning, a sign with the Lord's Prayer on it and hands clasped together. A thick black Bible rested on the table as well.

We don't go to church. We don't really pray. I'm not sure why she would make such a religious tribute to them, but maybe she's dealing with her own guilt.

I understand that. Far more than she even knows.

I watch from my window as droves of students head for the football field for tonight's game. So many, I feel confident in leaving my dorm in search of food in the dining hall once the game starts. No one is in there, save for a couple of very young-looking students, all of them I assume are freshmen, and they're clustered together at a table, whispering furiously, watching me with suspicious gazes as I walk by them.

They probably know I'm the enemy too. And they're freaking freshmen.

With no one else around—such as Whit and his posse of henchmen and herd of sheep—I'm able to grab a fresh salad and soup, and I eat it in peace, my AirPods in, watching a new series on Netflix.

Once I'm finished, I head back to my room and change into leggings and a hoodie, then tie on my favorite running shoes. It's pitch black out, but the storm is over, and everyone's at the game.

No one will bother me.

My AirPods still in, I jog my way through the gardens, the lights above the many statues casting them in a golden glow. They're beautiful. A delicate angel. A weeping woman. An angry young man, his face angled as if looking in the distance, his jaw hard.

He reminds me of Whit.

They all do. Aching beauty etched in stone. Cold and unfeeling. Though every time he touches me, I feel nothing but heat. Fire from his fingertips, incinerating me.

Making me burn.

I jog faster, my heart rate kicking up as I make my way toward the forest. It's so dark. Darker than usual, thanks to the clouds still lingering in the sky, and I squint into the night, trying to see. My feet pound on the pebbled trail beneath me, and as long as I stay dead center, I won't lose my way. I can see the white pebbles, even in the darkness.

The path winds through the thicket of trees that lines the campus and separates it from the beach. Even with my AirPods in, I can hear the pounding surf, the waves riotous, the sea angry from the storm. I turn off the music and stop, breathing heavily, absorbing the rhythmic sound.

If I walked into the swirling water right now, no one would miss me if I disappeared. The school would most likely have a party, led by Whit. My mother would be sad, and add my photo to her shrine, but otherwise she'd move on. Everyone would tell her she was so strong.

And she is. But maybe all that strength is a mask for what she really is.

Devoid of emotion. Exhausted.

I don't know which.

The ocean tempts me, especially after such a harrowing day, but after a few minutes of listening to the waves, even taking a few steps toward them, I turn away from the beach path, and head back toward campus. I tell myself I'm stronger than that. If I walked into that water and let it swallow me, then they would win. And while I told Whit it wasn't a game, maybe he was right after all.

Life is one big game, and I'm too young to give in. I can't lose.

Not yet.

Knowing I was tempted yet didn't succumb, somehow makes me feel stronger. Gives me more power. I keep my pace steady as I head back toward the campus, choosing the trail that jags to the right and doesn't meander through the gardens. Instead I run through a tunnel made of towering trees and bushes, and they come across at the top, creating a canopy over the trail that I'm sure is refreshing during the summer.

Not that I'll ever witness it. Summers in Newport. Summers on campus. They offer a program, but I didn't attend, and soon I'll graduate. I'll never have to look at this campus again come the beginning of June. I'll have my diploma in hand and leave with my head held high.

Hopefully. If they don't break me first.

They won't. I won't let them. I won't let *him*.

A crack of thunder sounds overhead, startling me and I make a little noise, picking up my pace. Rain starts to fall in steady sheets, lightning shining in the sky again and again, accompanied by furious rolls of thunder, and I realize I'm putting myself at serious risk out here.

I could get struck by lightning, electrocuted on sight. Farfetched, but knowing my luck lately, entirely possible.

I break out of the covered path, rounding a giant wall of ivy, when another loud boom sounds, rattling the earth as lightning streaks across the black sky, illuminating the ground below. I see someone. Tall. Dressed in black. He's there.

And then he's gone.

Swallowing hard, I slow down and carefully approach the spot where I saw him, my heart racing. I hit my AirPod to stop the music, glancing around as I pull the buds out of my ears and shove them in my hoodie pocket. Wherever he went, he can't be too far. Probably someone else out for a run.

Right?

Thunder cracks, startling me and then an arm comes around my neck from behind, holding me to a firm, lanky body. A mouth settles at my ear, his voice low as he murmurs, "Gotcha."

I go cold, recognizing his voice immediately.

Elliot.

Closing my eyes, I remain completely still, telling myself to stay calm. I can figure this out. He's hellbent on getting revenge, I assume, and I can play along for a little bit. I need to gather my strength and take my chance when the timing is right.

"You're so fucking stupid," he says, his tone menacing. "Out here all alone. No one else around. Everyone at the football game."

"Why aren't you at the game?" I ask, proud of how calm my voice is.

"I got suspended for one game thanks to what happened earlier," he says, his grip tightening around my neck. His thick forearm presses against my throat, threatening to cut off my air. "Fucking bitch. You're not worth the trouble."

Another boy suddenly appears in front of us, completely unfamiliar. He's also dressed in black and he approaches us slowly, a disturbing smile on his face.

"Is this her?" he asks Elliot.

"Yeah. What do you think?"

His gaze scans me from the tip of my head down to my soaked Nikes. "I'm not one to hit a woman, but she looks like a royal bitch who deserves a smack or two."

"That's what I'm saying," Elliot practically growls with a laugh. "You hold her and I'll get the first hit?"

"Deal," the other boy says with a nod.

That's my cue to act.

I struggle against Elliot's grip, slipping right out of his hands, but the other boy quickly grabs me around the waist, whirling me around and lifting at the same time, my feet dangling in the air. He drops me to the ground, following after me, pinning me in the center of the graveled path. The little rocks dig into my scalp and my body, making me wince and the boy thrusts his face in mine, the rain dripping off his skin and onto my cheeks.

"Keep going. I like it when they struggle," he leers, as if he's done this sort of thing before.

"Get the fuck off her. She's mine first," Elliot yells, yanking at the other guy and pulling him off of me. I start to cry when Elliot straddles my hips, looming over me with a fist cocked back. I thought they wanted to rape me, not beat me up.

Anger fills me, drying up my tears and I try to buck him off but it's no use. He's got the upper hand and he knows it.

"Little bitch," he whispers, his teeth flashing in the darkness. "I'm going to fuck you up."

He sounds pleased, like he's getting off on this, which only infuriates me further. I put up a huge struggle, lifting my hips with all my might and sending him sideways, tumbling off of me. I kick out at him with one foot, nailing him in the stomach, so he falls back with a loud grunt, his face twisting in fury as he lunges for me once again.

Just as fast, he's gone. The other boy yells.

"Watch out! What the fu—"

A fist connects with the boy's mouth, and he crumples to the ground. I watch it all unfold in shock, the rain falling steadily upon us in fat drops, lightning flashing frantically above us.

Illuminating Whit, clad in his white button down and navy trousers, turning at the last second toward Elliot right before he hits him in the face.

"Whit!" I scream his name, just as his head rears back from the force of Elliot's fist making contact with his pretty face. I leap to my feet, heading straight for Elliot, ready to pull him off Whit.

Whit shoves Elliot off of him and they roll onto the ground, their legs and arms entangled as they each struggle to get the upper hand. I stand over them, feeling completely helpless, not sure what to do next. I pull my phone out, and start to dial 9-1-1 when Whit yells at me.

"Put that fucking phone away now!"

I slide out of the call, glaring at him. Worried for him. The other boy is staggering to his feet, his face already swollen thanks to Whit's fist, and I scream when Elliot swings for him yet again.

Whit's prepared this time. He stops the swing of Elliot's arm, thrusting his fist into Elliot's stomach with all his might. They keep hitting each other, the sickening thud of hands connecting with flesh sounding again and again as they try to destroy each other. Until Whit is the one left standing over Elliot, who's lying on the ground clutching his stomach, his body curled inward as he tries to protect himself.

"Fucking cocksucker," Whit says, breathing hard, pushing his wet hair out of his face. "You were going to beat the shit out of her."

"Bitch fucking deserves it—" Elliot starts but Whit kicks him in the stomach, making him groan.

"Asshole. You're finished. Through." Whit spits on him, right in his face. "Rot in hell, Elliot. You're done here."

"Come on, man. She's just some little bitch you wanna fuck. What does it matter what happens to her?" Elliot whines.

"More like she's a little bitch you want to fuck." Whit kicks him again, the rain picking up speed and becoming so loud I can barely hear him. I hit a button on my phone and somehow, I accidentally turn the music back on. The song "Streets" by Doja Cat starts playing on low from my Airpods still in my pocket, but I can hear Whit yelling at Elliot. "You have twenty-four hours. I never want to see your face again."

Whit turns on the other guy, who's watching all of this with a scared look on his face. "Never want to see your fucking face again either. Get the fuck out of here. Both of you!"

Elliot stands, rubbing his hand against his jaw with a wince. "You're making a mistake."

"My only mistake is that I trusted you in the first place," Whit says with a faint sneer. "Fuck off, asshole. I'll take my chances."

I watch, breathless as they stare each other down. Scared they'll start fighting all over again. Hurriedly I put my AirPods back in my ears so I won't lose them, watching the boys stare each other down.

But eventually, Elliot slowly walks away, the other guy following him, until they disappear into the darkness. Once they're gone, I turn to study Whit carefully, noting the way he cradles his front, his arm curved around his ribs.

He's hurt.

The prodigal son. The posh prince, still standing after he fought not just one, but two boys off of me.

I suppose I should be grateful. I probably should thank him.

His back is to me as he watches Elliot and his buddy run away, the pounding rain drenching his clothes, making his white shirt completely see-through. The fabric clings to his torso, emphasizing the lean muscle just beneath and I stare, unable to look away. I lift my gaze to his profile, sucking in a breath when I see the bruise forming on his cheek. The scrape on his jaw.

I go completely still, contemplating my next move. I should run. I can pretend I never saw him or Elliot tonight, and I never witnessed this fight. We can continue on and act like this never happened. I'm poised and ready to make my escape when he lifts his head, his nose in the air as if he scents me, like a wild animal.

I'm frozen. Like the nearby statues. Immobilized, quaking with fear inside. Today has already been too much. So much for me to deal with, and to end it with another horrible encounter with Whit Lancaster...

I don't know if I'll be able to stand it.

His startling blue gaze meets mine. Our gazes lock, and I can't look away. Neither can he. The song keeps playing, the words filling my head, so apt in this moment.

LIKE YOU, *like you*

Like you, ooh

I found it hard to find someone like you

THERE'S a cut on the side of his mouth. I can see blood dripping down his chin. He turns his head to face me fully, and I gasp, covering my mouth with my fingers.

Whit always reminds me of the statues in the campus gardens. Beautiful. Perfect. Cold.

Heartless.

Seeing him now, the untouchable god among us peons, broken...bleeding.

Human.

Staggering on his feet, he walks toward me, larger than life. Powerful despite the damage that's been done to him. His right eye is starting to swell shut. There's a red, bruising scratch on one sharp cheekbone. His lips are moving, as if he's speaking to me, so I rip one of my AirPods out of my ear only to catch the last few words he says to me.

"...you shouldn't have been out here alone. Are you okay? Fucking Elliot." He spits, the color of his saliva solid red.

I'm immediately furious. Who is he to tell me what to do? To act like he cares? So he ran to my defense and got his face battered in thanks to me. Really?

He could give a shit about me.

Whit has admitted he's the leader of my schoolwide torment. They're all bullies, but he's the biggest one of them all.

"At least I'm not the one who's bleeding all over the trail," I retort, waving a hand at him.

He grins. There's blood staining his teeth, reminding me of a beautiful devil. A fallen angel. As if he can read my mind, he spreads his arms out, looking like he might take flight. His position only emphasizes how soaked through his white shirt is, and I can see his flesh beneath. The dark shadow of his nipples. The muscle and sinew, the rise and fall of his chest as he breathes raggedly.

My skin prickles with awareness, and I mentally tell myself to stop.

"That mouth of yours is going to get you in trouble one day, Savage," he says, the maniacal grin still on his face. "Can't even say thank you for saving your ass. Those two were going to beat you into a bloody pulp, I hope you know."

"You probably called them on me and then ran in to break it up, hoping I'd believe you were my savior," I throw at him. "I don't trust you."

"I should've let them have you," he says, the smile slowly fading.

"Asshole," I mutter as I start to move past him, eager to jog by and forget this entire interaction ever happened.

But we both know I can't ignore him, and he can't ignore me. I can't leave him out here alone, even if he is the one who organized this in the first place. We have too much history between us.

Whit grabs my arm as I try to walk past him, stopping me. "Where do you think you're going?"

"As far away from you as possible." I try to shake him off, but his fingers tighten around my upper arm. "Let go of me."

"Gimme a minute," he says with a grimace, stumbling on his feet, and I reach out to clasp his other arm, steadying him in place. He's still cradling his stomach with one arm, his expression grim. "Fuck, I think that dick cracked my rib."

Shock washes over me, along with the rain. His injuries are worse than I thought. "Why did you do that?"

"Do what?" he asks, his expression incredulous. "Save you from two assholes who were going to tear you apart in the middle of a rainstorm? Oh I don't know. I thought you'd be glad I showed up."

"What were you doing out here?"

"I should ask you the same question," he retorts.

"You never answered my first question," I remind him, my voice calm, my thoughts chaotic.

We stare at each other, the rain falling. Falling. I blink the drops out of my eyelashes, watching him carefully as he shifts. Winces. I reach for him, my fingers brushing against his mouth and he jerks his face away from my touch.

"It doesn't matter. I'll be fine." He doesn't answer me, and having him so close, dependent on me, needing me, fills me with panic. He doesn't need anyone. He's above this.

Above me.

But even the god of this school bleeds, and I'm witnessing it now. The rain washes the blood away, but I can tell he's hurting. That black eye is going to be a doozy. How will he explain that?

"You don't look fine," I tell him. "Maybe you should try and see the nurse—"

"No," he interrupts, his voice firm, his eyes cold. "And don't you fucking dare tell anyone what you just witnessed. Got it? This stays here. Between us."

Who the hell does he think he is? God, he's infuriating. "You're such an asshole," I scream at him.

"Don't ever forget it, Savage." He jerks away from me, stumbling backward, landing onto the trail on his ass with a loud thump. "Fuck," he groans, lying flat on his back in the middle of the path, his arms spread wide.

He doesn't move. Just lies there on the pebble path amongst the puddles which are slowly turning into mud, with the rain coming down on him, his eyes closed. I study him for a moment, a war waging within me. I could offer him a hand and help him up. Walk him back to his fancy suite that isn't even a part of the dorms, and forget this encounter ever happened.

Or I could leave him out here and let him figure out how he's going to get back to his room. Not like he'd tell anyone I left him. He doesn't even want anyone to know any of this happened.

Making my decision, I turn on my heel and head toward my dorm hall.

"Where the hell are you going?" he yells over the rain.

I glance over my shoulder to see he's sitting up once again, his knees bent. His feet in puddles. "Why do you care?"

"Get back here!" he demands.

"Go to hell." I start walking, but guilt eats at me. Gnaws at my stomach. At my heart.

At my soul.

He's the worst human being on this planet. He's made my life a living hell since I first started at this stupid school. He got the entire school to torment me every single day, and he's not going to stop. Not until he gets what he wants.

And what he wants is...

Me.

On my knees, submitting to him. Letting him humiliate me. Making me do dirty, sexual things that I'll no doubt enjoy, and then feel swamped with guilt when it's over. He's a sick, twisted fuck. Damaged. Broken.

But he pulls at something that's deep within me. Something I don't understand. He makes me *feel*. Our one moment together when we were fourteen probably only lasted fifteen minutes tops, but it's burned into my brain forever. I want to know what it's like to kiss him now. Touch him now.

To have him touch me.

I should hate him for what he's done. The names he's called me. The things he's put me through.

But I can't just...leave him out here. He *saved* me. Despite everything he's put me through, in the end, he helped me. And the weather is terrible. What if he's seriously hurt? Internally bleeding?

Like an idiot, I turn and head back toward him. He watches me approach, shock registering on his handsome features as I draw closer and closer.

"Give me your hand." I hold mine out.

He stares at it with a grimace before lifting his gaze to mine. "You came back."

"I shouldn't. You're a complete dick."

He laughs. "My charm won you over."

"That and you coming to my rescue." I wiggle my fingers at him. "Give me your hand or I'm leaving. And I'm never coming back."

Whit isn't stupid. He takes my hand and I brace my feet in the mud, trying to haul him up. But he weighs more than I do and the ground is slippery. Of course, my hand slips out of his grip and I'm the one who goes stumbling backward, my ass landing in the mud with a loud plop.

Despite his pain and the wounds on his face, despite the rain beating down upon us, he starts to laugh.

"Should've seen your face," he says, shaking his head.

God, he's the worst.

I'm sure I look completely undignified as I push myself out of the mud and rise to my feet once again. He does the same, struggling and groaning in what I can only imagine is tremendous pain as he eventually staggers to his feet.

Good. I hope he hurts so bad he can't sleep tonight. It's the least he deserves for what he's put me through. I don't care if he did save me from that asshole Elliot and his little friend.

"You gonna make it?" I ask him once he's taken a few careful steps in my direction.

"Will you ah..." His voice drifts and he glances down for a moment before he looks back up, rain droplets clinging to his thick eyelashes. Of course, I would notice this. Despite the beating he took and the fact that he's covered in mud, he's still gorgeous. The fallen angel determined to lure me into darkness.

"Will I what?" I toss back at him, crossing my arms. I realize the rain has become lighter. And the thunder and lightning have completely disappeared.

"Walk me back to my room?" He takes another step toward me, his arm brushing mine and I grab hold of him, realizing that he's actually pretty unsteady. "I know I weigh more than you and I don't expect you to carry me, but it would help if you could maybe guide me there?"

I do not want a glimpse into the inner sanctum that is Whit's exclusive dorm. I'm guessing Sylvie must live in one of the private dorm suites as well.

"I shouldn't help you," I tell him warily, keeping my distance. Watching him as if he's a snake prepared to strike. I don't trust him. He'll turn this around on me somehow. Make it look like I snuck into his room and then I'll become the campus whore.

Though I wouldn't doubt I already hold that title.

"You shouldn't," he agrees.

We stare at each other, rain dripping off of us. He still cradles his arm against his stomach, and I wonder how bad his ribs are. Bruised? Broken? He'll be in really bad shape if they're broken, and what if moving him makes everything worse?

I glance over my shoulder, my dorm hall looming in the near distance. A thought forms in my mind, one that is absolutely ridiculous, but now would be the time to make it happen. No one's around. They're all at the game. We have plenty of time.

"Can you walk?" I ask as I go to him. I slip my arm around his waist and hold him steady, trying to ignore the heat of his skin that burns through his saturated shirt.

We start to move, his steps halting, his face wracked with pain. He leans into me, almost too heavily, and I brace my feet, trying to remain stable. "Feels like I can't breathe," he mutters.

That's his ribs. Has to be.

My mind made up, I steer him gently toward my building. "We're going to my room," I tell him.

"What the hell? No way." He laughs, immediately clamping his lips shut. I'm sure that hurt. "They catch me in your room, you'll be expelled."

"No, I won't. And you'll make sure of that." We walk side by side, his heavy arm slung across my shoulders, my arm still around his waist.

"What do you mean?" There's a pause between each word, as if it took a lot out of him to say that, and I try not to let that little detail worry me.

But it does.

"You're a Lancaster. Untouchable. We'll tell the truth, and nothing will happen to me," I say simply as we approach the double doors of my building.

"Don't you have an advisor watching the front desk?" he asks.

"They're all at the game." When I left for my jog, the front desk was empty.

I'm hoping it still is.

"You're taking a chance, Savage," he says admirably. "I don't know if that's brave or fucking stupid."

Probably both, is what I want to tell him.

But I keep my mouth shut.

NINE

SUMMER

SOMEHOW, I get him into my room, though it's not easy. We had to pause a lot. He coughed once, and I thought he might pass out, but maybe that's me being overly worried. I had to shove him against the wall and hold him there, praying he wouldn't lose consciousness. He's too heavy. There's no way I could've lifted him.

When I finally get him into my room, I guide him toward the chair at my desk, helping him sit. I realize quickly that he's shivering from the cold and his wet clothes.

I'm shivering too.

"I'll be right back." I hold my index finger in front of his face, trying to sound like I mean business. "Don't move."

"I couldn't if I tried," he croaks, trying to crack a smile and failing miserably.

I leave him in my room and go to the communal bathroom, where I grab a couple of towels and a washcloth. I go to the sink and turn on the water, running it until it's scalding, then saturate the washcloth with it, wringing it out quickly before I shut the water off. I scurry back down the hall, knowing we don't have a lot of time until the game is finished and everyone comes back to the dorms.

I need to get his clothes, and mine, into a dryer. I can't have anyone notice that I have boy's clothes either, so I need to mix them in with other stuff. It won't look unusual that I'm doing my laundry on a Friday night. No one likes me at this school. I have no friends.

What else am I supposed to do?

I enter my room to find he's still sitting in the chair, his pants puddled around his feet. He glances up at me with a grimace. "Get this shit off of me," he groans.

Irritation filling me, I go to him and kneel on the floor in front of him, pulling off his shoes first, then peeling off his socks. I go to grab his trousers and I realize his boxer briefs are there too.

Slowly I look up at him to find he's smirking at me. Despite everything. The pain and the wet clothes and the crazy situation we're currently in, he's got an arrogant look on his face and I know exactly why.

"Didn't imagine you kneeling before me for the first time like this, but it'll do," he drawls.

"You're such an ass." I tug his pants and boxers off his feet, letting them land on the floor with a wet plop. "Take off your shirt."

He cocks a brow.

"Take. Off. Your. Shirt," I repeat, a little slower this time.

"You want me naked? Don't know how well I'll be able to perform—"

I cut him off. "I want to throw your clothes in the dryer."

"Oh." He sounds disappointed. "Rich girl like you knows how to do laundry?"

"I do. Don't sound so surprised," I say with a huff, my eyes going wide when those long, elegant fingers reach for the front of his shirt and slowly start undoing each button.

"You going to watch?" he asks, his voice bored as he undoes the last button. The shirt hangs open and my gaze drops, but there are shadows in the room, thanks to the single lit lamp on my bedside table. I can't see anything. And I'm curious.

I want to see everything.

"I suppose," I say with indifference, like his near nakedness in my room doesn't affect me.

"I'll show you mine if you show me yours." He tips his head in my direction. "You're wet too."

My clothes are so soaked, fat water droplets are literally dripping onto the carpet.

Feeling defiant, I tug the hoodie off, dropping it onto the pile of Whit's clothes. I toe off my shoes, my no-show socks rolling right off with them. Resting my hands on the waistband of my leggings, I slowly work them down my legs, my gaze never leaving Whit's the entire time.

He doesn't look away. Just holds my gaze, as if we're in a competition to see who blinks first. He does, his gaze dropping to my legs for the briefest moment when I finally get the leggings off my body.

It was as if they were stuck to me like glue.

"You're really going to take off all your clothes. In front of me." He sounds like he doesn't believe me.

"I've got nothing to hide," I tell him, enjoying the dare—the way his gaze roams over me, as if he has no idea where to look first. I'm full of surprises, I think. I keep him guessing. He believes I'm some meek, stupid girl who he can push around.

He's wrong.

I take him in as well. How he's sitting on my chair completely naked, save for the open shirt, and I realize that's kind of weird.

This entire situation is weird.

"Neither do I," he says.

"Shall I go first?" I don't know where this bravery is coming from, but I'm going with it.

"If you insist." He smiles. Winces. The shiner he's sporting is deepening in color, giving him a gruff, rough-around-the-edges appearance.

The prince has been wounded in battle. And I'll have to pretend like I never witnessed it. As if I have no idea what happened.

It should be easy. Not like we talk in front of other people anyway.

Reaching behind me, I slowly unhook my bra. It springs away from my skin and I let the straps fall down my arms, then toss it into the clothes' pile.

"Just as pretty as I imagined," he murmurs, his gaze only for my chest.

Perv.

I am not ashamed of my body. It's been used, and I've used it. Right now, it's a weapon of mass destruction, and Whit is my target. I'm fully prepared to decimate him.

Though I suppose I have the advantage, considering he's injured and hiding away in my room. But still. When in war, you must take your opportunities where you can.

Resting my hands on my hips, I curl my fingers around the waistband of my panties. My heart slows, then kicks back into gear with a steady, heavy beat. His gaze is warm. Assessing. He leans back a little in the chair, and I know he should look ridiculous, practically naked with a drenched white shirt on and nothing else.

But he doesn't look ridiculous. Not one bit. I'm the one who's supposed to be in control right now, but he's the assured one, waiting for me to make the next move.

"You going to drop them?"

"You want to see?" I throw back at him.

"You fucking know it," he says with a grin.

Pissed, I push my wet panties down, irritated that they get stuck around my knees. I struggle with them, finally kicking them off before I just stand there and let him look his fill.

And he does. He blatantly stares at the spot between my legs, his brows lifting slightly. "You don't wax."

Why would I want to make my pussy pretty when no one was really seeing it? Well, the only person who was, I didn't want him to touch me. At one point, I wanted to make myself as repulsive to him as possible.

It didn't work. He didn't care. He still took what he wanted.

"I trim it," I say, which is the truth. "Groom it a little."

"I like it." His smoldering gaze meets mine. "Your confidence is a surprise, Savage. I like that too."

I shouldn't take pleasure from his compliments, but I do. And it's so cold in here, my nipples are hard, aching points. I rub my arm against them, trying to ease the pain, but it's no use. "Your turn," I tell him.

"I don't know if I can stand."

"Is that a cop-out I hear?"

With a grunt, he grabs the back of the chair and rises to his feet on unsteady legs. I'm tempted to help him, but he glares when I take a step forward, so I don't move any further. He shrugs out of the shirt, first one shoulder and arm, then the other. Very, very slowly.

Until he's just as naked as I am.

His shoulders and chest are broad. His abs...he has a six-pack. Flat stomach. His belly button is an innie. Hairy thighs. Long, thick cock that is semi-hard. And once my gaze latches onto it, it grows even harder.

"Impressed?" he asks, sounding annoyed.

"It would do," I say with a shrug and a yawn.

He laughs. Groans. Clutches himself, falling back into the chair with a heavy thud.

"Looks like nothing's going to happen tonight," I say with glee as I whip around and go to my closet, slipping on a fresh hoodie and grabbing a pair of sweat pants to pull on. I slip my feet into slippers and turn once more to face him. He's eyeing my fresh, warm clothing with obvious envy and I gesture toward my bed. "You should rest."

"In your bed?"

"No, in the chair." I roll my eyes. "Of course, in my bed. Oh! I almost forgot." I go to my dresser and grab one of the towels I brought with me, along with the now cool washcloth. "Do you need help?" I ask as he stands and starts to make the few short steps to my bed.

"I'm fine," he bites out, shuffling like an old man. My gaze drops to his ass, noting the shallow dimples at the base of his spine. I imagine kissing them. Biting the firm flesh of one butt cheek, then the other.

My cheeks flush, and I go to him, tugging the comforter and sheets back before he collapses on top of the mattress. I pull the sheet and comforter over his naked, damp body, tucking it around him. I offer him a towel and he frowns. "Dry your hair?"

He dismisses my offer with a single shake of his head. "No."

"Let me wash your face at least?" His frown deepens. "So I can clean up your wounds."

"Go put my clothes in a dryer first," he tells me, his voice weakening. His eyelids are heavy, as if he's suddenly been hit with a wave of exhaustion. "Before everyone comes back here."

His point is valid, so I do as he says, going to the communal laundry room and dumping our clothes into a dryer before I start it up. Forty minutes should be plenty of time to get everything relatively dry. Then we'll wait for lights out and I'll sneak him out of here. The advisor eventually goes to sleep, so no one will be at the desk by the time he leaves.

Though there are cameras. Someone could see us. How heavily are they monitored? Maybe Sylvie can help us with her hacking skills.

Maybe Whit won't want his sister's help. He might not want her to know what's going on between us.

And what exactly is going on between us anyway? I don't have a clue.

I rinse the washcloth with hot water once more and return to my room, going straight to him. He's lying there, his phone clutched in his hands, his fingers typing on the screen furiously. He glances up when I'm standing right beside the bed, a familiar scowl on his face that's oddly comforting.

I'm more used to him being cruel to me than anything else, and that is all kinds of fucked up.

"I have a warm washcloth to wash your face." I hold it up.

"I can do it," he says, dropping his phone beside him on the bed before he sits up to reach for it. The movement makes him wince, and I hold the washcloth out of his reach.

"Nope, let me play nurse for a minute."

"Only if I get to play doctor with you later," he mutters.

Ignoring his statement, I settle in next to him and he scoots over, giving me more room. I study his face. The deep scrape on his cheekbone. The reddish-purple bruises forming around his eye. The skin is swelling, causing his eye to become smaller, and I wish I had ice to put on it. It'll be swollen shut by morning. I'll start out easy, and move on to the bigger damage next.

"You're in bad shape," I murmur as I touch the washcloth to the cut at the corner of his lip.

"You should see the other guy," he says.

"I did. I saw both of them." I gently wipe at the scrape on his cheek. It's deep, and he bares his teeth at me as I clean it. "Why were you out there anyway?"

"It doesn't matter."

Irritation fills me. "I'm not going to tell anyone what happened."

"I can't trust you, Savage. I'm not telling you shit," he says irritably. "Just know—I'll take care of the problem."

"How?"

"Don't worry about it," he mutters.

Anger makes me swipe at the fragile skin beneath his eye a little too hard and he hisses in pain. "I don't want you to be my white knight."

He laughs. "Trust me. I didn't want to rescue your skinny ass tonight either."

I push away from him. "Then find someone else to nurse your wounds."

"I could get a hundred other bitches to do the exact same thing you're doing, right now. All it would take is this." He snaps his fingers.

The arrogant asshole.

I glance around the room, pretending to be in search of some-one. "I don't see anyone running to do it."

He silently glares.

I quietly gloat.

"Elliot is an asshole," he says after a few moments as I clean up the dried blood still on his face. I wonder if someone was wearing a ring when they hit him. There are tiny cuts among the massive bruises. "I had a feeling he was going to do some-thing to you."

I'm mystified by his statement. "What do you mean, you thought he was going to do something to me?"

"You made him look like a weak pussy earlier, in front of the library. He didn't like that." He smiles, his eyes sliding closed. "Stupid ass bested by a weak little girl. He's done for. Seriously, no one fucking fights me on this campus and gets away with it."

My hand stills, the washcloth still pressed beneath the eye. "What do you mean by 'he's done for'?"

His eyes slide open, brilliantly blue and glittering. "Elliot. He's finished."

"But I thought you two were friends," I say, confused.

"You kicked him in the nuts and took him down. And he retali-ates by trying to attack you. And look at you. Are you worth ruining his reputation completely?" He waves a hand at me before it drops limply on the bed.

I pull the washcloth away from his face and sit up straight, insulted. "You're such an asshole. I'm risking *everything*, sneaking you into my room and trying to help you, and this is how you repay me?"

"What did I do? All I said is look at you." His eyes slide closed, his lips purse, the ugly jagged cut in the corner red with inflammation. If he's not careful, it'll scar. "You're just a girl. A weak, whorish little girl who took him down with one knee as if he was powerless. That's why he was so mad. I don't blame him. You're nothing, yet you strut around campus like you own the place, and it's not yours to own, Savage. This is *my* campus. You should cower in fear every time I so much as look at you."

"You're a pig," I tell him, giving him a hard shove as I rise to my feet. He grimaces in pain, rolling over on his side so his back is to me, and I don't even care. I hope he hurts for all eternity. I hope a rib punctures his lung and they both fill with fluid. He'd die from that.

I wouldn't feel a single inch of remorse if he did. Not at all.

He deserves it. For how he talks to me. Treats me. The things he says about me. The things he gets people to do to me. I don't care if he helped me earlier. He only did it for selfish reasons. It had nothing to do with me.

Why should I help him? He's disgusting. The worst person I've ever met.

"The second your clothes are out of the dryer, I'm kicking you out of my room," I tell him.

"Someone will see me when I leave," he says to the wall, sounding annoyed.

"I don't care. You can be the one to explain why you're in the girls' dormitory this time of night. And you better not drag my name into it."

"Or what?" He glances at me from over his shoulder. "Are you *threatening* me, Savage?"

There's no point in denying it. "Yes. I am." I go to the bed and lean over hm, thrusting my face in his, our mouths so close I can feel his breath. So close, I could kiss him. I'm halfway tempted to. "I *am* threatening you. If you say I snuck you into my room, I'll tell them that you forced yourself on me. You held me down and made me swallow that giant dick of yours between my lips and suck you off."

His eyes narrow, but he doesn't say a word.

"You won't get in trouble, considering your goddamned name is all over this school and you're fucking untouchable, but at least I won't get in trouble either. I have no qualms in screaming sexual assault to anyone in regards to you, so don't tempt me," I tell him, giving his shoulder a shove before I stand tall once more.

His gaze tracks my every movement as I make my way toward the door, the washcloth and towels in my arms. "I think you'd get off on that," he says quietly. "Me holding you down, my giant dick between your lips. You sucking me off. I bet you'd drink every last drop."

I don't acknowledge his words. To do so would show that they get a reaction out of me. The image of him holding me down on the bed, feeding his cock between my lips, that arrogant smirk on his face the entire time...

A shudder moves through me at the thought, and I try to banish it, but it's like I can't. It's there, playing like a movie in my mind on a repeat loop. He'd get no greater satisfaction than dominating me, and I'd...

I'd love every second of it.

God, what the hell is wrong with me?

"I'm going to get your clothes," I tell him, my hand on the door-knob. "Don't move."

His soft chuckle follows me as I slip through the door.

I stomp down the hallway and into the laundry room, dumping the dirty towels in a giant bin. The dryer is still spinning and I open it, reaching in to feel his clothes.

They're still pretty wet. It's going to take a while still.

Frustrated, I slam the dryer door and hit the button, turning it back on. I watch the clothes spin and spin, chewing on my thumbnail, willing the clothes to dry faster.

I hate him so much. He's fucking despicable. He has major issues, and clearly hates women. Has zero respect for them, especially me. And he's surprised I could drop Elliot the idiot with one thrust of my knee? It had been easy. He dropped like a sack of potatoes, straight to the ground.

If Whit hadn't shown up earlier though, Elliot would've got his revenge against me. Dread floods my stomach, making it churn at the thought of what he might've done.

Whit rescues me, yet he treats me like garbage. I don't get it.

Is he a narcissist? Or maybe something else is wrong with him mentally. I wouldn't doubt his entire family is completely fucked up. Sylvie is kind of weird, though at least she's kind. My family is fucked up too, though—pretty sure everyone's is at one point or another.

Voices sound in the hall and I startle, realizing that people are starting to return. I grab the clothes out of the dryer—they're a little drier but not by much—and clutch them to my chest. No way can I leave them in the dryer for someone else to find.

I pause in the doorway, watching as girls pass by. None of them look in my direction. They're all so good at following instructions. Whit told them to ignore me and they do.

He's right. They're all a bunch of mindless sheep.

Once there's a lull in foot traffic, I dart out and make my way to my room, pressing flat against the door when a group of senior girls walk past me. Two of them are Caitlyn and Jane.

My so-called new friends from the first day of school.

"Slut," one of them murmurs beneath her breath just before they all burst into laughter.

I say nothing, my face hot. If they knew who was in my room right now, they'd die of jealousy.

And then have confirmation that I am, indeed, a slut.

At least in their eyes.

Reaching behind me, I slowly turn the doorknob, barely cracking open the door before I slip back inside and turn the lock. The room is dark. Quiet. The lamp is off. The window curtains are pulled back, letting in the bright moonlight and I go to look outside, surprised at the clear skies above us.

The storm has completely moved on. Almost as if it never happened.

I go to the lump beneath the comforter and give his shoulder a rough shake, but he doesn't respond. He doesn't even move. I grip his shoulder again.

Nothing.

Rounding the bed, I come at him from the other side, staring at his battered face. The moon gilds his features in a silvery glow, and I realize the asshole is in a deep sleep. In my bed.

Of course, he looks beautiful. Despite the wounds and the black eye, his lips are soft and his eyes are closed and he looks so...young. Like a little boy.

Vulnerable.

I hate him.

I sit on the edge of the bed, a loud sigh escaping me. He doesn't even flinch. I touch his nose. Tweak it. Poke at his bottom lip.

No response.

My eyelids are heavy and I toss his damp clothes on the floor. I'm so tempted to slip beneath the covers and sleep for a little while. This entire experience with Whit has left me mentally and physically exhausted. What's the difference if he goes now or stays a little longer? It might be easier if he just sneaks out in the middle of the night, never to be seen or heard from again.

I couldn't get so lucky.

Giving in, I tug the comforter and sheet back, and slip beneath them. Pull them up to my chin, and lie on my side. It's a double bed, very narrow, and he's sleeping on my preferred side.

Figures.

I study him in the moonlight through sleepy eyes, marveling at the realization that I have Whit Lancaster in my bed. Naked. Injured. Asleep. I despise him, yet I'm also glad for this moment. The two of us alone with no one else around to ruin it.

He can ruin it enough on his own.

What would it be like, to have this boy's heart? I wonder as I slowly drift off to sleep. Impossible, is what I tell myself.

He doesn't have one.

TEN

SUMMER

I WAKE up to fingertips on my cheek.

They walk a line on my face, one after the other. So light, I could almost believe it's not happening.

But it is. I remember everything before I fell asleep. Seeing Whit. Bringing him to my room. Stripping in front of him—still can't believe I did that—getting so pissed at him. He knows how to take something good and twist it into something awful. He self-destructs, and takes everyone else down with him.

It's a horrible trait. But he's a horrible person, so I shouldn't be surprised.

He doesn't seem so horrible right now though. I can feel his gaze on my face, heavy. Hungry. He touches the corner of my mouth. Skims my bottom lip.

Tingles rush through me and I'm tempted to part my lips, draw his finger inside and suck. That would surprise him. He'd probably love it.

That reason alone is enough for me not to do it. I'm still mad at him.

He touches my chin. Pinches it. As if he's trying to wake me up and he's frustrated it's not working. My eyes pop open to find him watching me, his lips curled into a faint smile, his eye nearly a slit, the bruises around it even worse. "Wake up, sleepyhead," he croons.

"Get out of my bed," I tell him evenly.

"You're the one who asked me to get into your bed in the first place," he reminds me.

"Your invitation expired. Go away." I'm about to roll over and show my back to him but he grabs hold of my shoulder, stopping me.

"You fell asleep." He gently tugs, his grip strong, and I have no choice but to roll over onto my back. He scoots closer, hovering above me and I glare at him, hoping he can't hear my heartbeat, which is currently racing. Or see how my breathing starts to accelerate at his nearness.

He's in my bed. Naked. I can feel his body heat. I'm fully clothed, but naked beneath the hoodie and sweats. It would take nothing for him to strip me bare and have his way with me.

And I'd let him. Despite what happened earlier, when Elliot nearly attacked me. Despite the anger and the bitterness and the loathing I feel toward this boy in my bed right now, even though he saved me, I'd kill to know what it feels like, to have Whit Lancaster inside of me. Claiming me.

Making me his.

"Why did you take care of me?" he asks, his voice firm. Cold. He sounds more like himself. Earlier, he showed weakness. He was feeling low. Who wouldn't, after getting into a fight in the middle of a thunderstorm?

I shrug one shoulder but don't say anything.

He shifts closer, lowering his head near mine. "Answer me."

"I couldn't leave you out there alone." I lift my chin, hoping he doesn't notice it's trembling. "Just like you couldn't leave me."

"You should've left me. I treat you like dog shit," he states matter-of-factly. "Yet you brought me into your room. Cleaned me up. Dried my clothes."

I stare at him defiantly, any words I could say are stuck in my throat. I have no answer for him.

"Cat got your tongue?" he asks, lifting a single brow.

I watch him, wary. Silent.

"You're stunning, do you know that?" His voice softens and he moves his hand toward my hair, making me flinch. He ignores it, stroking my hair away from my forehead, his gaze thoughtful as he stares at me. "You try to hide it, but there's no use. You're fucking beautiful, and it frustrates the shit out of me, Savage."

Now it's shock that's rendering me speechless. He thinks I'm fucking *beautiful*?

"It doesn't matter what I do, you don't back down. Any other person would've broke by now. It's like I can't break you, and that frustrates me too." His fingers go still. "What's happening in that mind of yours right now? What are you thinking? The same thing I am?"

I'm thinking I want him to never stop touching me.

"You stared me right in the eyes when you took off your clothes in front of me earlier, like you didn't give a fuck." He leans in, his cheek next to mine, and inhales. "All that smooth skin. Pink nipples begging for my mouth. Long legs I can imagine wrapped around my hips. Your body is all I can think about."

I close my eyes and he grabs my chin, shaking my face. "Open your eyes," he demands.

I do as he says, quaking. A shuddery breath escapes me.

"Do I scare you?" he whispers.

Deciding to be truthful, I nod.

"Good," he breathes across my lips, his mouth so close to mine, I can feel it move when he talks. "Because you scare me too."

The words hang between us, suspended in air, his mouth resting on mine, our gazes locked. His lips move, capturing my top lip between his and giving it a little tug. A sigh escapes me, bone-deep, my eyes falling closed. This is what I've been waiting for. What I've wanted since I saw him again. This.

This.

This.

He kisses me, his mouth seeking, his hand moving from my chin to cup the side of my face. I lean into his palm, needing to feel him, to feel something, anything. Whatever he can give me, I'll take.

His lips slowly work their magic, clinging to mine, soft, teasing kisses that surprise me. I open for his tongue, a gasp escaping me when he licks at my lips before sliding it into my mouth to meet mine. Our tongues touch. Dance. He shifts closer, lying halfway across me and I worry about him. Press my hands on his shoulders to push him off of me.

"Your ribs," I whisper against his mouth, but he swallows my words, the sound of our lips connecting again and again the only thing I can hear. I become lost in the sound, his taste, squirming beneath him, wishing I could get closer. Wanting to be as close to him as physically possible.

"Don't worry about me," he says at one point, his hand going for the hem of my hoodie. "Take this off."

He shifts to the side, helping me remove it. I'm braless, and his gaze goes straight to my breasts when the hoodie is gone. He kisses my neck. My collarbone. My chest. My nipples are so hard they hurt, and I arch my back, desperate to feel his mouth on them. He chuckles against my skin, I'm sure he can sense my neediness and he licks one nipple, making me cry out.

"Too loud, Savage," he whispers. "Might have to muzzle you if you keep that up."

"Put your hand over my mouth to keep me quiet," I tell him and he lifts away from me so we're face to face.

"You'd like that, wouldn't you?" He cocks a brow.

I like the idea of Whit's hand covering my mouth. I don't know why. He brings out something in me. He makes me want things I would normally never suggest, especially out loud.

He lowers his head to my chest once more, raining kisses all over my skin. His mouth is so hot, his velvety wet tongue painting my skin, making me pant. I clutch the back of his head, sinking my fingers into his soft hair, clutching him to me.

When he draws a nipple into his mouth and begins to suck, a keening cry falls from my lips.

He reaches up, his hand covering my mouth as he continues.

I moan against his palm when he sucks my nipple in earnest. I close my eyes, my entire body fixed on that one spot where we're connected. He licks and sucks. Bites. It hurts. It feels good. At one point, I try to pull away from him, but he just sucks harder, his cheeks hollowing out. Until he releases my nipple with an audible pop before moving to the other one, giving it the same treatment.

All while I writhe beneath him, my skin on fire, my heart beating between my thighs, an incessant throbbing that becomes more and more intense.

His cock is hard, pressing against my thigh and when he's finally through with my chest, he removes his hand from my face, watching me with swollen lips and that horrible black eye. The cut cheek and the split by his mouth, which I swear has started bleeding again. I reach out and touch the spot, pulling my finger away to see tiny drops of blood.

Despite the damage, he's still heartbreakingly beautiful. I can't believe we're doing this. That he's in my bed. That he wants to be here, and he's not calling me names.

That I even have to think that makes me realize what we have isn't normal. Far from it.

So what are we doing?

"I shouldn't do this," he murmurs. "I hate you."

His words hurt. They steal my breath. Make me want to turn away.

But I don't.

"Why am I so drawn to you?" I don't think he's really asking me this. More like he's questioning himself. And I don't have an answer. "Make me stop."

He kisses me again, his mouth brutally attacking mine. I accept his brutality. Revel in it. I respond to him, winding my arms around his neck. Tangling my legs with his, pressing my chest against his so we're skin-to-skin. He's hard. Blazing hot. His tongue rubs against mine rhythmically, making me think of sex, and I want it.

I want him.

"Make me stop," he repeats against my mouth, his hands going to the waist of my sweats and shoving them down my hips. I lift up, aiding him as he strips me bare, kicking the sweats off and shoving them aside with my feet.

He settles in between my thighs, his cock nestled between us and I spread my legs, giving him better access. He presses his forehead against mine, his hand going to my chin once more, squeezing until I open my eyes to find him watching me. His one eye swollen, the other one glittering, full of anger and so much hunger, it's overwhelming. I try to look away but he won't let me, his fingers gripping me firmly. "Tell me to stop."

I remain mute, arching beneath him, tingling everywhere. I want him all over me. Inside me. I want to feel him come. I want to watch his face when it happens. I want to know what he looks like when he loses control, and I want to know I'm the one who pushes him to his absolute limits.

"Summer." My eyes fly wide open. He never calls me by my name. It's always Savage. Or whore.

God, he's horrible. Terrible.

"Tell me." He lowers his mouth to mine. "To stop."

I slowly shake my head, and he kisses me. Softer this time, his mouth moving languidly against mine, our tongues sliding. He grinds against me, his cock heavy, pressed so close to my entrance it would take little effort for him to slip inside. He doesn't though. It's as if he's withholding himself on purpose, and I lift my hips, trying to get him in me. Frustrated whimpers leave me, and I can feel him smile against my lips. Know with complete certainty that he enjoys torturing me.

"You want it, don't you," he says after breaking the kiss, moving to my neck. He sucks and licks my sensitive skin, his hips working against mine. I stroke my hands down his smooth back, trace the dimples at the base of his spine before I skim my fingers along one firm ass cheek. "Despite everything I do and say, how I call you a whore. How I have everyone on this campus treat you like shit, how *I* treat you like shit, you still want my cock inside you."

I close my eyes, trying to ignore what he's saying. His words hurt. It's humiliating, how much I want him when all he ever does is treat me like garbage. I'm all twisted up inside over this boy, and I don't understand why.

He pulls away from me and I'm immediately cold. Lost. I open my eyes and watch as he crouches before me, his hand gripping the base of his cock, stroking. My gaze lingers on his fingers, watching him masturbate. His cock is huge. Veined. Beautiful. He squeezes just below the head, a little pearl of milky white liquid dribbling from the tip. I'm fascinated by how rough he handles himself and when my gaze lifts to meet his, I find he's already watching me.

"You're dying for a taste." His voice is flat, though his eyes gleam. He rises up, scooting closer, straddling me, his cock right in front of my mouth. "Take it."

I part my lips and he does just what I described earlier. He feeds me his cock, inch by inch, and I moan around him. His heavy flesh throbs, stretching my lips, settling inside my mouth. I can taste him, the salty pre-cum, my tongue rubbing against his velvety hardness just before I gag when the head bumps against the back of my throat.

He pulls out, strings of saliva sticking to his erection, and he looks so pleased, my pussy clenches. "Fuck, you're a pro. I knew you would be."

Whit teases. Thrusts in and out of my mouth and I take it. I suck him deep. I lick him like a popsicle. I grip the base and squeeze and stroke, just like he did only a few minutes earlier. He thrusts his hips, matching my rhythm, his gaze hooded, his lips parted, his gaze never straying from what we're doing.

I'm not a pro. Far from it. I've only given a couple of blow jobs in my life, so I don't have much experience. But I want to do this for him. Make it good for him. Seeing the pleasure wash over his face, the groans sounding low from his chest sends delicious little shivers racing all over my skin.

He increases his pace, fucking my mouth, and I let him. An unfamiliar feeling rises within me, threatens to overwhelm, and I realize quickly what it is.

Power. I may look submissive, as if I'm being forced to do this, but I'm the one who's giving him pleasure. I'm the one who's got his cock in my mouth. I'm going to make him come.

And that makes me feel strong.

His body grows tense, a growl falling from his lips as he practically rips his cock from between my lips, his hand working furiously over the length when a spurt of white shoots from the tip. He comes and comes, shuddering and moaning, semen splashing all over my chest. I lie there and watch him in utter fascination, agony etched all over his beautiful face, his eyes closed, his fingers still gripping the base of his erection.

So beautiful, I think. I did that. I made him come that hard.

His eyes slowly open and he studies the mess he made, his expression indifferent. The Whit I'm used to.

The Whit I don't particularly like.

He drags his fingers through his own cum and brings them to my lips. I part them readily, cleaning the musky, sour liquid from his fingers, my gaze never straying from his as I lick him.

"Dirty fucking girl," he whispers, his eyes still at half-mast, his expression pure satisfaction. "You want your turn?"

"Yes," I answer truthfully when he removes his fingers from my mouth. I'm throbbing between my legs so hard, I'm afraid he could touch me once and I'll come.

"Maybe I shouldn't give it to you. Maybe it's all about me tonight." He leans down and presses his mouth against mine in a feather soft kiss. "I'm a selfish bastard. I love nothing more but to take and take. It's the Lancaster way. I could make you give me head again. You'd do it. I know you would."

Anger rises, and I try to buck him off me with my body. He just laughs, the sound almost evil.

"Or I could fuck you until I come, and make sure you don't. It would be easy," he continues.

I don't know about that. I'm so on edge, I feel like I could shoot off like a rocket at one touch.

"I could eat you out. How about that?" He raises a brow. Like I'd say no. "Lick you everywhere. Finger you. I bet you're nice and tight, though I know I'm not your first. No way can I be your first. Not with how you act."

If he's trying to shame me, it's working. He'd probably be disgusted if he knew my backstory. Who I've been with. I've tried to blot it from my mind, especially right now, but he's not helping matters with what he's saying.

"Have you ever touched yourself and thought of me?" he asks casually, a smile spreading on his face when he must see something on mine. A flicker in my eyes. A twitch in my jaw. Some sort of tell. "You have. Tell me, is the reality as good as the fantasy?"

"I wouldn't know, since I'm the only one who's been delivering so far," I retort, referring to that epic blow job I just gave him.

My chest is still sticky with his cum, but I refuse to wipe it off.

"Let's test out the theory then," he says, shifting so he's lying on top of me.

He moves so fast, I don't have time to say or do anything but just lie there and take it. I wonder at his earlier injuries. He could barely move only a few hours ago, and now he's so quick. Was he faking? Was it some sort of ruse to get into my room?

Maybe.

Probably.

I don't care. He's currently kissing my stomach, his hand on my right hip, holding me in place. My breathing accelerates, I'm so anxious to have his mouth on me, and I'm afraid I might come too fast and miss out on all the good stuff.

But I'm also desperate to climax. My entire body is strung tight, my muscles straining. He touches my pubic hair, then shifts lower, settling that elegant, skilled mouth right on my pussy.

A choked sound leaves me and he lifts his head, glaring at me. "Stay quiet," he demands.

I do my best to obey. But oh God, it's so difficult. His mouth is the finest torture I've ever experienced. And his tongue. He spreads my thighs as wide as possible before he attacks my pussy with thorough efficiency, not missing a spot. He's everywhere, thrusting his tongue inside me. Searching my folds. Drawing my clit between his lips and sucking.

That's all it takes. A little orgasm quakes through me, making me cry out and I slap my hand over my mouth, riding the wave, hating that it's already happened.

That was so fast. Too fast. I won't come again tonight. I know I won't.

"Fuck, you're responsive," he murmurs against my flesh before he dives back in. He slips a finger inside me, his lips still on my clit. Another finger. Thrusting in and out, stretching me wide. His tongue flickers against my clit, faster and faster, his fingers keeping pace, until he curls them, nudging against something deep inside me that starts a tremble low in my body.

Oh. Keep doing that, is what I want to tell him.

But I don't.

It's as if he knows. He doesn't let up. He's relentless. Maybe he can tell by the way I'm moving, or the gush of liquid that's flowing from my body. I'm so wet, I can hear his tongue slicking through me, his fingers pushing inside me. The feeling keeps coming and coming, intensifying. I strive toward it, throwing my head back, my hand on top of Whit's head, holding him to me. My breath catches in my throat, my head spins, and I can't breathe. I can't bre—

Another orgasm slams into me out of nowhere, stealing every bit of oxygen and all of my thoughts. I'm mindless. Weightless. He doesn't let up, his tongue still flicking against my flesh, his fingers still thrusting. I rub against his face shamelessly, the orgasm rippling through me, tears squeezing out of my eyes. It's too much. Too overwhelming. Until finally I collapse, my breaths ragged, my head still spinning, my heart racing out of control.

I swear I thought I would pass out.

He kisses the inside of one thigh, then the other, his mouth gentle. As if he knows I'm coming down from the high, and my body is still so sensitive. He slides back up until we're face to face, and I can feel his heavy erection nudging against me.

"You came twice," he says with unmistakable pride, kissing me. I can taste myself on his lips. On his tongue. It's as if he wants me to, his kiss is so possessive. Forceful.

I return it eagerly, enjoying my taste on his lips, moaning into his mouth. He swallows my sounds, the kiss turning wild. Reckless.

That's how he makes me feel. Wild.

Reckless.

I've lost all control with Whit, and I don't even care. It's as if he's turned me into this needy, uncontrollable little thing, and the only way I'll be satisfied is by him.

He breaks the kiss first, smoothing my hair away from my face, studying me closely, as if he's trying to figure me out.

Don't bother. I'm hopeless, I almost say, watching him with glazed eyes, overwhelmed. Exhausted.

"Go to sleep," he whispers and my eyes slide shut as if he commanded them to, my already relaxed body seeming to melt into the mattress.

Until I don't remember anything else. Just him. And me.

ELEVEN

WHIT

WELL.

That was unexpected.

Once I know Summer is fully asleep, I slip out of her bed, not sure where to look first. She confuses me. I don't understand her whatsoever, yet I do. What just happened between us was unlike any sexual experience I've ever had in my life, and I've had quite a few. I'm no angel. No one expects me to be. I'm a selfish asshole who takes what he wants, whenever he wants it.

I never fully expected to take Summer Savage and definitely not tonight, though the temptation was always there.

Being with her, saying all that terrible shit, it felt...natural. She liked it too. I saw the flare in her eyes, the way she so readily agreed to everything I told her to do. She wants to be controlled. And I enjoy controlling her.

Somehow, even though we hate each other, it's as if we're a perfect match.

Maybe she imprinted on my brain when we were fourteen, that first night I kissed her. When she taught me how to kiss. I know now I had no clue what I was doing, and I only copied what I saw in movies. Porn. What the fuck ever. I kissed other girls like that, and they never tried to correct me. Maybe they didn't know any better. I didn't.

Yet she softened me. Taught me that kissing wasn't about brute force, but gentle persuasion. I owe her that lesson.

She owes me for saving her ass tonight from that stupid fuck Elliot. And she saved me too. I might've beat Elliot's ass, as well as his stupid friend's, but they got a few licks in, leaving me in pain. That she brought me back to her room to take care of me was surprising.

I hate being indebted to people. It's the worst thing you could ever do, a sign of weakness. And there's nothing more I hate than weakness.

So I need something, anything I can find in this tiny little room of hers. Something that belongs to her.

Something I can use against her.

I'm not above blackmail. We both know this. And now that she's lying asleep, blissful after that epic orgasm I just gave her, it should be easy to search through her belongings and find something personal. I know she has a secret in here somewhere. The girl is full of them.

I want to discover every single one.

I spot her backpack on the floor and go through it, grateful for the moon shining in the room and allowing me to see. It's full of notebooks and textbooks, nothing interesting, but I go through each one, making sure there's nothing hidden. I find a folded note that must've been passed between her and I think my sister. I recognize Sylvie's writing, and I frown as I read what they wrote to each other.

Sylvie is trying to become her friend. I won't have that.

I can't.

I leave the note where I found it and zip the backpack closed, my gaze going to her desk. It's cold as fuck in here, but I don't want to put on my clothes yet. I know they're still damp. I spot the oversized black hoodie Summer was wearing earlier on the floor, and I grab it, tugging it on. It's a little short, but it'll do.

Going to the pile of my clothes next to the bed, I grab my boxer briefs and slip them on as well, grimacing when I feel the damp fabric against my skin. I pissed Summer off earlier and I'm guessing she didn't dry my clothes all the way. Fucking sucks.

Still worth it though, after what happened between us.

The girl is an expert dick sucker. Does that sound awful? Yes. Do I still consider her a whore? Confirmed.

But now she's *my* whore, and I don't share.

I go to her desk and rummage through it. Not much on top of it. A couple of piled notebooks—girl is obsessed with them or some shit—and then I start going through the drawers, constantly glancing over my shoulder to make sure she doesn't wake up. I find a stack of old photos and I look through them. Photos of a younger version of Summer and her friends. They're smiling, their hair windblown, their gazes clear and carefree, with the exception of Summer's. There's something dark that lingers in her eyes. Mysterious. Her smile is wide, but there's pain in her eyes.

Anger grips me. Who hurt her?

I don't know.

Maybe I don't want to know.

Dropping the photos, I open the next drawer to spot a thick, black leather journal sitting there, just begging to be picked up. I do so without hesitation, holding it up to the light beaming into the window. There's a white sticker on the front cover, and someone wrote on it—I assume it was Summer.

Things I meant to say…

Jack fucking pot.

I open the journal, and all I see is words. So many words. I flip through the pages, realizing quickly that it's a journal, filled with her thoughts and dreams. Lists. Little bits of paper, a photograph here and there. Various dates. It started…over three years ago.

This is Summer's journal. A diary of her personal life, all in one little convenient book.

I snap it shut, and slowly close the desk drawer.

With quiet efficiency, I finish getting dressed. Don't bother putting on my uniform shirt. I leave it on her floor, since I'm taking her hoodie.

And her journal.

I've got what I need. This journal is full of information I'm sure, and all of it I can use against her. Tomorrow she'll try and pretend nothing happened between us. She'll act like I never touched her and made her burn. She'll pretend she never had my cock in her mouth, or my fingers inside her tight pussy. As if she never came against my mouth, her clit pulsating beneath my tongue.

She'll continue on as if what happened between us doesn't exist, but fuck that. I'm going to tell her I have something that belongs to her, and the only way her secrets are safe is if she continues to meet with me until I'm through with her.

Because that will happen—I guarantee it. I'll get bored. I'll toss her aside and move on, and maybe even give the journal back to her. Eventually.

Or maybe not.

I go to her bed and watch her sleep, ignoring the strange feeling stirring in my chest. As if my heart is being strangled. She means nothing to me. She *is* nothing to me. Except for a good lay. And I haven't even really fucked her yet.

My thoughts wander, and I think of Elliot and his townie friend who tried to beat the shit out of me. I fought as hard as I could, defending myself pretty decently, considering it was two against one. This only started because of Summer. Right after school, Elliot taunted me. Said he was going to fuck her first. Stupid fucker.

The hell he was. That piece of shit will be dead before he lays another hand on her.

She's mine.

I clutch the journal in my hand and bend over her, dropping a soft kiss on her forehead, inhaling her intoxicating scent. She stirs in her sleep, murmuring nonsense, rolling over on her side, the comforter slipping, her bare back to me.

The temptation to climb back into bed and have my way with her is strong, but I tell myself to stop. I need to get the fuck out of here. I've stayed too long as it is.

As silent as I can be, I exit her room. I already texted Sylvie about the cameras, and she said she'd take care of it. No one will know I was in Savage's room.

Except for her.

TWELVE

SUMMER

I WAKE UP SLOWLY, to the sound of chirping birds just outside my window, as if I'm living in a Disney movie, which I know is completely untrue.

More like I'm living inside a nightmare, one I can never seem to escape.

The curtains are still open and sunlight floods the room with way too much light. I crack open my eyelids and immediately close them, slinging my arm across my face, desperate to avoid the overly bright room.

It's too much. My eyes hurt. My head pounds. My entire body aches. I feel hungover, and I didn't even drink last night. Shifting beneath the covers, I realize I'm still naked, and my thighs are sore.

The memories come back, one after another. Last night. The storm. Elliot threatening me. Tackling me. Whit unexpectedly coming to my rescue. Until he was beaten. Bloody. Broken. Bringing him back to my room. Stripping naked for him. Watching as he stripped for me. Hating him. Wanting him. Waking up to him touching me. We took it further. I always knew we would. It was inevitable. It was also amazing.

Of course it was.

It feels like what happened between us was a dream. As if it never happened at all. He's not in my room. I don't know when he left, but he's gone. If he were still here, I would sense his presence. Feel him in the bed with me.

I slowly remove my arm from my eyes and open them, staring at the ceiling, thinking of last night. His head between my legs, his mouth on my pussy, licking and searching, leaving no part of me untouched.

My core clenches just thinking about it.

What Whit and I share isn't normal. I don't know how to define it. I also didn't know you could feel so much, being with someone you hate. Become aroused by someone who says such horrible things. It's as if he has complete control over my body, how it responds, and I'm not mad about it.

Not at all.

It's as if I crave him.

As my mind runs over what we said to each other, what we did, I start to feel sick. Maybe I should be ashamed of myself. I let him use me. He was essentially fucking my mouth, like some sort of porn clip come to life, and while I didn't mind at the time, now I feel nothing but shame.

We shouldn't have done that. I shouldn't have let him go down on me either. But oh, that orgasm had been amazing. I swear I lost all function of my body for a moment. I was flying. In the air. Soaring above. Just before I came crashing down.

Reaching between my legs, I touch myself there. I'm sticky. Wet. I tentatively rub my clit. It's swollen. Still sensitive from last night.

I don't stop touching myself, reliving the dirtiest moments Whit and I shared. It's like I can't. I remember at one point last night, when I opened my eyes to find Whit watching me, his mouth on the most intimate place of my body. I couldn't look away and he knew it. He stuck his tongue out, the gesture almost obscene as he thoroughly licked me.

A shudder moves through me and I squeeze my eyes shut, Whit's face haunting me. I'm coming. Oh God, I'm coming so hard. Not as hard as last night but the tremors move through my body and I stifle the moan that wants to escape.

I just think about him and I can make myself come.

What have I done?

Once I've composed myself, I climb out of bed, my steps tentative, the floor cold beneath my bare feet, despite the shining sun. I see the crumpled white shirt on the floor and I pick it up, realizing it's Whit's.

I slip it on over my naked body, doing a couple buttons. It still smells like him and I breathe deep, wishing he were still here.

But what would I do if he was? How would I act around him?

The bigger question: how would he act around me?

There's what I want to happen, and what will most likely happen. Knowing Whit, he'll probably make a mockery of the entire evening. To him, it was just a one-off. It means nothing.

I'm nothing, especially in his eyes. He'd make me feel like absolute shit, break me apart with his words and his sneers and his angry glares, and then leave me alone to pick up the pieces.

My skin suddenly crawling, I undo the buttons as quickly as I can, shucking the shirt off my body and flinging it onto the floor. I grab my robe hanging off the hook on the back of my door and slip it on, tying it around myself, and go to my desk.

I need my journal. I need to write down everything that happened between us yesterday so I don't forget. The library. Detention. Me finding Whit and bringing him back here...

I open the desk drawer where I keep my journal, but it's not there. Frowning, I dig through the drawer, the stack of notebooks and journals I love to buy and never use, but it's gone. I search the other drawers. The top of my desk. My backpack.

It's not here.

Dread consumes me as I look around the room. I know what happened. I know.

That bastard took it.

My hands clench into fists, and it takes everything inside of me not to scream as loudly as I can. But that will only draw people's attention, and that's the last thing I need right now.

Whit stole my journal. The most private thing that belongs to me. I'd let him steal my body, my heart, everything I've got, before I'd let him even get a peek inside my journal.

And now he has it. It's in his hands.

I collapse on the bed, my face in my pillow, and I wonder if I could suffocate myself with it. He could be reading it right now. I've kept that journal for *years*. Our first encounter is in it.

Before I knew who he was. I found out pretty quickly after I wrote that entry, but it didn't change how he made me feel.

Terrible. Wonderful.

Other things are in there too. Yates, and what we did. What he did to me. Those things are buried deep in the back of my journal where they belong, but they're there. For Whit to read whenever he wants. I talk about the divorce. My issues at school. How my friends abandoned me when I needed them the most. My mother. Jonas. My real father, who barely acknowledges my existence.

All my damage is in that journal, and it's not meant to be read by anyone else. I don't even like to re-read it much. The past belongs where it is—firmly behind me.

And it's in the hands of the boy who makes my life miserable every single day. A boy who will do whatever he can to ruin me completely. Including sharing my journal with others. I can only imagine him and his friends laughing over it as they read passages. He could make copies and share it with everyone. I would be the laughingstock of the school.

Worse? The authorities could be notified of what I did. I could be questioned. I could be...

Arrested.

I clutch the pillow to my face and scream and scream, the sound muffled. I yell until my throat is raw and aching. I yell some more, knowing it will hurt to talk, but not caring. What does it matter?

No one talks to me anyway.

AFTER TAKING A SHOWER, I spend the majority of my Saturday in my room, trying to do my homework. My concentration is shot, and I'm so tired. I end up sleeping the rest of the afternoon, only waking up to a sudden loud knock on my door.

I jolt up, pushing my hair out of my face, glancing around. The room is dark, and I see it's dark outside as well. Grabbing my phone, I check the time. A little past six. I should go to the dining hall and grab some dinner.

The knock sounds again and I go to the door, my steps quiet, and rest my head against the door, as if that could tell me who's standing on the other side of it. Saturday and Sunday the dorms are open, guests welcome until eight p.m. No one visits me though. I can only assume whoever's knocking is bringing trouble with them.

"Summer! I know you're in there," says a vaguely familiar voice.

Slowly I unlock and open the door to find Sylvie standing there, a faint smile on her face. She's clad in a pale pink oversized hoodie that swims on her thin body and black leggings, her feet clad in white Nikes. She offers me a little wave. "Your hair is a mess."

I rest my hand on my head, feeling my still damp hair. "I took a nap."

"I figured. Rough night last night?" She waggles her eyebrows, as if she knows everything that happened between me and her brother and I grab her hand, hauling her into my room and shutting the door.

"What did he tell you?" I ask, breathless. He talked about me with Sylvie, I just know it. That has to mean something, right?

"If you're referring to my closed-mouth brother who doesn't say boo to me, nothing," she says, walking around my room with curiosity shining in her eyes. She turns to look at me. "You have nothing hanging on the walls."

I shrug. I have photos in my desk. Of friends. My family. But my friends don't care about me any longer, and my family is fucked up. Why would I want to look at them every day? It's just a reminder of my old life. Was I happier then?

Sometimes. Sometimes not.

She drags her fingers along the edge of my desk, shuffling through the stack of notebooks there. Her obvious digging leaves me unnerved, but there's nothing for her to find. The most important thing to me in the world is gone.

In her brother's possession.

"I like your notebooks," she says, her gaze returning to mine. There's nothing deceptive behind it. She's not looking for my secrets. My shoulders relax, but I'm still on edge.

"Thanks," I say, defensive as always.

"I'm obsessed with them too, I have so many." She continues as her searching gaze sweeps around my room. "There's the cutest shop downtown. You should come with me sometime. You'd probably spend way too much money in there, like I do."

"Why do you want to be my friend?" I ask her warily, cutting right to the chase.

She's quiet for a moment, watching me. I do the same to her, noting yet again how thin she is. How her clothes hang off of her, the leggings only emphasizing how her legs look like narrow sticks.

"You intrigue me. I think you intrigue Whit too, though he'd never admit it out loud." Sylvie hesitates for only a moment. "He asked me to cut the security cameras at your building last night."

My heart bottoms out. I forgot all about the security cameras on us. Seeing me walk Whit inside. Watching as Whit left my dorm hall in the middle of the night.

"What do you mean?" I'm surprised I sound so calm. Inside, I'm quaking.

"He texted me last night around nine, asking if I would hack into the security system and cut the cameras on this specific building. The very one you live in. I did it for him, no questions asked. Anyone who was up to no good last night, they're not going to get caught," she explains, her eyes wide.

My face goes hot and I look away.

"This morning, I started to think. Why does Whit care about this dorm building? And why last night? I did a little investigating, and I saw you were one of the students who occupy a room. A private one." Sylvie smiles, reminding me of a cat. "He also specifically mentioned the cameras on the west end of the building. And look at you, with your room on the west end."

I say nothing. To protest would make me look guilty. Best to keep my mouth shut.

"I don't want nor do I need any dirty details, but I'm going to assume you and my brother were together last night." She raises a single delicate brow. Again, I remain mum. "And I have to admit, I'm impressed. Whit doesn't usually dip his wick in girls that go to this school, especially newbies."

"Who does he dip his wick in then, if not someone from this school?" I ask incredulously, wishing I could take the question back as soon as the words leave my mouth.

I shouldn't care. I don't care.

I do.

"Girls from families our family is close to. People we socialize with. Occasionally, girls he meets in town." She laughs, probably at the shock on my face. "That was last year. He slummed with the townies a lot, claiming they never asked questions, so they were the perfect girls to hook up with."

"He told you this?"

"He told his best friend, Spence, who told me." Her expression turns mysterious. "Spence and I are—*were*—close."

Interesting. "You like him."

"He likes me. I don't know how to feel about him. I'm dying you know, so there's no point." When my mouth drops open, she holds out a hand, laughing. "I'm serious. I'm in poor health, as mother says, and I've been on my deathbed already a few times in my life. I'm only sixteen."

"You and Whit are very close in age."

"Lina is fourteen. Mother had us, one after the other, like little chickens. Our eggs dropped, plop plop plop. Her and Daddy must've been very busy during that time in their lives. I suppose they were happy. I don't know. Probably not." Sylvie smiles. "She was hoping for all boys, so Carolina and I are a disappointment."

"My father was disappointed I was a girl too," I say, not knowing if it was true, but it feels better to think that.

"Men and their lineage. I don't understand. Girls can continue the family as well, we just don't continue the name, rendering us useless, I suppose." Her assessing gaze drifts over my room one more time, as if she's trying to find something in particular. "Want to go to dinner with me?"

"To the dining hall?"

"Ugh, no. How can you eat their dreadful food, day in and day out? Let's go somewhere." Her eyes dance and she clasps her hands together. "Please. There's an Italian place downtown that's my absolute favorite."

I haven't ventured out of here beyond the school, and the upperclassmen are allowed to leave on the weekends, with a curfew in place, of course. Besides, I didn't know where to go, and had no one to go with.

Truthfully? I was scared to leave. Scared to go somewhere unfamiliar, and chance getting cornered by people who hate me. There are too many people on this campus who despise me. Why give them a chance to do their worst?

"Come on, Summer. Please?" Sylvie says when I haven't responded. Her hands look like she's praying as she holds them up to me, a pleading look on her pretty face. "It'll be fun."

"Fine," I say with a sigh and she starts hopping up and down, just before she starts violently coughing.

I guide her to my bed and settle her on the edge of the mattress before I grab an unopened water bottle from my backpack and hand it to her. She cracks the lid open and takes a sip in between coughs. Then another. Until finally, she stops.

"I can't overexert myself," she says, wheezing. "Still getting over it."

"What exactly are you getting over?"

"Pneumonia, and it's not even winter yet. I usually get it a couple of times a year." She smiles, but it's weak. "You need to fix your hair before we go out. It's a wreck."

I touch my hair again, looking in the nearby mirror that hangs on my wall. It does look awful. I washed it and immediately fell asleep, so it's a mess. And still damp. "I'll braid it," I tell her, turning to face her. "I'll change too."

"Don't worry about dressing up. I'm going with this look." She waves a hand at herself. "Oh, this will be so much fun. Be prepared. I'm going to ask you endless questions."

I smile in answer, but it's forced.

That's what I'm afraid of.

THIRTEEN

SUMMER

THE RESTAURANT SYLVIE brings me to is small and quaint. Oh, and packed. It's Saturday night, and everyone's out, the sidewalks downtown crowded with people waiting to get into a restaurant or a bar. Sylvie glides into her chosen restaurant as if she owns the place, chatting with the hostess like they're old friends, and obtains us a table within minutes.

"It helps when you know someone," Sylvie tells me with a wink just before the hostess leads us to our table. The other people in the cramped lobby glare at us as we head into the dining area, pissed at us for jumping the line.

Sylvie is oblivious to their ire.

Once we're seated, she tells me her favorite dishes, making recommendations based on what I tell her I like. She orders us strawberry lemonades and fried cheese for an appetizer, my mouth opening in protest when the two words fall from her lips. She silences me with a look.

"Trust me. It's delicious."

I'm sure. And I'll gain five pounds alone from tonight's dinner.

My mother's words follow me everywhere I go in regards to food, especially in restaurants. Particularly ones that serve rich, calorie-laden dishes. My mother is so thin, she makes super-models look fat. Her diet consists of prescription medication and alcohol—that's pretty much it. She rarely eats. She used to be bulimic, she admitted that to me when I was thirteen and eating everything in sight. During those heroin chic days when she was younger, she referenced them more than once.

Meaning she was quite on-trend in the mid-nineties.

She believed I showed signs of bulimia as well, but it turns out I was eating like crazy because of a growth spurt. I'm prone to weight gain. She told me the summer I was thirteen, when I was lazy and spent the long, hot days in my room, rarely going out. I need to watch what I eat and exercise. She was a food tyrant, monitoring everything I put in my mouth. Griping at me when she caught me eating junk food, which back then was often.

Now I find I can't bring myself to eat bread or pasta without hearing her voice ring in my head, and that's a horrible thing. I'm not fat, but I'll never be as thin as Mother. Or Sylvie. She's so skinny, I can see the blue veins in her pale, thin arms. Her clothes hang on her, as if she has no meat on her bones, and her face is so angular, her cheekbones are razor sharp. Her pointy little chin and that lush, startlingly pink mouth against her pale skin really stand out. She's gorgeous, like Whit.

"You're staring," she tells me once the server leaves our table.

I blink her back into focus. "I'm sorry. It's just you're so—"

"Thin?"

"No," I deny, though it's true. She's thin as a rail. I could crack her in two. "You're beautiful."

"Oh." She appears taken aback. And pleased by the compliment. "Thank you. I haven't heard anyone use that word to describe me in a long time. Everyone's always so concerned with my weight. I know I look like a skeleton. Mother called me a bag of bones before I came back to school. I'm on protein supplements, but they're no use. I can't keep any weight on." She smiles. Glances around the room, as if she wants people to pay attention to her, but none of them are, which is fine by me. "Whit worries about me, but I told him there's no point. I'm dying."

My heart skips a beat at her casual mention of her brother. At the equally casual way she references her impending death. "I'm sure your family is very worried about you."

"There's no need. Like I said, I'm on the way out." She laughs at my horrified expression. "What? It's true! Death is something we all eventually have to face, Summer. I'm just having to face it a little sooner than most. And it's okay. I'll be lucky to make it to eighteen. Hopefully I'll have had sex by then. Have a boy go down on me, at least. Are you a virgin?"

Her question stuns me silent for a moment. I think of who stole my virginity and frown. "No."

"Oh, it was that bad? I'm sorry." She leans over the table, her voice lowering. "I thought I wanted to save myself for the right person, but I'm afraid the right person won't show up before my expiration date. Now I'm eager to get with whoever I can, just to get the deed over with. Really, I want to know what it's like, to have someone else give me an orgasm."

I kind of like how open she is. How honest. Sylvie is nothing like her brother.

"Don't you want it to be with someone special?" That's how I always felt before, when I was younger and incredibly naive. Until I was worn down and eventually gave in. A girl can protect her virtue for only so long.

"Trust me, there's no one special in my life, or I'd be banging him nonstop by now." The server stops by our table, delivering our drinks. They're beautiful, the glasses full of clear squares of ice, the strawberry lemonade a perfect layer of yellow and red liquid, the rim of the glass covered with sparkling pink sugar. Sylvie takes the drink eagerly and sips from the straw, a satisfied noise leaving her once the server walks away. "Now this drink? It's special. The boys I know? Not a one of them matters to me. Well, maybe one, but he fucks everyone else and puts me on a pedestal like I'm fragile and untouchable. He doesn't see me in that way." She hesitates for only a moment. "The fuckable way."

Her casual use of the word fuck is surprising for such a delicate little girl like her, though I suppose I shouldn't feel that way. She's only a year younger than me. "Are you referring to Spencer?"

"He's the only one who I'd let see me naked. Whit says none of his friends are good enough for me, and he's probably right, but I don't want someone good enough for me. I just—want someone. You know?" She coughs, resting her fist in front of her mouth to contain it. "When you're someone like me, life is meant to be lived. Right now. I can't wait. It could all be over tomorrow."

I want to ask what's wrong with her, but I'm afraid that might be rude, and I don't want to pry. Instead I let her rattle on, eagerly grasping onto every morsel she shares about her family. Her brother. It's not enough, but it'll do for now, and I can't help but wonder where he's at. What he could be doing. Maybe he's sitting in his room, reading my journal.

I get angry at the mere thought, so I shove it away.

It's a Saturday night. I'm sure he's not alone.

"Tell me about you," Sylvie says once we've given our dinner orders and the plate of fried cheese is sitting on the table between us. She grabs one, dipping it into the thick marinara sauce before taking a big bite, the hot, stringy cheese staying connected before it snaps. "I know Jonas Weatherstone is your stepfather."

"Was," I correct her, taking a sip of the deliciously sweet yet tart lemonade.

"Yes. Was." Her expression turns somber. "That fire was just awful. You're lucky you weren't there."

"I was there," I admit, her eyes going wide. "I just managed to escape. My mother saved me." I duck my head, acting as if I'm overcome with emotion. And I suppose I am. With guilt. With anxiety. With worry. No one ever figured out what really happened, save for Mother. And she didn't tell.

We're both taking that secret to the grave.

"That's so awful. And to lose your stepbrother too," she continues. "When Jonas was still married to his first wife, they came to our house sometimes. Whit and Yates would play together when we were children."

My stomach churns, thinking of them knowing each other. How they each know me.

Intimately.

"As he got older, he had a—reputation," Sylvie continues. "Your stepbrother. I heard he was kicked out of a couple of schools for sexual assault."

I nod, wiping my mouth of imaginary food. I haven't eaten anything, my appetite completely leaving me.

"I suppose everything went to shit when his parents divorced. Same thing happened to our family," she says, shrugging. Very *c'est la vie* of her. "Whit turned into a complete control freak when Father first left. He would get into these raging fights with him. It was terrible. All Lina and I could do was cry. We were all eventually sent to counseling."

"I'm sure it wasn't easy," I murmur.

She picks up another piece of fried cheese, holding it with delicate fingers, tearing it into pieces and letting them fall onto her plate before she dips one into the red sauce. "It was a relief. When Daddy left, we could all breathe easier. Even Whit, though he's loath to admit it. The problem with Whit is he's cut from the same cloth as our father. He sees everything as black or white. There's no gray. Right or wrong. Yes or no. Do it or don't. He's extremely stubborn and hard to get along with."

She's describing him perfectly. I can only nod my head in agreement.

Sylvie smiles, her gaze knowing. "You tricked me. I'm talking about myself again and you've barely said a word."

"I don't mind. I'm a good listener," I tell her.

"But I want to know more about you." She reaches across the table, her fingers dancing on top of my hand briefly before she pulls away. "It's so exciting that you're here. It's always the same faces at Lancaster every year. I get bored *so* easily by them. The students. The teachers. The staff. That's half the reason I become terribly sick, I swear. I get tired of seeing everyone on campus. I need more excitement in my life."

"Like death?" I can't help but ask.

Sylvie laughs. "Yes. Like death. It's much more interesting, trust me. Now tell me about you. Don't hold back. I want to know everything."

"There's really not much to tell. I don't have any siblings." Save Yates, and he doesn't count. To think of him as my brother makes me want to vomit. "My father isn't in my life. My mother and I have a strained relationship."

Especially after the fire and the deaths and the reality that we're all each other has left, which is not very reassuring to my mother. I suppose she hates me for what I did. But that makes us even because I hate her for what she did too.

Or more like what she didn't do.

"You've dealt with death too, like me," Sylvie says, her expression curious. "With the fire. Tell me what that was like, the night it happened."

Unease slips through me. This is something I haven't talked about since I spoke with the police. It's a taboo subject between Mother and me. We'd rather forget it ever happened. "I don't remember much," I admit, my tone apologetic. "I woke up to a lot of smoke, and my mother dragging me out of the room."

I remember everything that happened that night, right down to the finest detail. It's just, I don't want to tell her.

"Your mother is a hero," Sylvie says, her voice full of awe. "She saved your life."

I shrug, brushing it off. "She did what any mother would do in a situation like that."

"Ha! I have a feeling my mother would let me burn," Sylvie says bitterly. "She'd save Whit. Maybe Carolina."

"She'd save all of her children," I say, my voice soft as I reach out and lightly pat her hand.

Sylvie pulls her hand from beneath mine, making a dismissive gesture. "This is getting too serious. Let's talk about something else. Oh, I know! Tell me about your trouble at Billington." Her eyes light up, little flames dancing in their pale blue depths. "I'm not going to pretend I didn't read your file when I hacked into the system, because I so did, and I'm positively green with envy over the experiences you've had. I love a lurid good girl gone bad story. Spill it."

The truth is so boring. I was the typical rebellious rich teen who acted out. It was the standard cry for help. The *any attention is good attention* type situation. I was a mess. Trying to escape the pressures at home, the pressures at school. Wanting to grow up too fast, too soon, yet needing my mommy because I was scared.

And of course, there was Yates. He was incessant. It started when I was thirteen and grew breasts. He wouldn't stop staring at them. He walked in on me taking a shower, watching me through the glass door. Sometimes, just because I could, I'd let him stare. It would satisfy him and he'd leave me alone.

Until the need became too great. Eventually, he was in constant pursuit of me. Trying to get me alone. Trying to sneak into my room.

Mother was too wrapped up in her own problems—and her affair with Augustus Lancaster, one of the richest men in the country, if not the world—to see what was happening right before her own eyes. In her own home. I'm still unsure if she realizes everything that happened between Yates and me. I tried to tell her once, but she began crying when I said Yates's name.

So I stopped.

I clear my throat and decide to tell her about the other boy in my life at that time. "There was a boy."

Sylvie's expression becomes excited. "Of course. That's how it always starts."

"He was a year older. Gorgeous. Confident. Arrogant." I think of Whit. He is all of those things and more. "With a hint of mean."

"They're the worst."

"Awful," I say in agreement. "He chose me out of everyone else, though, and I felt special. Wanted. Needed. He was bad—everything about him, my parents hated. He did drugs. Drank too much. I was only fourteen, and I turned fifteen when we were together. He convinced me to try things, and I was perfectly willing."

This is all true. There was a boy at school. A senior when I was a freshman, scandalous. Yates hated him, which made me love him even more. His name was Daniel. He taught me shot gunning—blowing smoke into each other's mouths—and how to stay drunk at school all day while keeping your composure. He had persuasive hands and an easy way about him.

He was the distraction I was looking for at that time. He was sweet, kind of dumb. Also kind of mean, just as I told Sylvie.

"Like what?" Sylvie's eyes are wide as moons.

"Drugs. Drinking. Sex." I shrug, hoping she doesn't ask for details. Knowing she will most likely ask.

"He's the one you were caught with in the gym."

I nod. We weren't actually having sex, but we were close. "They expelled him. He was eighteen. I was fifteen. A minor."

"Scandalous!" Sylvie covers her mouth with her fingers. "You were willing though, right?"

"Of course," I snap, feeling defensive. With Daniel, I was always willing, yet he was the one who got in trouble. Who was threatened with jail time by Jonas and my mother.

When the very one who was practically raping me every chance he could get lived under their own roof. Jonas' own son.

You can't call it rape when you enjoy it, Yates said to me once, after a particularly heated moment between us. *You want it. You want me.*

The guilt I still feel over that is so overwhelming, I suddenly rise to my feet, my thighs bumping into the table and making everything on top of it rattle.

"I need to use the restroom," I say before I hurriedly walk away, never once looking back. I don't need to. I'm sure Sylvie is wearing a shocked look on her face, wondering why I would just take off like that.

If you haven't been through it, it's hard to describe what it's like, dealing with haunting memories and how they make you feel. How they come out of nowhere, when you least expect it. Climbing up your throat. Crawling all over your skin. Swallowing you up whole. They linger on the edge of your mind, lying in wait with the potential to ruin everything. Like my dinner with a new friend.

How can I be friends with Sylvie when her brother is Whit? Who now has my private journal because he stole it? Who, if he wanted to, could go to the very back of that journal and read those extra secret entries, and figure out exactly what happened between Yates and me. And what I did to finally make it stop.

I find the tiny restaurant bathroom in the back of the building and lock myself away inside, leaning against the door, staring at my reflection in the mirror on the opposite wall. I look so young tonight, my hair in French braids, no makeup on my face, a gray North Face hoodie on and black leggings with my black and white Dior sneakers, much like what Sylvie's wearing.

We both look like babies. We *are* babies. But I've seen and done so much already, inside I feel old. Jaded.

Disgusted.

Pushing away from the door, I go to the sink and turn on the water, washing my hands before I splash the icy cold water on my face. It puts some color into my cheeks, and after I've dried myself off, I smooth my hair back. Stand a little straighter. I remind myself of the girl I was two years ago. Chasing dreams and running from nightmares.

I'm still that girl. Though my dreams are all gone and the nightmares are always just behind me.

With a resolute sigh, I open the door to find two middle-aged women standing in the hallway, waiting to use the restroom. They glare at me with contempt, their eyes narrowed, their lips curled. Judging me when they don't know me. Most likely hating me for my youth, while they hang on to it as tightly as they can with their claw-like fake nails.

I return the glare, flipping one of my long braids over my shoulder, putting a bit of saunter in my step as I walk past them. I exit the short hallway, making my way out into the dining area and head toward Sylvie when I spot someone sitting at a table on the complete opposite side of the building.

Whit Lancaster.

Watching me.

I stop short, in the middle of the restaurant, struck dumb by his presence. Our gazes lock. He smirks. I frown. He's sitting with his friends, and a few girls accompany them too. Including Jane and Caitlyn. They're flanking either side of him, both of them laughing, touching him, their hands like butterflies, hovering just above him, as if they're not sure where to land next. Jane makes her decision first, her hand settling on his forearm. Caitlyn rests her hand on his shoulder, leaning her head toward his, her mouth right at his ear. Her lips move as she whispers something to him, but he doesn't acknowledge her. They're both desperate to capture his attention, but it's as if he doesn't realize their existence.

He can only stare at me with that beautiful face, temporarily battered. The black eye is obvious, and he wears it like a badge of honor. No shame in Whit Lancaster's game. If anyone is talking about the obvious fight he must've engaged in, no one is saying a word to him about it.

I tilt my head. He does the same, away from Caitlyn, as if he's trying to avoid her and her nonstop moving mouth. I blink.

So does he.

All right. I can play this game.

My mouth falls open the slightest bit, and I curl my tongue at the corner, just the tip peeking out. I bite my lower lip, dropping my eyes from his for the quickest moment, just before I glance back up at him.

He licks his upper lip, his eyes gleaming. Reminding me of a wolf, ready to launch his attack.

At me.

This all happens in a matter of seconds, but it feels like minutes. An agonizing tease.

I hate him.

Seriously, I do.

Not caring that I'm giving in first, I tear my gaze away from his and march over to Sylvie, settling into my seat. I smile at her, noting her frown. "Sorry about that," I say. "I really had to go."

"It's the strawberry lemonades. They make me pee almost immediately." She easily accepts my lame explanation, tapping her mostly empty glass. Mine looks the same way. "I ordered us another round."

"Thank you."

"Too bad they don't have vodka in them." She laughs.

"I don't drink much anymore," I admit.

"Why not?"

"I don't like feeling like I'm not in control," I answer.

"My brother says the same thing. Drinking, drugs. They are of little interest to him lately. He wants to remain in control, at all times. But that's so typical of Whit. He's the ultimate control freak."

Truer words were never spoken.

She rests her chin on her hand, contemplating me. "Do you like my brother?"

"No," I say immediately, glancing to my right. He can see me perfectly. I wonder if he realized that. If he's been aware of my presence in this restaurant from the moment he walked in, while I've been over here, completely oblivious.

Probably. I'm sure he's been watching me, and I'm also sure I've looked absolutely hideous. Laughing and carrying on. Sucking down strawberry lemonade. Dressed like a hobo, minus the designer sneaks on my feet. I'm sure he prefers his girls pretty and perfect, who drink water and nibble on a leaf. Who wear dresses and no panties so he can have easy access.

The perv.

Sylvie laughs. "I love your honesty. It's so refreshing."

"Are you surrounded by liars?" I ask.

"Mostly. People who'll say anything to please me—I've dealt with them my entire life. It's quite annoying. I've always wanted a friend who will be honest with me. Who'll have an opinion instead of agreeing with me all the time." Sylvie rolls her eyes. "Girls like that drive me crazy."

"Same here," I say truthfully, the two of us going silent when the server appears with our dinners.

We dig in once she's gone, and my appetite comes roaring back. I'm famished, craving carbs, and I devour the pasta dish embarrassingly fast, consuming plenty of bread as well, not caring if Whit can see me stuffing my face.

Fuck the lettuce leaf. Give me all the pasta.

Sylvie matches me bite for bite, exceeding me with her appetite, since she also downed all of that fried cheese. We keep eating until we're both stuffed, resting our hands over our distended bellies and moaning and groaning.

"I feel terrible," I say.

"Same, but it was totally worth it," she whimpers.

"You're right." I do my best to not look in Whit's direction, and it's driving me crazy. I hope my not looking at him drives him crazy too. He deserves to think I don't care that he's in this restaurant. I'd love to go talk to him. Demand that he tell me where my journal is and return it to me right away. But that's not how I have to play this with Whit. Confrontation won't work. I need to be sly. Cunning.

As sly and cunning as him.

The server drops off the check and Sylvie flashes a heavy black credit card, giving it to her. "Let me pay for mine," I tell her.

"No, my treat. You can get it next time," Sylvie says with a faint smile.

I like that. That she mentions there will be a next time. I finally feel like I have a friend. Someone who won't be intimidated by Whit or fall under his influence so easily.

As his sister, she can defy him.

And so can I.

We're waiting for the server to return with Sylvie's credit card when I feel him approach—the air electrifies, and my head buzzes. Shadows fall over our table and I glance up to find Whit standing there, Spencer by his side. Chad is standing on the other side of Spence. The girls are behind them, giggling and tittering nervously, most likely excited by the possibility of a confrontation.

Wouldn't they just die to know I had Whit's dick in my mouth last night?

"Whit. Chad." Sylvie smiles. "Spence." She scowls at him, the look on her face reminding me of her brother. "What brings you boys to this lovely establishment?"

I love that she didn't acknowledge the girls whatsoever.

"Hunger," Chad says with smile. Spencer scowls at her in return, shoving his hands in his jeans' pockets.

Whit doesn't say a word. His expression is cool. Stoic. He won't even glance in my direction, the prick.

"Have you met my friend?" Sylvie says jokingly, indicating me. They all know who I am and she knows it. Maybe she's trying to be nice. At the very least, get them to be polite and acknowledge me. I hear a few murmured *yeahs*, though none of them will actually look at me.

"Can't say that we've ever met before," Whit says, turning so he's staring right at me, his expression indifferent. Downright blank. As if he never had his mouth on me last night. As if I wasn't the one who let him come all over my chest, like an animal marking his territory.

"Whit," Sylvie snaps, but he ignores her.

"What was your name again?" he says to me with a flick of his chin, his gaze roving over me. Last night's hunger is completely gone, replaced by that familiar cold stare. "Nice braids," he says snidely. "You look like a child."

I don't even think. I just grab my leftover lemonade and stand, throwing it in his face, making direct contact. He closes his eyes at the last second, the drink splashing him, and even the girls behind him. They gasp.

Right before they start squealing.

"Fuck you," I tell him between clenched teeth, glancing over at Sylvie to find she's watching us with open glee on her face. The girl loves drama. "I'm leaving. Thank you for dinner, Sylvie."

And with that, I turn and walk away.

FOURTEEN

SUMMER

I'M OUTSIDE IN AN INSTANT, the cool late fall air wrapping around me, making me tremble. We drove here in Sylvie's Mercedes and I could easily call an Uber, but not out in front of the restaurant. I don't want to chance running into Whit again so quickly after I threw a drink in his face.

I can't believe I did that. It was stupid but also...exhilarating. He deserved it. I hate how cold and callous he is. As if I don't matter. As if he didn't have his mouth all over my skin. As if he didn't kiss me like he couldn't get enough.

Not looking back, I walk fast, getting as far away from the restaurant as possible, threading my way through the crowds of people on the sidewalk. I swear I hear someone shout my name —a male someone—and I pick up the pace, not wanting to be found.

At the intersection, I turn right, blindly running down what turns out to be a quiet residential street, finally glancing over my shoulder to see no one is behind me. I slow my pace, breathing hard, thinking I'm in the clear when he steps out from behind a fence, directly in my path.

Whit.

I come to a complete stop, the shock at seeing him freezing me in place. He must've figured out a shortcut. The motherfucker.

"Don't come any closer," I warn him, taking a few steps backward.

He smiles. "You got another drink hiding behind your back?"

I say nothing. I'm poised, ready to take flight, and as if he can sense it, his smile fades.

Just before he lunges for me.

I try to run, but he grabs me around my waist, holding me in place, pushing me against the fence. I go willingly, all the fight leaving me at first contact of his hands on my body. My skin prickles where they rest, my body familiar with his and responding in kind. His heat seeps into my flesh, his fresh clean scent surrounding me, making me feel drunk. High.

"Why'd you throw the drink in my face?" he asks me, his eyes blazing with unrestrained fury. He didn't like the public humiliation. I'm sure not much gets past Whit Lancaster, and it feels good, that I threw him off. That I made him look like an asshole in a public restaurant, in front of his friends and those stupid girls. In front of other people. People who probably know exactly who he is.

He already hates me. I'm sure the feeling is magnified times ten.

"Why'd you say you didn't know me?" I throw back at him. There's my humiliation, and why I had to get back at him. He tries to act like he's something special, but he's really just like all the rest of them. Only wanting one thing in private. Ignoring me completely in public.

I won't have it. I refuse to let him play that game with me. I'm a master at it now.

"Because I don't know you. Not at all." He leans in so close, I can feel his minty breath waft across my face. "I'm sure I'll learn more about you when I continue reading your journal tonight."

Continue? Oh God.

I struggle against him, which makes his arms grow tighter, and it's as if he's trying to squeeze the life out of me. "You *stole* it from me, you fucking prick."

He ignores my insults. From the glee I see dancing in his eyes, I think he's enjoying this. "Hiding all your deep dark secrets in there?" His voice is taunting.

It's my turn to ignore him. "I want it back," I say, my voice firm.

He grins, as if he derives great pleasure from infuriating me. "No."

"Give it to me!"

He clamps his hand over my mouth, thrusting his face in mine. "You are in no position to make demands. I am controlling the narrative here, Savage, and you're going to do what I say. Is that clear?"

I don't answer. I can only stare at him, my eyes wide, my heart thumping wildly. The neighborhood is quiet. No one else is around. He could probably do whatever he wanted to me and no one would hear us. Or catch him.

I'd give in anyway, so what's the point.

"You want the journal back?" he asks.

I nod, my head rubbing against the rough wooden fence behind me, and I can feel it snagging on the splintered wood.

"You'll have to earn it back then." His hand relaxes against my face, his thumb stroking my cheek, my jaw. His touch is gentle, despite how firmly he's holding me. "Want to ask how?"

We watch each other warily, and I witness his expression slowly change. The anger dissipates, replaced by that familiar hunger, and my body betrays me, answering in its own way. I relax beneath his hold, my bones languid, my thoughts full of nothing but what he could possibly do to me next, anticipation rippling down my spine and settling between my legs.

As if he can sense my giving in, he removes his hand from my face completely and I whisper, "How?"

"By doing whatever I want you to," he whispers back, his gaze raking down my body before he returns it to mine. "I'll own you, body and soul. When I want you in my room in the middle of the night, you'll come running. Begging for it. When I want a blow job, you'll deliver, no questions asked. If I want to eat that pretty pussy of yours, you'll offer it up on a silver fucking platter and I'll feast on it for hours. When I want to fuck you, no matter the time of day, or where you're at, you can't refuse me. Understood?"

My body warms at the promise in his words, and I will myself to stop. What he's proposing is...

Degrading.

"For how long?" I ask, surprised at how calm I sound. Inside, I'm a riotous, excitable mess. To be at Whit's beck and call whenever he wants me, doesn't sound like a bad proposition.

Which means something is desperately wrong with me. I just know it.

"For however long I want." He smiles, and the sight of it makes my heart lurch. He cups the side of my face and tilts it back, leaning in to whisper against my lips, "My own personal whore, to use however I like, whenever I want. It'll be fun, Savage. I'll fuck you in every hole you've got. And you'll take it. Willingly."

My core clenches and my panties are wet. "No," I say, breathless.

He laughs. "You know you want it. I can tell."

He thrusts against me, showing me his strength, how he has complete control over me, and I close my eyes, pressing my lips together to stifle the moan. This is so incredibly fucked up. What happened to us to leave us so damaged? I see this sort of thing in porn, in movies, and I've even read it in books. But I've never experienced something like this before in real life. I've never let someone control me so completely that I'll do whatever he demands to be with him, even if he looks at me as if I'm nothing but his worthless plaything.

"Answer me, Savage. Do we have a deal? Or do I get to make copies of your journal and pass it out to everyone at school?"

Oh God, no. Talk about humiliating. Once everyone knows what happened to me, what I really did, I could get in serious trouble.

"You could just agree, you know. Things would be a lot easier for you. I know what a sick fuck you could be. You have so much potential." The words almost sound like a compliment, and I take them that way considering I'm warped beyond belief. Especially when it comes to him. He rests his hand against my throat, reminding me of that moment between us in the library yesterday. His fingers drift, making gooseflesh rise, and I whimper. "No one else likes it when I do this. Yet you seem to."

If he would squeeze my neck just a little bit tighter...

I hate myself for wanting this. Wanting him.

I close my eyes, a soft gasp leaving me when he leans in and traces my lower lip with his tongue, just before he bites me there, his teeth sinking, tugging on the fleshiest part of my lip. Not hard enough to break skin, but it still hurts.

"I'm not a whore," I whisper when he releases my lip, and he chuckles.

"Please. You're just like your mother. She destroyed my entire family, and didn't give a single fuck over what she did. As payback for her sins, I'm going to destroy you. The only thing she has left in her sorry ass life that she cares about." He slides his hand down my side, curling it around so he can grip my ass as he hauls me to him. "Soon you'll become so addicted to me, no one else can have you. You'll crave everything only I can give you, and when it's over, when I eventually deny you this..." He thrusts against me again, and I can feel his erection straining beneath the front of his jeans. He's huge. Throbbing. "I'll know I've broken you completely, and only then can you have your stupid journal back. I'll have discovered all of your secrets anyway, so it won't even matter anymore."

He springs away from me, taking a few steps back, leaving me a shaky mess pressed against the fence.

"I hate you," I tell him with all the sincerity I can muster, because it's true.

I hate him more than any other human being on this planet. He's awful.

Terrible.

"I know." He chuckles. "You *really* hated me last night. When my dick was in your mouth and you were moaning. Or when I came all over your tits."

"You're disgusting." I spit the words like bullets.

"Right, especially when I tongue-fucked you. What a sick twisted asshole I am, right? When you were coming all over my face?" He rubs his chin. Licks his lips. As if he's savoring the memory. "Twice, I believe? Next time, we should try for three."

Three? God, I couldn't be so lucky.

"Do we have an agreement? Or do I need to get started on all those copies I'll have to make." He rubs his hands together in relish, as if he can't wait to put my entire journal on blast, for all of Lancaster Prep to read.

"Yes," I whisper, the sound raspy. My throat hurts. My entire body aches. I don't have a choice.

I have to agree.

Pleased, he approaches me once more, cupping my chin as he likes to do, and drops a single kiss on my upturned lips. "You're such a good girl," he practically croons, his mouth brushing against mine as he speaks. "So agreeable when you want to be. Always defiant though, when you feel cornered."

My heart flutters at his compliment and I close my eyes, telling myself I can't fall into this trap. I can't let another boy try to control me. This situation is different than the others, right? I'm stronger now. I can take this.

I can take him.

"I like it when you put up a fight," he continues, his mouth settling on mine once more. As if he can't resist. I open to him, his tongue sneaking in, licking mine. He reaches for my hair, tugging on one of the braids, so hard I break away from him with a muttered, "Ow."

He backs away from me, that evil smile on his face. "I'll be in touch."

I don't say anything as he walks away. I watch him retreat, until he turns the corner and he's back on the main drag. Only then do I sag, ducking my head, staring at my feet, counting my heartbeats, scared my heart might pop out of my chest.

What did I just do?

FIFTEEN

WHIT

I HAVEN'T CONTACTED Summer Savage in four days. Not since the night when I had her pressed against the fence, a vulnerable, shaking little thing. Staring up at me with those big brown eyes, my hand clamped over her mouth, her body softening for me. I could've fucked her there, and she would've let me. She probably would've begged for more. I neglect her on purpose. Testing her. Testing myself. The all-consuming need that fills me just looking at her is too much, and I must learn how to gain control of my urges.

She brings them all out. Every single dark thing that lives inside me bubbles to the surface when I'm with her. I want to hurt her. I want to soothe her. I want to taste her. I want to be inside of her.

I want to consume her. Make her mine and no one else's. Primal, unfamiliar urges course through me, heating my blood, making my heart roar.

It's hard for me to understand. Harder for me to ignore. But I've endured worse. I can withstand this...whatever it is we have. I can't let her see what she does to me.

I must have the upper hand. Always.

Instead of contacting her right away like I want, I do my best to ignore her in the two classes we share, my gaze skimming right past her as if she's not even there. I can feel her angry glare every time I enter the room. Can sense her presence immediately. Smell her scent. I'm like an animal, desperate to mate with the only female who sets me on fire, yet I refuse to touch her.

It's a test in control. I will myself to remain indifferent when it comes to her. I'm proving something. To myself.

And to her.

I immediately called off the sheep, telling them the ostracization of Summer Savage is over. They're disappointed, but they do what I say. She's not necessarily accepted around campus, but she's no longer shunned anymore either. I halfway expected a thank you from her, for allowing her room to breathe once more, but of course, she says nothing to me. She ignores me right back.

It's maddening. *She's* maddening.

Elliot, on the other hand? He tried his damnedest to talk to me that Saturday afternoon, eager to explain why he did what he did, stumbling over his words, a babbling idiot full of excuses and apologies, his face bearing as much damage as mine.

There was no explanation necessary. I understood why he ambushed me. I embarrassed him, and in a way, supported the girl who humiliated his ass by kicking him in the nuts. I showed my supposed allegiance, and it pissed him off. I guess I can't blame him.

But the stupid asshole took it too far. His attack on Summer and subsequent attack on me ruined him in my eyes for good. I made a few calls, and next thing I knew, Headmaster Matthews was having a special meeting with Elliot first thing Sunday morning. By that evening, he was seen packing up his belongings, his parents arriving around dinnertime in their older model Range Rover to pick him up and take him home.

By Monday, he was gone for good.

That's how easy it is for me to rid this campus of someone I don't like. Removing Elliot was a message—to little Miss Savage more than anyone else. My father got her on this campus, but it would take nothing at all for me to have her removed.

In fact, it would be too damned easy.

I'm in American Government at this very moment, my gaze going to her as it always does. The back of her head, the sleek dark hair pulled into that ponytail, her entire demeanor contained. Her shoulders are hunched, as if she's trying to disappear inside herself.

I see you, I want to say. *You can't hide from me.*

I try to pay attention to the lecture, but my thoughts linger on her, as always. She mystifies me. I don't understand her. I don't understand myself when I'm with her. Seeing her at the restaurant Saturday night enraged me. Caitlyn and Jane made me an offer, one I thought I couldn't refuse. I thought it would be the perfect thing to banish all memories of a naked Summer coming on my face once and for all.

Two girls instead of one. Two sets of tits. Two wet pussies. Two mouths on my cock. How could I refuse? I took them to dinner, bringing Spence and Chad with me. Rubbing it in their faces that I was about to have a threesome.

My debauched plans were ruined at first glimpse of Savage, her hair in braids, laughing and talking with my sister, oblivious to my presence. Downright joyous, despite how everyone at Lancaster treats her. It was as if it didn't matter—as if *I* didn't matter.

And that infuriated me.

Caitlyn and Jane were sorely disappointed. I have no idea if they propositioned Chad and Spence. I didn't care. I abandoned them at the restaurant, chasing after Savage like a madman. Creating another delicious memory between us. Me terrorizing her. Her becoming aroused by it.

She's a mystery. One I know I could eventually figure out. She can't hide from me. I will eventually lay her bare and open. Until every little secret she hides comes pouring out. I have power over her, and she knows it.

Does she realize she has power over me?

I understand my sister's fascination with her. Sylvie likes strays. She always takes them in. They make her feel better, as if she's not so sickly. My sister's health is a constant concern of my mother's, yet she never seems to get better. She's actually getting worse. And Sylvie's fascination with death is morbid. Seeing her with Summer, which is happening more and more, gives me a little bit of hope. I swear, Sylvie's gaining weight. She smiles more. I can only assume it's because she has a friend.

But I don't like it. I don't want them getting too close. It'll hurt my sister that much more if I have to break them apart, and that's the last thing I want to do. My family is the most important thing to me. I'd kill someone to protect my entire family, especially my sisters. I'm their older brother, and it's my responsibility to watch over them.

I just hope Summer doesn't try and get information about me from Sylvie, not that Sylvie would say anything.

She knows better.

Four days is a long time to go without touching someone, but I could go longer. Human beings and their need for comfort, for touch, for consolation, for sex, for love, for *feelings*—I don't get it. Needing someone is a sign of weakness. Protecting someone —such as my mother, my father, my sisters, that's different. I love them, but don't need them. My closest friends? I care about them too. I need them like soldiers and I'm their general. We're an army and their singular goal is to protect me.

And my job is to protect them.

Yet there is something about Summer that makes me want... more. From that first moment with her at my parents' apartment in Manhattan, I felt changed. Charged. A little girl sitting in a woman's dress, sneaking drinks from discarded champagne glasses like a thief. As I drew closer, I realized she was around my age, and her tits were spectacular. She was all limbs and bare skin and big breasts. Doe eyes and dark hair and flickering interest. She oozed sex to me, and I can't even explain why. We were young.

Kids.

All I could think about was consuming her that night. How could I inhale her, keep her, mark her so that no one else would touch her? I didn't know then, and I don't exactly know now.

I still feel that way, all these years later.

I'm back in my suite after school, my gaze going to the journal, where it lies on top of my desk like a bomb I'm afraid to detonate. Do I dare open it and consume her secrets? Oh I taunted her that night, saying I would *continue* reading it, but I hadn't cracked it open beyond my initial discovery of it in the first place. Looking at the nondescript journal sitting on my desk every evening, seeing it first thing every morning, I told myself I didn't care. Who is she? Nothing. What does she mean to me?

Also nothing.

All lies I tell myself.

I stop at my desk, the journal taunting me, the title scratched across the front like a dare.

Things I wanted to say...

The need to read it grows, rising inside of me. Growling, I snatch it up and crack it open, finding a subtitle on the inside of the cover.

...but never did.

Settling on my bed, I start to read. Bits and pieces at first, flipping through the pages impatiently, eager to find something salacious. In the front of the journal, the words are written in girlish cursive, with rounded letters and tiny hearts instead of dotted i's. Doodles in the margins, quotes and favorite lyrics. Lists of the boys she liked. Traits she wanted her future boyfriends to have.

None of those traits really apply to me. She wanted them all to be nice and caring and smart, with a great smile and soft hair. She wanted them tall, with a good body and kind manners and a sense of humor. A boy who knew how to kiss, who gave great hugs, who had a caring family.

Hmm. Guess I nabbed a few of the physical traits, and failed all the rest.

I count back through the early passages, aligning the dates of her entries to our ages, and realize she started this journal midway through eighth grade. She talks of bad grades and the future and friends and dances. She writes about traveling in Europe for the summer and where she'll go to high school and how badly she wants to attend Lancaster Prep, but she couldn't get in.

Interesting.

She makes no mention of her mother or Jonas beyond them going somewhere as a family. She talks of her stepbrother, a boy I knew, but didn't particularly like. A boy who's now gone.

Dead. As is his father.

In the late spring of our eighth-grade year, she complains incessantly of Yates. How he won't leave her alone. How he sneaks looks at her in the bathroom, always busting in when she's showering. How she didn't yell at him to go away one time. Instead, she said nothing, and he stayed in there. Watched her through the rippled glass of the shower door, trying to make out her naked body, she assumed.

The moment I shut the water off, he left, slamming the door behind him. I was so relieved. What a perv! Not like he could see anything through the glass, but maybe me letting him look for once will satisfy him. At least for a little while. Y definitely needs a girlfriend, so he'll leave me alone.

Interesting. Why does it not surprise me that Yates Weatherstone lusted after his stepsister? It figures. He was always odd. Overly eager to prove his worth, his strength, his wealth. Loud and brash, a braggart when he'd done nothing to brag about. His father was in real estate and had amassed a small fortune. He was a smart man, a quiet man and my father respected him, which shouldn't be taken lightly. He used Jonas Weatherstone in a few business dealings to acquire some properties in the city, and when my parents had parties and business get-togethers, the Weatherstones were almost always included on the guest list. I remember Yates' mother—a strange woman who would gawk every time she entered our home. As if she'd never seen such a thing.

I supposed she hadn't.

I have to force myself to stop reading it, and I leave campus, needing the escape. I drive aimlessly, and end up downtown, though I always knew this was my destination. Last year I did this—too much. In search of a townie. Someone to lose myself in. It's getting darker earlier and earlier, and the streetlights are already on. Most of the stores are already closed. Only a few restaurants and bars remain open. I slow down when I spot a group of girls standing by a seafood place, their heads swiveling toward my car as I approach, all of their faces familiar. One of them in particular stands out.

Dark hair. Dark eyes. Pouty, dick sucking lips. She always reminded me of someone, but it never dawned on me until this very moment.

She reminds me of Summer.

I pull over directly beside them. Roll down the passenger side window. My gaze locks with hers and I tilt my head, indicating I want her to come over.

They know the drill. As I've mentioned, I've done this before. I realize quickly that I've done this before with *her*. She's pretty.

But she's not who I really want.

"You again," she says, her voice full of boredom as she leans into the open window. She's smiling, her makeup garish. Her gaze sly. Knowing. "You want another blowie?"

It all comes back. The last blow job she gave me. How I pulled out of her mouth and came on her face. She became angry. I didn't give a shit.

We watch each other coolly, and I try my damnedest to realign her features, but it doesn't work. She's not a puzzle.

She's not Summer.

"More," I tell her.

"Like what?" She lifts her brows.

I want to degrade her completely. "Your ass."

She makes a face, pulling away from the window. "Ew. No."

Such a prude.

"Get the fuck out of here then," I tell her fiercely, and she rolls her eyes, pushing away from the car.

"Fuckhead!" she yells as I pull away from the curb.

I return to campus, hungry. Annoyed. Hard. I take a shower and jerk off to thoughts of Savage. With the lush mouth and soft tongue. With the vacuum quality suction and delicious pussy. I still don't know what it feels like to be inside her.

And I want to know. I'm dying to know. I want to violate her in every way possible. The beauty of it?

She'll let me. And she'll enjoy every goddamn minute of it too. She's not a prude. She's sick.

Like me.

Once I'm finished with my shower, I slip into bed and pick up the journal, reading until I can't take it anymore. It's difficult, being in her head. Reading her joys. Her complaints. Her dreams. Her hopes, and how slowly but surely, it erodes. Until she has no hopes or dreams left. She's just trying to survive.

I dream about her. Now I'm the one who's watching her in the bathroom instead of her stepbrother, the glass wall clear, her beautiful body on complete display, only for me. Her dark eyes never leave mine as she runs her hands over her slick body, suds forming, dripping down her arms. Her legs. She reaches between her thighs and touches herself, her lips curled in a barely-there smile. Coy. Teasing.

I go to her. She gets farther away. The bathroom stretches on and on. I reach out but touch nothing. It turns into a long hall that's never-ending and I run to her, calling her name, and when she turns around, it's not Summer any longer.

It's the townie. She smiles, her eyes turning red.

I wake up in a cold sweat, wondering what the fuck that was about. I'm jittery. Wide awake. I grab the journal from where I left it on my bedside table and open it, finding the spot where I left off.

It's closer to the end of the school year, and her entries are less frequent. She's busy with various activities, and I remember doing much of the same. There's one journal entry that's concerning as I read it. Again and again.

He won't leave me alone, no matter what I say to him. I can't take a shower without being scared he's going to watch. I lock the door but he still slips inside. I can hear him breathe. It grows louder and louder, and I know what he's doing. Mia says he's jerking off. Touching himself when he watches me, which is so gross.

He's my brother. Stepbrother, but still! I've known him for years. We've lived in the same house for a long time. I don't think of him like that. He's kind of gross, and weird, but I think all boys are that way. He's worse than other boys though, because he's too quiet, always watching me, no matter where I am. Touching me in the most obvious way.

Y leaves the bathroom every time I turn the water off, and sometimes I wonder if I'm hallucinating. Imagining it. I want to tell Mother, but she probably won't believe me. Or she'll accuse me of making a big deal out of nothing, which is what she always says.

Maybe I shouldn't shower at all. Then he'd find me disgusting, and eventually stop coming near me.

Alarm flashes through me each time I read the last passage. This goes beyond a stepbrother wanting his stepsister and having a little lusty fun. There were three years between them. He knew better. She was practically a child when he started doing this.

I keep reading, despite how late it is, and how soon I have to get up for class.

Maybe I'll skip.

There's a familiar entry about a warm June evening. A night I lived through too.

I met a boy. He was so hot. And so cold too. Mean. He called me a whore. Who does that? And he was dead serious too. Said I was like my mother and claimed that she was having an affair with his father. I don't want to believe it. I love Jonas like he's my real father, and if she were to break up their marriage over a stupid affair...

I would miss Jonas so much, and our life. He gives us a good life. But maybe that would be a good thing if he found out. It could get me away from Yates. But I don't want to talk about him or my problems.

I want to talk about the boy.

He was tall. Beautiful ice blue eyes. I felt his dick when he kissed me. It was hard, pressed against my stomach, and I touched it. I touched it! Not for real, just over his clothes. His tongue was soft, and I liked how it felt in my mouth. He was my first real kiss, and he made my stomach dip. Made my entire body feel fuzzy when he rubbed his tongue against mine. It was like my body didn't belong to me, but to someone else. Him?

I belong to myself, I know this, but it felt so good to be pressed against a boy like that and let him kiss and kiss me. My head was already spinning thanks to all the champagne I drank, so maybe it wasn't the kiss at all, but the alcohol. I don't know. I just liked it. It was a fun party.

A deep breath escapes me and I slap the journal shut, tossing it onto the bed next to me. That's all I manage to rate. A few paragraphs, mostly about us kissing and how she felt my dick. That encounter with her that night feels like it altered my entire life. I was young and angry then, and eager to blame someone else for my father's infidelities. To blame him would be to acknowledge that he's not perfect, and I didn't want to do that. Not yet.

I blamed her mother—and her. That's why I called her a whore. I wanted to see what she would do. How she would react. I wanted to make her hurt, because I was in pain and no one saw it. No one ever sees it.

Instead, her eyes flared and her breathing accelerated. I held her against the wall and she gave in to me so easily. Kissed me. Clung to me. Taught me how to kiss, when I had no clue what I was doing.

That one night changed everything. I wanted to find someone just like her, yet I never could. As I got older, I became angrier. Saw things I shouldn't. Did things I shouldn't either. No one stopped me, so I kept going.

I'm still going. No one stops me now. Definitely not Summer.

I think of what I want to do with her and it makes me smile. Seems like she has bad memories when it comes to sex. Maybe I could do her a favor. Help wipe away any old memories she shares with that asshole stepbrother of hers, and replace them with me. And her.

Us.

SIXTEEN

SUMMER

FOUR DAYS. He's ignored me for four days, and it's beyond infuriating. Not that I want him to contact me.

I'm a liar. Of course I want him to contact me. He left me a needy, trembling mess Saturday night, slumped against the fence. Despite the threats. Despite the aggressive way he touched me. Talked to me. He's a horrible human, but for some reason, it feels like he's *my* horrible human. I don't know why he'd make so many demands, only to leave me completely alone.

The kiss is what destroyed me. His lips are a weapon, and when they touch mine, I become lost. Weak. I think about his kiss. His fingers on my throat. His hard body pressed against mine. My entire body aches just thinking about him.

Monday morning I show up to Honors English an amped up mess, worrying over his reaction.

He doesn't show up.

I pass him in the hall between classes. Spot him in the dining hall. He doesn't even look in my direction. His gaze flits over me as if I'm not even there. It's like this the rest of the day. Every day this week so far. Eventually, I do the same to him. Going about my business. Walking through the halls, into classrooms, around campus with my head held high.

Fuck him and his deal. He's trying to teach me some sort of lesson, and I don't get it. He demanded I be willing to do whatever he wanted, whenever he wanted, and then he doesn't even bother with me.

It's confusing. *He's* confusing.

I saw Sylvie on Monday. She spent lunch and the study period with me in the library. Whispering and gossiping. I wanted to ask her about Whit, but I kept my mouth shut. And after Monday, I don't see Sylvie again. I can only assume she's sick once again, and now she's a ghost on this campus. One minute she's there. The next, gone.

I miss her. She's my only friend.

Instead of worrying about Whit Lancaster and his endless bullshit, I concentrate on school. I have a paper to write. A few projects to finish. Surprisingly, no one at school is treating me terrible anymore. It's a relief, yet one I don't understand. Did Whit call off his dogs? Is that all it takes? One snap of his fingers and they leave me alone?

He wields so much power on this campus, it's mind-blowing.

Terrifying.

I'm working on my paper on my laptop when a text message comes through from an unidentified number. Frowning, I open it.

Come to my room. 9 p.m. WAL

Excitement sparks in my stomach. Between my legs. I've been summoned.

Finally.

I don't respond to his text. What's the point? He probably wouldn't answer me anyway. He expects me to show up, and I will. I will do whatever it takes to get that journal back. There's too much incriminating evidence in there. Things I don't want anyone to know. If he were to find out and leak that information? I'd be done for.

Ruined.

I'm sure that's exactly what he wants, too.

Curfew is at ten on a weeknight, so I have no issues walking out of my room or exiting the dorm in general. What will be hard is getting back into the building. The security isn't the best, considering how old the buildings are, and they don't want to destroy the structure, the old-world feel, blah blah blah, but still. There are cameras, but Sylvie & I are not close enough friends to ask her to work her hacking magic for me.

Besides, if I make the request, then she'll start asking questions. And I don't want to answer them.

So I'm taking my chances, and praying I won't get caught.

I'm dressed like I'm going for a jog, much like what I wore the night I found him in the rain. Leggings and Nikes and a hoodie. The only difference is I'm not wearing a bra. No panties. I considered wearing something sexy underneath my clothes, but

I don't have much in that department. Besides, I'm sure he just wants easy access.

I enter the building where his suite is. It used to be the old staffing quarters, but no one lives on campus who works here anymore, besides advisors and security. And they're housed in another building.

The only ones who live in this building now are Whit and Sylvie, and half the time, she's not around. The rest of the rooms are used for storage, or stand empty. Unused.

Wasted.

I walk down the darkened hall, unsure which room is his. I keep my footsteps light, not wanting to draw attention to myself in case Sylvie is in her room. She is the last person I want to run into right now.

A door suddenly swings open, allowing light into the hallway and I come to a complete stop, waiting to see if he might appear.

But no one appears. No one speaks either. Yet the door remains open.

I start to move again, slowly. Cautiously. I press my lips together so no one can hear me breathe, drawing closer and closer to that beam of golden light that's cast upon the floor. I take one step into the light and then he's there, filling the doorway.

Glaring at me.

"You're late." His voice is flat. His gaze heated.

I pat my hoodie's front pocket, but it's empty. Like an idiot, I didn't bring my phone. I have no idea what time it is.

"By what? A minute?" I challenge, feeling feisty.

His lips draw into a line. "By three minutes, if we're being precise."

I roll my eyes, my attitude a mask for my nervousness. "Are you disappointed? Want me to leave?"

I start to walk away and he steps out of the room, his hand settling on my shoulder. His touch burns, locking me in place and I glance up at him to find he's already watching me. "You're not going anywhere. We have a deal, remember?"

He wraps his fingers around my upper arm and escorts me inside, shutting the door behind us and turning the lock. I glance around the room, releasing a slow, shuddery breath, drinking it all in.

My single room is larger than the rooms where the girls have to share, but this is massive. There's a king-size bed in the center of the room. Two bedside tables, two dressers. A full-length mirror propped against the wall, opposite the bed. A desk with a giant iMac computer. There's a sitting area with a flat screen TV and a couch. A bookshelf filled to the brim with actual books. I can see the connecting bathroom, a closet. He has everything he needs here.

"Does it meet your approval?" he asks, his voice snide.

I turn to face him. "It's really nice," I say truthfully.

"It'll do."

I watch him walk to the bed. He's clad in light gray Lancaster Prep sweatpants and a black T-shirt that clings to his shoulders and chest, showcasing every muscle he has. He settles on the edge of the mattress facing me, his legs spread wide, his hands braced behind him as he contemplates me, a bored expression on his gorgeous face.

"Strip," he demands.

I raise a brow. "Getting right to business?"

"No backtalk. You agreed to do whatever I asked of you, whenever." He pauses. "Now strip."

My gaze never leaving his, I toe off my shoes, letting my socks slip off with them. "Maybe I wanted you to undress me."

"You don't get to choose in this scenario," he says, his blank gaze unnerving me. "Quit stalling."

His snappy tone stiffens my spine with anger and I whip the sweatshirt off without hesitation, tossing it onto the floor. His gaze settles on my chest, lingering there for a moment before it returns to mine.

"Keep going."

I turn, pretending to keep my modesty, I guess, but really wanting him to get a glimpse of my bare ass. I grip the waistband of my leggings and bend over, tugging them down my legs, hoping he enjoys the view. I kick the leggings off the rest of the way, nudging them aside with my foot before I stand up straight.

"Turn around." He sounds exasperated. I'm enjoying how much I'm annoying him. Probably too much.

Slowly I turn around and face him, not hiding my body whatsoever. Just like the last time we did this in my dorm room. Only now he has the advantage. Fully clothed to my naked. I rest my hands on my hips, contemplating him as much as he contemplates me, the both of us silent. Straight faces. Dim gazes. No smiles.

No emotion at all.

"Come here," he finally says, his low voice rippling along my nerve endings.

I approach the bed, stopping directly in front of him. Fully prepared for him to demand I get on my knees next. I'm sure he'll want to degrade me completely by fucking my mouth and coming on my face.

He's sick. Worse?

I'm turned on by the mental image.

"Straddle me." He brings his legs closer together and pats his right thigh, demonstrating where he wants me.

Frowning, surprised by his demand, I swing my leg over both of his, resting my hands on his broad shoulders, my center nestled right on top of him. I can feel his cock beneath the thick sweats, nudging up against my pussy and a ripple of wanting washes over me. I'm bound to leave a wet spot on his pants before this is through.

He settles his big hands on my waist, his touch light, though his fingers seem to burn against my bare skin. Goose bumps rise as usual, all over me, and I sit there on him, face to face. Unsure of what to do next.

Without a word he nuzzles my cheek with his nose, his intimate touch causing me to inhale sharply. His mouth rests at my ear and I can hear him breathing. "I can smell you," he murmurs. "Here."

He rubs his nose on my neck.

"And here."

Reaching between us, he settles his hand on my pussy, cupping me.

I grip his shoulders tighter and dip my head, watching as my breasts rise and fall. Rise and fall with every hurried breath. My nipples are hard, aching points, and I remember when he sucked them last.

"What do you want me to do now?" I ask when he resettles his hand on my hip once more.

"Stay still," he says, his mouth moving against the sensitive skin just below my ear. He's silent for a moment, our breaths comingling, keeping pace with each other. "Do you hear that?"

"What?" I ask weakly.

"Your heart beating." Whit touches my chest, his fingers resting in between my breasts. "So hard, Savage. Do I still scare you?"

Slowly I lift my head, my gaze meeting his. I bite my lower lip and nod once.

Whit smiles, brushing across my nipples with the back of his hand. "If I told you what I really want to do to you right now, you'd run screaming from my room. You'd never want to come back. I'd haunt your nightmares for the rest of your life."

My heart trips over itself at his words, the promise behind them. "Tell me."

He smiles, and the sight of it steals my breath. No wonder he doesn't do it much. It's absolutely devastating. "I want to mark your skin."

"With what?"

"My mouth." Leaning in, he touches his lips to my jaw. "My teeth." He nips me there. "My hands." They grip my hips tighter, pressing into my skin. "I'd tie you up, so tight. Then you can never run from me."

"I wouldn't want to," I admit softly.

He lifts his head once more, those icy blue eyes staring at me, as if he can see down into my soul. It's black and dark, just like his. His words don't sound like a threat.

They're a promise. One I'm desperate for him to fulfill.

"I'd tie you to the bed. Your hands. Your ankles. I'd want you spread wide, that pretty pussy on complete display. Just for me." He drags his lips along my neck, and I close my eyes, my entire body tingling in anticipation of what he might say next. "But I wouldn't touch it. Not yet. Not for a long time. First, I'd want you crying. Sobbing. Begging for me to touch you there. To let you come."

His mouth sucks on the spot where my neck meets my shoulder, hard. Painfully. I squeeze his shoulders with my fingers, savoring the pain. "I'd touch you everywhere," he continues. "I'd drive you out of your mind with wanting me. You'd drip all over the bed. I'd run my mouth across your stomach. The inside of your thighs. All over your ass. I'd kiss and bite you there, and leave bruises."

I shift against him, nudging closer, as close as I can get, and his hands slide down to cup my ass. "Look at me," he demands. I do as he says, my gaze locking with his, my entire body on fire for him. "You want me to fuck you tonight?"

My nod is furious, though I can't find my words.

"Make yourself come then." He lets go of my ass, reaching behind him to brace his hands on the mattress. His new position thrusts his hips up, his thick cock straining against the front of his sweatpants, pressing into me. "I won't touch you. I won't kiss you. I want you to use me."

I gape at him, frowning. "Wh-what do you mean?"

"Get creative, Savage." He grins, and my heart stops. "Rub that wet pussy all over my dick. Do whatever you want to me, but I'm not touching you. Won't kiss you either. And don't try to take off my clothes. Got it?"

This will be absolute torture for me, and he knows it.

It will also be torture for him.

Leaning in, I hover my mouth against his, whispering, "Got it."

He doesn't even flinch. Just watches me with that cool, assessing gaze. I press my feet against the floor, lifting up, until just my toes are on the ground, my torso pushed forward. I tilt my hips, gliding my pussy along the front of his sweats. Up and down.

Up and down.

Making me shake.

I lean my head back and close my eyes, shamelessly rubbing against him. I'm tits up, nipples pointing at the ceiling, my thighs shaking, straining from the position, and oh fuck, it feels so good. My clit rubs the seam of his sweats, his thick cock just beneath. My hands still grip his shoulders and I swear I can feel them grow more tense beneath my hold. Am I driving him crazy?

I hope so.

A moan escapes me, followed by a whimper. I drop my head so I'm facing him once more, and lower my feet, settling more firmly on top of him as I open my eyes. He's still watching me, his eyes stormy. Full of hunger that I know he's fighting. I circle my hips, gyrating against him, increasing my speed.

He doesn't say a word. No encouragement. No nothing. Just that stare. He's trying to remain impassive, but how can he, when I'm blatantly rubbing my naked body all over his? I can feel the tension in his muscular frame. See the storm brewing in his eyes.

"Oh God," I whisper, my eyelids fluttering. I want them to stay open so I can watch him, but the sensations filling me are overwhelming. I let go of his shoulder to cup my breast. Pinch my nipple. A hiss leaves my lips and I lick them. Let my mouth hang open. "Fuck."

Still he does nothing. Just watches me with that same expression on his face. The beautiful, cold statue in the garden. Cold. Unmoving.

It's a façade though. His eyes give him away.

There's a hitch in my breath when I shift up, my clit hitting the head of his cock. Oh yes. Right there. A string of dirty words leaves me as I grind on his cotton-covered dick, my entire body tense, the breath stuck in my throat as I strive toward my release. It's close. I'm close. My clit throbs in time with my heartbeat, and I cry out when it hits me.

I'm falling, the orgasm wrapping itself around me, rendering me stupid. My cries pierce the air, again and again, gasping breaths leaving me as I rub on top of him like a cat in heat, my thigh muscles tight. Shaking. My entire body trembles and my fingers curl into the fabric of his T-shirt as I grip him like an anchor. If I let him go, I'll fall to the floor.

When it's over, I open my eyes, exhaling loudly. Our gazes meet.

"Stand up," he says calmly.

I rise on shaky legs, staring at the giant wet spot that stains the front of his sweats. But that's not all me. He did that too. His cock is leaking, I know it is.

He glances down at the spot, frowning, his gaze returning to mine. "You made a mess."

"I'm a messy girl," I say, my voice scratchy, my breaths uneven.

"Take them off." He points at himself. "Get on your knees."

Ah, here it is. I kneel down, reaching for the waistband of his sweats. I tug, and he lifts his hips, allowing me to pull them down, past his thighs. His cock pops up, straight and thick, the tip gleaming and wet. I back away when he kicks off his sweats. Reaches behind his neck to take off his T-shirt, until he's just as naked as I am.

And what a glorious sight he is. His body is beautiful. A work of art. Elegant muscle and firm sinew. Those six-pack abs. His lean hips and thick thighs and that giant cock.

"My turn," he whispers. "Lie on the bed."

Confused, I stand once more and go to the side of the bed. He stands as well, going to the other side. "Dead center, Savage. Hurry up."

I lie on the bed, sticky between my thighs, my nipples hard and throbbing. I could come again in seconds if he so much as barely touched my clit.

"Spread your legs," he says and I do it automatically, opening myself to him.

He settles on the end of the bed, his fingers wrapped around the base of his cock as he begins to stroke. "Touch yourself."

I frown. "What?"

"Do as I say."

I rest my hand over my pussy, the heat licking at my fingers. "What do you want me to do next?"

"Do I need to command your every move?" he asks.

I say nothing. Just wait for his next order.

"Trace your clit," he says, his voice low.

I do it, using just my index finger. "Like this?"

"Yes. Not too hard." I increase my pace immediately, unable to stop myself. "Not too fast either. Stop."

I pause, the tiny bit of flesh pulsating beneath my fingertip.

"Move your hand away. I can't see you."

He can't make up his mind what he wants me to do. I drop my hand, moving my legs so my feet are flat on the mattress, my knees bent, legs still spread, giving him an eyeful. I watch as he begins to stroke himself in earnest, his hungry gaze glued to the spot between my thighs.

Without warning he rises up, crawling up the mattress. Crawling over me. Until he's straddling my shoulders, my neck, his cock right in front of my mouth. "Let me come on your face."

I knew he'd want this. Sick fuck.

But I want it too.

He strokes himself furiously, grunts sounding low in his throat. He's so close. I can smell him. Feel him. His cock brushes my face and I lick my lips. Purse them together. A guttural groan leaves him as he teases my mouth with the head of his cock and I stick out my tongue, licking it. Tasting it. Tasting him.

"Fuck, Summer." He chokes the words out on a gasp, and I feel his cum hit my face. Across my cheek. My lips. Streams of it. Again and again. He groans loudly and I open my eyes, watching him as he loses himself in me.

On me.

When it's over, he reaches out, dipping his fingers in his own cum and smearing it on my lips, tracing their shape. "So fucking perfect," he whispers, his compliment lighting me up inside.

He climbs off the bed without another word, leaving me there. My entire body throbs with the need to come, and his semen is all over my face. I think about wiping it off with my fingers and I'm about to do just that when he returns, a wet washcloth in his hand.

"I'll wash you off." His voice is cold. Almost clinical. As if he's a doctor and I'm his patient, not the girl he just came all over.

I lie there and take it, closing my eyes as he wipes the cum off my face. His touch is impersonal, and he doesn't say a word. Doesn't even breathe hard. He's in complete control of himself.

It's infuriating.

When he's finished, he's off the bed and back in the bathroom. I roll onto my side, propping my head up with my hand, contemplating my surroundings. The room is completely shrouded in darkness, and I wish I knew what time it was.

"You should go."

I sit up when I hear his deep voice, searching for him in the dim light. I find him standing in the open doorway of the connecting bathroom, stark naked and his arms curled in front of his chest.

"I thought—"

"You thought wrong," he interrupts, pushing away from the doorframe and approaching the bed. "I'm done with you." He bends over and grabs my clothing, tossing it at me. "Get dressed and get out."

I scramble off the bed and do as he says, slipping my clothes back on as fast as I can, my entire body shaking, but for a different reason now. Any pleasant feelings I might've had, have left me. Now I'm just angry.

Enraged.

"I want my journal," I tell him as I slip my shoes on, not bothering with my socks.

He actually laughs, the bastard. "You think one beat-off session gets your journal back? I don't think so."

"You treat me like shit," I spit at him, hating the pain coursing through me. "Like I'm worthless."

"Familiar, right? Isn't that how you treat yourself?" He lifts a brow.

I march toward him, my hands clenched into fists. "What the fuck do you know about me?"

"More than you know. I watch you. You walk around this campus as if no one can touch you, but deep down, you have zero self-worth." He takes a step forward, bending down so his face is in mine. "Find your value, Savage, and prove to me you're worth more than a meaningless jerk off." He waves his hand at me, dismissive. "Now get out."

"I hate you," I say, my voice quaking with anger.

"You hate yourself even more because you enjoyed every second of this," he says with an evil smile. "Now go."

I turn and leave without another word.

SEVENTEEN

SUMMER

FRIDAY AFTERNOON and I'm in the library alone, sitting at my usual table. My American Government textbook cracked open in front of me as I try to read, but my eyes want to cross, the chapter is so boring. And I'm tired from last night with Whit.

I ran across campus back to my room, terrified someone would catch me. I returned to my dorm building almost exactly at ten. The advisor on duty gave me a stern look when I walked in, and I thought for sure I was busted.

"You were almost late," she said and pointed at the clock on the wall right above her head.

It was ten o'clock on the dot.

"Sorry. I was studying with a friend." I smiled at her, hoping I was convincing.

I guess I was. She let me go back to my room without another word.

I'm just grateful I didn't come stomping in there like an enraged Incredible Hulk. The entire exchange with Whit made me so angry. His attitude is bullshit. And what does he know about how I feel about myself? Trying to tear down my self-esteem? Most of the time he compliments my attitude, and now he's claiming I don't love myself enough or some shit?

God, I can't stand him. He's not my therapist, that's for damn sure. He's a psychotic sex fiend who treats women as objects and not as actual human beings. Talk about fucked up.

Even more fucked up? How much I want to see him again. If I think he has issues, then I know for sure I do too.

Irritated with myself, with everything, I slam my book shut, earning a shush from Miss Taylor for my efforts. I ignore her, unzipping my backpack and shoving the textbook inside. I shove my notebook in there too. I still have forty minutes until class starts, but no way am I going to be ready for the quiz we're having today. Screw it.

Besides, who gives quizzes on a Friday afternoon? Sadistic assholes, that's who.

Grabbing my backpack, I pull it toward me and wrap my arms around it, resting my head on top of it like a pillow, closing my eyes. I'll take a quick nap. No one will bother me.

Hopefully.

But hopes are for dreamers and idiots, because mere minutes into my spontaneous nap, I hear someone whisper my last name. A male someone. I open my eyes and spot Whit standing in the stacks. He tilts his head to the right, indicating he wants me to come to him.

I lift my head, my gaze never leaving his as I mouth the word, *no*.

His jaw clenches and he marches toward my table, standing over me like a lord looking down upon his lowly servant. As in me. I'm his servant. Meant to entertain him whenever he wants me to.

"You don't have a choice," he says between clenched teeth. "Come with me now, or pay the price."

"Maybe I want to pay the price," I tell him calmly.

"Savage," he practically growls, his deep voice washing over me.

As if I have no control over myself, I rise to my feet and go to him. There's no point in fighting this. Fighting him. We're going to do whatever we do, no matter how much I protest. It will happen.

We are happening.

He grabs my hand the moment he can reach me, his fingers tangling with mine before he jerks me deeper into the endless rows of books. I let him drag me as he turns left, then right. Then another left. Until we're so deep into the library, I can see no light from the massive windows that line the building. I can't hear any voices either. Just the electric hum of the pendant lights hanging above us, and the sound of my blood roaring in my ears.

Whit turns to face me, pressing me into the books, his body so close it brushes mine. I tilt my head up, defiant as I stare at him. "What do you want?"

His lips curl into the barest smile. "Your panties."

I roll my eyes. "Seriously?"

He nods. Leans down so his face is directly in mine, his lips close as he whispers, "Not yet though."

"Why not?"

"I want to get them nice and wet first," he says, just before his mouth lands on mine.

His lips are electric, sparking energy between us. This is what I craved last night, and he wouldn't give it to me. He was so cold. Distant. Infuriating. No kissing. No closeness. I may have come, but it wasn't enough for me.

I wanted this. His mouth on mine. Devouring me. A kiss is intimate. It brings people closer, even strangers. He was the first boy I ever really kissed, and I've been addicted to his taste ever since.

I part my lips for his entry, and his tongue slides against mine, circling. Thrusting. I moan into his mouth, my hands reaching for him, resting on his chest, curling into the lapels of his uniform jacket. He slips his hands under my skirt, resting them on my ass, kneading my flesh, pulling me into him.

He's hard beneath his trousers. Of course he is. When is he not when we're together? Knowing I do that to him makes me feel powerful. Strong. Despite how terrible he treats me, how cruel and indifferent he is, I still affect him.

Knowledge is power, Jonas used to tell me. And he's so right. I just never thought it would apply to something like this.

With little effort, Whit lifts me, and I wrap my legs around his waist, clinging to him, letting him consume me.

I consume him right back.

We kiss and kiss for what feels like hours. He never stops devouring my mouth. It's almost as if all of this energy was pent-up inside of him, dying to get out. And I'm the receptor, eagerly wanting more.

"Last night wasn't enough," he murmurs after breaking the kiss.

I say nothing, a sigh leaving me when he licks his way down my neck.

"I can't stop thinking about you," he continues, his voice hard. Full of irritation. "You make me insane."

The tiniest laugh leaves me and he yanks on the end of my ponytail, thrusting his face in mine. "And not in a good way."

I glare at him, my heart racing, my lips swollen from his kisses. His gaze drops to my mouth, lingering there, and he leans in, sinking his teeth into my lower lip. Hard. Harder. Only until a whimper escapes me and I swear he breaks skin is when he finally releases his hold.

"I hate you," I whisper, because it's the only thing I can think to say.

"I hate you too, Savage," he returns impassively, lowering me to the floor and removing his hands from my body before he steps away from me. "Now take off your panties."

Never taking my eyes off of him, I reach beneath my skirt and tear them off, stepping out of them awkwardly and nearly toppling over. I reach out and brace my hand against the shelf before I thrust my underwear at his chest. He catches the ball of black cotton, rubbing his fingers over the crotch.

"Wet." He brings them to his nose and inhales. "Smells just like you."

"You're fucking disgusting," I spit at him, though I don't mean a word of it. Watching him sniff my panties actually makes me wetter. God, I'm just as depraved as he is. If I don't watch it, I might end up dripping down my thighs, and I still have to go to class.

Shit, I still have to take a quiz.

"You like it," he says knowingly. "I'm leaving this weekend."

Disappointment crashes within me, but I remain outwardly ambivalent. "What a shame."

"You'll miss me?" he asks.

"Not in a million years." Feeling brave, I try to push past him, but he grabs me with one hand, stuffing my panties in his pocket with the other.

He grins. "I'm positive you'll miss me."

"In your dreams," I retort, hating how accurate he is.

"You will." He crowds me, his body pressed to mine. "You'll be alone in that narrow bed of yours, touching yourself to memories of us being together. Crying out my name when you make yourself come, though it won't be near good enough. Not without me there." He nuzzles my cheek with his nose, the touch oddly sweet. Almost comforting. "You need my fingers deep inside you. My mouth, my tongue on your wet cunt."

I swallow hard, my eyes falling closed when I feel his mouth drift across my face, until it pauses at my ear. "You were made for me, you know. You're just as sick and fucked up as I am."

I'm trembling. A shuddery breath leaves me and he bites my ear, making me whimper. "When I come back, I'm fucking you."

Arousal lights me up inside at his words. "Where are you going?"

"None of your damn business," he says, pushing away from me with a sneer. "Thanks for the gift."

He turns and leaves me there, walking away without a backward glance. I watch him go, shaking like a leaf, despising how easy it is for him to just...abandon me.

Typical. They all eventually abandon me.

He's just like the rest.

I wait a few minutes before I make my way back to the table I abandoned. My backpack still sits there untouched, and I know it's because of Whit that no one bothers me anymore. I can appreciate that, but the only reason they bothered me in the first place is...

Because of Whit.

He's somehow become both my protector and my nightmare.

Fitting.

Grabbing my stuff, I go to the bathroom and try to piece myself back together. I'm a mess. My hair is falling out of my ponytail and after washing my hands, I fix it, studying myself. My eyes are sparkling and a little wild. My cheeks are pink and my lips are still swollen, all from our kissing session. Why do I want him, when he treats me so terribly? What is wrong with me? Is it the whole, *we always want what we can't have* scenario?

I don't know, but the thing is, I can have him. I have had him. Not in every way I want, but we're getting there. We're going to have sex. I'm going to know what it feels like to have Whit inside of my body.

My pussy clenches at the mere thought, reminding me that I'm standing here with no undies on. A strong breeze could come up while I'm walking on campus and catch my skirt, and everyone could see me.

I sort of don't care.

The bathroom door swings open and in walks Caitlyn. Our gazes connect and she rolls her eyes, stopping at the sink next to mine to wash her hands. I watch her blatantly, annoyance filling me. One second she's my friend and now she's my enemy. I don't get it.

I don't get any of the people at this school. They're all fucking terrible, truth be told.

"What are you looking at?" she snaps at me.

"I haven't done shit to you, yet you hate me," I say truthfully.

She shuts off the tap and shakes her hands into the sink before going to the paper towel dispenser to tear off a piece. She wipes her hands, her back to me, and I wait for her response. This has to be some sort of stall tactic.

Whatever. I've still got time.

Finally Caitlyn turns to face me, her face blank. No one at this school has emotions, I swear to God. "I don't hate you."

I'm taken aback by her simple statement. "I don't believe you."

She shrugs. "It's true. I feel nothing for you. My problem is, I don't understand why Whit is interested in you so much."

"He's not interested in—"

"Don't bother saying he isn't when you know it's not true. I saw the way he stared at you at the restaurant. How he asked everyone on this campus to make your life a total nightmare, only to turn around and call us all off," she says, admitting to everything I suspected. "He feels something for you, and he doesn't feel anything about anyone beyond his friends and his family. Certainly never for a girl. He's a user."

I stare at her, stunned by her words, though they're not necessarily a surprise. I've just never heard anyone say it so blatantly before.

Caitlyn is describing Whit perfectly.

"So why you?" she asks when I haven't said anything. "I don't get it. No one does. You're not anything special. No offense, by the way, but I don't see why he's so fascinated with you. Who are you anyway?"

I remember the first time I saw Whit, at the party at his parents' apartment. Did it begin then? When we were only fourteen?

"I'm no one," I finally say, making my way toward the door. "I don't matter."

"You do to him," she reminds me.

Reaching for the handle, I smile at her as I open the door. "I suppose I do," I say just before I walk out.

EIGHTEEN

WHIT

I'M in the city for the weekend, summoned by my very own lord and master to make an appearance at his apartment. I show up at my father's late Friday night, delaying my visit as much as I could, grateful to see he's already in bed by the time I arrive.

I make myself a drink and go to my room, tossing my duffel on the edge of the bed and pulling a few things out, settling them on the bedside table, along with my drink. I mechanically strip out of my clothes completely and pull back the bed covers, slipping in between them. I grab my glass from the table and sip the aged whiskey at first. Until it turns into me consuming it, draining every last drop and licking my lips, savoring the burn that coats my throat.

Like a fucking degenerate, I grab the crumpled panties from where I left them on the table and bring them to my nose, inhaling deeply. I can still smell her scent. Musky sweet. Like sex. The memory of her taste floods my mouth and I close my eyes, sliding her panties down my chest and wrapping them around my already hard cock.

I'm fucking obsessed with her and the way she talks to me, like she wants to piss me off. The defiant look on her face earlier in the library filled me with the need to tame her. Make her mine. The night before, when she used my body to get off, shamelessly rubbing her wetness all over the front of my sweats—fuck me. It took every bit of willpower inside of me not to reach for her. Touch her.

Fuck her thoroughly.

Last night, I didn't know what I wanted, and it showed. I lost control of the situation mentally, and I was all over the place. That frustrated me. Made me angry at myself.

At her too, though I know it wasn't fair.

When is life ever fair though?

My head fills with images of her last night. The pleasure on her face when I jerked off above her, how she pursed those lush lips, her tongue darting out for a lick. She winced when the first splatter of semen hit her face and then she just laid there and took it. Like the perfect little submissive she must be.

Fuck.

The first time we were together, when she blew me, my cock hitting the back of her throat, making her gag. Coming all over her perfect tits.

Jesus.

The orgasm slams into me unexpectedly and I come in her panties, a quiet groan leaving me. I lie there afterward, pissed that it's already over. Hating how quickly I'm losing control now, but only when it comes to Summer.

She's becoming a weakness. One I don't want or need. Maybe this weekend in the city with my father will reset me. Distance is the key. Disgust is a close second.

If I keep away from Summer, I won't want her as much. If I remember how needy she makes me, it'll disgust me.

Taking a deep breath, I clean myself up, then let the panties drop onto the bedside table. I grab her journal and crack it open, finding the spot where I last left off.

My mother refuses to listen to me, turning me away or changing the subject every time I try to talk to her. I think she knows what's going on, yet she won't do anything to stop it. Heaven forbid she upset Jonas. All she does is flutter around him, trying to keep the peace, but she's hiding secrets too.

Just like I am.

That's okay. I don't want anyone to know about Daniel. I skipped school again today, and we went on an adventure. Just before he took me back to his apartment and went down on me. It was good. I liked it, but I didn't come. He tried and tried to make it happen, but it wasn't meant to be, I guess. I finally made him stop, and I gave him a hand job. He came in less than five minutes.

Boys have it a lot easier than girls, I guess.

I slap the book shut, annoyed to read about her experiences with someone else. A jackass who can't manage to get her off. The dumb fucker. I feel like I could breathe on her and she'd come, she's that responsive.

Only when it comes to me, I think, pleased.

Only me.

There's a knock on my door and without waiting for my response, my father bursts into my room. I sit up, shoving the journal under the sheets, scowling at him as he paces my room.

"Already in bed?" He pauses, watching me with his brows raised.

"I'm tired." I shrug.

"Not out finding an heiress to fuck?" He sips from the glass he's clutching. Scotch, I'm sure. "That's your usual plan when you come into the city."

It never even crossed my mind to reach out to any of the heiresses I know and see if they wanted to go out. "None of them interest me."

"Your mother would beg to differ." He drains the glass completely, setting it on my nearby dresser, his back to me. His shoulders are a straight line, and full of tension. "She's exerting pressure."

"On who? You?"

He turns to face me once more. "Your birthday is coming up. You'll be eighteen. Coming into your own."

As in, coming into my trust fund.

"So?" I've known this was the first step in the many layered inheritances I have since I was a child. I was eight years old, maybe? First is the trust fund left by my mother's side of the family. Then when I'm twenty-one, I come into money from my paternal grandfather. At twenty-five, the rest of my rightful fortune floods my bank account.

My parents won't be able to control me financially ever again. The freedom is so close, I can practically taste it.

"Your mother has—expectations for you. They were brought upon her. They'll be brought upon your sisters as well," Father says, his expression blank.

I know what he's referring to. Mother was paired with Father when they were in college, though everyone knew they were getting married even before that. The Lancasters are American royalty. We can't marry any commoner off the street. My future wife has to come from a certain family, be of a certain age and pedigree, and go to a certain school. She must be questioned, vetted and trained. Mother will be in charge of all of it. She's already chosen the perfect girl for me.

This girl does nothing for me whatsoever.

"Leticia." I say her name. My body, my mind, nothing responds. She is a zero in my equation.

"She's a lovely girl, Whit. Smart. Beautiful. Her lineage is impeccable."

"She's boring." I sulk like a little boy, pissed that my entire future has been planned out for me. "I don't want her."

"She's not a doll that you return to the store when you're done playing with her," Father says drolly.

"She's a doll I have no interest in touching at all," I retort, crossing my arms.

He settles on the edge of the mattress, contemplating me. "I know this isn't how you want things to be. I'm just telling you what your mother says to me. This is what she wants. What she expects. She's determined to preserve the Lancaster name."

"Right. Because you two did such a bang-up job keeping it untarnished," I toss at him.

He winces. "That statement is fair. And it's my fault we divorced. I'm the one who cheated on her."

God, the man is infuriating. He speaks out of both sides of his mouth. He takes full responsibility for the affair, as he should, but I see it now. How my mother drove him away from her. Shoved him into another woman's arms. I didn't see it then, when it happened, but I'm starting to get it now.

"You're encouraging me to do the same thing, don't you see? I have no interest in Leticia. She's nice, but I'm not attracted to her. I can't imagine being married to her, fucking her on occasion while I have affairs on the side." I thrust a finger at him. "I don't want your life. Stop trying to force it on me."

We contemplate each other silently and Father glances over his shoulder, staring at the empty glass on the dresser. I'm sure he'd love nothing more than to gulp more liquor down his throat so he wouldn't have to feel anything. "Sometimes we have no choice, son."

"That's bullshit and you know it," I spit out. "You and Mother are pushing your agendas on me, and you both ended up miserable and divorced. I'm never getting married."

"Son—"

"I'm not." I feel like I'm having a tantrum, but fuck it. "Marriage is a trap. A façade. Something society came up with that rarely stands a chance of surviving. Do you know I don't have a single memory of the two of you happy together? Not one. Most of my memories are of the two of you fighting. Arguing."

Seething at each other through clenched teeth. Whisper-shouting so other people wouldn't hear them, but we always heard them. Their arguments scared my sisters. Servants were fired for eavesdropping. Other women's names were always brought up by my mother, and my father would always deny he was having an affair.

But he was. He did. He stuck with Janine Weatherstone for years. Like he was addicted to her.

If she's even remotely like her daughter, I understand the feeling.

My father's gaze, so much like mine, narrows on me. "Fine. You want some fantasy advice? What I would tell you if money and family weren't involved and we were just regular people?"

I nod. "Tell me."

"Fuck the proper lineage and important family names. Find someone who sets you on fire every time you so much as look at her. Someone you can talk to, fight with, and fuck just as fiercely. And once you find that woman, don't let her go," he says vehemently.

He grabs his glass, rattling the ice before he drinks the last dregs of alcohol. "You can either do what you're supposed to and please your family, or do what you want and fuck the whole world. It's your choice, Whit."

Before I can say anything else, or ask him any questions, he exits my room, slamming the door behind him.

NINETEEN

SUMMER

MY NAME WHISPERED in the darkness rouses me. I thought I was dreaming at first. The voice was deep. Familiar. Reminded me of Whit's.

I hear my name again and I squirm beneath the covers, struggling to remain asleep. The dream will be good, if Whit's involved. I don't want to miss a thing.

Firm fingers grip my shoulder. "Savage."

My eyes pop open to find a dark figure looming over me. I part my lips, the scream crawling up my throat and a gloved hand settles over the lower part of my face, silencing me. My heart races, my scream muffled behind the glove and I struggle beneath his hold.

He thrusts his face in mine. Sharp cheekbones. Angled jaw. Plush mouth and ice cold eyes.

Whit Lancaster. In the flesh.

"Be quiet," he whispers, his tone a threat. Deadly.

I thrash about, marveling at how strong his hand is, pinning my head to the bed. The scent of rich leather fills my head and I'm tempted to bite his gloved fingers. He reaches for me, using his other arm to hold me down, his body draped over mine to keep me from moving. "What the fuck, Savage?"

My heart races so hard it feels like it's going to burst from my chest. He has to feel it. Has to know how scared I am.

"It's just me," he whispers. "Calm down."

His tone is softer than usual and I immediately do as he asks, my body growing still, as do my thoughts. I take a shaky breath, which is a struggle beneath his leather-covered hand, and as if he can sense my sudden compliance, he removes his hand from my mouth.

I exhale loudly, watching as he rises to his feet and begins to pace the room. He's dressed all in black. Black hoodie and joggers. Black Nikes on his feet and a black beanie covering his hair.

"Why are you dressed like that?" I ask, my voice raspy from sleep.

"I didn't want anyone to see me," he says, his back to me as he goes to the window and pushes the curtains aside to stare outside.

"Have your sister hack the security system," I tell him.

He glances over his shoulder. "She's not here. I literally snuck inside your dorm hall, keeping to the shadows."

"Why?" I ask incredulously. "It's Saturday. I thought you were gone for the weekend."

"I came back early." He rests his gloved hands on the edges of the window, one foot cocked forward, his gaze on the view while he speaks to me. "I couldn't stop thinking about you."

I sit up in bed, his admission making me blurt out the only word I can think of.

"*Why?*"

He pushes away from the window and returns to my bed, his hands cupping my face, forcing me to look at him. "It's like my thoughts are consumed with nothing else but you. I jerked off last night thinking of you. I jerked off again this morning thinking about you. We haven't even fucked yet, and I'm fucking obsessed."

Whit releases my face, springing away from me as if I might be diseased, on his feet and pacing the floor again.

"You're dressed as if you're going to rob the place," I say, my voice shaky. "You're risking a lot, sneaking into my room."

"I'm not risking shit, considering my family owns this school and I wouldn't get in trouble. They could find me in your bed with you impaled on my cock and they wouldn't do a damn thing about it." He thrusts a finger at me. "What I am risking is my entire fucking future right now. Not that you give a damn."

I frown, not sure what he's referring to. "What do I have to do with your future?"

"You fuck with my head, when I shouldn't be thinking about you whatsoever, Savage. You're nothing to me."

The words are cruel, but there isn't any real feeling behind him, so I take no offense to what he just said.

"Then why are you here?" I ask softly.

Whit thrusts his hands into his hair, pulling it away from his forehead while he studies me. "I don't know." He sounds positively tormented.

His torment is my power. I'm the one who does this to him. Not quite sure what he means by the future comment, but it doesn't matter right now. What does matter is that he's back. He returned to campus because of me. For me.

I shove the covers back and rise onto my knees, reaching for the hem of the oversized T-shirt I wore to bed. With one fluid movement, I remove the shirt, tossing it aside. I'm only in a pair of panties and nothing else, and his gaze drops to my chest, his eyes flaring with heat. I get on all fours and crawl across the bed, until I'm on the very end, and he stops directly in front of me, his black leather gloved hand slipping beneath my chin and tipping my head back so I have no choice but to rise up on my knees.

"Are you an offering?" he asks, his voice deceptively soft, his eyes glittering.

The cool air whisks across my body, making me tremble. Making my nipples harden to almost painful points. "If I'm what you want, then yes."

"You're always what I want."

I blink up at him, shocked by his admission, the obvious yearning in his eyes as they skim over my face. He drifts his hand along the length of my neck, across my collarbone. The smooth black leather is soft and cool against my heated skin and I close my eyes, a gasp leaving me when he drifts his knuckles along my breast. "You make me want things I can't have."

He pinches my nipple with his thumb and index finger, pulling on it. Making me wince. He does the same to my other nipple, twisting it until I cry out before he releases it, ducking his head and tonguing the throbbing bit of flesh for not nearly as long as I want him to.

Whit steps away from the bed, his gaze still on my glistening nipple. "Why the fuck do I always want to hurt you?"

He sounds tortured. And if he's trying to threaten me, it's not working.

I cup my breasts, fondling myself. "You can't."

"Why not?" He frowns.

"Because I like the way you touch me too much." I brush my thumb across my wet nipple, my pussy flooding from the warmth of his gaze as he watches my every move. "I even enjoy the pain."

His eyes darken with heat. "You're as fucked up as I am."

I nod. "We're one and the same."

He swallows hard, his Adam's apple moving before he utters, "Slip your hand in your panties."

I do as he says, diving my fingers into the front of my pale pink panties. They're nothing special. But he's looking at me as if I'm wearing expensive lingerie just for him. It's that look that has me soaked, and my fingers sink into my folds, slicking through my juices. I'm so wet, I'm sure he can hear it.

"Give me your hand," he demands and I pull my hand from my underwear, my coated fingers shiny. He inhales sharply, his chest rising before he reaches for my wrist and brings my hand to his mouth.

He sticks his tongue out and drags it slowly along each of my fingers. My breath comes in little pants, my gaze on his tongue, aroused by the way he laps at my fingers as if he's savoring my taste.

"Do it again," he murmurs against my palm. My gaze jerks to his and he gently kisses my hand. "Let me hear just how wet I make you."

Once again my fingers are between my thighs, my hand busy as it stretches the pink cotton tightly. My clit throbs as I rub it, and I increase my speed, the wet, sloppy sounds filling the room. He leans in and circles his gloved fingers around my wrist, stopping me, his face in mine, his breath fanning across my lips.

"I'm going to fuck you tonight," he whispers.

I nod, my eyes wide and unblinking.

"I want to make you come first," he continues, his grip tightening around my wrist. "Do you want that?"

"Yes," I breathe out with no hesitation.

"Don't move," he says.

I remain still as he removes his hand from my wrist, watching as he climbs onto the bed behind me. He lies down and pushes his head between my legs, his face right at my pussy. "Remove your hand," he demands and I yank it out of my underwear, breathless with anticipation.

He remains fully clothed, his gloved hands pressing on the inside of my thighs, spreading me wider. With careful fingers he nudges my panties aside, exposing me and I watch as he studies my pussy, his lips parting, tongue sneaking out to touch the corner of his mouth. "So fucking wet."

My thighs tremble—my entire body shakes as I wait for him to make a move. He lifts his head, his mouth landing dead center on my pussy and he nuzzles me. Teasing, light strokes that send my head spinning and my heart rate kicking into overdrive.

"Sit on my face," he whispers, but I don't. What if I suffocate him? What if I—

His hands grip my ass and he presses me down, so I have no choice but to do what he demands. He sticks his tongue out, licking my folds, my clit. Circling it, searching every part of me. His fingers slide closer to my crack, stroking me, teasing me as I basically grind on top of his face. Our gazes lock and I'm fascinated by the heat in his eyes, the way he watches me so intently as he devours me.

He draws his index finger up and down my ass crack, his touch as light as a feather. A shudder moves through me, a warning sign that my orgasm is already close, and I spread my legs wider, throwing my head back as I shamelessly rock against his mouth. He grips my ass, moving me against him, his tongue increasing in speed and I strain toward his magical mouth, desperate for more.

The orgasm hits, his name falling from my lips as I slide back and forth on his face, his tongue fluttering against my clit, his finger pressing against my asshole. My pussy clenches, my vision turning hazy as I toss my head back, a moan sounding from deep within me. He doesn't let up. His mouth still works me, his gloved finger stroking my ass, his other arm coming around my waist and holding me to him as he fiercely eats me.

Another orgasm follows the first one, almost immediately, surprising me. It's not as strong, but it still sends shudders rippling through me, leaving me a gasping, helpless mess. My thigh muscles strain as I try to lift away from him, and he loosens his hold on me so I can collapse beside him. I close my eyes, trying to calm my thoughts, my heart.

God, that was intense. The way he looked at me. Touched me. No one's touched me back there before, and I never knew it could feel so...good.

I hear him roll off the bed. Peel off the gloves, the leather making a slapping sound as he tosses them on my desk. Clothes rustle as they're removed and I remain still with my eyes shut, anticipation curling through me as I wait for him to return.

The mattress dips from his weight and I feel his fingers brush my hips as he tugs my stretched-out panties down my legs, removing them completely. He rolls me onto my back and climbs on top of me, his heavy weight almost a comfort, pressing me down onto the bed. He pushes my hair away from my forehead, his touch strangely gentle and I slowly open my eyes to find him watching me, all the usual iciness in his gaze melted away, replaced by unmistakable heat.

"You alive?" he asks sardonically.

I stretch beneath him, his firm cock resting against my belly. "I don't think so."

"You're a filthy fucking girl, how eagerly you rode my face." He leans down, his lips on mine, his tongue dipping inside my mouth. My scent is all over him, and I can taste myself. Salty sweet.

"It felt good," I murmur against his lips as I reach around him, my hands sliding down his back.

He lifts up, his hands braced on the mattress on either side of my face, hovering above me. "I shouldn't have come here tonight."

I ignore his words, choosing instead to close my eyes and arch my body into his.

Whit presses my shoulder down onto the mattress, holding me with force. "What we have is meaningless."

There he goes again, trying to convince himself.

"I'm only using you because I have your journal," he reminds me, his mouth suddenly at my ear. "I'm finding out all of your dirty little secrets, Savage. You've been a grade A whore since you started high school."

Anger suddenly floods me. Why does he have to open his mouth and say such shitty things? He's ruining everything. I try to buck him off my body, but he's too heavy. Too strong. "Get off me."

"Little freshman Summer Savage enjoyed sneaking around campus, getting fucked by her eighteen-year-old boyfriend," he croons in my ear, his fingers drifting down my arm gently, finding my wrist and clamping it like a vise. "Ol' Daniel was a stupid fuck, was he not?"

All of my earlier tender feelings toward Whit evaporate with every cruel word he says. "Shut up."

"Truth hurts? Your entries are just getting better and better." He lifts my arm above my head, holding it there as he rakes his gaze over me. "Though I feel like there are certain things left unsaid in that journal."

Fear wraps its tendrils around my insides, cinching tighter and tighter. After my relationship with Daniel ended is when Yates finally sunk his claws into me completely. And once Whit reads those entries?

I assume he'll want nothing to do with me.

"You even keep secrets from yourself, don't you?" He presses his torso against mine, and I can feel his cock nudging at my pussy. He grabs my other wrist and pulls it up over my head, so he's clutching them both and I feel trapped. Powerless.

Aroused.

I don't understand why his anger and mean words turn me on so much, but I'm helpless to it. We're sick. What we do is just...depraved.

Whit shifts down, his mouth on my breasts, covering my sensitive skin with downright sweet kisses. He draws one nipple into his mouth and sucks and sucks, making me writhe beneath him. He does the same to the other one, biting the flesh, sinking his teeth into it as I struggle against his hold, crying out.

He releases my nipple, blowing a soft breath across it, the flesh throbbing from his bite. He returns his attention to the other nipple. Licking. Sucking. Biting. Hurting. I feel his teeth sink into my flesh and it turns into an ache between my thighs. I wrap my legs around his hips, wishing he'd slip inside me.

"I'm not using a condom," he mutters, releasing his hold on me so he can reach between us, his hand gripping around the base of his dick. "I want to feel you."

"I'm on the pill," I tell him.

Whit laughs. "Of course you are. Pretty little whore. Fully prepared to fuck whoever you want with no consequences."

Without thought I strike out, ready to slap him, but he's faster, catching my wrist before I can smack his smug face. His expression darkens as he holds me, our gazes locked, me silently fuming. He makes me so incredibly angry when he says such awful things.

But deep down...I also like it. Too much sometimes.

"Don't like it when I call you a whore?" he asks with a sneer. "Well, too fucking bad."

He thrusts inside me, filling me completely, all the way to the hilt. A gasp escapes me and he releases my hand as he begins to thrust, pulling almost completely out before he pushes his way back in. He's relentless, hammering inside of me at a steady pace, the force of his thrusts pushing me up the mattress and I take it.

Damn it, I *enjoy* it. Whit sinking inside my body feels so good. He's not hesitant in his movements at all. There's no fumbling, no asking if I'm sure, if I'm okay. No careful touches or gentle caresses. He's brutal. He fucks me like a machine, his hips working, his thick cock driving inside of me again and again. It's as if my entire being comes alive the more that he thrusts, until I'm clinging to him, our sweaty bodies stuck together as we move as one.

"Fuck, you're so tight," he says on a groan, burying his face against my throat as he presses me deeper into the mattress. I let my hands drift down, until they settle on his ass, and I feel the muscles there flex with every push inside my body. I press down, wanting more, wanting all of him, and he licks my neck. Sucks it.

My hands wander everywhere I can reach. His body is beautiful. Smooth and muscular and flawless. His cock fits perfectly, as if we were made for each other. Every time he pushes inside me, I see stars. My belly trembles. I'm going to come again.

I grip the back of his head, my fingers sinking into his silky soft hair and tugging. He grunts, going completely still above me, his cock throbbing, pulsating deep within my body just before he's racked with shudders.

"Aw fuck," he mutters through his teeth, his hips bucking wildly as he loses all control. A spurt of hot liquid floods me and I realize he's coming. I clench my inner walls around him, purposely trying to milk him and a string of curses leaves his lips as he thrusts once. Twice. A third time.

And then collapses on top of me.

I lie there for a moment, trying to gather myself. I didn't come. My entire body is on edge, eager to fall, but he doesn't move. Disappointment crashes over me and I push at his shoulders, desperate to get him off of me.

He pulls out of my body, a gush of semen spilling out of me and leaving a wet spot. I roll away from it, plastering myself to his side, both of us trying to catch our breath.

"You didn't come," he says after a few seconds, his voice a whisp of sound.

I shake my head. "No."

His hand lands between my legs, his nimble fingers finding my clit. He rubs it in circles, his pace quickening until he's furiously trying to get me off. It takes nothing. A few assured strokes of his long fingers and I go off like a rocket, chanting *oh God, oh God* again and again as my orgasm rattles through me.

I crack open my eyes when he removes his hand from my pussy, just in time to watch as he sucks our mixed juices off his index finger. "Told you there would be three."

My mind scrambles, remembering what he said only after he's already climbed off the bed and casually putting his clothes on. I sit up, clenching my trembling thighs together as I watch him get dressed, trying to come up with something to say.

"Do you hate me?" he asks casually as he tugs his joggers on, foregoing his underwear.

I stare at him, unsure of what he wants from me.

"You should," he continues, tugging the hoodie over his head, that beautiful torso disappearing from my view. "I treat you like shit, and still you come for me. Multiple times."

"I hate you," I agree, scooting away when he plops onto the edge of the mattress and puts his shoes on with his back to me.

"Good." He sounds pleased. "I'll eventually fuck you out of my system, give you back that drivel you call your deep thoughts and we can forget this moment in time ever existed."

I watch as he stands and stretches his arms up toward the ceiling, his hoodie lifting and revealing a sexy sliver of his flat stomach. My mouth practically waters at the thought of licking him there.

Licking him everywhere.

"Because trust me, you are that forgettable." I blink him into focus, realizing too late that he's incredibly close. He grabs hold of my chin, forcing me to look at him. "Thanks for the fuck."

He delivers a punishing kiss upon my lips before letting me go, striding toward the door without a backward glance, carefully opening and closing it as quiet as a church mouse.

His words run through my mind again and again, and I realize he's full of shit. The only reason he came back to campus early was because of me. He couldn't stop thinking about me. Those were his exact words.

I'm unforgettable. He's just trying to convince himself that I am.

My lips start to curl and I rest my fingers on them, trying to stop the smile from spreading, but it's no use.

Stupid, bratty boy.

TWENTY

SUMMER

HE IGNORES me for three days.

Of course he does—this is what he's done before. Now he fucks me to within an inch of his life and then pretends I don't exist in class. On campus. At lunch. In the halls. It's his usual mode of operation and I'm not even offended. At least everyone else still leaves me alone.

I let him have his way. He's like a pouty little baby who has to have a tantrum—after he got what he wanted. Giving me the silent treatment, treating me like a stranger. He can pretend all he wants, though. We're so aware of each other, I swear the air between us crackles and sparks with electricity every time we're in each other's presence. In American Government he's always in his seat before I am, his eyes trailing after me as I walk past, my entire body lighting up from just a look.

He unnerves me completely, and I think I do the same to him. The awareness between us grows each day, and I'm more daring when he passes by me in the hall, or in class. I blatantly stare, not caring who notices. Who would say anything? He can't help but look at me either, his eyes going to my chest. My legs. I roll up the waistband of my skirt just for him, the hem dancing around my thighs as I silently hope I drive him out of his mind.

One day after my French class, the hall floods with people, all of us seemingly moving as one. He approaches, head above everyone else, his gaze locked on mine. We pass by, his fingers finding mine briefly, so quick I could almost believe it didn't happen. His index finger curls, snagging around mine briefly. One second we're touching...

The next, he's gone.

Whit Lancaster has become a dangerous obsession, and I don't know how to get him out of my head. My blood. He said he was going to fuck me out of his system, but how is that possible? With our every interaction, it only gets worse. He becomes...more.

I can't help but think I affect him the same exact way.

Mid-week we're struck by a hot spell. It's that last bit of summer before we're slammed with frosty mornings and brisk late afternoon winds. Followed by endless rain and then eventually, nothing but snow. Everyone on campus is outside every chance we can get, grabbing at those last bits of warm temperatures and shining sun. At lunch, during free periods, after school.

Thursday during lunch, I'm in line at the dining hall, paying the cashier before I turn to head outside when I run smack into Chad, nearly sending my wrapped sandwich and bag of chips clutched in my hand flying onto the ground.

Chad grabs my elbow, steadying me. "You all right?"

I glance up at him. Chad is attractive. Not as handsome as Whit, but he's close. He has warm hazel eyes and rich brown hair. He's from a prominent family with British royalty connections—his aunt married a duke. His family also makes frequent appearances in gossipy magazines and sites, thanks to his sister, the social media influencer, who hangs out with Kylie Jenner and her crew.

But his hand on my elbow does nothing to me. Not even a spark. His touch is meaningless.

"I'm fine. Thanks." I offer him a faint smile, but he doesn't react whatsoever. He just drops his hand, nods at me once, and leaves.

I watch him go, as he heads for his friends, Whit of course, being one of them. His gaze snags on mine, his expression unreadable, and I stare back at the beautiful boy who's blackmailing me. A boy who calls me shitty names, all while he touches me as if I'm the most beautiful thing he's ever seen and drives me wild with his mouth. His fingers.

God, I despise him. He's so confusing.

The rest of the day I catch Whit watching me with almost disgust in his gaze. Or anger. I can't tell. He's so incredibly frustrating, and now I'm the one who ignores him, determined to enjoy the day and its beautiful weather while I can. It's late in the afternoon and I'm sitting on the grass close to the library with Sylvie, the backs of our thighs itching from the grass.

"I should've brought a blanket," I grumble as I scratch myself.

Sylvie laughs. "I like the itch. Makes me feel alive."

I send her a look, but she seems dead serious. She's so—odd sometimes. I wonder if she lies about the dying stuff, but she's always so sincere when she mentions it. "How are you feeling?"

"Oh, I'm fine." She waves a hand, dismissing my question. "Mother found me a new doctor."

Frowning, I pluck at the grass. "For what?"

"No one can ever figure out what's wrong with me. When they don't deliver the answers she wants to hear, she moves on and finds a new one." Sylvie shrugs. "It's just her way. She wants to make sure I have the best medical attention out there, and we can certainly afford it."

I can only imagine the money that's been spent on Sylvie's health. "Do you have a disease?"

"Oh, I have all sorts of them, with names I can't pronounce and they're almost all incurable." She presses her hands together almost in prayer, her fingers dancing against each other. "I have a copy of my medical file if you'd like to look it over sometime."

"I don't think so," I say, making her laugh more. "Is that why you were gone over the weekend? Were you with your mother?"

"How did you know I was gone? I told no one. Mother showed up Friday morning and said we had to go. She whisked me away in the Rolls. Mommy always travels in style." Her eyes narrow as she contemplates me. "Wait a minute. Did you speak to Whit? Is he the one who told you I left?"

"No." I am in complete denial with Sylvie when it comes to her brother. "We don't talk."

We really don't. Not much anyway. We just argue. Say mean things to each other. Get naked. And give each other orgasms. Now that we've progressed to full-on fucking, it's all I can think about.

I can't wait to do it again.

"Sure you don't," Sylvie says, her voice ringing with doubt. "He looks at you as if he wants to eat you up."

My cheeks warm, and I know they must be red. "He does not."

"He does too. He stares at you every time you walk past him. He even turns his head and watches you leave, and he never does that. You don't have to confirm or deny, because I already know. You two are together." She laughs when she sees the mortified expression on my face. "Mother will have an absolute fit and I'm sure he's doing it to spite her, so enjoy him while you can."

Her words cut deep, though she didn't mean for them to. He's only using me to upset his mother? And I should enjoy him while I can?

God, he's such an asshole.

Sylvie holds her hand above her eyes and looks around, her face lighting up when she spots someone. "Hey! Over here!" She holds her arm up and waves.

I glance over in the direction she's facing to see Spencer and Whit making their way toward us. My heart falls into my stomach as I watch him saunter over, his expression bored as usual. As if he'd rather be anywhere else but here. Near me.

"Brother dearest. Spencer." Sylvie inclines her head toward them and they do the same. "What are you two gentlemen doing this fine, warm afternoon?"

"Looking for girls to fuck," Whit says, his gaze on me and no one else.

Sylvie makes an irritated noise while Spence laughs uncomfortably. "I told you I don't want to hear about your latest conquests, brother dearest." She glances over at me, her lips curling. "You're just trying to shock my friend with your crude language."

"Not too sure about that. I don't think much shocks Savage," Whit says with a shitty grin.

I glare at him, wishing I could hit him.

I also wish he would touch me.

More uncomfortable laughter comes from Spencer, causing Sylvie to set her sights on him. "Are *you* looking for a girl to fuck, Spence?"

"Uhh." His cheeks redden. He's clearly flustered, which I find endearing. He's also not as smooth as Whit. Nothing bothers him. Of course, this is the boy made of stone so I'm not surprised.

Sylvie's tinkling laughter fills the air as she bounds to her feet and makes her way to Spence, stopping directly in front of him. He's tall, and he towers over sweet little Sylvie. "Let's go get ice cream."

"We're not supposed to leave campus," he says.

She pats his chest, making a tsking noise. "I'm a Lancaster, Spence. I can leave whenever I want. Let's go. Will you drive?"

Spence puffs up his chest, his brown eyes only for her. "Sure, Syl."

Whit shoves at his friend's shoulder before thrusting his finger in Spence's face. "You touch a hair on her head, I'll break every bone in your body."

Spence rolls his eyes. "Lighten up, fuckface. I'm not interested in your sister like that."

"You're such a dick, Whit. Leave him alone," Sylvie fumes, her gaze cutting to me. "Sorry to abandon you, but ice cream calls. Bye!"

I watch Spence and Sylvie leave, hyperaware of Whit's eyes on me. Only when they're out of view do I dare look over at him. "I'm surprised you want to be seen in public with me."

He shoves his hands in his pockets, his expression impassive. "Sylvie called us over. What was I supposed to do?"

"Ignore her?" I arch a brow.

His gaze drops to my legs, lingering. "I've been trying to ignore you all week."

His honesty is surprising. "Trust me. I know."

"You're rolling up your skirt." His glittering eyes meet mine. "Trying to catch my attention?"

"Is it working?"

"Spread your legs a little and I'll let you know," he drawls, his gaze, once again, returning to my skirt.

I clamp my thighs together, drawing my knees up. "You're disgusting."

He laughs. Actually laughs. And it's a joyous sound that reaches deep into my belly and tugs at something unfamiliar. "You fucking like it, considering you're just as disgusting as me."

His words hit home because they're true. "Why have you ignored me?"

"I tried to convince myself I was done with you." He shrugs. "Guess I'm not."

Anticipation fills me, and I sit up straighter.

"Take a walk with me, Savage," he says, his voice casual, the light in his eyes anything but.

Unease slips through me, along with a healthy dose of arousal. "I don't think so."

"I'll show you something you've never seen before," he practically croons, trying to lure me away.

I laugh. "I've already seen your dick, Whit. You don't need to tempt me."

He scowls, his lips twitching at the corners.

Almost as if he wants to...smile? Laugh again?

Well, he's in a mood.

"Come on." He offers his hand to me. "Let's go."

His voice is firm. A demand, not a request. I settle my hand in his and he pulls me to my feet, tugging me toward him. "You want people to see you take me somewhere on campus?"

"I don't care what people think of me. Or you." He lets go of my hand and starts walking.

I hurry to keep up. "Is that why you've ignored me the last few days?"

"I've been—busy." He avoids looking at me.

"Busy ignoring me."

"Maybe you're not worth my attention."

"So why are you with me now?"

His grin is evil as he aims it in my direction. "You're the one who's taking a risk. You shouldn't go somewhere alone with me. Who knows what I might do?"

"You don't scare me," I say, my voice light and airy, as if I don't have a care in the world.

It's a lie though. He *does* scare me. He makes me uncomfortable. Nervous. He makes me want things I have no business wanting.

He makes me feel alive.

"I should," he says nonchalantly, making a left once we're at the back of the library. "Come on."

I follow him as we take a path I've never been down before, toward a large grove of thick trees. He says nothing, his walk determined, as is the look on his face. I hurry beside him, not wanting to trail behind, curious to where he might be taking me.

"There are old buildings back here," he says. "That used to be part of the campus."

"Really?" My curiosity piqued, I wonder if I can ask more questions. Or if he will just shut me down. "Where are they?"

"We're almost there."

Birds are chirping as they fly over our heads, landing in the trees that surround us. The sunlight is warm, the sky a vivid blue, and I glance around as the trees become thicker, the buildings farther away, until I can hear the ocean waves in the distance.

A damaged building suddenly looms up ahead, its roof completely gone, as are most of the walls. I come to a stop, staring at it. A little spooked.

"Come on," he says, tilting his head toward the building.

He leads me closer to the decaying structure, and I follow him as he walks around the crumbling walls. The brick is faded almost to white, parts of it covered in fuzzy green moss. I look around at all the destruction as I follow Whit up a set of rickety wooden stairs that I can feel giving way beneath my feet until we're actually inside the building, though it's completely open. No roof, no real walls, nothing remaining inside.

It's a shell. A ghost from another time.

"What happened here?" I lean against an old window sill, the glass long gone. Glancing back, I prop myself up, sitting on the edge, watching him.

The air between us shifts, becoming electric. Whit approaches me, slow and methodical, much like a tiger stalking his prey. Carefully he undoes the already loosened knot of his tie, whipping it off his neck completely. He stretches the silk taut between his hands, stopping in front of me. "A fire. Happened over one hundred years ago. It was the original Lancaster Prep, the first building established here. At the time, my family and the staff didn't have the heart to destroy it completely, so they left it standing and rebuilt elsewhere, buying up surrounding acreage to add to the school."

I glance around, seeing the prominent chapel spear in the far distance. "It's far from the rest of campus."

"The entire staff used to live on campus. Where we stand housed part of their living quarters at one point. The building was close enough to campus, far enough to pretend they had some privacy," he explains.

A bird chirps in the distance, and another bird answers him. Or her. Secret lovers, like us? Searching for each other in the forest?

My mind loves to spin a fantastic tale when it comes to my situation with this boy. Whit and I aren't lovers. There are no emotions between us. We're merely addicts, desperately seeking each other to help stave off the darkness that festers inside of us.

"I never knew it existed." I trail my fingers along the wooden edge, careful not to give myself a splinter.

"Of course you didn't, new girl." His smile is treacherous and makes my heart pang in anticipation.

"Have you brought other girls out here?" I try to keep my voice casual, as if my question means nothing, but he knows. I've given myself away, wanting to learn more, anything about him.

"No. Why would I bring any girl out here?" He sends me a measured look.

"Why did you bring me out here then?" Because he wants to fuck me. When does he not? Outside, in secret. I imagine him lying me down in the nearby field, my legs spread, his head between them, his mouth hungrily licking my flesh. I love it when he goes down on me. Almost as much as I love it when he fucks me.

"Privacy. You made such a big deal about us being seen together earlier, and I realized you're right. I need to keep us a secret." He's basically throwing my earlier concern back at me, and I suppose I deserve this.

"You're ashamed of me." I lift my chin, glaring at him.

"Aren't you ashamed of me? Of what we have? We hate each other, yet here we are." He gestures toward me.

"We make no sense," I say in agreement.

"Yet you're all I can think about." He sounds disgusted with himself. With me. He yanks on either end of the tie, drawing my attention to it. "Sometimes I'd rather you didn't exist at all. Then I wouldn't have to obsess over you."

His words light me up inside. They prove he's drawn to me despite everything. "What exactly are you saying?" My words are a taunt. As if I want him to say something horrible and cruel.

Secretly, I do. I want to hear what sort of devious, awful thing he could come up with and see how it makes me feel.

"I could choke you right now with this and no one would ever miss you." He curls the tie around his fingers, running the silk between them.

"You're right." My voice is cool, though deep down, I tremble. Can't help but wonder yet again what makes someone so young so fucking diabolical.

He was dark even back then. When I first met him. When he called me a whore and kissed me to shut me up. He was brutal, but still unsure.

Now it's as if he knows exactly what he wants, and exactly how to do it. It's terrifying.

And exhilarating.

Whit steps closer, his body heat, everything about him invading me, and I draw myself up, my muscles braced as he presses the warm fabric against the delicate skin of my throat. "You're not scared of me?"

It takes everything within me not to quiver. "No."

"Are you stupid?" He raises a brow. "Or do you trust me that much? Same thing, really. Trusting someone gets you nowhere. You know this."

We say nothing to each other. I stare into his icy gaze, a breath leaving me when he draws the silken tie completely around my throat. His fingers brush the back of my neck, sift through my hair and I close my eyes at the gentle touch, reminding myself it means nothing.

He hates me. This is torture. He gets off on seeing my pain. He's almost eighteen and completely fucked in the head.

But then again, so am I.

"No one will hear you scream out here." He tugs on either end of the tie, the fabric tightening. Just enough to let me know it's there. Not tight enough to hurt.

Yet.

"You won't hurt me," I say with far more confidence than I actually feel.

"What makes you so sure?" He dips his head, his mouth hovering just above mine. "I'll smother your screams with my lips. Swallow them whole."

He sometimes becomes poetic when he speaks of hurting me. "I won't scream."

"I've made you scream before." He drops one end of the tie, his fingers sliding beneath the hem of my skirt.

Gooseflesh rises where he touches me and the dull ache that's always there between my thighs when I'm with Whit roars to life. "That's a different kind of scream."

"Pleasure. Pain. It's interchangeable. You of all people should know this by now." He rests his hand against the front of my panties. "You're wet."

I reach for him, my hand settling over his erection. "You're hard."

"I got hard when I thought about choking the life out of you." His lips curl in the barest smile.

I don't believe him. Maybe this makes me foolish, but seriously. It's more the fantasy that turns him on versus actually wanting to hurt me. "You won't kill me."

He raises a brow. "What makes you so confident?"

"You don't want to destroy the family name. Whittaker Augustus Lancaster, murderer? Your parents would disapprove."

Anger flares in his beautiful eyes and his mouth touches mine in a brutal kiss. It's all tongue and teeth, his fingers slipping beneath my panties to stroke my bare flesh, toy with my clit at the same time he bites my lower lip so hard, I cry out.

And come all over his fingers in a gush.

He laughs, shifting away from me, removing his fingers from my panties. My cheeks burn with shame at how easy that was, my entire body a shaky mess and when he shoves his fingers between my lips, I suck them, tasting myself, hating how badly my clit throbs in anticipation of what other punishments he'll deliver upon me.

"You hate me so much, yet I barely touch you and in seconds, you're squirting all over my fingers." He drops a kiss on my nose, smiling. Though it doesn't quite reach his eyes. "Little whore. I bet you like it when I tell you how much I want to hurt you."

My throat is clogged with too many protests, and I swallow them down. There's no point in saying them. He'll just laugh. Call me a liar.

Deep down, I know he's right.

"Want me to fuck you now?" He tilts his head to the side, contemplating me. "Maybe you want to get on your knees and choke on my cock."

I furiously shake my head, like the ideas he's just put into my head terrify me.

They don't. I want him to fuck me right here, in the dappled sunlight and the hushed quiet of the forest. I can smell the ocean nearby, hear it lick at the shore. In and out. Rhythmic.

Like sex.

I'm not surprised when he reaches both of his hands beneath my skirt and grabs at the thin waistband of my panties, tugging them down my thighs and off my legs. I watch as the delicate fabric falls to the ground, my mind buzzing. I'm breathless. My heart beats so hard, I swear it'll burst from my chest. I keep my head angled away as Whit undoes his belt, the clank of metal making me wince.

All the while, he talks. Of how much he hates me. How badly he wants to fuck me. Hurt me. Split me in two with his cock.

He's damaged. Scary. More intense than usual. I don't understand his thoughts, his desires. They're wrong. Demented. Sick.

But they satisfy something inside of me I've never experienced before. Something I struggled with for years. Something I fought against. I always called it 'the darkness,' and when he reads my journal, he must recognize it.

We're the same, Whit and me.

His trousers drop, forming a puddle around his feet. When I dare look at him, I see his cock, thick and long, the head glistening, a drop of pre-cum pearling at the tip. His pale blue boxers are shoved just below it, and he's coming for me.

My legs fall open in welcome. He sneers, his hands rough on my hips as he angles my body to take his. He thrusts, a sharp push of his hips against mine, filling me completely and I scream so loud, a flock of birds flutters away, their flapping wings frantic as they make their escape.

"You're soaked," he says through clenched teeth as he thrusts and thrusts, my body, my desire making it easy. It's not a challenge when he fucks me. I'm never dry, and I've experienced that before. The dryness. The resistance.

I don't imagine that will ever happen with Whit.

"Why do I always want to fuck you? Why?" He increases his pace.

Slowly I come to life. When he's inside me, it's like fuel. Nourishment. I lift my head, my gaze meeting his and I wonder what he sees. His expression softens. His movements slow. I reach for him, trailing my fingers along the side of his face and his eyes fall at half-mast. His lips part. His cock throbs inside of me and I shift, my ass dragging against the rough brick beneath me, scraping my flesh.

"Tell me you hate me," he says just before he kisses me. His hot lips on mine feel like a gift, and I don't reply. I just take what he gives me, wrapping my arms around his neck, sinking my fingers into his silky hair.

He's hard everywhere but his hair. And his mouth—it can say such cruel things and do so much damage, but when he kisses me like this, they remind me of a cloud. Fleeting.

Ethereal.

I think of those other soft spots he tries to keep hidden. The skin on the inside of his arms that tickles when I touch him there. The dark, secret spot behind his balls that makes him groan when I touch it. His inner thighs.

His heart.

The realization slams into me. I don't care how dark he claims to be, or how cruelly he treats me. There's a wall there, but it's crumbling. Much like the remnants of this building that surround us. I'm patient. I'll tear down those walls and I'll find the soft underbelly of his beating heart.

"Fuck." He breathes the word against my mouth like a curse. A prayer. "You feel so good."

I smile and open my eyes to find him watching me. His thrusts are rhythmic, pushing me against the brick, and I know my backside will be scratched and bruised by the time he's finished with me.

"Tell me you hate this," he says, his voice desperate.

"I hate it." I don't sound like I hate it at all. My voice caresses each syllable, as if I gain pleasure in saying it.

"Say you hate me."

"No."

"Say it, Summer. You fucking despise me."

Once upon a time and very recently, I did. And sometimes, I still despise the things he does to me. But I don't hate him. It's like I look forward to this. The taking. The cruelty. The soft touch behind it.

"I'm not using a condom," he hisses. "I could get you pregnant."

"I'm on the pill," I remind him. I know he enjoys fucking me bare, and I like it too. It's something I've never done before. Yates was always careful about using condoms.

"I could give you a STD," he continues.

I go still at those words, my gaze widening, panic making my heart trip over itself. When I meet his gaze once again, I see the deep satisfaction pooling in his ice blue eyes.

"Didn't think I'd be fucking anyone else, did you? Would I really save this all for you?" He withdraws from my body, his fingers curling around the base of his cock as he drags it against my pussy. "Selfish little slut. This doesn't belong to you."

I say nothing, hating how my mind immediately gets carried away with thoughts of Whit doing this to someone else. Claiming someone else. Fucking her. Making her his.

I'm a fool. An idiot.

Reaching out, I try to hit him, but he grabs hold of my wrist, stopping me. He keeps me in place, pushing his way back inside me, his thrusts rougher. I press my lips together to keep from crying out. Not from the brutality of his cock, which I crave, but because of the little rocks and bits of brick cutting into my sensitive flesh.

"You can't hurt me no matter what you do. Haven't you learned that by now?" He laughs. Then sighs. I don't know how he has so much control. I'm sure any other boy his age would be coming like a geyser by now.

Not Whit.

He's unlike any boy I've ever known.

His movements increase and he buries his face against my throat, his soft hair tickling my cheek. He fucks and fucks, ruts like an animal, his hot breath coating my skin. I squeeze my thighs around his waist, letting him take me, my orgasm rushing forward, rising higher, like the birds I scared earlier, scattering in the sky in fear. It frightens me, this feeling, but I chase after it anyway. Needing it. Wanting it. I moan with his every stroke, not holding myself back, savoring the letting go, the orgasm building, growing, overwhelming me.

It's going to be big. The biggest one I've ever had.

I'm teetering on the edge, my breath gone, my head spinning, when he pulls out of me, his fingers squeezing around the base of his cock, semen spilling out, all over my stomach, my pubic hair. He makes a mess of me, groaning, pleasure written all over his beautiful face and I stare, transfixed.

Aching. Empty.

He finishes with one last shudder, his eyes slowly opening to reveal the familiar, lazy gleam they get after he comes. He licks his lips while I watch him, and my fingers itch to claw over his face. Mar all that beauty.

I was so close, and he stole it from me.

"You're a mess," he says with disgust, his gaze dropping to my pussy. "You got cum all over you."

He dips his fingers in his own semen and brings them to my mouth. I lick them delicately, savoring the slightly sour taste, in agony that I didn't find my release. This is the first time he hasn't let me come, and I'm sure he's reveling in his newfound power.

"You need to learn your place." He sounds bored. Looks like he could practically fall asleep as he watches me suck the cum off of his long, elegant fingers. "You hate me. You hate what I do to you. And while you belong to me, I definitely don't belong to you."

I don't acknowledge what he says and he reaches for me, his wet fingers curling around my chin so tightly, I almost cry out. "Say it," he whispers. "You belong to me."

There's no hesitation. "I belong to you."

"If I catch you talking to Chad again, I'll make you watch while I fuck his little sister." He gives my face a shake. "Do you understand?"

I blink at him, confused by his mention of Chad. I didn't even know he had a little sister on campus. What is Whit talking about?

He sees the confusion and it somehow infuriates him even more. "Tell me you understand!"

"I u-understand." The stutter is a weakness, and I close my eyes in shame.

"He touched you," Whit says, his voice low. Broken. His fingers loosen their hold and he strokes me. Touches the corner of my lip, whisper soft. "I saw it. He touched you and no one touches what's mine."

It all rushes back to me. The moment in the dining hall earlier. When I almost dropped my lunch. It meant nothing. I'm not interested in Chad. Whit knows this.

But then I also remember how he watched us in the dining hall, anger shining in his eyes the entire time. I didn't recognize it in that moment.

He didn't like seeing Chad touch me, because he believes I belong only to him.

"It was nothing," I whisper, noting the pleased gleam that fills his gaze. "I belong to you. Only you can touch me."

"Don't ever forget it." He kisses me, meaning it as a punishment, but I drink from his lips, taste his tongue, grateful for it.

The kiss, his possessive words, are like a balm. They piece me together when all he's trying to do is tear me apart.

I watch as he puts himself back in order, my core still throbbing, in desperate need of release. That first little orgasm was nothing. Now my entire body hurts from the anticipation—and of my release being ripped away. All while he's completely collected, as if nothing fazes him. Not me. Not anything.

The truth is there though, in his words. Chad touched me. And while it meant nothing, that innocent touch infuriated Whit.

He's jealous.

A smile curls my lips and I avert my head, exhaling when he yanks the tie from my neck and winds it around his own.

His jealousy is my power too, I think as I hop off the window's edge, reaching beneath my skirt to rub my sore and scratched butt. I won't forget this moment.

Ever.

TWENTY-ONE

WHIT

WE WALK BACK to campus in silence, me fuming the entire way, Summer seemingly unaffected. I was mean to her just now. Cruel. Crueler than I've ever been, and she took everything I gave her. She seemed to enjoy it.

I definitely enjoyed it. Every twisted word and brutal touch. How I slammed into her without finesse, no foreplay, no nothing. My cock enveloped in all that tight, wet heat. She'd been ready for it. She wanted it.

So fucking bad. Just as bad as me.

All because I was jealous. No. It was more than that. The territorial feeling that rose inside of me at seeing Chad touch her had made me want to tear him apart. And what happened between them was nothing. His fingers on her fucking elbow didn't mean shit.

Yet witnessing him put his hands on her made me see red. Like a bull, I wanted to charge. Run up on him and slug him right in his smug face. Chad can have whoever he wants, and he has no business even looking at her.

I told him as much once I calmed down, when we were outside. He laughed at me, the motherfucker, and said he didn't give two shits about Savage. That infuriated me too.

My feelings for her confuse the shit out of me.

We come upon the library and Summer veers right, about to head for her dorm hall, when I grab her around the elbow, stopping her.

"You okay?" I ask, my voice low.

Jesus, why am I asking her that? Why do I fucking care?

I don't.

Her smile is faint. "I'm fine."

I pull her in closer, unable to resist. "Don't tell anyone I took you out there."

She frowns. "Who would I tell?"

"Sylvie." It still bothers me that she's friends with my sister. What is she doing? Trying to get closer to her, in order to get closer to me? It won't work. And she better not be using Sylvie either. My sister is fragile. Sick. I don't know what the fuck is wrong with her, but our mom has been taking her to an endless list of specialists over the last few years, trying to figure it out. Sylvie treats it like one big joke, like she's going to drop dead at any minute and she's perfectly fine with it. But I know the truth.

She's terrified.

"I don't tell Sylvie anything about us," Summer says. "She makes her own assumptions."

"What the hell does that mean?"

"Your sister isn't blind," Summer hisses, stepping even closer to me. So close, I can smell her. Her own light fragrance mixed with the scent of her cunt. I breathe deep, savoring it, my dick hardening.

Jesus. My need for her is overwhelming, and I fucking hate it.

"Blind to us?"

"At the restaurant, it was fairly obvious, with your fuck-me stare aimed right at me," Summer says, her voice hostile.

I can't help but chuckle. "Fuck-me stare? Really."

"It's true. You eye fuck me every chance you get." We remain silent for a moment, watching each other. "Like now."

Narrowing my eyes, I release my hold on her, pushing her away. She nearly stumbles, righting herself at the last second, a demonic glare in her eyes. I want her to hate me. She should tell me to fuck off and leave her alone.

But that'll only make me push her more. It's a game we play.

A game we're both destined to lose.

"Don't talk to Sylvie about us," I demand. "Don't even mention my name to her."

"She's the one who always brings you up first," Summer starts, but I shake my head once, silencing her with a look.

"Change the subject. I'm fucking serious, Savage. What happens between us, stays between us. Don't involve anyone else."

I don't bother waiting for her reply. I turn and walk away, my steps hurried, as if I'm desperate to get away from her. I feel that way. Having her close is what it must feel like for an addict trying to kick the habit, yet a fresh pile of coke always appears before him. I want to inhale every bit of her every goddamn time I'm next to her.

It's exhausting.

I make my way back to my suite, barging through the door and slamming it so hard I swear to fucking God the entire building rattles. I go to my desk and grab the journal, flipping it open to a random spot, near the back. I'm sick and tired of reading about her experiences with Daniel. Or the step-brother. How mad her mom makes her. How no one under-stands. It's teenage drivel at its finest, and I'm bored to fucking tears.

I want the meat of the story. All of her secrets. The darkest ones she has.

There's a bunch of pages folded in the back, tucked within the pages. Big bold words are scrawled across the folded outward page.

DO NOT READ!!!!

Frowning, I stare at the words. How did I not notice this before? She's so obvious. Almost as if she wants someone to find her secrets.

I flip the pages out to find them covered in her girlish writing, mostly in pink pen. It's light, hard to decipher and I squint, flopping down in my chair and turning on the lamp so I can see better.

Yates came to my room last night. He snuck in after Mommy and Jonas went to bed. I locked the door to keep him out, but he got in anyway. I wasn't asleep. Just pretending. I could feel him standing over my bed, hear his heavy breathing as he watched me. He did nothing at first, and it was so hard to stay still. I couldn't breathe. I could tell he was touching himself, which is so gross. He was jacking off while he stood over me, and I had to lay there and listen to him the entire time. It was awful, but over in minutes. He came into his hand, and then he wiped his fingers on the edge of my comforter.

The moment he left my room, I flung the comforter off onto the floor, kicking at it with my feet. I lay there, humiliated, the scent of his cum filling the room, and...it kind of turned me on, which is so fucking gross.

I'm sick. Seriously. But it makes me feel powerful, knowing Yates wants me so bad he'll sneak into my room and jerk off while he stares at me. He must think I'm beautiful. Special. Daniel said I was, but now he's gone, and I think he said that just to get in my pants, though we never had actual sex. We messed around. He told me I was beautiful. Special.

I have no one now. Mother says I need to work on everything. My grades, my manners, my clothes, my makeup, my hair. All of it. I'm not good enough. Jonas is too busy working, or paying attention to my demanding mother.

And then there's Yates. Poor, lost, weird Yates.

He wants me.

And I might let him have me.

. . .

I SNAP the journal shut and lift my head, breathing deep, vaguely disturbed. And nothing disturbs me. But knowing Yates was in such hot pursuit of Summer fills me with disgust.

With myself.

I treat her terribly.

Sounds like everyone else does too.

TWENTY-TWO

SUMMER

HE SUMMONS me later that evening, like a king calling his court. The moment I opened my room door after returning from the dining hall, a note fluttered to the ground, thin and sharply folded. I open it with shaky fingers, knowing exactly who it's from.

Come to my room.

No please. No thank you. No signature. His handwriting is distinct, so I know it's from him. That he dares come into the dorm hall and slips a note into my door is bold. No one knows about us. We try to keep ourselves discreet, but it's getting more and more difficult to keep up the pretense.

I wait until lights out before I sneak from my room and leave the building. The air is chilly, the tang of salt from the sea in the air and I breathe deeply as I make my way to his private suite.

Pausing in front of his door, I raise my arm, my fingers curled into a fist to knock, but the door swings open before I can, Whit grabbing hold of my arm and pulling me into the room. I stumble inside, practically falling into him and he pulls me close, holding me to him as he shuts and locks the door.

"You're late." He sounds irritated as he lets me go, practically pushing me away from him.

"I had to wait until lights out," I remind him, rubbing my arm from where he touched me. "I'm not as privileged as you. I can't walk around campus as if I own the place."

He smirks, and my heart stutters to a stop before it slowly starts back up again. He looks young right now. Almost carefree. I don't know why the change, but I swear he appears as if he could break out into a smile at any moment. Much like how he laughed earlier when we were together.

What in the world is wrong with him?

"You sound downright jealous, Savage," he taunts.

"And you sound like an asshole, Lancaster," I toss back at him.

His gaze dims. "You have a smart mouth."

"So do you." My voice is cool and I fold my arms so he won't see my shaking hands.

A sigh escapes him and he paces around the room. I think of our first night together. How it was a realization.

We were alike. In the scariest way possible.

When he still hasn't said anything, I speak up.

"Why did you summon me?"

He stops his pacing, turning to look at me. "*Summon* you? Is that what you call it?"

"You gave me no choice."

"You always have a choice." He approaches me slowly, stopping directly in front of me. He's wearing black sweatpants and a white T-shirt. His hair is still damp, and he smells fresh and clean, as if he just came out of the shower. I want to shove my face into his neck and inhale him, but I restrain myself. "You don't have to come here."

I lift my chin, my gaze meeting his. "That's not true."

"It is. Like I said, you always have a choice. But you want to be here. With me."

I don't say a word.

"I fucked you earlier. Was that not enough?" He raises a brow.

"You're the one who demanded I come to you," I remind him. "So maybe you should answer that question yourself."

His chest rises and falls, his breathing shallow. His frustration is a living, breathing thing, swirling around us, and I wonder what's bothering him.

What did I do to him? What happened earlier at the crumbling building was no different from any of our other experiences together. I don't know how many more times I have to do this for him until he'll return my journal to me.

Maybe it's not even about the journal anymore. Maybe it's about something else.

Something more.

"Drop your pants and bend over the chair," he demands and I startle, shocked by his request.

"Why?" I ask quietly, not able to contain the tremble in my voice. My ass is killing me. I picked out tiny bits of rocks that were embedded in my skin in the shower earlier, and I have a bruise on my right butt cheek that's going to make sitting on those hard desk chairs in class extra difficult for the next few days.

All thanks to the way he brutally fucked me against that ledge. And while I could accuse him of hurting me and taking me against my will, we both know none of that is true. I wanted it.

I wanted him.

"Just do it," he says.

"Why?" I ask again. If he threatens to spank me or whatever other deviant thing he has in mind, I'm going to have to refuse him.

I won't be able to take it, no matter how much I want to.

"I want to see..." His voice drifts and he throws his head back, staring at the ceiling. "I want to see what I did to you earlier."

"Oh." My heart squeezes. I'm confused, but I go along with what he asks, going to the chair that's pushed in close to his desk. I shove my leggings and thong down all in one push, so they puddle around my feet and I slowly bend over, showing him the damage.

He sucks in a breath, and I feel his hand come close. I wince, bracing myself, but his touch is surprisingly gentle. He traces a scratch. Another one. He touches a particularly deep one and I hiss. He draws the perimeter of my bruise. He exerts no pressure, his fingers a soft caress upon my skin and I close my eyes, savoring it.

This means nothing, I tell myself. He just wants to see his destruction. Revel in it. And that's okay. He doesn't feel bad for what he did to me, and I guess he shouldn't. I agreed. He just wants to look at it. Maybe he even wants to take a photo of my scraped and bruised flesh as a keepsake.

"I hurt you," he says, his voice raw.

"You've hurt me before," I remind him, ducking my head when his fingers come closer to the spot between my legs.

"I've never marked you like this." He smooths his hand over my butt, the touch somehow more intimate than usual. "Are you okay?"

I remind my riotous thoughts to calm down. He doesn't care.

He doesn't. Care.

"I'm fine." I open my eyes and stare at his desk. There's a stack of papers sitting on top of it. A haphazard pile of textbooks. A familiar, battered black journal tucked at the bottom of the stack.

My journal.

I stand up straight and turn on him, not caring that I'm basically half-naked. "I want my journal."

He blinks, and it's as if his face transforms into an impenetrable mask. "No."

"Give it back to me." Anger rises and my voice is fierce. "Haven't I done enough?"

"No," he says, stepping closer. "You haven't. You always seem to forget your place when it comes to me."

"Trust me, I haven't forgotten," I spit at him, hating the disdain that drips in his words. "We've been doing this—whatever it is for a while now. I think I've paid back my debt."

I don't even know why I owe him anymore. What we do is like a game. I'm just a toy he enjoys playing with before he sets me back on the shelf and forgets all about me.

"You haven't even come close to repaying what you owe me." He cups my chin, reminding me of how he touched me earlier. Everything within me comes alive at first contact and I'm trembling. My nipples harden beneath my T-shirt. I didn't wear a bra.

I'd hoped for something to happen between us. I'm that sick.

That needy.

He tilts my head back, his examining gaze trailing over my face. "I did some online searching earlier. Regarding your mother."

I press my lips together so I don't say anything.

"You look so much like her, it's eerie. I see why my father fucked her for so long." He leans in to breathe the next words across my mouth. "And why I fuck you."

I blink at him. Where is this coming from? We haven't talked about our parents in a while. In Whit's eyes, I'm still the whore daughter of the whore mother who destroyed his family.

"You only do this with me to get back at your *father?*"

I don't believe him.

"Your mother ruined my parents' marriage," he reminds me.

"I think that marriage was ruined long before my mother came along," I retort.

His face hardens. "You don't know what you're talking about."

"Neither do you." I pause. "I want my journal back."

"No."

"I've done enough with you."

"You've barely scratched the surface."

"Fine." I yank my face out of his grip and take off my T-shirt. Kick my leggings and thong away from my ankles. Until I'm standing before him completely naked. "Is this what you want?"

He says nothing, but I see the hunger simmer in his gaze. Mine drops to the front of his joggers. I can see the outline of his cock. He wants me.

Nothing new there.

Lifting my chin, I march over to his bed and sprawl across it. My legs spread wide so he can see all of me. I'm wet, but I don't care. We're beyond humiliation now. I lie there, spread-eagled and vulnerable just for him. My ass smarts, but I ignore it. I want him to fuck me.

Fuck me for one last time and be done with this.

Lies. You don't want to be done with this. You want it to go on and on and on...

"What the hell are you doing?" he snaps.

"Fuck me," I tell him. "You know you want to."

He approaches the bed, his expression impassive, his hands in the pockets of his joggers like he doesn't have a care in the world.

I want to sock him in the face.

"Nice," he drawls, his gaze zeroed in on my pussy. "You think this is what it'll take for me to give the journal back?"

"I don't know," I practically wail and I snap my lips shut, irritated with myself. I can't show weakness, yet here I am, crying to him. Sacrificing myself to him. "Just get it over with."

"What? Now you're nothing but a fucking martyr," he says, his voice hard. "You just want to lie there and take it? That's not like you."

"Isn't that what you want?" I taunt.

"No," he says firmly. "When have I ever told you that?"

I think of our other interactions. Most of the time we end up together because of something I say or do. What's so different about tonight?

"You want me." I sit up and reach for him, cupping his erection. His cock jerks beneath my touch. "I can feel it."

"Not like this. Not like a sacrifice."

"You don't want me willing? God, you're such a sick fu—"

He grabs hold of me, so roughly I shriek. His hands grip my arms and his face is in mine. "Don't you dare call me sick when you're just as fucked up as I am. We're both like this. You love it when I tell you what to do. And I like it when you fight against me."

"I didn't fight earlier," I whisper. "When you told me to say I hate you."

"You should hate me," he says, his voice harsh. "All I can think about is how much I want you to resist."

I struggle against his hold and squeeze his cock at the same time. "Like this?"

"Let go of my dick," he whispers.

"No." I smile. Slip my hand beneath his sweats and encounter nothing but bare flesh. I stroke him, loving the way his eyelids flutter. I smooth my finger over the head, smearing sticky pre-cum everywhere and I want to suck him into my mouth.

He's right. I'm as sick, as fucked up as he is. I could accuse him of making me this way, but that would be a lie.

I was already like this. I just didn't understand how. Or why.

"Summer." His voice is a warning.

"Whit." My voice is a tease.

He lets go of my arm and grips the back of my head, pushing me forward. "You want it? Suck it, then."

I do as he asks, rearranging myself so I sit on the edge of the bed. He stands in front of me, his expression like stone. Like the beautiful angel statues in the campus gardens.

I shove his joggers down, exposing him completely, and I reach out to touch his erection. Warm, hard skin. Velvety soft.

He's human, I remind myself. No matter how much he tries to convince me that he's not.

Dipping my head, I let my hair fall forward as I wrap my lips around the head of his cock. He drips onto my tongue, and a surge of triumph runs through me. He wants this.

I lick him. Grip him tightly. Suck him. Glancing up, his cock filling my mouth, I find he's watching me, his expression still blank, though I see something flicker in his eyes. Heat.

Want.

He wants *me*.

I take a deep breath and suck him even deeper into my mouth, until the head bumps the back of my throat. What's funny is I'd only given exactly two blow jobs before I met Whit. Now I feel like an expert.

"Fuck." His favorite word falls from his lips and I gag on his cock when he thrusts his hips forward. "Jesus."

He pumps in and out of my mouth, again and again, until I pull away, a shuddering breath leaving me. "Stop."

He stands there, his dick glistening from my mouth, his face one of pure shock. I've never refused him. I've never told him stop. Ever. He probably thinks something's wrong with me. "What the fuck, Summer?"

I lie back on the bed, my hand going to my pussy, testing it. I'm so wet. My clit is throbbing. Closing my eyes, I begin to stroke myself, my thoughts filled with images of Whit. Earlier today, how much I enjoyed what he did to me. I always enjoy what he does to me. Too much. He sees my darkness, and he matches it. Exceeds it.

"What the fuck are you doing?" he asks angrily.

His words fuel me and I stroke myself harder, pinching my swollen clit between my fingers. "I need to come," I tell him and he laughs.

"You are unbelievable," he utters.

There's rustling, and then he's right there, in front of my pussy, his hot breath wafting across my sensitive skin. He shoves my hand away and attacks me with his mouth, devouring me, licking me everywhere. I squeal in delight. In pain. In pleasure. It feels so good, his lips, his tongue. He thrusts a finger into my pussy and strokes. Tickles the skin between my pussy and my asshole, making me jump.

Making me lean into his touch.

"I want to fuck you here," he says, his finger drawing closer and closer to my ass. "Taste you here."

"Do it," I tell him, closing my eyes in shame when he pushes me backward, my legs over my head, my ass completely exposed to his gaze.

His mouth.

He contemplates me, deathly quiet, and I want to squirm. He loves nothing more than to humiliate me, and he's doing that right now, as he studies my body, not saying a word. I wait in anticipation, my heart thumping wildly, my throat dry as I try to swallow. Until finally, *finally* I feel his mouth there. His breath. His tongue.

He licks. A delicate flick that makes me jump. He licks again, bolder this time, exploring, his tongue teasing the ridged skin and a moan escapes me. Oh God, it feels so wrong. So fucking wrong.

So right.

He continues his gentle assault on my untouched flesh, working me into a panting, squirming mess, until suddenly his mouth is gone, and he's pulling me into position so my back is pressed against the mattress, my legs sprawled.

I could've come if he kept that up. I'm desperate to.

"Does your ass hurt?" he asks, his fingers briefly skimming over my scrapes and bruises.

I forgot all about my wounds. "No."

He rubs his mouth with the back of his hand, his chest heaving, his dick standing straight out. Licking my ass must've made him impossibly hard. "I fucked you roughly earlier. You want it again?"

I nod, overcome. Unable to speak. I want it so badly.

He slides inside my body, no condom yet again, the asshole. Not that we've ever used them. He fucks me steadily, his gaze never straying from mine, his hair hanging around his beautiful face. I arch up into him, my hips meeting his, my entire body tingling, anticipating the orgasm he's about to give me. I don't think it'll be as good as the one promised this afternoon. There was something so primal about doing it outside, among the ruins. Exposed and open to nature, the breeze bathing my skin, making me feel so alive. I want to do it again there someday.

Maybe tomorrow, if I'm lucky.

"Fuck," he whispers, his gaze racing over me, as if he doesn't know where to look first. "I hate you so goddamn much, Summer."

I pretend he tells me he loves me instead. He loves me so goddamn much. It's what sends me over the edge. My entire body goes still, the orgasm sweeping over me without warning and I'm trembling, crying out with my pleasure. He keeps up the pace, still watching me, his fingers going to my hair, tightening. Pulling. Hard. Making it painful.

Making my orgasm go on a little longer.

"You like it when it hurts," he whispers as he still fucks me.

"I love it."

"You liked it when I licked your asshole?"

I nod. "I want to lick yours."

He grins. Actually grins. "Dirty fucking girl. Seriously?"

"I want to do everything with you," I admit softly.

Whit lifts his upper body away from mine, gripping my hips as he pounds inside of me. I cup my breasts. Press them together. Pinch my nipples. He watches, fascinated, and I smile. That's all I do. Just smile.

He comes. Falls over me in a heap, his big body shuddering over mine as he spills and spills. Endless amounts of cum shoot inside me and I hold him close. Stroke his back. Murmur dirty words close to his ear.

How much I love his cock. How good he feels inside of me. How I want to tongue his asshole and jerk him off at the same time. Is that even possible? I'm sure I could make it work, and he likes it because his body jerks forward, a little "ahh" falling from his lips with that one final, weak thrust.

I made him come like that. Me. Watching me. Being inside of me.

And he best never forget it.

TWENTY-THREE

SUMMER

IT'S ALMOST HALLOWEEN. My favorite time of year. The school doesn't recognize the actual holiday with garish decorations of ghosts and black cats and jack o' lanterns, but it does decorate the campus with giant pots of colorful mums and bales of hay stacked on either side of the doorways, a variety of pumpkins scattered about. There are scarecrows that one of the dining hall ladies makes every year according to Sylvie, and they're cute, with friendly faces and straw hair, plucky little hats sitting on their heads. Some of the teachers burn fall scented candles in their classrooms, making me nostalgic every time I smell one.

My mother used to do that when I was younger. Burn all of her fall candles throughout the season, before she switched to Christmas scents. She'd decorate the house with cute Halloween-themed items she picked up over the years, and I'd get excited every October when she pulled the orange and black storage boxes out. I loved dressing up for the holiday the most, becoming someone different every Halloween, even if it was just for one night. I still yearn to dress up. To pretend to be someone I'm not.

I think I'm having an identity crisis at the ripe age of seventeen and three quarters.

Whispers start among the students on campus as the days draw closer and closer to the thirty-first. Of a party planned, out among the ruins Whit took me to, which makes me assume he's the one who organized the party in the first place. Not that he's ever mentioned the party to me.

We meet at night, once, twice, sometimes three times a week. We mess around. We fuck. We don't really speak to each other. He's keeping his distance from me on purpose, as if he showed me too much vulnerability that one night. When he was visibly upset that he hurt me, marked me, despite his earlier threats that he craved to do exactly that.

We don't really communicate in class either. We're wooden. Acknowledging each other in the barest of ways, his eyes flat, his expression impassive. It feels like I'm losing him, and I don't know why. I don't even know why it matters. I should be glad. But he still hasn't returned my journal to me. We don't mention it.

It's not even about the journal anymore. I don't care. He can read every last word of it, and it wouldn't matter. Not any longer. I wish he'd talk to me. Act like he cared, like he did before. I don't want him to forget me.

But I think he already has. I've become a rote habit for him and nothing more. A girl to fuck. He doesn't even threaten me anymore.

I'd rather have him be mean toward me than act like I don't matter to him at all. Ambivalence is the worst feeling you could ever have for someone, and I think that's what Whit has for me.

It's awful.

The weekend before Halloween, Sylvie comes to me in the library Friday afternoon, her eyes bright, her face pink with vitality. Life. She's in high spirits, and I don't think I've ever seen her look so pretty. So alive. "You're coming shopping with me."

"Where?" I ask, hating how apprehensive I feel. What does she want from me? Why do I think everyone's out to get me?

"Thrift shops. One of those temp Halloween costume stores they always have in town." She bounces up and down, looking terribly pleased with herself. "We need costumes for Halloween night."

"And what exactly is happening that night?" I need confirmation of this party once and for all. Whit certainly isn't going to tell me about it.

"Haven't you heard all the rumors? Whit came up with the *best* idea, and I've been helping him. We're having a party on campus, among the ruins from the fire that happened a long time ago." She tilts her head, contemplating me. "Have you ever been out there?"

"No," I say solemnly, desperate not to give myself away.

"Oh. Wait until you see it. It's beautiful. Creepy. Perfect Halloween scenario. Whit already asked Father, who gave his approval. It's going to be so much fun," Sylvie practically squeals.

I smile, but it's weak. Being out there will just remind me of what happened between us last time, and it'll make me sad. It'll make me miss him, which is so incredibly stupid. Why do I miss a boy who clearly doesn't give a shit about me?

Maybe Whit was right. My self-esteem is for shit. If I don't care about myself, then no wonder no one cares about me either. My father. My mother. Daniel, my first supposed love. Yates—ugh. I don't even feel bad that he's dead.

He was a terrible person. Awful. Selfish. Demanding. Strange.

The only person I truly miss is Jonas. He cared. He had faith in me when it felt like no one else ever did. And now he's gone.

It's my fault too.

I sniff loudly, on the verge of tears when I feel Sylvie's hand settle lightly on my arm.

"Are you okay?" she murmurs.

I lift my head, shaking my hair back, unable to hide the tears shining in my eyes. "I'm fine." I swipe at the corners of my eyes, catching the tears that don't fall. I can't remember the last time I actually cried. "Homesick, I guess."

What a bunch of shit, but I need an excuse.

"Aw." Sylvie squeezes my arm, her touch gentle. "It's okay. We all feel that way sometimes out here. Well, not me since I go home all the time thanks to my mother, but you know what I mean."

"Right." I nod, sniffing again. "Sure."

Sylvie changes the subject and starts rattling on about Halloween costumes, but I'm not really listening. Though I should. Getting caught up in her excitement would be the perfect distraction I need. I swallow hard and turn to look at her, forcing myself to listen.

"...and so I was thinking I could be a sexy angel? But like, a devil's angel, because when I die, I doubt I'm going to heaven," she says with a laugh.

"Why would you say that?" I know for a fucking fact I'm not going to heaven, but I have my reasons. None of them I'd share with her.

She leans in close, pressing her forehead to mine. "I'm not a nice person, Summer. Haven't you realized that by now? I'm spoiled and mean. Over-indulged and dumb. I'm not going to amount to anything in this world, but the bar is set pretty low, so what would anyone expect?"

I blink at her, taking in her words. They don't feel like anything she'd think about herself. "Who told you that?" I whisper.

Sylvie pulls away from me, her eyes gleaming with approval, like she wanted to shock me. "The woman who birthed me, of course. She hates me. I have serious middle child syndrome, haven't you noticed?"

"If she hates you so much, why does she take you to the doctor all the time, looking for the cure to your mystery ailments?" I ask, genuinely wanting to know.

"She's not looking for the *cure*, Summer," Sylvie practically drawls, glancing toward the window. "She's trying to kill me so she doesn't have to deal with me any longer."

A gasp leaves me and she turns her head, her eyes narrowed into slits. "Don't act all surprised. Isn't it obvious? Whit is the golden child. The only boy. The heir apparent to the massive

Lancaster fortune. And then there's Carolina. The tiny dancer. She'll become world renowned, queen of the ballet. She's already on her way. Everyone adores her."

"Sylvie." My voice is a harsh whisper and I scoot closer to her, not wanting anyone to overhear us. "You don't believe your mother is really—"

"You're right, I don't," she interrupts, laughing so loud, she sends Miss Taylor into shushing fits. "I just wanted to see your reaction when I said it. Though I really do suffer from middle child syndrome. No one gives a shit about me. They never really have."

I blink at her, trying to process what she said, what it all means. If she's being serious or not. "Your brother cares about you."

"Because he has to," she retorts, watching me carefully. "You've accomplished something major, you know that right?"

I rear back from her, frowning. "What do you mean?"

"You've earned the approval from not just one, but two Lancasters." When my frown deepens, she continues, "Me and Whit."

"Whit doesn't approve of me," I say quickly.

"He approves enough to sneak you into his room." Her smile is knowing. I'm sure she's seen me.

"It's nothing," I tell her. "Meaningless."

"He's just using you?" she asks, raising her brows.

"We're using each other," I correct.

"Whit doesn't attach himself to the same girl more than once. Twice, and usually that's by mistake. He's very much a one and done kind of guy," Sylvie says. "Not that I pay too much attention to my brother's sex life, because ew. But I do know what's going on, because I can't help but see it. And what's going on between you and my brother? Is not the norm for him."

"He treats me like garbage most of the time when we're together," I mumble, feeling stupid for even admitting it.

Whit won't be happy that I'm talking about him to his sister either.

"He treats everyone like garbage. Including me," Sylvie says. "Don't take it too personally."

Easy for her to say. I take everything Whit says and does personally, especially lately.

"I'm just a habit. I scratch his itch, so to speak." My cheeks grow warm and I clamp my lips shut. I should quit while I'm ahead.

Sylvie giggles. "He must have a freaking rash then, because you're scratching his itch on a regular basis."

I wad up a piece of paper and toss it at her. Laughing, she bats it away. Miss Taylor shushes us, even says Sylvie's name, but we ignore her.

When you're with a Lancaster, you can ignore everyone.

FRIDAY NIGHT and everyone's at the football field—our last home game of the season. I don't go, because there's still no one for me to sit with. I haven't made any friends beyond Sylvie, and I'm okay with that. Sylvie hates football, so she doesn't go to the games. I think she does it on purpose.

Spencer plays football so she stays away and it drives him crazy.

Their interactions make no sense to me, but I have zero room to talk, considering the fucked-up supposed relationship I have with Whit. So I say nothing.

It's none of my business anyway.

There's a soft knock on my door around eight-thirty and I climb off my bed, ready to answer it when the door swings open.

Whit stands in the doorway, watching me. He braces his hands on the doorframe, leaning away from the door and remaining in the hall. For anyone to see.

"Get in here," I whisper-hiss.

"You gave me permission," he says as if he needs to remind me, his tone nonchalant as he strolls into my room, slamming the door behind him.

I stay rooted in place, not moving when he walks right up to me, so close, his shoes brush against my toes. "Why are you here?"

"Why am I always here?" He reaches for me, his arm going around my waist, his hand sliding to my butt and pulling me into him, but I resist, desperate to keep space between our bodies. "What the fuck, Savage?"

"I'm not in the mood." I rip myself out of his grip and return to my bed, tugging the covers over most of my body.

"You're not in the mood?" He actually scoffs. "Please. Don't pout. It's not a good look for you."

"I'm on my period," I tell him, which is a lie. I had it last week. And the one night we were together when it was at its heaviest,

I gave him a blow job and that was it. Not like he protested. He loves nothing more than having my lips wrapped around his dick.

He studies me, his expression fierce as he slowly approaches my bed. "So if I slipped my hand in your panties, I'd encounter blood?"

I roll my eyes. "I use a tampon, asshole."

"Right, so I'd find that little string then?" He lifts a brow.

He has way too much knowledge of the female body. This should bother me. But I can't judge him for his past sexual conquests, just like he can't judge me for what I've done.

"It's my first day," I tell him, wanting to gross him out. "Heavy flow and all. You don't want to risk it."

"Risk what?" He sounds genuinely interested.

I make a face. "It's *really* heavy."

If he tries to dive beneath my panties, he's going to find nothing. And he might be pissed that I'm lying.

"I'm curious though," he says.

"You're also gross."

"It's a natural bodily function." He shrugs. "Are you freaked out by the sight of blood?"

"Of course not. I bleed out of my vagina on a monthly basis," I retort.

"I'm not scared."

"You're a perv," I spit out.

"So are you." His voice is annoyingly calm.

I glare. He watches me with that ever present impassive expression on his face. "Come on, Savage. Let me see."

"Absolutely not."

"Right. Because you're lying." He literally pounces on top of me on the bed, a yelp escaping my lips. He settles his big hand over my mouth to keep me quiet, thrusting his face in mine. "You were on your period last week. That's why you gave me the BJ and wouldn't let me touch you."

I narrow my eyes, hating how observant he is. How he remembers every little thing.

"And you were a grumpy little shit. PMS is real and you suffer from it mightily," he continues.

I try to buck him off my body and he laughs, the asshole. Doesn't remove his hand from my mouth either.

"You're grumpy tonight too. What the hell is your problem?" He drops his hand from my face.

"I don't want to do this anymore," I tell him, my voice weak. It's hard, denying yourself something that you actually enjoy. Yes, for some weird reason, I enjoy Whit's cruelty. His mind games. His terrible words and soft touch.

But what we're doing is fucked up. I'm tired of feeling like a mess all the time. I just want to be normal.

"Really." His tone tells me he doesn't believe me.

"Yes, really," I retort. "And I want my journal back."

His gaze narrows. "I haven't finished reading it yet."

"Just—what's the point anymore? Give it back. You've found out all my secrets already. What more is there for us to do? Haven't you blackmailed me enough?" I ask, my gaze flickering away from his, my stomach knotting with nerves. I hate the idea of him finding out what I did to Jonas and Yates, but it's bound to happen. He's had my journal for almost two months. I almost don't believe him when he says he hasn't finished it yet.

He's probably ready to reveal he knows my biggest secret right now. He'll drop the bomb, it'll detonate, and none of this will ever be over.

Whit slides off my body and off the bed. He's on his feet, staring down at me, his gaze contemplative as he rests his hands on his hips. "You want this to be over."

I nod, pulling the covers up higher, until they're at my chin. "Yes. I do."

"My father said I should stop fucking you."

I drop the covers and sit up straight, shock coursing through my veins, chilling my blood. "What the hell, Whit? You told *your father* we're together?"

"I told my father I was fucking someone, not that I'm with someone. Big difference," he corrects, his words a weapon. Reminding me of my place. "And I never mentioned your name."

"Thank God," I breathe out, trying to ignore the pain his words made me feel.

He doesn't care about me. We're just fucking. I know this.

Yet it still hurts.

"I'm marrying someone," he announces, and my jaw drops. "Not right now, but it's already been arranged."

"You're not even eighteen," I point out.

"I will be soon."

"And what, you'll get married then?" I ask incredulously.

He grimaces. "Of course not. We're too young for that. But we're expected to be together. Me and my future bride. We need to start making a show of it—of our relationship. We'll go to college. We'll be a couple the entire time. I'll ask her to marry me. We'll have a big wedding at the Newport house. It'll be everything my mother could ever want."

He describes it in such a monotone voice, I know he doesn't believe a word he's saying. He doesn't want this.

So why is he doing it?

"Is that what you want?" I ask him.

He shoves his hands in his jeans' pockets, averting his head. As if he can't face me. "I don't have any say in it."

"You're heir to one of the biggest fortunes in the world, and you don't have a say in who you marry?" I climb out of bed and start pacing, overcome with what he's telling me. "That's fucking ridiculous."

"You're the one being fucking ridiculous right now," he says, his voice dark, his eyes cold as he watches me. "You can't judge me. My situation may sound crazy to you, but it's normal in our social circles, of which you're no part of. Matches are created, mergers are necessary. Lineages must be preserved."

I ignore the insult. When it comes to Whit, I'm definitely getting a thicker skin. "So if you were to marry a lowly girl from say...New Mexico, then it would make every Lancaster in the ground roll over in their graves?" I toss out at him. I don't know why I came up with New Mexico. I don't even know what I'm saying, but what he's telling me is straight out of a historical novel. Like British royalty stuff.

He actually chuckles, the smug bastard. "Most likely. Life isn't as simple as you think, Savage. There are expectations set upon me, right from birth, especially being the first male. The only male from my father. I have to maintain a certain image, and there are promises I must keep to my family."

"Totally understandable." I don't get it, but whatever. It's easier if I just accept it and move on from this once and for all. "You can leave now." I point at the door.

He watches me carefully as he says, "I'll give you back your journal."

"You will?" My voice is scratchy and I swallow hard against the sudden emotions rising within me. Returning the journal means he really won't see me anymore. I'm the one who made that demand in the first place, but God help me...

I'll miss him.

"Give me till Halloween." I start to complain, but he lifts his hand, silencing me. "We're putting together the party right now, and I have a lot going on. I can return it to you after that. It's only a few days, Savage. You can wait."

"Okay," I whisper, watching as he makes his way to my door. He pauses there, his hand on the handle, his back to me.

"This is really it?" He says it as a question, as if he wants me to do something. Say something. Like beg him to stay.

There will be no begging on my part. I won't stoop that low. If he looks back though, I'll say no. If he says he'll miss me, I'll invite him into my bed.

But he does none of that. He remains in place, hand still on the handle, back and shoulders stiff with tension.

"Goodbye, Whit," I say firmly.

He doesn't respond. Simply opens and closes the door without a backward glance.

TWENTY-FOUR

WHIT

IT WAS the right thing to do, walking away from Summer tonight. These last couple of weeks, I was trying my damnedest to throw up walls, doing my best to avoid her. When that didn't work, I'd fuck her without feeling. Using her as if she's nothing to me. I wouldn't look her in the eyes, wouldn't say the shitty things I usually do. Those words she feeds off of.

I feed off them too. I feed off *her*. Her greedy sounds and the way she kisses me. How she gobbles up my dick, and she's always so wet for me. Every time I sink into her welcoming body I think how perfect she is. As if she were made just for me.

She's not. She doesn't really belong to me. Despite the need for little Summer Savage that pumps in my veins, settles in my dick, we can't last. She's like the worst craving. Driving me to desperation, always ready—no, fucking eager—for that next hit.

It was difficult, going to her yet keeping myself removed. Fucking her as if she didn't mean anything to me. Using her without any emotion, good or bad. She could tell something was wrong. I saw it in her eyes, in the way she'd watch me. She closed herself off too. She's good at that.

So am I. We both are.

The idea that what we had was almost over always lingered in the back of my brain, and I wasn't ready. Who's ready to give up on the best sex they've ever had? I have a connection with that girl. I can't describe it, but it's there. It's always been there, from the very beginning. When we first met at the age of fourteen.

I knew I couldn't keep fucking her. Spending time with her. I'd want her more.

More and more and more.

She's something I can't have. Yet she's the one who said she didn't want to do it anymore. I pushed her away and she knew it. My Savage is so much smarter than I give her credit for. She beat me to the fucking punch. I'm the one who got dumped in this situation.

We're over.

I return to my room and shed my clothes, climbing into bed and reaching for her journal, where I last left it on my bedside table. I haven't read it in weeks. Reading her entries keeps her in my head, and lately that was the last place I wanted her. She's burrowed deep, and I want her out.

Gone.

Yet here I sit, holding her journal, going to the secret entries near the back. I know now that Yates fucked her, and it left her an emotional mess. I don't want to read about that anymore. I don't want to know exactly what he did to her, or how much it ruined her. She's damaged goods, I know this, but fuck.

So am I.

Maybe that's why we're drawn to each other. We've seen and done so much for being so young. I'm jaded as fuck, and so is Summer. But to *really* be with her...

Would send my mother into a complete fit and my father would tell me I'm fucking crazy. Which I am.

I know this.

Why the hell am I so drawn to the one girl I shouldn't want? Why?

I toss the journal across the room. It hits the wall with a loud splat, dropping to the floor. I can't read it any longer. Reading her words leaves her haunting my thoughts. She's already in them enough.

I need to find someone else. My father said I should fuck around as much as I can before I make things serious with Leticia. Once I'm with her, once it's public and we become engaged, I have to act like the faithful fiancé. The perfect future husband. Keep up the pretense for as long as I can stand it. Once we make a couple of babies, maybe even before that, all bets are off. As long as I'm discreet, I can have as many affairs as I like. Even if Leticia finds out, she'll understand. This is how it's done. Leticia knows what she's getting herself into, just like I do.

My life is mapped out. There will be no surprises. Nothing unusual. Hell, my father recently received a report from Leticia's gynecologist, informing him that she's still a virgin, and everything appears in good shape—Father's exact words. She'll give me plenty of children, he said with a laugh.

He had her examined—like an animal. Fucking unreal.

Frustration ripples through me and I close my eyes, trying to focus on something else. Anything else but my fucked-up future. I've been consumed with arranging everything for that stupid party. The only reason I'm doing it is for Sylvie. She wanted to celebrate Halloween so badly, as if it will be her last one.

All I care about is getting fucked up, especially after tonight.

The party is happening in mere days, and while I'm disappointed I can't have the girl I want, I can find someone else Halloween night, and hopefully I'll fuck Summer Savage right out of my system.

Once and for all.

TWENTY-FIVE

SUMMER

I MEET Sylvie in her room to get ready for the party Halloween afternoon, after class. Anticipation rippled throughout campus the entire day, reaching a fevered pitch by last period, and no one could concentrate. The teachers pretend they don't know about the party, but they have to. It's all anyone can talk about. I wish I were more excited, but with Whit and me over, I don't have much to look forward to.

I pretend to be excited for Sylvie's sake instead.

We do our makeup first, sharing the bench at her vanity table, the both of us applying heavy eyeshadow and layering on red lipstick. Her excitement is palpable. It fills her entire room, giving me nervous energy, and I glance at my duffel bag sitting on the floor, almost afraid to put on the costume I know is going to cause a scandal among everyone who attends Lancaster Prep.

They might've never really noticed me before, but they're going to see me tonight.

"Tonight is ripe for a scandal," Sylvie announces once she's finished applying her lipstick. She studies me, rubbing her ruby red lips together, her eyes sparkling. "This will be a life-changing party."

"If you say so." I'm reluctant to agree, because I need no life-changing events right now. I've already had one, thanks to Whit and I agreeing we shouldn't spend time together anymore.

I'm loathe to admit this, even to myself, but I miss him. It's stupid, when I'm the one who pushed for it.

My emotions for him make me feel stupid.

"Things are going to happen tonight, Summer. I just know it," she continues. "If Spence makes a move, I'm going to let him."

"Let him what?" I ask warily.

"Let him touch me. Kiss me. Fuck me. Whatever. I'm ready. I'm tired of saving myself." She starts putting away all the cosmetics, shoving them back in the drawer with one sweep of her arm. "I've been preserving my virginity all my life, and I'm sick of it. I might not have much time left. I want to know what it feels like to come with a boy inside me."

"When it's your first time, you might not come when he's inside you," I tell her drolly.

She laughs. "Says the girl with *allll* the experience."

Ouch. That sort of hurts.

I say nothing, dropping my lipstick into my makeup bag and zipping it a little too fiercely.

"I'm sorry. I didn't mean to hurt your feelings," Sylvie says, her voice low, her expression contrite. "I was just teasing you."

"I know." I give her a grim smile. "It's okay."

She didn't mean it. I know she didn't. I'm not proud of my past fucked up experiences, but how is she to know that, when I haven't told her everything?

She puts her hands together, her smile stretching wide. I can tell she's trying to shift the mood. I'm a complete buzzkill and she's so excited for this stupid party. "Let's put on our costumes!"

I rise from the velvet bench we shared, going to grab my duffel bag before I head for the bathroom, but her voice stops me in my tracks.

"Where are you going?"

"I'm going to change in the bathroom." I wave my bag. "I want my costume to be a surprise."

"Oh, good idea." She claps her hands as she jumps to her feet. "I can't wait to see it."

"It's kind of sexy," I add, frowning. "Probably too sexy."

"Ooh, I seriously am dying to see it now," Sylvie says, wagging her eyebrows at me. "Trying to drive my brother crazy?"

"Not even," I say with a scoff, though that had been my original intent.

I ordered the costume online, before Whit and I ended things. I imagined he'd take one look at me and be unable to resist.

Now he'll probably be all over some other girl tonight, giving her his undivided attention while I'm standing there looking pitiful with too much skin exposed.

Ugh.

Sylvie offers me a knowing smile and I ignore it, slipping into the bathroom and shutting the door with a quiet click. I remove all of my clothes hurriedly, even my bra and panties. The costume doesn't allow for any undergarments. I take my time with the fishnet stockings so I don't snag them, and hurriedly put on everything else, staring at myself in the mirror when I'm finished.

So much skin is exposed. Too much, really. This costume isn't appropriate for a high school party, I'm sure. But there will be no chaperones or staff on hand to cast their disapproving looks. Whit and Sylvie are Lancasters. They can do whatever they want on campus, whenever they want to.

Taking a deep breath for courage, I walk out of her bathroom and do a little twirl. "Ta da. What do you think?"

I finish turning and face Sylvie, who's mouth is hanging open as she studies me. "Oh my God, Summer."

My stomach cramps with nerves. "Is it too much?"

She slowly shakes her head, snapping her mouth shut. "If you're trying to get someone's attention, it's going to work. That costume is a freaking guarantee. And I thought my costume was revealing."

Sylvie mutters that last bit under her breath.

I go to the giant full-length mirror propped against her wall, noting that it's one similar to what Whit has in his room, not that I mention it. I tilt my head, studying myself, knowing that yes, I am absolutely pushing my limits when it comes to this costume.

But I look damn good. I stand a little taller, wobbling on the narrow boot heels. I keep myself under wraps constantly, not wanting anyone to notice me, but Sylvie's right. I'm going to get someone's attention.

Maybe someone different. Someone new. I don't need Whit. Not anymore. He has no claim on me.

Of course, deep down I know he's the one whose attention I'm trying to get. Maybe that makes me pitiful, but I sort of don't care.

Fuck it. I want all of their attention tonight. Every single boy in the senior class. Maybe the juniors too.

"You'll get cold," Sylvie says as she stops to stand beside me, staring at her own reflection.

"So will you," I tell her. She's dressed as a dark angel, with skin tight booty shorts and a black corset that plumps up her breasts. Her skin is pale, downright translucent, as I can see the blue veins in her arms. Across the tops of her breasts. Her legs look long and thin, and she's wearing black sky-high stilettos on her feet. "I love your costume."

"You look amazing," she says, her voice almost reverent.

I'm clad in a red-sequined cropped tube top, my belly on display. I thought about wearing red booty shorts, but I upped my game, and am basically wearing red bikini bottoms. It's skimpy, I'm barely decent, really. Fishnet stockings and thigh high boots complete the look. A golden pitchfork and red sequin horns atop my head are the final touches.

"You're completely exposed." She slaps my ass, making me flinch. "Does Whit know what you're wearing tonight?"

"We're not—involved anymore," I say, unsure how to describe us. "We broke it off with each other a few days ago."

"Huh. We'll see how long that lasts. He's going to take one look at you in that outfit and lose his damn mind," she says with an evil laugh. "Did he break it off with you because of Leticia?"

I frown, deciding to play it off. "Who's Leticia?"

I turn the name over and over in my mind. Leticia. It's pretty. I'm sure she's beautiful. Poised and elegant and polished. She wears twin sets and pearls and is modest. She wouldn't be caught dead in a revealing Halloween costume that is basically begging for someone to proposition her.

"His future wife. Crazy right? They've been chosen for each other since we were all little kids. She's nice. Pretty. *Bland.*" Sylvie rolls her eyes, bumping her hip against mine. "Nothing like you."

"What do you mean?"

"She doesn't have a personality. She just agrees with all of us. My parents. Me. And of course, my brother. She stares at him with dopey eyes while he barely pays her any attention. It's pathetic. There's nothing wrong with her, she's just boring," Sylvie explains. "Oh God, I keep running my mouth and hurting your feelings. You probably had no idea Whit has someone else."

"It's okay," I say with a shrug, oddly reassured by Sylvie's description of Leticia. I'd much rather be the more exciting one. Though I guess Leticia is wife material, while I'm more like, mistress material.

Like my mother.

"I know one thing. Leticia would never wear a costume like you've got on. She's really modest," Sylvie says.

Just as I suspected.

"And I'm not?" I raise a brow, turning to the side. My butt cheeks are literally hanging out, covered in fishnet.

I sort of don't give a shit.

"You normally are. You don't play up your features at all, when every other girl at this school is trying her hardest to make herself stand out. Including me." She smirks, her gaze meeting mine in the mirror. "But you? It's like you're always trying to blend in."

"Not tonight," I say.

"Definitely not tonight," Sylvie says with a little laugh. "You ready to go? I snagged the keys from one of the staff golf carts earlier. Whit loaded the back of it with extra liquor, so we have to bring it out there. At least we won't have to walk that far in our heels." She kicks up a foot, a pointy stiletto aimed right at me.

"Great idea," I say, glancing around. "Are you ready to go?"

"As ready as I'll ever be." She rubs her hands together. "Are you bringing your phone?"

"Where would I put it?" I hold my arms out. There's absolutely nowhere on my body for me to stash a phone. "I left it in my room."

"Good idea. Oh!" She runs over to the mini fridge in her room and pops the door open, bringing out a bottle of vodka. "Let's pre-party first."

We chug from the bottle, the icy cold vodka slithering through my veins, mellowing me out. Sylvie can't stop giggling as she sips delicately from the bottle.

"Let's take a couple of photos before we go. We must document this moment," Sylvie suggests.

We pose in her room in front of the mirror. Sweet and innocent at first, with beaming smiles and wide eyes. Then we turn things raunchy and wicked. Hands on our hips, chests thrust forward with our tongues out. I help Sylvie put her wings on and take a photo of her standing with her legs braced and her arms crossed in front of her, the wings rising behind her. She looks amazing.

It's fun, spending time with Sylvie. She helps me forget all my troubles—and so does the vodka. She can't stop laughing, and I get caught up in her happiness. I've been mopey since Whit and I called it off, but tonight, I'm on top of the world. I'm going to strut into that party and he's going to swallow his tongue when he looks at me.

I just know it.

When we're finally done taking photos and she posts a few of them on social media, we go outside and climb into the golf cart. Sylvie drives it like a mad woman, constantly going off the trail and laughing uncontrollably. The day started off gloomy, with gray skies and a constant drizzle, but it stopped just after lunch. The air is chilled and the ground is still wet, but at least it's not raining.

We arrive at the ruins to find the party already in full swing. People are everywhere. Standing outside, surrounding the old building. Sitting on the steps. Almost every single one of them clutches a beer can or a red solo cup. Loud music comes from inside, and so many people are crowded in there, all I see are bodies. Moving against each other as they dance. Clustered in tight circles as they talk. Almost everyone's in costume, many of them wearing masks, and I barely recognize a soul.

"The party has arrived, bitches!" Sylvie screams when she pulls up directly in front of the steps, throwing her arms up after she locks the cart's brakes with one push of her foot.

A boy dressed all in black, including a cape, pulls away from the crowd near the steps, and I realize it's Spencer. His face is ghostly white, little strips of fake blood dripping from the corners of his lips. He smiles when he sees Sylvie, revealing his vampire teeth.

"Looking fine as hell tonight, Sylvie."

"Why thank you, prince of darkness." She hops out of the golf cart and runs up to him, patting Spencer's chest as she smiles up at him. She glances at me from over her shoulder. "Check out Summer."

His gaze shifts to me and his eyes widen as I carefully climb out of the golf cart. "Uh, holy shit."

"Is it too much?" I ask as I approach them, resting my hands on my hips and stopping to pose.

His gaze is everywhere, as if he doesn't know where to look first. "Does Whit know about this?"

Irritation simmers in my veins and I push past Spencer, shoulder checking him. "Fuck Whit Lancaster. I don't care what he thinks."

I leave Sylvie and Spencer behind, marching up the rickety steps and into the building with my head held high. People stare as I walk past, launching into furious whispers once I'm past them, and for the quickest moment, I second-guess my costume choice.

A group of girls sneer at me when I approach. One of them coughs into her hand, "Slut."

I send her a death glare but she only laughs.

A makeshift bar is set-up in the closest corner of the room and I go to it, grabbing the already poured glass and shooting it. The alcohol burns as it slides down my throat, making me wince and I grab another one, drinking it in one swallow as well.

There. More liquid courage should help. My brain is already swimming. Doesn't help that I haven't eaten anything since breakfast.

"Hey, sexy."

I jerk away from the hand that tries to settle on my hip, turning to find a boy from my English class smiling at me. I try to remember his name, racking my brain as I study him. He's wearing all black too, but that's it. As in, he's not really dressed up at all. He's watching me with dark heated eyes, his thick hair falling over his forehead. He's not a bad looking guy, but he's staring at me as if he can already imagine me naked.

He probably can, considering how skimpy my costume is.

"It's Bryan," he offers when I still haven't said his name, glancing over at the bar nearby. "How much have you had to drink?"

"I just got here," I answer with a smile.

"It's my lucky night then," he says, his gaze snagging on my chest. "Why haven't I noticed you before? You're new here, right?"

Of course, he fully expects me to know who he is, yet he doesn't know who I am. Whatever. These boys are all the same.

"Yes," I say truthfully. "Brand, spanking new."

"I like, I like." His hand goes to my hip again, and this time, I don't pull away. I like his attention. At least he's not shunning me or calling me names. "Tell me, Miss Brand Spanking New, do you have a name?"

"Summer." I reach around him and grab yet another drink, sipping from it this time. Every pour in these cups is strong, not diluted by much and the alcohol is going straight to my head. I've always been a lightweight. "Like the season."

"The season where we're half-naked most of the time because it's so hot?" His gaze rakes over my body. "I get it."

Laughter escapes me, and I smother it by taking another drink. "You know who I am. I'm sure Whit told you."

"Whit Lancaster?" He raises his brows. "I hate that fucker. Thinks he owns the world."

"Right?" I laugh, loving that he hates Whit. We could form a club. "I mean, he does own this school."

"His parents do," Bryan amends with a sly smile. "Big difference."

"He didn't try to get you to snub me?" I ask him point blank.

His expression doesn't change a bit at my words. "Right. You're that girl. Why the hell would I snub you? Look at you."

His appraising tone makes me grow warm inside.

The music changes up, a fast song that was popular a few months ago starts playing and I smile at Bryan. "Let's dance."

Without waiting for his reply, I drop the cup on the table and take his hand. He follows me into the throng of people, until we're in the dead center. I start moving, the alcohol loosening my muscles, making me feel free. He barely moves. Just stands there and watches me as I sway from side to side, raising my arms above my head as the beat consumes me.

"Fuck," I hear him breathe, which makes me laugh. All these girls at Lancaster are a bunch of stuck-up prudes. We're almost eighteen. Shouldn't we be free to do whatever we want? To dress skimpily and have fun without repercussion?

Having male approval is something I crave, I realize as I see the way Bryan stares at me. My daddy never gave it to me. Jonas' attention was fleeting. Yates was annoying and even scary, yet I still wanted it.

And then there's Whit. His disapproval was a turn-on. His approval, necessary.

God, I'm so fucked in the head. Why would anyone want to deal with me? Be with me? Be my friend?

I dance and dance, letting myself get lost in the beat of the music. Other bodies brush against mine and I smile at them. They smile at me in return if they're male, and scowl at me if they're female, their gazes full of hatred.

God, I am so over people judging me.

Bryan has barely moved from his spot and I go to him, draping my arms across his shoulders, my face in his. I tilt my head close to his ear. "You don't dance?"

"I'm too busy watching you." He settles his hands on my hips, his fingers pressing into my bare skin.

I feel nothing at his touch, but I still chase it. Chase the approval, chase the smile on his face. The way he looks at me. He wants me. He's imagining fucking me right now and I smile at him, tipping my head back as he leans forward, his mouth barely brushing mine.

"You're a fucking tease," he tells me.

"I'm a fucking sure thing," I return saucily.

His grip tightens and I pull away from his hands, turning so my back is to his front. I sing along with the chorus, rubbing my butt shamelessly against his crotch, and I can feel him beneath his black jeans. He's hard.

Good.

I keep it up, my gaze searching, looking for the one person who I want to witness this, but of course, I don't spot him anywhere. He's probably already cozied up with some idiot girl who's willing to suck his cock in front of everyone else.

Poor thing. I know what it's like, wanting him. It's painful.

Wonderful.

I shut my eyes, trying to banish him from my thoughts. I basically grind my ass on Bryan's dick and he settles those hands on my hips, his fingers sliding brazenly beneath the waistband of my bikini bottoms. I pull away some, his hands dropping and then I turn to face him once more, bending my knees and dipping low, so my face is right at dick level.

"What the fuck?" he yells with a laugh. I can tell he's enjoying this. "Were you a stripper in a former life or what?"

"You wish," I tell him as I slowly rise, my body brushing against his the entire way. "I'm the devil, don't you know?" I point at my sequined horns atop my head with an evil grin.

"You're fucking tempting, that's for sure." His grip is firm as he slams my body into his, his voice a low growl. "Come with me."

I mock pout. "I still want to dance."

"Let's get out of here for a few minutes first. I need to cool down. Then you can dance all you want, Satan." He grins.

I grin too.

Glancing toward the doorway, I spot Whit. Dressed all in black, with black devil horns on his head. Anger surges through me and I curl my hands into fists. Of course, we match.

Of course.

His gaze finds mine, narrowing when he sees me, his upper lip curling in apparent disgust. I grab Bryan from behind, resting his hands on my hips as I begin to gyrate, putting on a show for Whit. I want him to know I've moved on.

I have.

Whit glares as I continue to dance, Bryan's hands toying with the waistband of my bikini bottoms. I let him, reveling in the heat I see in Whit's eyes, wishing he was the one whose hands were on me. I part my lips and raise my arms, lifting my hair up off my neck, swaying back and forth to the song. My eyes fall closed for a moment and I lose myself, wishing for Whit's hands, not Bryan's. Wishing for Whit's mouth on my neck, not Bryan's.

When I open my eyes once the song ends, Whit is gone.

Bryan takes my hand, leading me out of the crowd. I spot Sylvie standing with Spencer and wave, but she stares at me, her eyes wide as she shouts, "Summer, what the hell are you doing?"

"I'll be back," I tell her, pointing at the back of Bryan's head, mouthing, *he's cute.* I give her two thumbs up and her expression turns horrified.

"Don't go outside with him!" she yells at me.

I ignore her warning, laughing when someone slaps my ass as I walk past. Some guy with a lecherous grin on his face. I have no idea who he is. The first one gets away with it, so another guy slaps my ass. Yet another touches my waist. They're all trying to grab at me, and I let them, not caring, too busy laughing, basking in the attention. Nothing bothers me. I totally want Bryan to touch me. I might even let him fuck me. I want to forget about Whit once and for all and let someone else give me what I need for a change.

Bryan comes to an abrupt stop at the top of the steps, causing me to run into the back of him. "Move out of my way," he demands.

"What the fuck are you doing, McAllister?"

I shrink behind Bryan, recognizing that deadly voice. It's Whit.

And he sounds furious.

"Trying to leave with my new friend. Now move." Bryan doesn't sound scared of him whatsoever, which is kind of shocking.

Everyone bows down to a Lancaster.

"You're not going anywhere with her," Whit says quietly.

Everyone outside goes silent, eager to watch, ready for drama, as always. I cower behind Bryan, not wanting Whit to see me. Not wanting to see Whit.

"Who the fuck are you to tell me who I can and cannot fuck? Just because you're a Lancaster, it doesn't mean shit to me." Bryan glances over his shoulder, snagging my hand in his and tugging. "Come on, Satan. Let's get out of here."

I follow behind him, Whit shockingly enough stepping aside to let us pass, his gaze landing on me. Burning me where I stand.

"You're really going to go with him." His words are aimed at me.

"You have no claim on me anymore," I say haughtily, pausing so I can give him the full effect of my costume.

He barely looks at me, and that hurts. Doesn't he notice? Can't he see?

Bryan tugs on my hand. "Come on," he mutters, but I don't move. I'm rooted to the spot.

A girl approaches, settling herself right beside Whit, and I squint, my vision a little blurry from the alcohol as I really take him in. Accompanying the black horns is a red pitchfork that he's currently clutching in his hand. I suppose the devil himself doesn't have to dress up, but it's so damn annoying how we match.

The girl's face is heavily made up, and she's wearing a sexy witch costume, complete with a pointy witch's hat on top of her head. I realize in an instant it's Caitlyn, and she's smirking at me, curling her arm through Whit's.

"Nice costume," she sneers at me. "You may as well have come naked."

"Gee thanks," I taunt. "Your costume is scarily...accurate when it comes to your personality."

Her expression turns murderous. Whit doesn't say a damn thing, appearing amused by the both of us.

"Right, and yours is accurate too, since you look like a complete slut," she says, but her insult is weak.

Laughing, I give her the finger and she scowls in return. Bryan wraps his arm around my neck, pulling me in close and kissing my forehead. Whit's gaze is murderous as he watches us, and I smirk at him, unable to help myself.

"Come on, Satan," Bryan says, his lips moving against the side of my face. "She's just jealous."

"Have fun with my leftovers," I tell her as Bryan releases me.

Bryan grabs my hand and I let him lead me down the stairs, feeling Whit's furious gaze upon me the entire time.

We walk through the soggy grass, Bryan's steps hurried as he practically drags me behind him. I can't stop giggling, thinking of Whit's face when he saw me on the dance floor. How angry he looked. How he has Caitlyn now, who probably has no idea who she's dealing with. He's so fucking dark and twisted.

A ripple of unease moves through me as I think of all the things Whit and I have done. I love his brand of dark and twisted. I have no idea what Bryan's like, but I'm sure he doesn't even come close to what Whit's capable of.

We approach the grove of trees, the damp air hushed, the sound of the ocean in the distance. I breathe in the scent of pine, the cold air making goose bumps rise all over my exposed skin and I gasp when Bryan shoves me against the thick trunk of a towering pine, the bark scratching my back as he pins me to it with his body. "Ow," I complain, reaching to rub the back of my head, glaring at him.

"Sshh," he says, his mouth on mine before I can say another word.

His kiss is hard. Punishing. I gently bat at his shoulders, trying to make him stop, to push him off me, but he won't let go. He tightens his hold on my waist, his fingers pinching into my skin. He thrusts his tongue into my mouth, searching for mine, and I tentatively touch it. I try to pretend he's Whit, hoping it makes my response easier, but it's no use.

He's not Whit. Not even close. His tongue is too big in my mouth, and he's so pushy. I hate the feel of his hands on my body, how he gropes every part of me. I shove at his shoulders, trying to avert my face away from his to end the kiss, but Bryan is persistent.

"You said you were a sure thing," he whispers against my cheek, right before he dips down and drags his too wet mouth along my neck.

Alarm fills me at his words. I don't like this. Not at all. I press my hands flat on his chest, desperate to push him away, but he's too strong. "Stop."

"Aw come on," he says with a low chuckle. That sound fills me with dread. "Don't be such a fuckin' tease. Give me a show. Dance for me like you did earlier."

"Let me go," I demand.

He goes completely still, pulling away from me slightly to glare at me. His gaze is unfocused, and I realize too late that he's smashed. He's had a lot to drink tonight. Probably something else too. Coke? I noticed a few people wiping white stuff away from their noses earlier on the dance floor.

"You said you wanted this." His voice is quiet. Disbelieving.

"I-I changed my mind." I curl my fingers around his shoulders and smile, a tremor moving through me at the dark look in his eyes. "Let's go back inside. We can dance some more, okay?"

"No." He says, reaching for my tube top and tugging it down. My breasts pop free, the cold air making my nipples harden and I cry out as I try to cover myself, but he won't let me. He grabs hold of my hands, keeping them at my sides. "Fuck me," he says, his gaze on my chest. "Look at your tits."

His voice is reverent, as if he's never seen a set of boobs before. He starts to reach for them.

"Stop." I break free from his grip and grab at my top, ready to yank it back up, but he stops me, his hand crushing my wrist, his mouth back on mine as he presses me firmly against the tree.

"Don't fight it," he mutters against my lips, his other hand going for my bottoms. He slips his fingers just beneath the fabric and I lift up my knee, trying to fight him off. "Don't fight me. Calm down, Satan. You're going to like this. I promise."

He pins me in place, overwhelming me with his strength.

My thoughts are frantic as he exerts pressure on my wrists, pulling up so my arms are above my head, completely exposing me. I start to tremble when he holds my wrists together with one hand, his other hand sliding down. Along my face. Across my shoulder. Down my chest, until he circles one hard nipple with his index finger.

"You want it," he murmurs, a whimper leaving me when he pinches my nipple. He glares at me. "You like it rough."

I gape at him, horror consuming me. How does he know? Did Whit tell his friends? And then the rumors spread?

"Any girl who's fucked Lancaster likes it hard." His fingers pull tighter on my nipple, making me cry out. He smiles. "She likes it when it hurts."

"Please," I whisper when he cups my breast, kneading my flesh roughly. "Don't do this."

"You want it," he says, leaning in so his mouth is just above mine. "Remember? You promised you were a sure thing. I expect you to deliver."

He kisses me and all I can do is take it, sobbing into his mouth, but he doesn't even notice. His hand is too busy, his mouth too greedy. I should've never worn this stupid costume. I was asking for trouble from the moment I appeared at the party like this, and I honestly thought Whit would've stopped Bryan from taking me away.

But he didn't. He let me go. He doesn't care about me. He probably never did, I think as Bryan runs his lips down my neck, across my collarbone, his mouth getting closer and closer to my breasts. Oh God, I think I'm going to be sick.

Bryan squeezes my right breast, his fingers brutal, his head dipping down and his mouth open so he can suck on my nipple when he's suddenly gone, ripped away from me.

"Motherfucker—" Bryan utters, right before a fist connects with his mouth, the sickening sound of flesh hitting flesh filling the air before he drops.

I shriek, more with relief than anything else, when I realize it's Whit punching the shit out of Bryan. He hits him again. And again, his knuckles red, his eyes blazing with fury as he stands over Bryan, who crumples into a ball on the ground, trying to protect himself.

"She said no, asshole," Whit says, literally spitting on him, reminding me of the time he saved me from Elliot. He kicks Bryan directly in the ribs and he rolls over with a grunt, away from us. "Sick fucker."

"She wanted it," Bryan says with a groan. "She promised me she was a sure thing. She grinded on my dick."

"Doesn't mean shit if the girl says no. Ass face." Whit nudges Bryan's backside with his booted foot before lifting his head to glare straight at me.

I stare at him in return, breathing heavily, my top around my stomach and my breasts exposed. Tears stream down my face and I know I must look a mess.

His lips firm and he slowly shakes his head as if he's disappointed in me, kicks Bryan one more time for good measure, and then turns.

And walks away.

What the actual fuck?

Tugging my tube top back into place, I chase after him, calling his name.

He keeps walking, his back stiff, his shoulders straight. Tension radiating off of him as if it's a living, breathing thing. I pick up my pace, desperate to catch up to him, and I snag his hand, my fingers curling around his.

He whips around, yanking his hand from mine, his expression one of pure anger. I've never seen him so mad before. "What the hell, Summer?"

I go completely still, shocked he called me by my first name. He never does that. Surely never in public. Not that anyone's around.

"T-thank you," I whisper, just as my entire body starts to quake. "He was going to—going to—"

I choke on a sob.

Whit pulls me into his arms and I collapse against him, his familiar smell wrapping around me, making me feel safe. I cling to him, crying into his soft black shirt, my tears flowing uncontrollably. He just lets me cry, holding onto me, his arms around my waist, his chin resting on top of my head. I feel his fingers tangle in my hair and that just makes me cry harder, my stomach roiling at the realization of what just happened to me.

Whit's right. Bryan was going to rape me against that tree. I should've never left the party with him. I only just got there, and I'd already had too much to drink. My entire night is ruined, and I'm sure I ruined Whit's too.

I don't know how long I cry like that, but it feels like an eternity. Shuddery breaths leave me and I hiccup as I slowly pull away from him so I can look into his face.

It's the same unfeeling, cold Whit staring down at me. "Are you through?" he asks.

I nod, hiccupping once.

He grips my chin, forcing my gaze to meet his. "Don't fuck around with strangers. I won't always be around to rescue you."

Overwhelming hatred races through my veins, making my blood boil. "You're not my hero," I spit at him.

"I am tonight. Was last time too. I can't keep saving you, Savage. Eventually, you're going to find yourself in this position again, and I won't be around. What will you do then? Huh?" His fingers squeeze my chin, but I remain still, not about to show more weakness in front of him. "That asshole almost *raped* you. He had his hands all over you, and you fucking asked for it, dressed like you are. What did you expect?"

Tears start flowing again, streaming down my face, but still I say nothing.

"You're a fucking mess, Savage. Figure your shit out. Before you end up dead and buried in the ground."

He shoves me away from him, heading back toward the house.

And this time, I let him go. I refuse to follow after him.

Fuck Whit Lancaster.

Fuck him.

TWENTY-SIX

SUMMER

LATE NOVEMBER IS when they all say the first snow comes to campus, but this year, it arrives a little earlier. On the eighteenth to be exact, in the middle of the day while I'm in class, bored and staring out the window, light flurries begin to fall, eventually turning into bigger flakes. They stream steadily from the dark sky throughout the afternoon and by nightfall, the entire campus is blanketed in winter white.

The teachers can't stop talking about the unusual cold front as they mess with the hissing radiators in our classrooms, complaining about the temperature. Lancaster Prep is housed in beautiful historic buildings, their heating and cooling systems archaic. This prompts a debate in American Government, my last class of the day. Students want modernizations to the buildings, arguing that it's the twenty-first century. Don't we deserve central heat and air? The teachers agree, but say modernizations would destroy the integrity of the buildings.

This turned into a debate for the rest of class, and I was bored out of my skull. As usual. All I can think about is how badly I want out of here.

But I have nowhere to go.

It's a strange day. We're all distracted, staff included. We're two days away from Friday, the last day before Thanksgiving break. Everyone is anxious to leave the newly formed winter wonderland our campus has magically turned into. Conversations buzzed during classes throughout the day, louder than usual about vacation plans. Tropical getaways, shopping excursions, visits with family—though those are deemed boring. Passe. It's as if we're in prison and they're about to finally let us out.

I wish I could go somewhere. Anywhere. But I'm not leaving. Mother and I spoke often leading up to this week. Stilted conversations on the phone I wish I could replace with the occasional text, they're so awkward. I don't mention the break, and neither does she, but it's there.

We both know it.

As the date draws closer, it hovers between us, until she finally mentions she's going on a short trip to the Caribbean with a group of friends. Will I be okay alone? She needs the escape, she's quick to explain, not allowing me to answer her yet. After everything she's been through, all the suffering throughout the last year. The fire, the insurance claims, handling the estate, the legal fight she's facing with the first Mrs. Jonas Weatherstone.

What can I say to that? How can I protest? Of course, I tell her to go. I even remind her to take sunscreen, like I'm the parent and she's the child. I'm the responsible one in our ever-evolving relationship.

That would be hilarious, if it wasn't so sad.

The dormitories stay open during the break for any students without a place to go, and I let my dorm advisor know I'll be staying. The sympathetic look on Ms. Thompson's face annoys the shit out of me, and when she opens her mouth, the words, "I'm sorry," about to fall from her lips, I cut her off and tell her I have to go or I'll be late for class.

It's not true, and we both know it. I met with her during the last part of lunch, Sylvie nowhere to be found, as usual. The thought of spending another lunch hour alone, fed up with the monotony that has become my life since the first of November, almost becomes too much.

It doesn't help, how on edge I've been, waiting for Whit to say something, anything to me. But of course, he remains quiet. Elusive.

A puzzle I can't put together no matter how hard I try.

He saved me on Halloween night, and the next day, Bryan wasn't in class. He hasn't been seen or heard from again, and I know without a doubt Whit got rid of him. Much like he did the poor, stupid Elliot. No male crosses Whit, or challenges his authority on this campus. To do so would mean your end.

Looks like Bryan met his. He won't be missed. Sometimes I can still feel his hands on me, his tongue in my mouth. How he kept repeating I was a sure thing. I remember how I acted toward him at the party. Dancing, grinding on him. Rubbing my ass against his dick, wearing practically nothing. Maybe Whit was right. Maybe I did ask for Bryan's attack. I was desperate to get Whit's attention, but I got someone else's instead. Someone unwanted.

Whit may have come to my rescue, but he also made me feel like shit. I still feel shitty all these weeks later, thanks to him not talking to me. He's moved on from me anyway. He's with Caitlyn now. I see them everywhere together. All over campus. She flutters all around him, eager for his attention, yet he rarely gives it to her. Always with that impassive expression on his face, as if he'd rather be anywhere than there with her.

I know the feeling. I hate that I have that in common with her.

At least he's seen in public with her. He never really wanted anyone knowing we were together, and that hurts. More than I care to admit. The asshole always did think he was better than me.

Right till the bitter end.

Sylvie still disappears frequently. Whereas she was looking better, now she appears worse. Her health is going rapidly downhill, she tells me when she reappears on campus for a day. Sometimes only an hour before she leaves again. Always haggard and pale. The circles under her eyes grow darker and darker, and I grow more and more concerned. She's avoiding Spencer, and I don't know what happened between them on Halloween night, because she's not talking. Not to me.

Not to anyone.

If she's not out sick, she's at endless doctors' appointments. Specialists. Centers that specialize in this, that and the other. Poked and prodded, x-rays scanned, vitals tracked, new medications introduced. But they still claim they don't know what's wrong with her.

"Oh, I could tell them, but no one listens," she said to me a few days ago, after we ate lunch and were sitting outside together, the brisk wind whipping our hair all around us. The sun was out for approximately fifteen minutes that day, and everyone was soaking it up before it disappeared again. The dark, cloudy days are notorious here. "So I just wait for the day I die, and then maybe someone will figure it all out."

Her words scare me, but I don't understand what exactly she's referring to. And every time I try and ask, she changes the subject.

So I remain quiet, and secretly pray that my only friend at this godforsaken school doesn't die before the end of the year. I don't even know if she and Spence had sex yet. She's never mentioned it.

Whit also still hasn't returned my journal.

Our deal is finished. He's not interested in me anymore, that is abundantly clear, yet he won't return it. Of course I don't ask for it either. He just goes about his business, spending time with his new plaything, or with his friends, and we don't speak. No more sneaky, heated glances in the halls or in class either. We're over that.

I'm over him.

That's what I try and tell myself.

It's in American Government where I suffer the most. He sometimes sits directly in front of me, switching up his seat, as if he's taunting me, reminding me that he's still there. Larger than life and out to haunt me. I remain at the same desk every single day, arriving to class early, hoping he'll avoid me. His gaze will meet mine for the briefest second, just before he drops a kiss on Caitlyn's upturned cheek and they go their separate ways. She sits on the opposite side of the room, directly in front, like a good little student.

While Whit comes to the back of the room on the left side, always sitting directly in front of me.

So close I can smell him. Can stare at the soft hair that lies against his nape. I know the silky feel of his hair around my fingers. I know the groans he makes when he comes. The taste of his mouth when he kisses me. The taste of his cock when he slides it between my lips.

Sometimes I wonder. Maybe I just imagined it. Maybe what happened between us was a dream. Or a nightmare. After he left me by the trees in the middle of the forest, I staggered back to my dorm room, a broken, crying mess. No one came looking for me. Not even Sylvie. She was too wrapped up in her own bullshit with Spencer, so I can't be angry at her.

Besides, being angry at Sylvie means I have no other friends, and I can't risk losing her.

I just...

I can't.

The missing journal burns a hole in my brain and I want it back. Every time I open my desk drawer and see it gone, I become infuriated. I wonder how much of it he's actually read? If he really does know all of my secrets?

Or did he tease me the entire time and never cracked it open once? That makes more sense. He doesn't care about me. Why would he care about anything about my past?

He doesn't. He's an unfeeling, giant dickhead who deserves a miserable life with a woman who's been chosen for him versus one he could actually fall in love with on his own. I hope he fucking hates her. I hope she can never give him children. I hope someday he thinks of me, and is filled with burning, mad regret.

I hope.

I hope.

I hope.

After speaking with Miss Thompson and letting her know I'm not going anywhere next week, I go to the library and pretend I'm doing homework. I'm really reading a book on my Kindle app, something dark and disturbing yet totally romantic. I can relate to it. The woman is strong. Defiant. The man is a total alpha, billionaire businessman who barks orders at people instead of speaking to them like a rational human.

With the exception of the woman. He treats her like a queen. Like a fragile, precious thing that only he can protect. And while she's perfectly capable of taking care of herself, she lets him treat her that way. She enjoys it. He makes her feel special. Cared for.

Loved.

I think of Whit. When he said I was fucking stunning. When he made me feel like I was the most beautiful girl he's ever seen. How I can't hide my beauty, no matter how hard I try. I didn't focus on those words so much then, but I do now, replaying them over and over again in my mind. Did he really mean them? Or was he just trying to charm me into giving in to his every need?

"There you are."

I glance up to find Sylvie standing by the table, a wan smile curling her pale lips. I tuck my phone away, not wanting to get caught reading a dark romance when I should be doing school work, even if it's just my friend who's catching me.

"Hey," I say, my voice ringing with concern, just with that one word. I see annoyance flicker in her gaze. She hates when people ask her about her condition. "Where have you been? Are you okay?"

"I'm fine." She jerks the chair away from the table and settles in, dropping her backpack onto the table with a loud clatter.

I hear the unmistakable shush from Miss Taylor, and Sylvie rolls her eyes.

"Another doctor's appointment. I told Mother to bring me back here. I wanted to go to class," she continues.

"We only have one more day," I remind her gently. "Nothing's really happening around here anyway. You could've skipped it."

"I needed to get away from her." Sylvie glances at her phone, the tip of her tongue sticking out between her lips as she types a reply to someone and sends it. She plops her phone on the table next to her backpack. "I'm so tired of her. Spending time with my mother is exhausting."

I know the feeling.

"I've missed you," she says, her voice gentle. "I know we haven't had much of a chance to talk lately, but I know you went through...a rough time Halloween night, and I'm so sorry that happened."

I want to ask her what exactly she knows, but then again, I don't want to know what's been said about me.

Instead, I smile tightly and nod once. "Thanks."

"You're okay?" She glances over her shoulder before scooting her chair closer to mine. "Whit took care of the problem."

"You mean Bryan?" I ask, my brow arched. "I figured."

"He doesn't do that for just anyone, you know. He saves those drastic measures for people who terrorize me usually." She pauses for only a moment. "Now he's done that for you twice."

"I don't know why," I say airily, trying to act like none of it matters. "He's with Caitlyn now. I suppose he'll protect her instead."

Sylvie dissolves into giggles, shaking her head. "He could give a shit about Caitlyn. I think he likes having her around because she gives him all of those ego strokes he enjoys."

"Don't be naïve, Sylvie. Caitlyn is stroking more than his ego," I snap like a jealous shrew.

Her giggling come to a full stop as she contemplates me. "She wishes she was stroking other parts of him. He always keeps her at an arm's distance. I asked him why recently. He said he can't have sex with her. She'd be too clingy."

I say nothing, desperately wanting to believe Sylvie, and telling myself I don't care what Whit does anymore.

He's none of my business.

Her face lights up as she studies me. "Oh my God, I just had the *best* idea. You should come home with me for Thanksgiving!"

I watch her in stunned silence, her invitation rolling over and over again in my mind. She's not paying attention to me, having pulled out a piece of plain white paper and resting her hand on top of it. With a pencil, she begins to trace her hand slowly. I recognize what she's doing and can't help but smile.

She's making a turkey.

"I don't want to intrude," I start, but she jerks her head up, her gaze imploring.

"*Please* intrude. I'm dying for you to intrude. It's so boring at the Newport house. We used to spend the summers there all the time, but after the divorce, now we only go there for Thanksgiving. Mother and Father always spend the holiday together with all of us."

My mouth pops open. "I thought they were divorced."

Sylvie concentrates on her turkey once more. "Mother is always saying my father needs to think of the children. As if we're still a perfect little family unit when Mummy and Daddy are under the same roof. Please. It's more like she wants to pretend they're still together. Their divorce is a giant stain on her social status."

Her voice is laced with bitterness.

"What does your family do for Christmas?"

She lifts her head. "Father draws the line at Christmas. He never spends it with us anymore. He always goes on an exotic vacation with his girlfriend of the month. Since their divorce, he's living it up, and I suppose I can't blame him."

"What about the rest of your family?" I ask.

"Oh. We spend the holidays in Manhattan usually. The city is alive during Christmas. It's my favorite time of year."

"It's beautiful during the holidays," I agree absently, my mind racing with the possibilities. Is it crazy to contemplate going with Sylvie so I can possibly be near Whit? Though why would I want to torture myself like that? And would he be angry that I showed up during his family vacation, or would he be glad to see me?

I'm going for the former. After our last encounter, I'm sure he's absolutely sick of my shit. Just as I'm sick of his.

"So? What do you say?" I look up to find Sylvie watching me. "It'll be the perfect distraction."

"For what?"

"For me. I need someone to spend time with. Lina is too busy dancing all the time. She's in London and can't get away. Even if she did come to Newport, she's not the same. She's never up for hijinks anymore." Such an odd, old-fashioned word, though I suppose it doesn't sound all that odd, falling from Sylvie's lips. "You could meet my father. Oh, now that would be a sight to see."

She laughs, shaking her head, while I sit there, knowing exactly what she's thinking.

Bring the daughter of the woman who destroyed the Lancaster marriage to Thanksgiving dinner. Gee, great.

"Sylvie. Are you using me to upset your parents?" I ask calmly.

Her eyes widen and she rests her hand against her chest. "I would never. I genuinely enjoy your company, Summer. You know this."

"It's rather convenient, bringing me for Thanksgiving break, when both of your parents will be there," I say, feeling the slightest bit played. "I don't want to be used as a tool to get back at them."

"Oh come on, why not? What's the harm in it? My mother will be *so* furious." She throws her head back and laughs, the most joyous sound I think I've ever heard come out of her. I watch her, the incessant shushing coming from Miss Taylor as background music, until finally her laughter slows. Fades. Her eyes still dance though. "My father will try to sleep with you."

My mouth pops open. "Disgusting."

"Are you eighteen yet?" Sylvie raises a delicate brow.

I squirm in my seat, not wanting to admit this, but she's giving me no choice. "Um, I will be."

"Of course you will," she says, like I'm a stupid child. "But when? Soon?"

"Tomorrow, actually." I've kept it quiet. No one cares about my birthday at this school. No one cares about my birthday anywhere, not even my mother. She hasn't mentioned it. Not once.

And I'm her only child.

How could she forget?

"*No,*" Sylvie breathes. "Tomorrow? Oh my God, we *must* celebrate! This is so wild! You know who else's birthday it is tomorrow?" I shrug, confused. "Oh, you're never going to believe it!"

Her voice is so loud, Miss Taylor actually recognizes it. "Sylvie Lancaster, be *quiet!*"

"Oh shut it, you old hag," Sylvie mumbles under her breath, making us both laugh.

My laughter fades quickly though. I don't know who she could be referring to, but something tells me I should already know.

"Who do I share a birthday with?" I ask, curiosity eating at me. Maybe it's Spencer, Sylvie's not-so-secret crush, though she hasn't even mentioned his name once since Halloween.

Could it be her little sister? The mysterious dancing Carolina? Oh God, I hope it's not her father. That would probably make things worse, since she said he would most definitely hit on me if I was of legal age.

"Like I said, you're *never* going to believe it. Like ever." Sylvie pauses for full effect, a giant grin on her face. My heart races, pounding uncontrollably as I wait for her to say it. "It's Whit. He's turning eighteen tomorrow too."

TWENTY-SEVEN

SUMMER

THE FRIDAY before break and Lancaster Prep drops all pretense of being a place of learning. Half the student body is already gone, many of them on a jet to an amazing trip, all of them wanting to get an "early start of it." I woke up at seven and stared out my window at all of the cars in the nearby parking lot as they came and went, parents picking up their children with smiles on their faces. Some of them scowl. Some of them send servants in place of themselves, a few of them escorting sulky girls and annoyed boys into gleaming black Mercedes.

I press my hand against the glass, wondering where they're all going. Wishing I could leave too.

Then I remember I *am* leaving, and it's a giddy, blissful feeling, mixed with swirling dread. Escaping this campus for a week sounds like a true vacation.

Spending the entire week with Whit and his family?

Absolutely terrifying.

This is the dumbest thing I think I've ever done in my life, and I've done a lot of dumb things. I tried to tell Sylvie it was a bad idea, but she was persistent. She didn't want to go home alone, and she reassured me Whit wouldn't be around much. I'm sure once he realizes I'm there, he'll believe I accompanied Sylvie to be close to him, when that isn't true.

I'd rather face Whit's fury than spend the holiday week alone at Lancaster Prep, depressed and feeling abandoned.

It'll be okay. I can handle spending the week with the Lancasters. I'll have Sylvie. She says their house is so huge, I probably won't even run into Whit.

Perfect.

There's a knock at my door and I frown, checking the time on my phone. It's barely seven-thirty. I go to the door and unlock it, then slowly crack it open.

It's Sylvie, perfectly dressed in her uniform, not a hair out of place, and a smile on her face. "Happy Birthday!" she says, holding a white bag in front of her.

"Thank you," I say with a faint smile, opening the door wider so she can come in. "What do you have?"

"Open it and see," she says excitedly, handing over the bag before she walks into my dorm room. She stops short, glancing around. "There's still nothing in here."

I open the bag to find a donut with pink frosting and sprinkles inside. "Thank you. And what do you mean, there's still nothing in here?"

"On the walls. On your desk." She gestures. "No photos. No candles or plants or knickknacks. It's like you don't even live here, and you've been in this room for months, Summer. It looks like a prison cell."

"It's only temporary, my being here," I say with a shrug as I reach into the bag and pull the donut out, taking a big bite. It's sugary sweet. The crunch of the sprinkles makes me want more. I devour it in four bites, wishing I had something to drink.

If my mother saw me right now, she'd probably have a coronary.

Sylvie's not even paying attention. She's wandering around my room, touching everything. The iPhone charger cord draped across my bedside table. My backpack sitting in the desk chair. My light blue comforter, the bed still unmade. I try to see my room through her eyes, and realize quickly she's right. It's boring. Plain. No personality.

"Swear to God, it looks like you're staying in an institution," she says, spinning in a slow circle in the middle of my room. "Not even a calendar on the wall with the days marked off by a giant X."

I know she's trying to make a joke, but I'm instantly defensive. "I have, what? Six months left here? What's the point of trying to make it cute?"

"So it'll feel like home," she says, emphasizing the last word.

Before I came here, I didn't feel like I even had a home anymore. There was nothing for me to bring, and Mother suggested nothing. She bought me new bedding, and looking at it now, I realize Sylvie's right.

"Did you like the donut?" she asks, changing the subject.

"I already ate it all," I admit, feeling gluttonous.

Sylvie laughs. "You're welcome. We're going out to dinner tonight as a family to celebrate Whit's birthday. Wait until you see the menu! It's my favorite place to eat."

Oh God, this all sounds incredibly awkward. "Are you sure it's really okay that I'm coming with you?"

She makes a face and waves her hand, as if I'm making a big deal out of nothing. "Trust me, it's fine. I already talked to my parents. Daddy loves when I have friends over. He's always worried about my social status. Afraid that I'm too isolated because of my ailments."

Her father is probably right. She doesn't have a lot of friends, much like me, but her reasons are different than mine. A little more foreboding and gloomy.

"What about Whit?" I ask, my voice barely above a whisper. I rarely say his name out loud in front of Sylvie. It almost feels like an invocation. His name passes my lips and the spirits will rise. The devil will swirl in the air before lunging for me.

So dramatic but every time I think about Halloween night, it leaves me quaking.

"What about him?" Her tone is overly innocent.

"Have you told him I'm going home with you?"

"No." She laughs when she sees the horror on my face. "Don't worry! He'll be fine. You two might have secret, clandestine meetings while you're there, you never know. It'll be fun! I know he's still interested in you."

She shouldn't get my hopes up with stories of clandestine meetings. "He is not. He has a new girlfriend."

And please. The last word I would ever associate with Whit is "fun."

"His eyes follow you everywhere you go when you're in the same room together," she says.

I tilt my head, frowning at her. "What do you mean?"

"Exactly what I say. He watches you, Summer. All the time. And Whit doesn't care about *anyone*—at least none of the girls at our school. Caitlyn is a ruse. I don't know why he keeps her close, but he has his reasons. The only people he worries about are his friends and they're usually all that matter to him."

"I'm sure it means nothing that he looks at me," I say dismissively, refusing to get my hopes up. "He hates me now. Don't forget he turned the entire campus against me at one point."

"Right, and now they leave you alone. And you basically admitted to me you two had something going on. Now you don't. What's the deal?" she asks, her eyebrows shooting up. "Is it because of what happened with Bryan?"

My face flushes hotly at the memory. Everyone knows Bryan practically tried to rape me before Whit beat the shit out of him. "I don't want to talk about it."

"Uh huh." The knowing look on her face makes me even more embarrassed. "Well, whatever happened, I doubt Whit hates you."

"He definitely still hates me," I say way too quickly.

By the look on her face, I can tell she doesn't believe me. "Sure. Though I get what you're doing. And you're probably right. You shouldn't get your hopes up over Whit anyway. It's such a shame."

Sylvie's expression is incredibly sad.

"What's a shame?" I ask, hating how I always want every single detail I can get about Whit. She mentions his name and I lean in, always eager for more.

"That he doesn't have a heart."

I ENTER my first period class, Mr. Figueroa sitting behind his desk, chatting away with girls, as usual. They always surround his desk before class starts. They flirt with him, batting their eyelashes, laughing too loudly at his jokes, and they're not that funny. I've heard him tell a few and they're corny.

As usual, I walk right past them, headed for my seat when I hear him call my name.

Slowly I turn, my gaze questioning. He makes a gesture, indicating he wants me to come talk to him, so I approach his desk, while the two girls—they're not even in our class—stare at me with unmistakable disgust. I don't bother looking at them, keeping my focus on Figueroa, who's faintly smiling at me, his expression open. Friendly.

He's come a long way from that earlier hostility he'd felt at having me forced upon him the first day of school.

"Summer," he says my name, his tone pleasant. "Do you have a moment?"

I nod. Don't bother replying. He glances at the girls, sending them a look that sends them out of the classroom without another word. Once we're alone, he clears his throat, a faint smile curling his lips.

"I really enjoyed the last essay you turned in," he starts out, his compliment surprising me. "You have a particular way with words that makes everything come to life."

"Oh." I don't know what to say. "Thank you."

"Honestly? When you were first here, I thought you wouldn't be able to keep up with this class, but you've proven me wrong." His smile stays in place. "I notice you have a free period after lunch."

"I do," I say, frowning slightly. Was he checking up on me? How does he know my schedule?

"I was wondering if you'd be interested in being a TA during that period. I need some extra help organizing assignments and the like. Nothing too strenuous," he promises with a warm chuckle. "What do you say?"

I want to immediately tell him no, I'm not interested. I don't really like him, and I definitely thought he didn't like me either. But I'm guessing this is an opportunity I probably shouldn't turn away.

"Can I think about it?" I ask, scrunching up my forehead like I'm confused.

"Of course," he says easily. "Take the break and think on it. Let me know if you have any questions over break. I'll be available. You have my email, don't you?"

"Yes," I say with a nod. "And thank you for the opportunity."

"I don't offer this position to just anyone," he says, his voice lowering. "But I see something in you, Summer. Something special."

Unease slips down my spine at his words. *Something special.* They're vaguely creepy, especially coming from my teacher who has to be at least in his late thirties or early forties, and I literally just turned eighteen.

"Thank you," I say again before I turn away from him, running smack into someone who's just entered the classroom.

Whit.

His hands automatically go to my shoulders, lightly shoving me away. "Watch it," he snaps automatically, his expression softening when he takes a good look at me. I don't know what my face must look like, but his fingers tighten on my shoulders instead of letting me go, his head cocked to the side as he contemplates me. "You all right?"

I gape at him, thrown by his question, the gentle concern in his gaze. The fact that he's still touching me after he's all but ignored me for the last almost...three weeks? It feels like an eternity the last time we were face to face.

I don't understand him. Will I ever?

"I'm fine." I offer him a brittle smile and he lets me go. I decide to test the waters. "Happy Birthday."

He frowns. "How did you know?"

"Sylvie told me. It's my bir—"

"Whit. Summer. Please find your seats," Mr. Figueroa says, his voice full of annoyance.

Whit sends him a withering look, then turns and heads for his desk.

I'm left with no choice but to do the same. I walk on air the entire way though, my feet never seeming to touch the ground. For once, Whit didn't treat me awfully. He actually sounded like he was concerned for me and...

I'm probably reading too much into it.

It's hard for me to pretend he isn't in the classroom though, which is what I normally do. As Mr. Figueroa begins to lecture, pacing the front of the room, talking to only ten of us instead of the normal twenty, it's as if I can feel Whit's eyes on me, boring holes in my head, my back. Watching me.

Figueroa talks and talks, and every time I look up, I feel the weight of his gaze on me, his dark brows drawn together, as if he's trying to figure me out too. Maybe I stumped him by asking if I could think about being his TA. Good. All the other girls just fall at his feet, wanting a piece of him, a moment of his time, a laugh, a lingering look. They're starved for his attention, and I understand how they feel, though he's not the one I'm hungry for.

As subtly as I can, I angle my head to the left. Practically rest my cheek against my shoulder for a long moment, waiting there. Feeling like a fool. I lift my lids, my gaze seeking Whit out, finding him immediately.

He's already watching me, a pencil between his lips. I stare, fascinated as he rubs the pencil across his lips, almost as if he's kissing it. I even catch a glimpse of his pink tongue when he opens his mouth.

I turn away, my breaths short. My head spinning. I'm confused. Why is he suddenly acknowledging me now? He doesn't know I'm going with him to his house. I'll be there for a *week*.

With him.

Finally, the bell rings. Class is over. I take my time gathering my things, hating how Figueroa stands by the door, wishing everyone a happy Thanksgiving as they leave. I just want to make my escape without any acknowledgement.

Whit leaves his desk at the same time as I leave mine, the both of us meeting at the door and Figueroa doesn't even look at him.

His eyes are only for me.

"Think about it," he tells me mysteriously. "Have a happy Thanksgiving, Summer."

"You too," I say, shooting through the door as fast as possible.

Whit is right behind me, his fingers curling around my arm and stopping me from getting away from him. "What the hell was that all about?"

There are hardly any people in the hall, but he's still touching me in front of others, which is shocking. "How is it any of your business?"

"Don't play games with me, Savage." His fingers lock around my wrist and he drags me behind him, turning right down a short hallway, until we're tucked away in a quiet alcove with no one else around us. "What was Figueroa talking about?"

My pulse throbs beneath his touch. Can he feel it? Does he know how much he still affects me? God, I'm so weak. I should be pissed at him. Instead, I'm all amped up, hoping he won't stop talking. "It was nothing."

Whit steps closer, his chest brushing mine, making me suck in a sharp breath. "Tell me," he practically growls.

"He wants me to be his TA," I admit, wondering why he's acting this way. "It's no big deal."

"He's a perv who tries to sleep with his students. They almost always start out as his TA," he says, disgust lacing his voice. "It's a big deal."

My mouth drops open. "You're kidding."

"Would I really lie about that?"

"Why doesn't someone stop him?" Like you, I want to add, but I don't.

"No one's actually ever caught him in the act. And none of the girls he's been with tell on him," he explains. "Anytime someone brings it up, he's always got a story. An excuse. Same with the girls. He never gets with them when they're under-classmen. It's almost always with senior girls. It's this well-known secret that no one ever really talks about."

"You could do something about it, you know. Your name is on the sign out front. You can make people disappear," I remind him, thinking of Bryan. And Elliot.

"He's never actually done anything criminal yet—that he's been caught for. He's just creepy." Whit releases his hold on me and takes a step backward, as if needing the distance. He runs a hand through his hair, his frustration palpable. Frustration with me? With himself? With Figueroa? I'll never know, since he would never tell me. "And why am I bothering trying to explain this to you? Just—watch out, okay? His motives aren't pure."

Says the boy with the most impure motives I've ever seen in my life. "Are you giving me a warning?"

"For your own safety," he clarifies. "I'd do it for my sisters."

"So now you think of me like a sister."

He scowls. I smile.

"Absolutely not," he says irritably. "I don't want to fuck my sister, thank Christ."

My skin goes warm at his admission, and I decide to change the subject. "Did you know we share the same birthday?"

"What do you—it's your birthday?" He sounds confused.

I nod. Reach out and rest my hand on his chest, tugging lightly on his tie. "Eighteen and finally legal."

"Same," he says with the barest smile.

I don't release my hold on his tie. I don't understand where all this boldness is coming from either, but I'm going with it. I think about telling him I'm going with them for Thanksgiving break, but I decide to not push my luck. He'll find out soon enough, though I'm sure he'll be pissed when he finds out, no matter when. "We haven't talked in forever."

He snorts, slipping his hands into his trouser pockets. "After what happened Halloween night, I thought it best I avoid you. Figured you'd prefer it that way."

I just stare at him, my emotions conflicting. Warring with each other. "You saved me from Bryan, Whit. He was going to rape me. And then you got rid of him from campus. Just banished him as if you're the king and you can make people disappear."

"I can," he says with a menacing grin. "Keep finding yourself in trouble, Savage, and I can make you disappear too."

"You would never," I tell him, noting the flicker in his gaze. A sign of weakness? "You'd miss me too much."

"I have Caitlyn keeping me warm," he taunts. "She's not as depraved as you, but she'll do."

I frown, unable to stop it. "You pretend it's me when you kiss her?"

"I pretend she's you when I kiss her, when I eat her dry little pussy *and* when I fuck her," he says, making me flinch. He laughs. "Keep believing what you want, Savage. I'm enjoying it."

His words confuse me. I blink at him, unsure of what to say next.

"No flirtatious comeback? Or are you really worried I'm fucking Caitlyn every night now that you're out of my life?" He chuckles. "She follows me everywhere. She begs me to let her touch my dick, but I won't let her."

"Why not?" I snap.

"She's too eager to please." He shrugs.

"I thought you liked us submissive."

He grabs hold of my arm, yanking me to him. "I prefer them argumentative, so then I can put them in their place. Like you."

My skin warms at his words, at the way he looks at me. "You know," I say, reaching for his tie once again, running my fingers down the length of it, as far as I can reach. "You never did give me my journal back."

His gaze darkens, turning stormy. "Is that all this is about? You rubbing all over me, in the hopes I'd return your journal?"

My jaw drops. "I'm not *rubbing* all over you."

He glances down and I do the same, noting how close our bodies are. I'm practically standing on top of his shoes. "I'd beg to differ," he mutters, returning his icy blue gaze to mine.

I yank on his tie extra hard before I take hurried steps back, anger suffusing me. "I don't understand what you want from me."

"Not a fucking thing," he retorts. "Like I said, I'm trying to avoid you."

His words hurt, and I don't know why. "You have something I want."

"I'm not giving it back to you," he says with deadly finality. "So quit asking."

None of this is about the journal, and we both know it. "Why do you want it, huh? What does it matter? Just give it back to me. Please." I'm practically begging him, and I feel stupid. "Think of it as a birthday present."

"I'd rather give you something else for a present," he says, his tone low.

Dirty.

Frustrated, I turn on my heel and start walking.

He storms after me, his hand catching the crook of my elbow, turning me around to face him. I stare at his coldly handsome features, my lips parted, ready to call him an asshole, but he swoops in, his hands cupping my cheeks as he presses his mouth to mine.

My arms fall at my sides, helpless to the drugging power of his kiss. He devours me, his tongue sliding into my mouth, his fingers gripping my face firmly. He groans when my tongue meets his and we stand there, not touching at all, save for his hands on my cheeks and our mouths connected.

Whit ends it first, his breathing harsh as he lets go of my cheeks and slowly backs away. "Happy fucking birthday to me," he says.

I stand there, shaking, unable to speak. What would I say?

He stares at me for a moment longer, just before he turns on his heel and leaves.

TWENTY-EIGHT

WHIT

I SHOULDN'T HAVE KISSED her, I think as I'm sitting with my friends at lunch. Spencer gave me a giant sack of that good California weed he scores from his dealer as a birthday present. Dean gave me a box of donuts and a bottle of Clase Azul tequila. Considering that shit retails for almost two thousand, it's a generous gift.

"You'll need it, spending the week with your family," he tells me, his voice grim as he slaps me on the shoulder.

"Yeah. Thanks," I tell him, my thoughts drifting back to Summer. And that fucking kiss.

Soft lips. Slick tongue. She tasted sweet. Submissive. All those old urges came roaring back, silently asking me why the fuck I stopped seeking her out in the first place.

I get around her, and it's like I have no control. At one point, I had my hands in my pockets, thinking it was the only way I could keep myself from touching her.

Ultimately, that didn't work either.

I hate that I worried about her when it came to Figueroa, but someone needed to tell her. The guy is a perv. Scamming on girls every chance he gets, desperate for young pussy. It's amazing how many girls fall for his shit.

If he were to lay a single finger on Summer, I'd break every one of them. Crack a few bones in his hand too. Fuck that guy.

My gaze finds Summer immediately in the dining hall. Sitting with Sylvie, the two of them with their heads bent close, conspiring together. Sylvie says something to make Summer laugh and I wish I sat closer to her table so I could hear the sound.

Grimacing, I blink my friends back into focus. What the fuck was that just now? I *despise* how she makes me feel.

"When do you go home?" I ask Spencer, who frowns.

His parents are currently in the midst of a nasty divorce. He's not looking forward to the family holiday whatsoever. "I'm driving into the city tonight," he says. "My mom won't be there. She's with my grandparents in Kansas. Dad's taking his girlfriend to Ibiza for the holiday, so he won't be around. I'll have the place to myself."

"Maybe I'll come see you," I tell him, thinking of that giant apartment his parents own in midtown. We've had a few parties there in the past. Drinking and drugs and girls everywhere. Music pounding along with the throb in my head while I fucked some nameless, faceless girl to the same beat.

I think of fucking Summer in the guest bed at Spence's place. Her legs thrown over my shoulders as I pound inside her.

It had been going so well too. Avoiding her. Staying strong. Really shouldn't have kissed her.

Now I can't stop thinking about her.

"You should come see me. You too, Dean. We could have a party." Spencer smiles at the both of us, his gaze going to mine. "Bring your tequila."

"I'm saving that for Thanksgiving dinner with the folks, thanks," I say with a smirk, running my hand along the bottle sitting in front of me. I have it on the table in front of everyone. I don't give a shit. Like anyone's going to say something. I'd hand them their ass if they did. "No one is sharing this with me."

"Not even your sister?" Spence asks.

He's got a thing for Sylvie, though he's never flat out admitted it. And I don't encourage it either. He's not good enough for her. None of my friends are. He's a rude fucking bastard just like I am who has serious commitment issues. Why would I want to see my sister with someone like that?

Though I guess there's something to be said for the devil you know versus the one you don't...

"My sister doesn't drink. She can't because of all the medication she takes," I say, sending him a look. "You know this."

"She was drunk at the Halloween party," Spencer reminds me and I scowl.

"I know. That was a mistake," I say, my voice low. Thanks to the pre-party she had with Summer. That pissed me off. I yelled at Sylvie for a solid fifteen minutes about that shit. She cried and swore Spencer was protecting her. I didn't mention what happened with Summer that night to Sylvie. That's their conversation to have.

I wonder if they ever had it. If Summer admitted what Bryan almost did to her. If I hadn't come along when I did, that little asshole would've shoved his pencil dick inside her and fucked her against the tree.

If he'd done that, I'd have killed him. No joke. No one touches what's mine.

I shake my head once, noticing my hands are clenched into tight fists. I slowly uncurl my fingers, trying to relax.

Spence's gaze goes to the table where Sylvie and Summer are sitting. He watches them with longing in his eyes, and I hope to fuck I don't look as lovesick as he does. "She doing okay?" he asks, referring to my sister.

"She seems to be." I honestly don't know. Mother controls everything Sylvie does. She hates that Sylvie is here instead of at home, where she can keep watch over her precious, sickly daughter all the time. Carolina, on the other hand, is completely independent from our parents, far away at a prestigious dance school. And she's only fourteen. She told me once she hated being a Lancaster. It brought her nothing but trouble.

I can relate.

"I worry about her." Spence turns his gaze to mine. "Don't you worry about her?"

"My mother has everything under control," I say, my voice wooden, my eyes going yet again to Summer. She glances up at the same exact moment, our gazes locking. She doesn't look away.

Neither do I.

"Sylvie really likes Savage," Spence continues. "She told me Summer is her best friend. Her only friend, besides me."

"Fucking bullshit," I mutter, shaking my head. I know exactly what Savage is doing. Trying to get close to my sister to get on my good side.

It won't work.

"Right? It's ridiculous. Sylvie barely knows her," Spencer grumbles, irritable.

I study Summer. The elegant curve of her neck. The soft angle of her jaw. The stubborn jut of her chin. Her long, dark hair pulled back in the severe ponytail as usual, showing off that beautiful face. Her flashing dark eyes. Lush mouth. A mouth I kissed only a couple of hours ago. She opened to me like a goddamn flower, ripe for the taking. Eager whimpers sounding in her throat, her tongue licking mine like she wanted to swallow me whole.

Reminding me of all the things we've done together already. How she gives in so easily. The taste of her pussy. The breathy moans she'd make when I hit a particularly deep spot with my cock.

Discreetly I shift in my seat, reaching down to readjust myself as I tear my gaze away from her. She's a distraction I don't fucking need. I am so over her getting in my head and settling in like she belongs there. She's a nuisance.

A beautiful nuisance, but one I'm not interested in.

"What are your birthday plans?" Dean asks. I can tell he's trying to change the subject.

"Dinner with the fam, get drunk, get laid. Hopefully in that order," I declare, thinking of the impending evening ahead.

I'm not looking forward to it. Sucks that my birthday is so close to Thanksgiving. Since the divorce, our parents still spend this particular holiday together, and I can't fucking stand it. The snide remarks. The guilt trips my mother puts on Dad. The *let's pretend we're one big happy family* plan, though it never works.

There's always an argument. Sometimes a screaming match, though those have calmed down over the years. Tears. Always tears.

So many tears.

Carolina won't be there. Said she couldn't get away from school, their Nutcracker production is taking up all of their time, and she's the lead. Little Clara, dancing on the stage. My mother was terribly disappointed. She tries so damn hard to control all of us, and two out of three rebel against her cloying ways no matter how hard she tries. Sylvie deals with the brunt of it, and I'm starting to wonder if Mother has an unhealthy fixation on my sister.

I wouldn't be surprised if she does.

"You going to go trolling for a girl? Or do you already have someone lined up?" Dean asks, burrowing his way into my thoughts with his questions.

I contemplate his words, my thoughts filled with Summer. That's who I want for my birthday. But unfortunately, I've made prior arrangements. And I'm sure Summer has plans for the break. "I already have someone lined up."

"Bringing her as a guest to dinner?" Spencer asks. He knows how I operate.

I barely crack a smile. "Perhaps."

"Someone your parents won't approve of I'm sure," Spencer says with a chuckle.

"That's where you're wrong." My closed-lipped smile is smug. "My mother will die from happiness when she sees who I'm bringing. I'm already putting the plan into place."

Dean groans. "Tell me it's not Leticia."

My expression says it all. Of course it's Leticia Everett. My future wife. The future mother of my children, which is totally fucking crazy to think about, but my mother ensured this would happen when we were barely out of diapers.

Leticia's ancestors were land barons who bought up the majority of the east coast, then sold it off piece by piece for millions throughout the years. She's seventeen, pretty and virginal. If I were to even mention coming on her tits, she'd probably lose her goddamn mind. I fought against this relationship, but I recently realized I should try and feel this girl out. Maybe she's a freak like me.

Like Summer.

I couldn't be so fucking lucky, but it's worth a shot.

TWENTY-NINE

SUMMER

I FINISH PACKING my bag right when there's a knock on my door. Before I can answer it, Sylvie barges in, an impatient look on her pixie face.

"What's taking you so long?"

"I'm done," I tell her, slinging my duffel bag strap over my shoulder. I could've brought my suitcase, but decided it would be too large. Besides, it's only for a week. How much clothing will I need for a relaxing visit over Thanksgiving break?

Sylvie's eyes practically bulge out of her head. "That's all you're bringing?"

"What else do I need?"

She laughs. "You haven't spent a week with my family at the Newport house, have you? Just wait and see. We might need to take you shopping. Or you can raid my closet."

I look her up and down. "I don't think I could fit in your clothes."

"You could. Trust me. I have a variety of sizes, thanks to my weight always fluctuating." She sighs dramatically. "Dying is so hard on the body, no matter what age you are."

"Sylvie," I chastise, following her out of my dorm room. "I hate when you talk like that."

"Oh, when I speak the truth? Spencer doesn't like it either," she says nonchalantly.

We exit the building, the cold air like a slap to the face. I'm trembling, even in my thick coat, as we approach a sleek black Lincoln town car waiting for us in the parking lot, the trunk lid up, the driver standing beside it.

He rushes toward me, one arm reaching out. "Let me take that for you, miss."

I let him have my duffel, sending Sylvie a meaningful look once he walks away. She skips alongside me, laughing.

"Being rich has its advantages," she says. "Like servants at your beck and call and a private driver to take you to your destinations."

My throat suddenly feels like it could close up. "Is Whit joining us?"

"Oh no. He would never. Once he got his license, he drives himself to our family gatherings. Always."

Thank God. I don't think I could sit with him in the car for any amount of time while Sylvie is with us. I'd either jump him or scratch his eyes out.

"Why don't you ride with him?" I ask as I follow her into the back seat of the car. The driver shuts the door and then settles into the driver's seat, putting the car into gear and pulling out of the parking lot.

"Mother won't let him. He's too reckless, she says. Afraid he'll wrap one of his cars around a tree with me in it and I'll die instantly." More laughter, though it's tinged with sadness. "She's so ironic."

I don't quite know what she's referring to, and I'm almost afraid to ask.

So I don't.

We make small talk the entirety of the drive. It's slow going, the roadways clogged with people trying to make their escape just like we are. I can't stop looking out the window and marveling at all the traffic.

"If we would've waited any longer, the traffic only gets worse. Next week will be an absolute nightmare," Sylvie says.

"What are the plans for tonight?" I worry I didn't bring a fancy enough outfit for dinner, especially considering Sylvie's reaction to my lack of luggage.

"The restaurant we're going to is very expensive," Sylvie drawls. "But don't worry. It's also very casual. Outdoor seating. Firepits we can sit by and keep warm. Plenty of alcohol and appetizers to die for."

"Alcohol?" I ask, my voice weak.

"Daddy always manages to sneak me a few sips." She laughs. "I used to never drink, you know? Whit still believes I'm a good girl, but lately I've been allowing myself to indulge in...things. Specifically ones that aren't good for me."

I think of myself at fourteen, sneaking sips out of discarded champagne glasses like a little beggar. What must've the rich and snobbish Whit Lancaster thought of me? God, I was pitiful. Thinking I was so old in my tacky, strapless dress I wore as a bridesmaid at my cousin's wedding the year before. My boobs had grown since then, and that's why they were practically spilling out of my dress.

The memory has become painful. He saw me as a pitiful girl, I'm sure. One he could swiftly take advantage of, which he did.

"My parents are excited to meet you," Sylvie continues. "I told them all about you."

"All about me?" I feel like I'm walking into a trap. After all, I'm the idiot whose mother slept with Sylvie's father and essentially broke up their marriage.

What if her mother blames me for that, like Whit used to? I'm screwed.

"They know who you are, especially my father," Sylvie says. "Mother had a few choice words to say, but don't worry. She would never be anything but polite to you in front of everyone. 'To be rude is unseemly,' direct quote."

I press my forehead against the window pane, closing my eyes. I'm so stupid. Why would I do this to myself? I'm walking into a lion's den, and every single one of them will be hungry. Eager to take a bite out of me. And Sylvie is useless protection. I adore her, but she won't be strong enough to stave off her parents.

And especially not Whit.

As if I'll push him away though. He's my weakness too.

After a little over an hour on the road, we finally turn in front of double ornate black iron gates. Within seconds, they part, allowing us entry, and an endless stretch of black pavement curves through the green as far as the eye can see. I gawk out the window like a little girl, my face pressed against the glass, watching as we drive past gorgeous landscape. Lush green grass and giant trees barren of leaves, thanks to the recent turn in the weather. Towering green bushes appear as we make our way, lining the driveway on either side, and I know we must be getting close.

The driveway widens, and then it appears. The Lancaster mansion towers in the near distance, two, no *three* stories made of stone and marble, four massive pillars at the entrance, an endless amount of windows on either side. It's imposing, reminding me of one of those grand castles we saw when we went to England a few years ago for a family vacation. Before Jonas and Yates died.

It actually reminds me of Buckingham Palace, which is to say, it's mightily impressive.

"Like I mentioned before, we normally only come here for the summer," Sylvie explains as the car curves along the round-about, the house drawing nearer. "But Mother and Daddy prefer to use this house for our family Thanksgiving while we're at Lancaster Prep. So much closer for us to travel."

"You spend your summers here?" I ask weakly, my gaze trailing over the ornate front of the house. Angel statues stare down upon us, their beautiful faces forever caught in wonder, with their chubby cheeks and rosebud lips.

"Yes. Well, we used to, when I was younger. All of us would be here. Even Carolina, though she struggles throughout the season when she can't dance every single day. Mother turned one of the smaller ballrooms into a dance studio for her, and she spends pretty much the entire summer there. Waking up first thing in the morning, dancing and leaping and wearing herself out until she's a boneless heap of exhaustion," Sylvie explains. "Her dedication is mind-boggling. I can barely keep up with her after thirty minutes, and I used to dance too, before I became so sick all of the time. I just know she'll be a famous dancer someday."

Her family is so incredibly interesting, where mine has horrible secrets and deep shame, all of it locked up tight.

Well, not all of it, thanks to Whit getting his hands on my diary.

The Lancaster family seems so perfect. Beautiful. Yes, Augustus cheated with my mother and ended up getting a divorce, but that isn't so out of the norm.

I'm sure their family doesn't have as many dirty secrets as mine.

The moment the car stops in front of the house, Sylvie leaps out of it and starts pacing, stretching her legs. I follow suit, unable to stop from staring at the house. The massive front door slowly swings open and two women dressed all in black come out to greet us, taking our luggage and rushing back into the house.

"You'll have a guest room all to yourself." Sylvie laughs as I watch the servants scurry inside. "No pull-out couch or anything like that."

"How many rooms are in this place?" I ask as we make our way up the stone steps.

"Fifty? Sixty? I'm not sure," Sylvie says with a shrug as we walk through the open double doors. The foyer is two stories, her words echoing off the walls and the ceiling. A man in a black suit shuts the door, the sound ringing in the hollow room, nearly making me jump.

"Miss Lancaster, shall I show you and your guest to your rooms?" the man asks in a British accent.

"Please, Alfred." Sylvie indicates me. "This is my friend, Summer Savage."

"A pleasure, Miss Savage," Alfred says with a quick bow.

I blink at him. This entire moment is surreal. The have an authentic English butler at their beck and call. Servants everywhere. The biggest house I think I've ever been in, in my life. No wonder the Lancasters choose this holiday to spend together, and in this house. Augustus can have one wing; their mother can have another and they'd barely have to see each other.

"Nice to meet you too," I say to Alfred before he turns and leads us to the staircase.

"Your room is upstairs," he tells me. "The family has the west wing, and guests stay in the east wing."

I nod, mentally counting the steps as we climb them. They're wide, marble, covered in soft black fabric that resembles velvet. The black matches the ornate iron railings that also match the gate that blocks the commoners from coming in, and once we're at the top of the stairs, we're greeted by a massive painting of a stern looking man scowling down upon us.

"The original Augustus Lancaster," Sylvie whispers in my ear, steering me to the right. "Come on."

We go up another staircase, to the third floor, trailing behind Alfred as he marches ahead of us. I can't stop staring, drinking in the massive paintings of their ancestors. The ornate paneled walls, the chandeliers hanging above us, dripping with crystals. It's like something out of another time.

"The guest rooms are here," Alfred announces. "I made sure and gave you a room with an ocean view, Miss Savage. As per Miss Sylvie's request."

"Thank you, Al," Sylvie says, skipping right up to him. He stops, shocked, and she rises on tiptoe, giving him a pinch on the cheek. "You're such a peach."

Swear to God, the older man blushes.

We walk down the endless hall, until he stops directly in front of a towering door. With a flick of his wrist, he opens it, then holds out his arm. "Ladies first."

Sylvie leads me into the room and I stop in the center of it, my mouth hanging open as I slowly turn in a circle, trying to take it all in. But I can't. My eyes don't know where to settle first.

The rug beneath my feet is plush, the floral pattern faded, though that doesn't make it look shabby. No, more like you know you're stepping on something fine. Expensive. That's been in the family for generations. The walls are covered in subtle hydrangea printed wallpaper, with blue and pink and white flowers everywhere, allowing a bare glimpse of the pale green background. The bed is a massive four poster. The furniture is delicate, yet ornate. Painted white with gold tufted seating. Another chandelier hangs in the center and I gaze up at it, the crystals sparkling in the dim sunlight.

"I feel like I'm in a fairy tale," I say to no one.

Sylvie laughs and takes my hand. "Come see the view."

I follow her toward the slender glass double doors that open out onto a balcony. She grabs the black iron handle and opens one, leading me outside where the bitterly cold wind whips at our hair. Before us is a lush garden, reminding me of the one at school but even bigger, and beyond that, the ocean. It's wintry blue and whitecapped, the water churning. Restless.

"This is beautiful," I breathe, turning to find she's smiling at me, downright giddy.

"I love seeing it through your eyes for the first time. Everyone I know is so jaded. *Nothing* affects them. I mean, I can tell you're jaded in some ways, but not all," she explains.

I try to tamp down my joy and awe, feeling stupid. Their wealth shouldn't impress me. My mother is wealthy now too, thanks to Jonas and Yates' passing. Mother got everything. All of it. Jonas' ex-wife is suing, but she has no grounds for a lawsuit, according to my mother's lawyer, or so Mother says. The first wife's only son is gone too. She deserves nothing beyond what Jonas originally gave her in the divorce settlement.

"It's okay. You don't have to pretend." Sylvie reaches out, her hand gentle on my arm. "I like how open you are. How real. Everyone tiptoes around me, treating me like I'm a fragile doll about to break. You don't."

"You're the strongest person I know," I admit, my voice faint, swallowed up by the howling wind.

It's true. She's suffered so much, and still she skips around and acts like nothing bothers her. I'd be in a pit of despair if I believed I was dying.

She almost relishes in the fact that her time is near.

Sylvie visibly trembles and she tugs on my arm. "Come on. Let's go inside. It's freezing out here."

The moment the doors shut, the room is enveloped in complete silence. Alfred is long gone. My duffel bag rests on a bench that sits in front of the giant bed I get to sleep in tonight. It looks so small, downright shabby in the overt grandeur of the room.

"We're definitely going shopping this weekend," Sylvie tells me, her gaze locked on my bag. "You have a credit card?"

I nod. I'll should probably text Mother to make sure she's okay with me spending money, but I doubt she'd care. She's too busy vacationing with her friends, soaking up the sun. I didn't even bother telling her I was going to Sylvie's house for Thanksgiving. I don't think she'd really care about that either.

Or maybe she would, considering I'm interacting with Augustus Lancaster this week. I don't know.

Sylvie smiles. "Perfect. There are so many fantastic shops we can explore. We'll find you a new look for every day of the week. And a new suitcase to take it all home in."

"But I brought some clothes," I start, but she shakes her head, her expression firm.

"Meals are an event. There will be parties in the neighborhood. You'll want to dress up the entire week, especially at night." Her gaze skims me from head to toe. "You're so beautiful, yet you rarely play up your beauty. Please let me do your makeup tonight for dinner. What do you say?"

"I-I guess," I agree. "What should I wear tonight?"

"Oh, you can dress casual. Jeans. A sweater. And your hair down. You always have it in a ponytail." She reaches behind me and yanks the tie from my hair, so it cascades around my face, a bend in my hair thanks to the hair tie. "Your hair is gorgeous. Maybe I can curl it for you too. Please let me dress you up? I used to do this for Lina all the time before she went away to school. She was like my own personal Barbie doll I could make pretty."

"Fine, okay," I say with a laugh, overwhelmed. "What time is dinner?"

"I'll ask Mother what time the reservation is for. I'll go find her." Sylvie turns wide eyes upon me. "Would you care to meet her now?"

God, no. "I'd rather take a nap, if it's okay. I'm exhausted."

"Of course! You're the birthday girl. You can do whatever you want. I'll find out what time dinner is, and text you. You'll need to come to my room at least an hour before we leave so I can do your hair and makeup. Come dressed. I'll work my magic on you." She pulls me into a crushing hug, her face pressed against my hair. "I'm so glad you came with me. You'll be just the distraction I need."

I pull away from her with a frown. "From what?"

Sylvie's smile is mysterious. "My entire life."

THIRTY

SUMMER

AFTER SYLVIE LEAVES MY ROOM, I fall asleep within minutes of my head hitting the fluffy pillow, wrapped up in the sumptuous duvet that covers my bed. I sleep for over an hour, waking up disoriented, the room shrouded in complete darkness. For a moment, I forget where I am.

And then it all comes back to me. I'm at the Lancaster estate in Newport, and we're going to dinner tonight. All of us. Including me.

And Whit.

He still doesn't know I'm here. I'm sure of it. Sylvie won't tell him. She'd rather I appear at the restaurant like a little bomb, perfectly detonated and exploding in his face. I'm sure she'll get a great thrill out of that. I adore my new friend, but sometimes I wonder if I'm being used as a pawn in her games, gleefully starting family drama wherever she can.

I grab my phone to check the time. Just past six. I see a text from Sylvie.

Dinner reservations are at eight. We'll leave at 7:45. You have to be in my room no later than 6:30!

Yeah. Probably not going to make that, especially since I still need to wash and dry my hair.

I also have a text from Mother.

Happy Birthday my darling. I hope you're doing something nice to celebrate.

That's it. No I remember when you were born, no I love you, I miss you. I wish I were with you.

I'll answer her later. Instead I send a quick text to Sylvie.

Me: **Fell asleep. Just woke up. Hopping in the shower now.**

Sylvie: **OMG hurry!**

I gather my toiletries and enter the luxurious bathroom, my mouth hanging open as I take it all in. This isn't just a display of wealth. What the Lancaster family has goes far beyond that. It's heritage. Generational money that runs so deep, I'm sure it feels endless.

The house may be old, but it thankfully has modern plumbing and I can tell the bathroom has been recently remodeled. There is marble and glass everywhere. The shower is huge, two walls of clear glass. The cabinets are painted the palest robin egg blue, and the mirrors that hang above the two sinks are ornate gold. A fresh flower arrangement sits on the counter, with bursts of fall colors including giant sunflowers.

I open the shower door and turn on the tap, gasping when the water steadily begins to fall, reminding me of a rain shower. I quickly shed my clothes and step under the spray, tilting my head back and letting it pour all over me. The warmth relaxes my tense muscles, and so does the lavender scented body wash. By the time I'm finished and drying myself off, I feel languid. Relaxed.

Then I remember what's going to happen tonight—and who I'm going to see—and the tension is back, creating instant knots in my shoulders.

My phone buzzes and I check it. Another text from Sylvie.

Sylvie: **I'll dry your hair for you. Come to my room!**

Me: **I don't know where it is!**

Sylvie: **I will meet you at the stairs. I'm leaving now!**

Thankfully I've already slathered on lotion, face moisturizer and deodorant. I throw on my planned outfit—a pair of my favorite high waisted, light wash jeans and a tight fitting black mock turtleneck shirt. It's slightly cropped and I study myself in the mirror, turning this way and that, hoping I don't look too scandalous.

What's a little skin? At least my tits won't fall out.

Not that Whit hasn't seen them before...

Clumsily slipping on my old Doc Marten boots, I grab my phone and hurry out of the bedroom, jogging down the endless hall, slowing down when I see Sylvie waiting for me at the top of the stairs, just as she said. She's smiling, her entire body seemingly vibrating as she waves at me to hurry.

"Let's go," she says, grabbing my hand and taking me to her bedroom.

It's even more opulent than my room, which is, of course, no surprise. The walls are the palest pink, as is the bedding on the gorgeous white princess bed. The entire room is delicate and feminine and ethereal, just like Sylvie is.

"I love your room," I tell her as I drink it all in, my booted feet loud on the bare floor when I step off the thick rug. If my mother were here, she'd chastise me for stomping everywhere. She hates my boots.

I think that's half the reason I wear them every chance I can get.

"Thank you. Let's get you ready in the bathroom. Better lighting," she says.

I follow her into the gigantic bathroom, and she settles me into the built-in vanity, the counter covered with every hair tool imaginable. A hair dryer, a couple of straighteners and at least three curling irons, the barrels all of various sizes. She wastes no time, getting right to work on blow drying my hair and within minutes, my hair is sleek and straight, shiny under the bright lights.

"Why don't you ever wear your hair down?" she asks once she's turned the dryer off, setting it on the counter.

"I don't know," I say, hating how defensive I sound. "It always gets in the way."

Sylvie runs her fingers through it, her gaze meeting mine in the mirror. "It's beautiful. You should show it off. We have to wear those stupid uniforms so at least play up your best features!"

I say nothing as she begins to curl my hair, mulling over her words. Mother always harps on me about my looks. How plain I am without makeup, and she says the same thing Sylvie just did—I need to play up my features. How drab my hair looks pulled into a plain ponytail—don't I want to go with her to get a blow out? She wants me girly and feminine and beautiful, just like she is. My mother is a beautiful woman. I look a lot like her.

Defying her, turning down her constant requests, is some sort of control issue for me. I don't want people to be drawn to me only because of my face. I want them to see something else. Something more. I'm not just a pretty face or big tits or long legs.

I think of Whit. Is he only dazzled by my looks? I'm downright plain at school. No makeup, my hair pulled back. I don't roll up the waistband of my skirt to show off my legs except for that one moment in time, when I was desperate to catch his attention. Otherwise, I'm as dowdy as they come.

But he's seen me naked, plenty of times. He knows what I hide beneath the uniform. He saw me in that horrible Halloween costume too. He barely looked at me that night. For some reason, my appearance made him angry. My showing up as a sexy devil had the complete opposite effect than what I originally planned.

He confuses me. I don't know what he wants anymore. Actually, that's not true. I know what he doesn't want.

Me.

Sylvie curls my hair into subtle waves. Does my makeup, getting right into my face, her eyes on me. I sort of want to squirm under her assessment, but when I do, she chastises me and has to start all over again with my eyeliner.

So I remain perfectly still, my entire body a ball of anxiety. I'm going to end up looking like I'm trying too hard. I just know it.

When she finally allows me to turn toward the mirror, I suck in a sharp breath at first glance.

I look like myself, only enhanced. My eyes are brighter. My cheeks more accentuated. My lips redder. But it doesn't look like too much.

More like Goldilocks did her work on me and I turned out just right.

"Do you hate it?" Sylvie asks after I remain silent for a bit too long. I meet her worried gaze in the mirror. "I tried to keep you as natural as possible."

"It's...amazing," I say, my voice light. "I love it."

"Are you sure?"

I turn in my seat to smile up at her. "I'm sure. Thank you, Sylvie. I feel like a princess."

"You're welcome. Happy Birthday." She envelops me in a tight hug, almost crushing me to her.

"I appreciate it. But...can you make sure and not mention my birthday at dinner tonight?" I ask once I pull out of her arms.

Sylvie frowns. "You don't want anyone to know?"

"I don't want to make a big deal about it." This night isn't about me. I just want to be a quiet observer.

I also don't want to piss Whit off.

"I can do that," she says eagerly, pulling me in for another hug. "Thank you for coming here with me this week. I don't think I could've stood this alone."

I pull away from her with a frown. "What do you mean?"

"Oh, it's nothing. I'm being foolish." She makes a disparaging noise. "I'll be fine. Especially with you here. Just—don't abandon me for anyone else, okay? I-I might need you."

"I'm not going anywhere," I murmur, and I mean every word. I'll stick by Sylvie's side this entire week. No one will be able to separate us.

I'll make sure of that.

THE SAME DRIVER awaits us as we exit the house, and we take the town car that brought us here to the restaurant near the wharf, right on the water. It's freezing outside, and I wear the cropped black puffer jacket I bought online last month. Sylvie is similarly dressed in jeans and a dark blue, oversized sweater. Her blonde hair is pulled into a loose braid and it's draped over one shoulder. Giant diamond studs sparkle in her ears, bringing out the brightness in her blue eyes.

"Where's the rest of your family?" I ask nervously, gazing around the interior of the car. I figured we'd all go to the restaurant together.

Sylvie yawns. "Mother's already there. We got into a huge fight while you were napping. She wanted us to ride with her, but I told her you were asleep."

"Oh, I didn't mean to cause any problems," I start.

"Don't worry about it," she says, interrupting me. "Daddy is meeting us there. He just came in from London, so he had his driver bring him straight to the restaurant."

"What about Whit?"

"Again, driving his own car. In case he wants to make a quick escape." She rolls her eyes. "He might be bringing a friend or two. I have no idea."

This makes me nervous. Just the thought of seeing Whit fills me with trepidation. Will he be mad I'm here? Or will he not even care?

I don't know what's worse.

We arrive at the restaurant within minutes, both of us slipping out the back door of the car, shaking when the cold air hits us. We dash toward the front door, the warmth of the restaurant drawing us in. The front area is crowded with people waiting for a seat, reminding me of the last time Sylvie and I went out to eat. Sylvie speaks with the host, giving her name and he smiles broadly before leading us to a private room in the back of the building.

My nerves are beyond amped up. My legs are shaky and my breaths are rapid. I tell myself to keep it together, but I swear I'm going to hyperventilate if I don't watch out.

We enter the room and I see their mother first. An elegant, painfully thin woman clad in a black sweater dress, each slender arm dripping with gold bangles almost to her elbows. Her hair is cut into a severe, platinum bob and her delicate features remind me of Sylvie, though hers are more pinched.

A flash of annoyance crosses her face when she spots us. "There you are. Couldn't you have at least worn a dress?"

I ignore the jab, since it's not directed at me, but her greeting reminds me of my own mother.

"Mother." Sylvie's voice is firm. "I want you to meet my friend, Summer Savage. Summer, this is my mother. Sylvia Lancaster."

Her namesake. I step closer to the table, extending my hand out toward her. She takes it, offering a limp handshake. "It's nice to meet you," I say, my voice even. The epitome of polite. "Thank you for having me in your home. It's so beautiful."

"Any friend of Sylvie's is a friend of ours, dear," Sylvia says coolly, her ice blue eyes locking on mine. They remind me of her son's. Her demeanor does as well. Cool. Detached.

Judging.

"Have a seat," Sylvia says to the two of us, and we automatically sit next to each other, across from Sylvie's mother. "Tell me. How was your trip here?"

"Oh, it went perfectly smooth," I start, but Sylvie interrupts me.

"The traffic was awful, I already told you," she says, glancing around the small room. "Where's Daddy and Whit?"

"Your father should be here soon. He just texted me. Claims his plane landed late." Mrs. Lancaster's lips draw into a thin line. "And your brother is at the bar, ordering himself a drink."

"Oh, I want a drink," Sylvie says with a little pout, crossing her arms.

"I'm sure your father will pour you a glass of wine," Sylvia says, irritation flitting across her face. "Are you part of the textile Savage family?"

I frown. "No."

"The retail Savages then. Oh, their athletic wear is to die for."

"I'm not related to them either." I'm guessing she already knows this. She's just...what? Making me feel inferior?

"Oh." Sylvia wrinkles her nose. "Who's your father then? What's his name?"

"Lionel Savage. And I don't keep in contact with him," I admit.

"Hmm." Sylvia taps her finger against her pursed lips. "Doesn't sound familiar."

Last I heard, Lionel Savage was a gym rat and personal trainer somewhere in Jersey. Of course, his name doesn't sound familiar.

"What is your family doing for the holidays?" she asks me pointedly.

"My mother is in the Caribbean," I admit.

Her gaze flickers with irritation at the mention of my mother. No surprise.

"What about Jonas? Oh, I adored that man, especially when he worked with my husband. He was always so sweet," she says, her lips curling upward in what vaguely resembles a smile.

But her words are sharp. Carving at my emotions. Reminding me of what I've done, and how we can never get them back.

"Mother," Sylvie chastises, sending her a meaningful look.

Sylvia Lancaster's expression is one of complete and utter innocence. "What? I did adore Jonas so much. I know he and his first wife suffered through that horrible divorce, thanks to the affair." She sends me a quick look, full of ire. "But I assumed his new wife was keeping him very happy."

"He's dead," I state flatly.

Sylvia rears back, blinking at me. "What?"

"Didn't you hear? About the fire? He and—Y-Yates." I stumble over my stepbrother's name. I haven't said it out loud in so long. It feels odd on my lips.

"Oh. That's right. How could I forget? Such a tragedy." She frowns, but then it's gone. As if it never was there in the first place, her face is so smooth. She smiles pleasantly, resting her arms on top of the table, her hands clasped together. "I'm sorry for your loss."

She doesn't sound sorry at all. I'd take a guess that she mentioned Jonas on purpose, just to make a jab at me. Which is cruel, considering how much I adored Jonas, not that she knows that. He wasn't able to protect me from certain things, but he always treated me as one of his own.

"Did they catch who set the fire?" Sylvia asks, her brows shooting up.

My stomach twists. There's nothing in it, yet I feel as if I could vomit all over this table.

"It wasn't arson," Sylvie answers for me, sounding confused. She glances at me. "Was it?"

"An accident," I croak, ducking my head.

The word was tossed around at first, right after the incident. But then it was dropped. Not enough evidence, Mother reassured me, which was a relief.

Sylvie thankfully changes the subject, talking about school, filling her mom in on the latest gossip. Talking about people I have no idea who they are, but supposedly they attend Lancaster Prep, children of her parents' friends. I don't really pay attention, too preoccupied with watching the door, waiting and dreading Whit's entrance. Another man walks in first, though. Whit's father.

If I wanted to know what Whit will look like when he's older, he just entered the room.

"Aug, there you are," Sylvia says, sounding exasperated. "*Finally* you're here."

Augustus completely ignores her, walking straight toward Sylvie. She rises to her feet and embraces him, giving him a lingering hug. I can't help but feel envious, wishing I had a strong relationship with my father. Or that Jonas was still here. I miss having a father figure to go to for advice. For comfort.

I'm sure I have daddy issues. I won't bother denying them.

"You look well," Augustus says to Sylvie, clasping her cheeks with his hands as he stares into her eyes. She beams up at him. "You've gained weight."

"I feel well," she answers, her voice light. The lightest I've ever heard her. "I'm glad you're here."

Yesterday she looked like hell. Now she's sparkling with health.

I don't get it.

"The flight was terrible. Delayed at takeoff. Bad weather. Glad I made it back in one piece." He releases his hold on Sylvie, his gaze shifting to me. "Who do we have here?"

"Oh Daddy, this is Summer. My friend," Sylvie says, smiling at me.

I stand and take his offered hand. "Nice to meet you."

He tilts his head as he contemplates me, slowly releasing my hand. "You're terribly familiar."

"Her mother is Janine Weatherstone," Sylvie says, a knowing smile curling her lips.

"Ah." His brows lift in seeming surprise. "Well." He pauses, his gaze wandering over my face. "You look just like her."

Great. He realizes I look just like the woman he had a raging affair with. One that ruined his marriage and almost ruined Mother's.

I don't bother answering him, because what can I say? *Gee thanks, glad I remind you of your mistress?*

Talk about awkward.

We all settle back into our seats, Augustus sitting at the head of the table, as far away as possible from Sylvia. I watch as she tries to speak to him, and how he ignores her. Or says something dismissive, his gaze shuttered. Closed-off completely.

This is where Whit learned it from, I realize.

The server comes in to take our orders and Whit still hasn't entered the room. Augustus orders bottles of wine and a load of appetizers. Sylvie claps her hands in glee, while her mother chastises her ex-husband for ordering too many carb-loaded items.

I say nothing. A quiet little observer of the Lancaster family dynamics, trying to put it all together in regards to Whit and his behavior. He runs so hot and cold. He still wants me. I know that much after the blistering kiss we shared earlier today.

But his attraction toward me is always accompanied by anger and hostility. He's an absolute prick toward me most of the time. I don't understand it.

I still don't understand him.

"Oh, the birthday boy has returned!" Sylvia suddenly exclaims and I lift my head to see Whit standing in the open doorway, an absolutely stunning girl under his arm, staring up at him adoringly.

My stomach sinks and I keep my head averted. He brought a girl—and not Caitlyn. Of course he did.

"Father," Whit says, sounding surprised when he spots him. "You made it."

Augustus stands with a grin, going to his son. "Do you really think I'd miss my oldest child's eighteenth birthday?"

"I wasn't sure," Whit says truthfully, meeting his father half-way. He releases his hold on the girl and the two men embrace, slapping each other's backs in that purely male way. "I'm glad you're here."

"Happy Birthday, son," Augustus says sincerely. "I see you brought Leticia with you."

Dread consumes me. He's with Leticia. The girl who's been chosen as his future wife, like we're living in the middle ages.

"Hi, Mr. Lancaster," Leticia says sweetly, shaking Augustus's hand. "It's so nice to see you again."

"Lovely to see you too. Call me August. None of that mister talk. Always feel like my dad is nearby," he says jokingly, glancing around as if he's looking for him.

Leticia's tinkling laughter is, of course, delicate and pretty. Much like she is.

"Come, the both of you. Please sit down," Augustus says, taking over as host.

From the frosty expression on Sylvia's face, she doesn't approve.

"Your sister brought a friend with her," she says to Whit when he arrives at the table, gesturing toward me. "You know her, of course, since she attends Lancaster Prep. Summer." Her lips curl. "*Savage.*"

Whit turns his wide-eyed gaze upon me, his lips drawing into a thin line. "Barely," he bites out, his gaze flickering over me, as if I don't even exist. Typical. "Hello."

I nod toward him but otherwise don't say a word.

Conversation continues around me, but I don't hear it. I can't. All I can do is watch Whit out of the corner of my eye. He continuously sips from the glass of amber liquid he brought with him from the bar, his gaze on no one, anger radiating from him in palpable waves. It's as if no one else senses it though. Leticia makes a plate of appetizers for him like a good little girl-friend when they arrive, but he doesn't even touch them. She scoots closer to him, whispering in his ear, and his gaze drops to the front of her shirt, where it displays a healthy amount of cleavage. Her tits are enormous. Bigger than mine.

He touches her there, a casual caress, his fingers briefly skimming her skin, and seeing it jars me to my very core. I grab at the full wineglass sitting on the table in front of me and gulp from it, just before I push my chair back and stand, so quickly the chair clatters to the floor, effectively silencing everyone's conversation.

"Sorry." My cheeks burn with humiliation and I try to smile, but it just won't come. "I'll be right back."

I flee the room before anyone can say anything to humiliate me further, fully expecting Sylvie to chase after me, but thankfully she doesn't. I find my escape in the elegantly decorated ladies' bathroom. I stand at the sink, my shaking hands braced on the white marble counter, staring at myself.

What am I doing here? Why did I come? Did I really think Whit would be happy to see me? Clearly, I'm delusional. I should feign sick the moment we return to the house, and leave in the morning. They won't want me there if they believe I'm contagious.

Calmed by my new plan, I soap up my hands and wash them, turning away from the sink to dry them under the automatic dryer when I hear the door open and quickly close.

The quiet snick of a lock turning into place.

Glancing over my shoulder, I see Whit, leaning against the door. Watching me. Slowly I turn to face him, my heart racing, my chest heaving with every labored breath.

"What are you doing?" he asks, his voice deathly quiet.

"Washing my hands," I say calmly.

A flash of annoyance crosses his beautiful face. He's freshly shaven and smells crisp. Like fragrant fall air. If I could, I'd crumple to my knees in front of him and beg him to touch me again, but I refuse to be that sort of girl.

"You didn't tell me you were coming," he says, his voice flat.

"Sylvie invited me for the week. She wanted me to spend the holiday with her," I offer, but he holds up a hand, silencing me.

"You shouldn't be here."

His words are like a knife, carving into my stupid and always hopeful heart. You'd think I'd learn by now. "I know," I say, my voice trembling. "I'll leave in the morning."

We stare at each other, the silence, the tension growing between us, making it hard for me to breathe. He pushes away from the door, heading straight for me and I feel like a rabbit who's been ensnared by its prey. Stalking me as I stand rooted to the spot.

He crowds me, his big hands settling on my hips, his warmth seeping into me. My body lights up, responding to his familiar, devastating touch and I tilt my head back so our gazes meet.

"If I'd known you would be here, I would've never—"

Whit presses his lips closed, cutting off whatever else he was going to say to me. And I feel like I need to hear the rest of those words. I need some sort of confirmation that he doesn't mind finding me here.

But this is most likely wishful thinking on my part. He's not pleased by my appearance. I've probably ruined everything.

"What do you want from me?" I ask, feeling lost. Inept. Being around him, his family, I know I don't measure up. I'm no Leticia. I'm sure her family is prestigious, while mine is full of scandal. Shameful.

My mother had an affair with his father for God's sake. We're the epitome of scandalous.

A gasp escapes me when he grips my hips and pulls me to him. "Be my birthday present," he demands.

Before I can ask him what he means, his mouth is on mine, the kiss instantly deep. I moan when his tongue licks mine, his hands going to my ass and lifting, settling me on the edge of the counter. He comes to stand between my spread legs, breaking the kiss so he can stare at the space between us.

"I could fuck you right here," he says, cupping the front of my jeans, his thumb pressing against the seam. It hurts. It feels amazing. "You're at the perfect height."

My panties flood with moisture. I want him to fuck me right here. While his parents and the girl he's brought with him are in the next room. Waiting for us. "Please," I whisper and he smiles.

In less than a minute, his cock is out and my jeans and panties are down, bunched around my ankles, the marble cold against my butt. He slides inside of me with ease, his eyes falling closed as he pushes himself to the hilt, fitting his body to mine completely. I squeeze my inner walls around him, smiling when he groans.

Whit presses his forehead to mine, completely still, his cock throbbing inside of my body. I wait, suspended in time, unsure of what to do next. He sucks in a deep breath, licking his lips, and begins to move.

He fucks me in earnest. I grip his shoulders, watching him the entire time, completely fascinated by the myriad of emotions I see washing over his handsome face. It gets better between us every single time, I think, as I race my hands over his chest, wishing I was touching his bare skin. His movements become faster, the room filling with the scent of sex, and I moan softly with his every thrust. The drag of his cock in and out of my body makes my belly tighten and when I can't take it anymore, I close my eyes.

"Fucking beautiful," he mutters under his breath. "Addicted to your pussy, swear to fucking God."

He kisses me, his mouth frantic, his tongue insistent. I return the kiss, slinging one arm around his neck, anchoring myself to him. His breaths come faster and he ends the kiss, his face in mine, low grunts falling from his lips, matching the pace of his hips.

"Goddamn," he says just before he groans, spilling himself inside of me. I can feel his semen flood my body, our harsh breathing loud in the silent room, his body jerking with every wave of his orgasm.

Within seconds, he's pulling away from me, tucking himself back inside his pants and zipping them up. I sit there in a daze, watching him. My pussy throbs. I feel downright desperate to come, I'm so on edge. As if he can sense it, he reaches out and drags his fingers against my wet slit, stroking me once. "You want to come?"

I nod, wincing when his fingers toy with my swollen clit. "Yes."

He removes his hand from my body. "Later," he says with an evil grin.

Just before he turns and exits the bathroom without a backward glance.

THIRTY-ONE

SUMMER

AFTER I COMPOSE myself and wash my hands yet again, I return to the private room where the Lancasters are. I settle into the chair next to Sylvie on shaky legs, hoping no one can tell what just happened to me.

How Whit thoroughly fucked me in the women's bathroom, and then left me behind wanting more.

"I saved you some bread," Sylvie says, pushing the bread basket toward me. "Daddy over here was trying to eat it all."

He grins, chomping into a piece slathered with rich yellow butter. "You know your mother won't touch the stuff. Someone has to eat it."

Sylvie giggles. I smile, my gaze cutting to Whit and Leticia.

She's smiling up at him as he touches her cheek.

With the very hand that was just on my pussy.

I sit up straighter, wondering how in the world she can't smell me on his fingers. How can she not? Is she that oblivious?

God, he's such an asshole.

Reaching for my wineglass, I drain the golden liquid in three big swallows. Augustus immediately refills my glass, his warm gaze landing on me, his mouth curled into a barely-there smile. I sense his approval, and it makes me uneasy. So uneasy, I chance a glance in Whit's direction.

To find him already watching us.

I look away and drink more wine, needing it for strength. Sylvie is already buzzing, I can tell, but I'm sure it doesn't take much. She weighs nothing.

I'd like to be on my way to drunk too. So I can forget. Forget everything that's happened between Whit and me. He certainly forgets. He acts like I don't matter, which hurts. More than I'd ever want to admit. I'm sure he knows exactly what he's doing to me. How he destroys me with a few cutting words or rude gestures.

Such as not giving me an orgasm and then touching his date with my juices still on his fingers. Of course, I'm the one he just fucked in the bathroom, so I suppose I won this round?

I lurch forward in my seat as if I have no control of my body, the glass dangling from my fingertips before I bring it to my lips once more and sip more slowly. When I set the glass down, I see Sylvia watching me, her upper lip curled in barely restrained contempt.

"Sylvie, you shouldn't drink anymore," her mother scolds, her gaze cutting to her daughter. "You're on medication that could be dangerous if you mix it with alcohol."

"I'm not scared to die," Sylvie proclaims just before she downs the rest of her wine, setting the glass onto the table with a giggle.

"You need to watch yourself too, young lady," she says, her tone soft, but I hear the steel there, lying just beneath. "Don't drink too much."

"I'm good," I say to her, sounding like a drunk idiot already.

"Leave her alone," Whit snaps, making his mother's eyebrows shoot up. "Worry about your daughter."

"I'm fine," Sylvie says, giving him the finger. "Worry about *yourself*, brother dearest."

He bares his teeth at her in a feral smile, his gaze sliding to mine.

My entire body flushes hot, my core still throbbing. I'd do anything to drag him out of here and have him put his mouth on me. Specifically, between my legs.

He has a talented tongue and I miss it.

I glance over at their mother to find her smile is forced and she's glaring down the table at Whit. I'm sure she didn't approve of him telling her to leave me alone, but she doesn't acknowledge the comment at all. "Please say you and Leticia are *finally* serious about each other."

I'm still. Frozen. The entire table goes quiet at Sylvia's words, and Sylvie giggles uncomfortably before she murmurs, "Way to put him on the spot, Mother."

Leticia glances over at Whit and settles her hand over his. The very hand that touched me in my most intimate place only a few minutes ago. "He's not that easy to capture," she says with a light laugh, her gaze never straying from his handsome face. He doesn't smile at her in return. It's that same, stoic, unemotional expression. At least he treats all of us girls the same. "But I'll get him someday."

Oh this girl knows how to play it off. I could learn a thing or two from her, I'm sure.

Whit smiles tightly, his gaze alighting on every single person sitting at the table, lingering on me the longest. "I'm not ready to get serious yet, Mother. You know this. Stop putting me and Leticia on the spot. Let me enjoy my birthday dinner in peace."

"A mother can dream. After all, I'm the reason you have a birthday in the first place," Sylvia says, her voice sharp.

"You remind me of that almost daily," Whit says, equally sharp.

I duck my head, wishing I was anywhere but here. This sort of thing makes me uncomfortable. The jabs. The insults. Innuendo. My mother loves this sort of thing. She'd fit right in.

Well, Sylvia would probably stab her with a steak knife if my mother dared to set foot near her, so maybe not.

A wistful sigh escapes Whit's mother as she stares at the golden couple sitting next to each other. "You two are such a beautiful pair. I cannot wait to see the babies you'll make one day."

Despite the jealousy racing through my veins at her words, she's not wrong. Whit and Leticia are stunning together. They would make beautiful babies.

"Jesus, Syl," Augustus mutters under his breath.

She turns to glare at her ex. "What?" When he remains quiet, she prods him further. "If you have something to say, just say it."

"The kid barely turned eighteen. He's not thinking about marriage and babies yet. Give him a fucking break," he says.

Her eyes flare with irritation. Sylvie giggles again, covering her mouth with her fingers. The smile on Leticia's face is frozen in place. She'll do anything to guarantee a spot within this family, I realize. Including keeping her mouth shut.

I chance a look at Whit.

His gaze is still on me, his eyes hungry. He licks his lips, and my pussy clenches, as if his tongue made a direct hit.

This is going to be a long dinner.

WE'RE in the town car headed back to the Lancaster residence after our birthday meal is finally over, just Sylvie and me. She sits slumped in the back seat, giggling to herself as she taps away on her phone. I check my phone as well, contemplating sending Whit a message, but what if Leticia saw it? Would she be mad?

Would he?

Besides, what can I say? Come meet me in my room later? I don't think so. I don't want to look desperate. And right now, that's how I feel. Desperate. Needy.

Stupid.

I shouldn't have come here with Sylvie. It's too much, being with his family. Witnessing their dynamics, having to deal with him bringing another girl as his date. The girl he fully intends on marrying someday. He told me that himself.

Will she be here the entire week too? Will he sneak into her room and fuck her like he fucks me?

I can't bear the thought.

"What happened when you went to the bathroom?" Sylvie asks me out of nowhere.

I go still, searching for the right thing to say.

"Did you fuck Whit?" she continues.

I jerk my head in her direction to find her watching me, her lips curled into a suspicious smile. "No," I lie.

She tosses her head back and laughs. "Liar. You two are fucking on the low, and everyone knows it."

Alarm races through me at her words. "What do you mean, everyone?"

Sylvie holds her hand up in front of her and starts counting. "My father. My mother. Leticia. Me. The server. The bartender." She laughs, sounding pleased with herself. "It was super obvi, Summer. You ran out of the room when Whit was all over Leticia. Within a minute, Whit leaves too. You were both gone for a while. He returns first, his cheeks red and his hair mussed."

I don't remember touching his hair.

"And then you come slinking back in smelling of sin and you won't look anyone in the eye." Sylvie reaches out and pats my leg. "You're playing with fire, my friend. And you're going to get burned. My brother hurts people. I told you he has no heart."

"What do you mean?" I ask warily.

"Whit is a disaster. All Lancasters are disasters. We're cursed. We all hurt people eventually, even the ones we care about." She hiccups. Giggles. Squeezes my knee. "My father was eyeing you with interest, did you notice? God, he's such a perv."

I knew I wasn't imagining things. "I'm sure I just remind him of my mother."

"That's the problem. You remind him of his ex-mistress—no offense."

"None taken," I say.

"And you remind my mother of her too. I probably shouldn't have brought you," she says, casting a glance in my direction, her blue eyes wide. "They'll all come for you, at one point or another. Looks like Whit already did."

"You really think Leticia noticed?" I whisper, hating the shame that wants to wash over me.

"Ha! I knew you fucked him." Sylvie thrusts her finger in front of my face. I bat it away. "She's tolerated my brother's shit for years. Mother has put the two of them together since they were practically born. She wants them together so they can, and I quote, create a legacy."

Sounds like complete bullshit, but I say nothing.

"My daddy likes them younger and younger. You're perfect for him. He'd love to rub it in my mother's face that he had the mother and the daughter."

I wince. So gross.

"So I advise you to stay out of his way," she warns. "You definitely shouldn't let him get you alone anywhere."

Her warning is cryptic.

"I won't," I reassure her, taking a deep breath. "But what about Whit?"

"You've already dabbled with him enough that you have to know what you're dealing with," she says wryly. "It's your funeral if you continue."

We're silent for the rest of the drive, me staring absently at my phone and Sylvie lightly snoozing. It is my funeral if I continue what Whit and I are doing. He's treated me terribly, pretty much the entire time—but then there are the tender moments. The almost sweet moments. They're rare, a tiny glimpse of Whit without his usual brashness. His walls come down, offering me the vulnerable, raw version of this man who is so incredibly dark.

His darkness matches my own. We're kindred souls. We see each other for what we really are. Driven by our needs. Faintly disturbed. He disturbs me in the best possible way.

I hope I disturb him too.

By the time the car pulls around to the front of the house and stops, rain is falling steadily, and we dash inside, doing our best to avoid getting wet.

Sylvie clings to me as we approach the massive staircase, struggling to remain upright. She drank way too much tonight, and I remember what her mother said. About mixing alcohol with her medication. "Help me walk?" she asks.

"Of course."

I guide her up the stairs, which seem endless. Down the corridor leading to her bedroom, which takes forever. I help her get undressed and into bed, noting how thin she is despite everyone saying she's gained weight. She's light as air, her arms like sticks, and when I tuck her into bed, she grabs hold of my hand and squeezes it to her chest, keeping me there.

"Thank you for being a real friend," she murmurs, her eyes falling closed. I wonder how many real friends she's actually had. "I'm sorry I made you come with me."

"Maybe I should leave early," I start and she jerks on my hand, her eyes flashing open as she sits straight up.

"No. Please don't leave me. I know this was a terrible idea and you probably hate me for torturing you, but it won't be so bad. I promise. As long as we stick together, I can protect you. And you can protect me." She pats the empty side of her giant bed. "Sleep with me."

I don't want to. I want to be alone in my own room, with my own thoughts. She must see the hesitancy on my face because she pouts, her lower lip actually trembling, as if she might burst into tears.

"Please," Sylvie whispers.

Sighing, I climb into bed with her. We talk a little, but she falls asleep fast, and within minutes, she's lightly snoring. I watch her, with her angel face and thick black lashes. Her tangled blonde hair and rosebud lips.

Sylvie is beautiful. Fragile. Delicate. Like a doll. I want to protect her, but from what?

I slip out of her bed carefully so I don't disturb her and take off my shoes, carrying them in my hand as I tiptoe out of her room. I shut the door behind me, glancing to my left, then my right, pausing when I see movement in the shadows.

The sound of soft footsteps echo on the marble floor and Whit slowly emerges from the dark, his hands in his pockets, his gaze intent. He stops, there's at least twenty feet between us, but I can feel his presence as if he's actually touching me.

I stare at him, saying nothing. He does the same. I turn away and with my head held high, leave the family wing, heading for my bedroom. I cross past the stairs, and the massive portrait of the original Augustus Lancaster. He stares down upon me, those light blue eyes so like Whit's, and a shudder moves through me as I pick up my pace.

The portrait is intimidating. I don't like it. There are all sorts of portraits around the house, all of them foreboding and giving me the creeps.

I'm practically running down the hall by the time I draw closer to my bedroom, aware of Whit's presence. He stalks me like a cat in the jungle. Quiet. Patient. Confident.

It's unnerving.

I slip into my room and shut the door, but I don't lock it. Deep down, I want him to come in here. I want him to do whatever he wants to me, whenever he wants it. It's still his birthday. I'll give him whatever he wants, as long as he doesn't stay mad at me. I'll let him use me in any way possible for the entire week. I won't refuse him.

It's like I can't.

I push away from the door and go to my duffel, tossing it onto the bed and unzipping the top. I rummage through my clothes, finding the one pair of panties and matching bra set I own. I'll take a quick shower and change into this, I think, lifting my head when I hear the door slowly open.

Whit enters my room as if he owns it, which I suppose in a sense, he does. He closes the door behind him with a soft click, turning the lock into place. My heart rate ratchets up, my mouth going dry as I watch him. He leans against the door, much like he did earlier in the restaurant bathroom, contemplating me silently, his stance casual. As if he has all the time in the world.

I watch him in return, my underwear still clutched in my hand, my legs trembling at his nearness.

"It's your birthday too," he finally says and I blink at him.

I'd completely forgotten.

"Yes," I finally say. "It is."

"Was it everything you wished for?" he asks, his tone faintly mocking. He has to know that's the furthest thing from the truth.

"Not at all."

He approaches me, walking to the other side of the bed and pausing directly across from where I'm standing. "Were you hoping for a gift from me?"

"No." I actually laugh. He doesn't care enough about me to give me a present.

His gaze lands on the frilly cream lace I'm holding. "What are you doing?"

"I was going to take a shower."

"Go take one then," he says, inclining his head toward the bathroom.

"What are you going to do? Wait for me?" I ask incredulously.

"Is that what you want?"

I shrug.

"I need a yes or no answer, Savage." He pauses. "Do you want me to wait for you?"

"Yes," I whisper.

"Go take your shower then." He runs his hand along the sumptuous duvet cover. "Lock the door, though. There's no telling what I might do, knowing you're naked and rubbing soap all over your body while I wait for you."

My skin prickles at his words and I head for the bathroom, his next words stopping me.

"And don't bother with that."

I glance over my shoulder. "With what?"

"Whatever is in your hand. I want you completely naked when you come to bed."

"I thought it was *my* birthday."

"It's mine too," he says with a selfish smile. "But don't worry. You'll benefit from my wishes. Trust me."

If I only could trust him, is what I want to say.

But I don't.

THIRTY-TWO

WHIT

SEEING Summer sitting at the family table when I entered the room with Leticia by my side had shocked me. She was the last person I expected to be there. Though I should've known. I love my sister, but she's a secret schemer. She knew bringing Summer Savage for Thanksgiving break would tilt the entire family on its axis.

Mother is beside herself at having to host the daughter of her ex-husband's mistress for a week. Father is most likely interested in getting in Summer's pants. He already conquered the mother, why not conquer the daughter too? I know how he thinks. We're similar, him and me.

I won't let that happen.

And then there's me.

My earlier interactions with Summer at school had set me on edge. Made me angry. I'd fully planned on demanding Leticia give me a blow job tonight. I wanted her to prove she wants to be with me. She's agreeable, but we haven't done much beyond share an occasional kiss, and that was a while ago.

I wouldn't have fucked her. Not yet. But I would've probably imagined Summer's lips wrapped tight around my dick the entire time I was with Leticia.

Jesus, I have issues. All of them stem from my need for Summer.

Didn't have to demand a blow job from Leticia tonight though. Seeing Summer had done something to me. It did something to her too. She flew out of the room and I waited barely a minute before I went chasing after her. Like I couldn't resist.

I suppose I can't.

Fucking her in the bathroom had been necessary. Once I came inside her, I calmed. I could get through the torturous dinner. Deal with Leticia's fawning ways and whispery words of encouragement. The girl is dying for me to make it official. Her parents want us married as soon as possible, as does my mother. Father is the one who told me to pump the brakes and enjoy myself before I get tied down. Before we left the restaurant, he mentioned if I was really smart, I should try and marry for love.

Fucking hilarious, that guy.

I pace around the guest bedroom and go to the giant window, flinging back the thick silk curtains. It's coming down hard outside, the sound of the rain hitting the house loud in the quiet stillness. A streak of lightning crosses the sky, followed by a roll of thunder, reminding me of the night I protected Summer in the gardens, beat to shit by Elliot and his idiot friend.

That feels like a long time ago. A lot has happened since then.

Without thought, I take off my clothes, letting them all drop in a pile, until I'm completely naked. I go to the bed and slip beneath the covers, propping myself against the pile of pillows, the sheet and duvet draped across my lap. I wait patiently, watching the storm play out. Attuned to every sound that comes from behind the bathroom door.

The water shutting off. The glass shower door opening. I don't wait for girls. I've never done this before. They come to me, we fuck, it's over. For once, anticipation curls through me, settling in my cock, my balls. I'm going to push aside my needs tonight, and make this night good for her. I could tell she wasn't lying when she said she forgot it was her birthday. My family is overwhelming. I am overwhelming. Savage is strong, but not always.

She needs to learn how to be stronger.

The bathroom door finally opens, and she steps into the room, wrapped in a stark white terrycloth robe my mother leaves for all guests to use, like we're a goddamned hotel. Her hair is wet, her face scrubbed clean and her exposed skin is pink from the hot water.

I wonder if she's pink everywhere.

"I said I wanted you naked," I drawl, raking my gaze over her.

"I am." Her fingers play with the knotted belt. "I just didn't want to walk out of the bathroom naked."

I raise a brow. "Why not?"

A flash of lightning illuminates the room, followed by a shaking boom of thunder. "It's cold."

I flip the covers back on the empty side of the bed. "Join me." She makes to crawl on the bed, but I stop her. "Take the robe off."

She slowly undoes the belt, the fabric parting, offering me a glimpse of her naked form. I watch, completely entranced as she shrugs the heavy robe off, letting it fall to the floor, revealing herself completely.

"Do I pass inspection?" she asks saucily.

"Come here," I growl and she crawls under the covers, my fingers curling into her wet hair and pulling her to me so I can give her a scorching kiss. "What do you want?" I murmur against her lips.

She blinks open her eyes and pulls away. "What do you mean?"

"For your birthday. What do you want? I'll give you whatever you desire."

I think of all the things I want from her. I'd love for her to be on her knees for me and do whatever I demand of her. I'd love to take her ass. We've never done that, and I want to lay claim to the one spot no one else has ever touched. If she wants to sit on my face for hours, I'd comply, giving her so many orgasms she'd barely be able to walk after I was through with her.

"I want you to cuddle with me," she finally answers, her voice small.

"What?" I frown, not understanding.

She shifts away from me, shrugging one bare, smooth shoulder. My gaze drops to her tits. Her nipples are hard, begging for my mouth. "I want you to hold me."

When she remains quiet, I say, "And what else?"

"That's it."

"Really?" I sound skeptical.

"It's not always about sex, Whit," she says shyly.

"It is for me," I return.

"Is it really though?"

I snap my jaw shut, contemplating her. Wondering what's going on in that mysterious head of hers. She throws me for a loop every fucking time I think I have her all figured out.

It's maddening.

"You want to cuddle?" I say it like it's a dirty word.

She nods. "Please."

I open my arms to her and she comes to me, her fragrant curves nestled close, her head resting on my shoulder as she places her hand on my chest. I wrap my arms around her and hold her there, hating how fast my heart beats from her nearness. Hating more that she can hear it, thanks to her cheek pressed against the center of my chest.

"You're like a child, needing cuddles," I say with a faint sneer.

She laughs, her nails skimming my chest. "I'm the same age as you. Exactly."

"What time were you born?"

"Just after noon."

"I was born at four in the morning. I'm older," I say smugly.

"Not by much."

"By just enough."

"Mmm." She readjusts herself before she settles in further, her hair tickling my face, her nose in my neck. "You're so warm."

Her words spoken against my skin make me squirm. "You really only want to cuddle?"

"Isn't it nice?" she asks, her mouth moving against my neck. "We never do this."

"I don't like it." I stare at the ceiling, trying not to react to her touch. How she's practically draped across my body.

My cock reacts though. I'm rock hard and aching for her.

"Really?" She pulls away slightly so we can look into each other's eyes. Lightning flashes, silver streaking across her face and I notice the doubtful expression. "You hate this."

"I don't cuddle or snuggle or whatever the fuck you want to call it with any girl," I practically growl.

She leans into me, her mouth close to mine as she whispers, "You cuddle with me."

"Reluctantly."

"You're still doing it." She presses the faintest kiss to my lips and I immediately want more. "However reluctant you may feel."

"I'd rather do something else."

"So demanding."

"It's my birthday too."

"You made your offer, and now you have to stand by it." She sounds very pleased with herself.

No way can I admit how good this feels, having her lie with me, our naked bodies close. She tangles her legs with mine, before slinging one across me. The heat of her pussy presses against my thigh and my cock grows even harder. I want inside her. I'd love nothing more but to fuck her all night long.

Yet she seems perfectly content being with me and keeping it chaste between us.

"Are you officially with Leticia?" she asks out of nowhere.

I drape my arm around her shoulders, remaining silent on purpose. I want to torture her just as she tortures me. "We are not together, no."

"Do you want to be with her?" She asks this in the barest whisper.

An exhale leaves me as I ponder my situation with Leticia. "We've known each other forever. You know she's been chosen for me. It will happen between us, but not yet. I brought her tonight because I knew it would make my mother happy."

"Was she happy?"

"No. Because you were there."

"I know why she hates me. I get it." Summer traces my skin with her nails. Little circles. Straight lines. She's driving me insane. "So she wants you with Leticia based on her pedigree."

"Leticia is very nice," I say, wondering why the hell I'm defending my future wife to my current fuck buddy.

No. Summer is more than that. What we share...is hard to define.

"I'm sure she is." Summer doesn't sound jealous, which is surprising.

I hate seeing her even talking to someone else. I want to tear things apart—including the guys she speaks with who mean nothing to her.

"I don't know if I want to be with her for the rest of my life," I admit, running my fingers up and down her arm.

She curls her body into mine, smothering me with her warmth. Her scent. I inhale deeply like a junkie, chasing the high that only she gives me. "Have you been with her since—you've been with me?"

I could lie. I could destroy her with a few choice words and I'd still be able to have my way with her tonight. But I decide to tell the truth.

"No." I could tell her I've never been with her, but I decide not to.

She exhales shakily. "Have you been with anyone else?"

I think of the things I've said to her, just to hurt her. Just to watch the horror and pain flash in her eyes. I wanted to tear her down to make myself feel better, and did that really work?

"No," I repeat.

Her body seems to melt into mine and her hand drifts down, fingers dancing across my stomach. "I don't like the idea of you with anyone else."

"I fucking hate the idea of you with someone that isn't me," I say fiercely, my arm tightening around her shoulders.

Her fingers tease through my pubic hair, touching the base of my cock. "I know."

We're quiet as she plays with me, and I remain still. Letting her have her way with me. She firmly grips my cock, sliding her hand up and down my shaft, jacking me slowly and I close my eyes, breathing in her delectable scent. She does this for minutes, her hold loosening. Tightening. Her fingers tracing the flared head, smearing precum all over it.

And still I do nothing. I don't push. I don't demand.

I let her do what she wants.

Eventually she kicks the covers down, the cool air washing over our hot bodies and she releases her hold on me, my dick bobbing forward, toward my stomach. I watch as she streaks her sticky fingers across the flat plane of skin beneath my navel, her touch making my cock jump.

I want her mouth on me. I want inside of her. So fucking bad, I'm borderline desperate with need.

Summer touches my face, startling me, turning me to face her. I can smell myself on her fingers and she wraps those fingers around my nape, pulling my head down so our lips meet. I let her take the lead, the kiss soft. Playful. Languid. Her tongue sweeps into my mouth, searching, sliding against my own. We kiss like this for minutes, with no urgency. No insistence.

It's different, being with her like this. A slow wave of pleasure washes over me when she climbs on top of my thigh, straddling it. She rubs her pussy against me, riding my leg, her mouth fused with mine, our tongues dancing together. I reach for her, cupping one breast, thumbing her nipple. She whimpers into my mouth and I swallow the sound, running my other hand down her back, across her ass, pulling her tighter to me.

"See?" she whispers against my lips. "Cuddling's not so bad. It can lead to other things."

"Were you trying to prove a point?" I ask, nipping at her lower lip.

She smiles. "I was trying to show you that there's more to sex than just demands."

I feel as if I've been put in my place. My hands spring away from her and I rest them behind my head. She lifts up, her thighs still wrapped around mine, her hands braced on my chest. "Have your way with me," I tell her.

This moment reminds me of the night I told her to use me. When she grinded her pussy on my dick, and came all over me. God, she'd been so hot that night. She drives me out of my mind with lust when she does shit like this.

She's driving me out of my mind with lust right now, but in a different way. It's slower. More deliberate.

"I want you to touch me," she whispers, her eyes glowing when they meet mine.

"I want to be inside you," I whisper back.

Summer leans over me, her damp hair a curtain around my face as our lips connect. She straddles my hips, her pussy on my stomach, my cock probing her ass. It would take nothing for me to slip inside her body.

I lift my hips, seeking her. She scoots down, finding me, angling her torso so she slides down my length, until I'm fully inside her. She sits up straight, her ass on my balls, my dick throbbing inside her body and she watches me, her hands coming up to lift her hair, her back arching, thrusting her tits toward me.

Fuck, she's stunning. Gorgeous. I rest my hands on her hips as she starts to move. Hesitantly at first. Searching for her rhythm. I let her find it, wincing when she shifts, her inner walls squeezing, strangling my dick. I can't take my eyes off of her as she rides me, her knees pressed into the mattress, her hips lifting up and down. My gaze drops to where our bodies are connected and I watch in utter fascination as my cock disappears inside her body before it reappears, glistening with her juices.

"Whit," she moans, dropping her head back as she increases her pace, her hands falling to my stomach. She's making the bed bounce with her movements, the box spring lightly squeaking and I stare, helpless to her. Overwhelmed by her.

I always take command of the situation and she lets me. She's a willing participant every single time. But this...

This is different. This is *her* taking charge. Taking over. It's softer. Sweeter.

Like she is.

My grip tightens, my fingers pressing into her skin so hard, I'll probably leave marks. She's oblivious, lost in herself, lost in me and I see the transformation happen right before my eyes. The rosy flush that coats her skin. The little gasps and whimpers falling from her lips as she gets closer. She's lost in the sensations she's experiencing as she rides my cock hard. Fast. Her eyes are tightly shut in concentration as she strains toward it and I reach for her pussy, desperate to help her along.

I swipe her clit with a firm touch, her inner walls strangling me just as they begin to pulsate. She cries out, her body shuddering above mine, her pussy milking my cock. My chest tightens, the air leaving my lungs until I feel like I can no longer breathe and only when she collapses on top of me in a boneless heap does my orgasm wash over me, racking my body completely.

We lie there, our bodies still lightly shaking, tangled together, her hair in my face, in my mouth. My dick still semi-hard and inside her body. I'm covered in sweat. So is she.

Fuck.

Finally she lifts her head, a satisfied smile stretching across her face. I reach for her, brushing the hair away from her forehead, confused by the sudden tender feelings that fill me at seeing her like this. Her lush body sprawled across mine, her breaths matching my own as she watches me.

"Happy birthday," she whispers, dipping down to kiss me.

THIRTY-THREE

SUMMER

I THINK HE'S BAFFLED.

He certainly looks baffled. And still turned on, despite the orgasm we both just experienced. God, it had felt so good to take the reins and have my way with him. That he even allowed it is a huge moment for us. He doesn't seem comfortable in ever letting me have even an ounce of control when we're together like this. He's in charge.

Always.

The cuddling hadn't been a ruse either. I'd really wanted to just lie there with him and snuggle for a few minutes. Silly, I know, but who do I ever get to snuggle with? No one. No one has held me like Whit just did in so long. It felt good. Being in Whit's arms, wrapped all around him, felt...

Like I belonged.

With him.

He's currently frowning, his mind blown I'm sure, and I kiss him again, my lips clinging to his as I breathe in his breaths, inhaling him. Like I want to keep him forever.

"You confuse me," he murmurs against my mouth, his hands wandering, lighting me up despite what just happened between us.

"You confuse me too," I say, kissing him, parting my lips for his tongue's entry.

His hand clutches the back of my head, his fingers tightening in my hair in that familiar way of his. He's back. In command. In charge. His kiss is ferocious, his mouth demanding, his tongue thrusting much like his cock does inside of me.

He commandeers my body, taking over and flipping me until I'm lying on my back, his body pressed on top of mine. "Did you like it?" I ask him breathlessly.

"You drive me out of my mind." He thrusts against me, his mouth attacking my neck. My chest. My breasts. He sucks my nipple into his mouth, his hands wandering along my sides, and a wave of euphoria fills me at his touch, his damp lips and wet tongue. He lifts his head, his intense gaze meeting mine. "Watching you fuck me like that..."

I smile. It's true. *I* fucked *him*, and he's always the one who fucks me. The shift in power was deliberate. "You liked it."

"I fucking loved it." He grabs my hands and pulls them above my head, holding me captive as he stares into my eyes. "I don't want you to leave tomorrow."

I frown, my eyes fluttering closed when he thrusts his cock against me. He's already so hard again. A shift of our hips and he'd be inside me. "You said I should."

"I take it back." He kisses me, his mouth on mine as he says, "I want you to stay."

He enters me at the same time I open my eyes. A moan leaves me when he strokes, deep and slow, pulling almost all the way out before he slides back in. He keeps his pace lazy, doing to me what I just did to him and oh my God, it feels so good.

Whit keeps my arms pinned above my head with one hand, working his hips as he grips my side with his free hand. I wrap my legs around his waist, anchoring myself to him, sending him deeper. He changes positions, angling his body so he can hit a particular spot that has me seeing stars and his languid strokes are forgotten. He fucks me in quick, deep jabs, pounding me into the bed. The box spring squeaks rhythmically, the sound of our skin slapping together filling the room just before he goes completely still and spills inside of me with a deep, shuddery groan.

I don't come. I wasn't even close, but it doesn't matter. All I can think about is what he told me.

I don't want you to leave tomorrow.

I want you to stay.

And how good those words made me feel.

"WAKE UP SLEEPYHEAD!"

Something soft smacks me in the head, jolting me awake and I automatically jerk the duvet up, making sure I'm covered. A figure is standing by my side of the bed and I blink it into focus.

Sylvie. Bright-eyed and with a mischievous curl to her lips as she studies me.

I glance to my right, panic flaring inside of me at the thought of her finding me naked in bed with her brother but he's gone. I reach out, pressing my hand against the cold sheets.

He's been gone for a while.

"Reaching for your secret lover?" she asks, her tone knowing.

I ignore her question, flopping back onto the pillows, pushing my hair out of my face. "What time is it?"

"Almost ten. You must've been exhausted to sleep this long. Especially since you went to bed so early."

I don't bite at her baited statements. "I guess so."

"I thought you were sleeping with *me* last night." She offers up a mock pout.

"I was. But I left because you were snoring."

Her mouth drops open. "I don't snore."

I laugh. "Yes, you do."

"Oh." She frowns. "How unladylike of me."

I decide to give her a taste of her own medicine. "Hasn't Spence told you that before?"

Sylvie sniffs, her nose in the air. "I've not spent any amount of time with Spence that would offer him a glimpse into my sleeping habits."

"Such a pretentious way of saying you haven't slept with him yet," I tease. She bops me on the shoulder with the pillow I didn't realize she was still holding. "Come on, fess up. What have you and Spencer done, exactly?"

"Nothing. That's the problem. I want to do something, but he always resists," she says drolly. "I think he's terrified of my brother coming for him."

Whit is definitely terrifying. Though he wasn't last night, in my bed. He was almost...

Sweet.

"I see you getting all dreamy-eyed. Stop thinking about him." Another bop of the pillow, this time on top of my head. "You missed the family breakfast."

My stomach growls as if on cue. "I'm starving."

"We can grab something before we go shopping." She hesitates for only a moment. "While we were eating, Mother suggested Whit invite Leticia for Thanksgiving dinner."

My appetite leaves me. "What did Whit say?"

"He said no. He doesn't want her here." Sylvie plops onto the edge of my bed, making it bounce. "Then Mother suggested I send you home. Claims you make her, and I quote, 'uncomfortable.'"

My stomach twists into a painful knot. God, that woman is awful. Though I suppose I shouldn't blame her for not wanting the daughter of her former husband's mistress at her home for a fun-filled family holiday.

Talk about convoluted.

"Whit told her no. You're staying. They got into an argument." A little smile dances across her face. "Over you."

I remain quiet, taking her words in. I'm sure yesterday he would've fought for me to leave and Leticia to stay. What changed? One night of cuddling? Is that really all it took?

I find that hard to believe.

"Whit and I—"

"Are together," Sylvie finishes for me. "He also mentioned that to Mother."

"*What?*" I gasp, my eyes going wide. "He did not."

"He kind of did." Sylvie shrugs. "He said you were his guest too, and he refuses to send you back to school so you can spend the holiday alone. You're staying. He shut her down every time she tried to argue her point. It was rather amusing."

"I'm glad you enjoyed the moment," I say, my thoughts riotous. "Where is he now?"

"With our father. Whit just went to his office. He said they had some business to discuss." Sylvie's gaze is shrewd. "I'm thinking it has to do with you."

"Doubtful." I roll my eyes, refusing to get excited about any of this. Sylvie could be exaggerating. Whit might treat me terribly when we see each other next. That's his normal M.O. Passionate one minute, awful the next.

Why would he change?

"Do you want to go shopping with me?" Sylvie asks. "Or are you going to hang around outside Daddy's study and hope Whit comes out soon?"

She sounds vaguely jealous, which is a side of Sylvie I've never seen before. "I'm *your* guest," I stress. "And I'd love to go shopping."

Her smile is genuine. "Yay. Well, get ready, sleepyhead."

I realize she's fully dressed, while I am most decidedly not. "Um..."

"What?"

"I need a few minutes. I'm uh." I wave a hand at myself. "Not decent."

Sylvie laughs. "Why, are you naked under those covers, Summer?"

My cheeks grow warm. "Maybe."

"So he did sneak into your room last night." Sylvie rises to her feet, making her way to the door. "I asked him if he did, but he denied it."

"He did?" I ask, my voice small.

"Yes, but he turned just as red as you are now, so I knew he was full of shit." She glances over her shoulder. "I won't tell on you two. Your secret is safe with me."

I certainly hope so, I think after Sylvie leaves.

It scares me though, that she knows so much. She could tell his parents. Everyone at school. She knows what Whit and I are up to.

She could ruin my life with a snap of her fingers. Of course, Whit could ruin my life too, after reading my stupid journal that he refuses to give back.

I take the quickest shower ever and throw on some clothes, leaving my hair down and in its natural state, which is haphazard waves that I don't particularly like, but for some reason, today they look good. Though I know my mother has never liked my hair like this, I think as I apply a coat of mascara onto my lashes. She always wanted my hair perfectly straight, or perfectly curled.

But I'm not perfect. I've done things, said things that I'm not proud of, and that's okay. We make mistakes and we're allowed, because we're only human, right?

I blink at myself in the mirror, thinking of one mistake I made in particular. The fire that night.

It was all my fault. I'm the reason Yates and Jonas are dead. And while I don't necessarily mourn the loss of my stepbrother —and this makes me feel even worse than I already do—I do miss Jonas. He was a good man.

Good to me. And my mother, despite everything she did to him.

Standing up straight, I drop my mascara into my cosmetics bag and zip it closed, telling myself I need to stop thinking about... everything. There's nothing I can do to change what happened in the past. I have to live with it.

No matter how difficult that is.

Grabbing my coat, I barge out of my room and pull the door shut, stopping short when I see Sylvia Lancaster standing in the hall, almost as if she was waiting for me. Our gazes meet, her dark blue eyes narrowing as I draw closer to her.

"Good morning," I say in greeting, forcing myself to be friendly.

"Slept in late, I see," she says coolly.

I stop right in front of her, taking her in. She's draped in pale pink silk, and I wonder if she's going somewhere. I stand up a little taller. No way can I let her intimidate me. "I was tired."

"I'm sure. Considering you were with my son throughout the night." I open my mouth to deny it, but she cuts me off with a short shake of her head. "My son does what he wants, and he also does *who* he wants. It's no surprise to me that the two of you are—involved."

Her voice drips with disgust.

I don't know how to reply. She's rendered me completely silent, and from the pleased expression on her eternally pinched face, I can tell she's extremely happy about it too.

"You aren't the first, and you won't be the last, you know. Somehow though, you've convinced both of my children that they should spend time with you, when we know the truth," she says.

I'm taken aback at her vaguely referring to me as a bad person. "And what's that?"

"That you're a whore, just like you're mother." She raises one thin brow, waiting for me to deny it.

But I don't. What's the point? She's going to think what she wants.

"Normally, this sort of thing wouldn't bother me. My daughter bringing home her latest pet, who just so happens to be fucking my son. Everyone all twisted up in each other's lives, though I suppose it's perfectly normal. You're all in school together. You're an attractive girl. Why wouldn't my son be interested?

And Sylvie's starved for attention. Everyone else has grown weary of her little mind games, and you're fresh and new. Easily manipulated. It's written all over you, you know. They can see it." Sylvia's gaze rakes over me, and it's as if everything inside of me shrivels.

"That's not how it is," I say quietly, swallowing the sudden lump in my throat. "You don't understand."

"I understand perfectly," Sylvia says, her voice tight. "Your mother was a naïve cow too. Dazzled by my husband's looks and charm and wealth. My children are the same way. Charming. Beautiful. Just as my husband seduced her, Whit—and even Sylvie—seduced you as well. You're just too blind to see it."

"See what?"

"The Lancaster family use people for their personal gain. Their personal pleasure. Entertainment. You're just a little toy they'll soon grow bored with. They will chew you up and spit you out once they're finished with you, and they're getting close. Whit will eventually have to straighten up and do his duty with Leticia. She's going to marry him someday, you do realize this, don't you?"

I lift my chin. "Yes. Whit already told me."

Her eyes flicker with surprise, but otherwise there's no reaction. "Then you understand your place with him."

"My place?"

"Yes. You're *temporary*, my darling. A fun little affair to indulge in. The dirty little girl who lets him do whatever he wants to her whenever he wants, because heaven forbid he could ever ask the future mother of his children to do...whatever it is you two do behind closed doors." Her tone is snide. Knowing.

The blood drains from my face, my knees growing weak. My head spins and I brace myself, praying I don't faint. How does she know what Whit and I do? There's no way he'd tell her just how depraved our interactions are. But she is his mother.

Maybe she just knows.

"So have fun being his filthy mistress. Once he tosses you aside, Sylvie will do the same. She's loyal to her brother to a fault." Her smile is cruel as she starts walking, shoulder checking me as she passes by. "Have a lovely day shopping with my daughter."

I turn and watch her go; my lungs clogged with air. I feel like I can't breathe.

My phone buzzes in the back pocket of my jeans and I scramble for it, hoping it's Whit.

But it's Sylvie.

Where are you? Meet me downstairs, the car is waiting!

With shaking fingers, I tap out a response.

I'll be down in a minute.

She can wait. I have some searching to do first.

THIRTY-FOUR

WHIT

"GET me out of this deal with Leticia."

This is how I greet my father as I stride into his study. No *hey dad, can you do me a favor?* None of that casual, help me out shit.

I'm demanding, just like he is.

Augustus Lancaster is sitting behind his mighty desk, in his mighty office with the mighty view. The recently installed floor to ceiling windows are uncovered, allowing in plenty of light, thanks to the clear skies outside. It's a crisp fall day with the threat of winter just behind it. All of the snow from last week has melted, as if it never happened in the first place, but it's coming.

"Shouldn't you be talking to your mother about this?" he says casually, leaning back in his chair.

I stop in front of the sprawling cherry wood desk, bracing my hands on the edge of it. "She'll tell me no."

"And what if I tell you no?"

"You'd be more inclined to help me, since you were pulled into the same damn deal I'm about to find myself in," I remind him.

My grandmother chose Sylvia Whittaker out of all the other girls at my father's private school when he was eight. *Eight.* My mother was seven, a grade below him and supposedly as pretty as a picture thanks to her mama's good genes. She was rich as shit thanks to her father's side of the family. Even then, she had a cunning mind and a tongue like a viper. She hid all of her unbecoming traits though and eventually, as time went on, my father knew who he was dealing with.

And still he went through with it. They were married at this very estate, on a gorgeous summer day. My father looks blitzed in all the photos—the man had to get blindingly drunk in order to go through with it. My mother was radiant, her smile stretching from ear to ear. She was finally a Lancaster. Her ultimate goal, met at the tender age of twenty.

Their marriage was miserable from the get-go. Supposedly she was a cold fish. They were rarely spotted together the first five years of their marriage, much to her dismay. His father forced him to return to their home they shared, demanding he pretend they're a happy family or he'd cut off his inheritance.

It took them a couple of years, but I was finally born when my dad was thirty. He fucked her only because he had to. He needed heirs, and she could give them to him.

Her mother turned in the gynecological report, just like Leticia's did.

We're a match, but only on paper. As if we're animals to be bred together.

The mere thought of marrying someone I don't really want, and ending up with that person for the rest of my life, fills me with major fucking anxiety.

And fury. Plenty of fury.

"Lancasters have a duty to produce heirs." My father says this as if it's a rehearsed line, one he's been forced to say for years.

"We're not the fucking British royal family," I spit out. "The supposed Lancaster monarchy won't die off if I marry someone I actually love and want to be with."

"Love?" He scoffs. "You're only eighteen. What do you know about love?"

He's not fucking wrong. I don't know dick about love, thanks to my fucked-up family and my shitty morals.

Being with Summer last night threw me for a loop. For the first time, I acknowledged my feelings for her. Not out loud, and not to her face, but within myself. They've been growing, despite my resistance. It was bound to happen, with how much time we spend together. I could be as cruel and awful as I wanted, and she took it. She seemed to enjoy it. She likes being with me. Every other girl would tell me to go fuck myself if I talked to them like that. Treated them like that.

And it's not because Summer is a pushover either. She's anything but.

Last night had been a realization. This girl is under my skin. We're connected. We share the same birthday for fuck's sake. I don't want to push her away because of some sort of obligation I'm being forced into.

Fuck duty. I want to live my own life.

"I know enough that I don't want to marry someone who I don't care about," I finally say.

"Is there someone in particular you have in mind?" He lifts a brow. I know exactly who he's referring to, the prick.

I press my lips together, refusing to say her name. I'm not doing this because of Summer.

I'm doing this for myself.

"I'm sure she's a lovely girl, perfectly willing to do whatever you want." The pointed look he sends my way irritates the shit out of me. He's of course, talking about Summer. "But she is not worth dumping your entire future over."

"I'm not dumping my future. I'm making sure I don't get caught up in an arranged marriage that makes me fucking miserable for the rest of my life," I tell him truthfully.

Witnessing Summer interact with my family last night at dinner had also been an eye opener. She's genuinely close to my sister. She put up with the bullshit flirtation my dad threw her way and the icy coldness from my mother. She took it all with a barely-there smile on her face, impressing me.

Leticia deals with my family too, but my mother lavishes her with compliments because she's her choice. Father pretends she doesn't exist. Sylvie avoids her at all costs.

My life, my future that's been chosen for me, makes no damn sense. I don't have to marry Leticia and ensure the family bloodlines are well-kept. What a bunch of horse shit. Mother treats our lineage as if we're in medieval times, and why the hell is that even necessary?

It's actually...insane.

"Sit down," my dad suddenly demands.

I frown at him. "I can stand."

"No." His voice is cold. Just like his eyes. "I said, sit down."

I do as he demands, anger flowing through my veins freely. I don't like being told what to do, and my old man knows it.

"You're not going to throw away a carefully made plan because you've been getting extra good pussy lately. I won't allow it." His voice is firm. Unyielding. "Trust me. Ultimately, her mother wasn't worth the chase. I lost my entire marriage because of Janine. Don't go losing your head and thinking this girl is what you want. She's not."

"It's not about the girl," I say. "It's more about the girl opening my eyes and making me realize I don't need to follow the same path as every Lancaster who came before me. I bet ol' Augustus the first didn't let his mother choose his future bride for him when he was a kid. I bet he lived his life and did whatever the hell he wanted. He eventually fell in love and got married like normal people do."

"We're not normal people any longer," he says drolly.

"Right. We're people with a shit ton of money and a fuck ton of drama that comes with it. Those are the only things I can think of that makes us not normal people." I fall back into my chair with an irritated sound. "I don't want to marry Leticia."

"We're not asking you to marry her *now,* son."

"I don't want to marry her now, or five years from now, or even twenty years from now. I don't love her," I stress.

"You barely know her."

"I know enough that I don't want to be with her. I'm sure she doesn't want to be with me either. And if she does, it's only because it's been drilled in her head that it's the right thing to do. She doesn't know me. She's probably not even attracted to me."

"You're a Lancaster. Trust me, you're attractive to her," he says with a chuckle.

"Only because of our money." I jump to my feet, letting my annoyance fly. "You're treating this like one big joke, when it's my *life* we're talking about here."

"And it's such a bad life you have, no? Oh wait, you have everything you could ever want. All the money in the world. You don't have to lift a finger for the rest of your goddamned life, and you're worried about your future bride? Who, I might add, is a very attractive young woman who will tolerate all of your bullshit with a smile on her face. Your only requisite is you must fuck her and make pretty Lancaster babies. That's it." He scowls at me. "Big fucking deal, son. Big. Fucking. Deal."

"You told me I should wait it out and marry for love, just last night," I say, my voice faint, my future flashing before my eyes. Boring. Cold. Just like my parents.

He frowns, as if trying to recollect what he said. "I don't remember saying that, and even if I did, I didn't mean it. I was drunk."

"Isn't that when we're being our most truthful?" I ask, trying to grasp onto something. Anything but my stark reality.

He sighs. "You caught me in a vulnerable moment. Love is for fools. Treat your marriage like a business deal, and it's a lot easier."

My head spins. No fucking way. I won't do it.

"I'm. Not. Marrying. Her," I say between clenched teeth.

My father's eyes narrow as he watches me. "Just because you turned eighteen yesterday doesn't mean you get to suddenly control your every move. You still have obligations."

"Like what? Marrying a complete stranger when I graduate college? Sounds like absolute bullshit to me." I tap my chest with my index finger. "I have money. Money you don't control, and you can't touch. And that infuriates you, doesn't it? When you turned eighteen, all the money was still under your father's control. Lucky for me, my mother comes from a wealthy family as well."

"Not as wealthy as a Lancaster."

"What the fuck ever. This song is completely overplayed. I'm not doing this." I turn and head for the door, my father's words stopping me cold.

"You're going to eventually marry Leticia," he says. "Whether you like it or not. You don't have a choice."

I glance over my shoulder. "That's the difference between you and me, Dad. Because we always have a choice. You just didn't see yours."

THIRTY-FIVE

SUMMER

"YOU DON'T THINK it's too much?" I stare at my reflection in the mirror, turning this way and that. We're in Sylvie's room, getting ready for a party that one of the neighbors is throwing tonight.

And by neighbors, I mean some giant palatial estate like this one, and there will be hundreds of people there, most of them close to our age. There will be booze and drugs and things will no doubt get out of control. Sylvie is beside herself in glee over all the potential this party has tonight.

Potential drama, I'm sure.

And one thing this dress will bring is major drama.

"You're covered," Sylvie says reassuringly, moving to stand right next to me so we can both stare into the mirror.

"It's super short."

"You have long legs. They look even longer in that dress." She smirks. "At least your tits aren't hanging out."

"Right, because the entire back is open instead. No biggie." I turn to the side, sinking my teeth into my lower lip as I contemplate myself in this dress. One wrong move and I'll expose side boob. My gaze meets Sylvie's in the mirror. "It's too much, don't you think? I want to make a good impression."

"All the girls will be wearing dresses that are too short or their tits will be falling out of the top," Sylvie says, rolling her eyes. "Don't worry about it. Besides, who are you there to impress?"

Easy for her to say. She grew up in this atmosphere, with these people. Her position among society and her friends is solid. Me? I'm the girl no one knows. Once they figure out exactly who I am, they'll be shocked to see me hanging out with the Lancasters.

But I'm the one who also bought this burnout black velvet patterned dress, thinking it was a solid choice. While it felt like the right purchase when we were in the store, now I'm worried.

Too late for that, I guess.

We finish getting ready. Sylvie's dress is a dark burgundy velvet, form fitting like mine, but with spaghetti straps and a low neckline. My tits would actually be falling out of that dress, but Sylvie is smaller than me and carries it off perfectly. I curl her hair and then she straightens mine, and we both put on heavy eye makeup, with lots of dark liner and shadow.

"Going for the sexy, smoky look," Sylvie says as she snaps her Chanel eye quad shut and reaches for a nude lip liner. "Pale lips though, or it'll be too much."

I follow her lead, applying a light pink lip gloss to my pursed lips before I check out the finished product.

Not bad, I think as I take myself in.

"You look amazing," Sylvie tells me, her voice sincere.

"So do you," I say.

"All the boys at the party will lose their minds when they see you. They love fresh meat," she continues, making me laugh nervously.

"I don't know about that." I fidget with the hem of my dress, uncomfortable at being called fresh meat. And there's only one boy I'm interested in. "Is Whit coming with us tonight?"

"He said he was," Sylvie answers, sounding bored. She doesn't even look at me. "I texted him earlier."

I haven't seen Whit all day. Not even a glimpse of him. After what happened last night, it feels like there's been a major shift between us. Like maybe we could acknowledge that we're...

Together.

Then again, after not seeing him all day long, I'm now completely unsure and annoyed with my insecurities. Or I'm just reading too much into our so-called relationship in the first place. We don't actually have a relationship. He's just using me for whatever reason. Though I definitely know it has nothing to do with my journal or getting revenge on my family because of my mother's affair with his father.

It's about us. And how we're drawn to each other, despite everything.

"We should go," Sylvie says, interrupting my thoughts. "It's already almost nine."

"When did the party start?" We had a late lunch and I should be hungry, but nerves killed that vibe.

"Eight, but no one shows up on time." Sylvie grabs her phone and texts someone, receiving a reply almost immediately. "Whit says he's ready too. We'll meet him downstairs."

Nerves now threaten to swallow me whole.

"Can I leave my stuff here?" I wave at my cosmetics bag, and my phone sitting next to it.

Sylvie frowns. "You're not taking your phone?"

"Where would I keep it?" I point at myself. This reminds me of our conversation on Halloween, which was not a good night for me.

I shove all of those unpleasant memories into the far recesses of my brain.

"True that. I'm leaving my phone too."

We exit her room and Sylvie grabs my hand before we start down the hall, stopping me. "Spence might show up tonight."

I raise a brow. "Your Spence?"

Sylvie scowls. "He's not mine. He doesn't belong to me."

"Right, he's just completely hot for you and dying to get with you," I tease.

Her scowl disappears, replaced by a sly smile. "Think he'll like the dress?"

"He'll freaking love it," I say firmly as we approach the staircase.

We pause at the top of the stairs and I see Whit standing down in the foyer, waiting for us with an impatient expression on his handsome face.

My breath catches in my throat at first sight of him. Wearing a black suit that fits him to utter perfection with no tie, his pale gray shirt unbuttoned at the neck. He's frowning as he types something on his phone, glancing up when he hears the click of our heels on the marble floor.

"Brother dearest, we're ready," Sylvie announces, shoving me slightly so I have no choice but to walk down the steps first, alone.

Whit's gaze never strays from me as I make my way down the stairs. The stilettos I'm wearing are high, but somehow I keep my balance, and I approach him with a faint smile on my face, fighting the nerves that make my stomach churn.

"Hi," I murmur.

He scowls, his voice low as he asks, "What the fuck are you wearing?"

His tone renders me completely still, and we stare at each other as Sylvie bounds down the stairs.

"You don't like it?" I whisper just as she approaches.

"We'll discuss it later," he snaps, going to his sister and offering his arm. "Let's go, Syl."

I follow behind them, trying to ignore the wave of disappointment threatening to overtake me. Why does he make me feel like this? Like all I do is fuck up every time I'm in his presence? It's maddening. *He's* maddening.

We climb into the back of the town car, the three of us occupying the passenger seat with me in between them. I'm pressed up next to Whit, absorbing his warmth and I wish I could lean into him. Beg him to tell me where I went wrong with my dress choice.

I thought for sure he'd like it.

He presses his thigh against mine for the entire drive, his heat seeping into me and making my blood hot. Sylvie chatters nonstop, oblivious to Whit and mine's quiet regard. The tension between us ratchets up. High. Higher. Until I can barely breathe.

Within minutes we're pulling into the front of the gorgeous estate and Sylvie is reaching for the door handle to get out of the car.

"We'll be out in a minute," Whit tells her, grabbing my arm to keep me from scooting across the seat and out of the vehicle.

Sylvie climbs out, turning to bend down and peer into the car, watching us with a frown. "If you say so."

She shuts the door, the car silent save for my shaky breaths. The privacy window is up, so the driver has no idea what we're doing and when I chance a glance at Whit, I find he's already watching me, that ever-present frown on his too handsome face.

"You're showing too much skin," he says, cutting right to the chase.

Relief floods me. I thought he was angry with me. And I don't think I can bear that. Not after what we experienced together last night.

"I'm pretty well covered up," I protest and he shuts me off with a look.

"Not here." He slips his hand behind me, his palm pressed against my bare back. "And definitely not here." He touches my thigh, the tips of his fingers slipping beneath the hem of my dress. A soft gasp escapes me when he slides his hand toward the inside of my thigh. "You're not wearing panties either."

"I-I couldn't. I didn't want panty lines to show." I close my eyes when his fingers gently brush the spot between my legs. "No one will know."

"I'll know." He strokes me, his fingers dipping between my lower lips, finding nothing but liquid heat. "Fuck, Savage. You're drenched."

I spread my legs, thankful for the dress's stretchy material. "Don't stop," I murmur, throwing my head back as he continues to stroke me. The wet sounds reach my ears and I'm not embarrassed. Not at all.

I'm aroused. Painfully so. I've missed him. Just having him look at me sets my skin on fire. The way he watched me as I walked down the stairs had nearly been my undoing.

And now here he is, stroking me as if he owns me. Commands me.

Which he does.

"You wear this dress for me?" he asks, his voice deep. Rumbling in his chest. He pushes a finger inside me and my mouth falls open when he strokes me deep. "Huh? Did you buy this for me today?"

I nod, a moan leaving me when he adds another finger to the first. "Do you like it?"

"I fucking hate it. I don't want anyone else to see you in it." He finger fucks me, his thumb pressing against my clit as he drives me wild with his seeking fingers. I ride his hand like the shameless girl I am, seeking the release I know he's going to give me.

"No one will touch me tonight," I tell him, reaching for his wrist so I can hold him to me. "I won't let them."

"You're damn right they won't. But they'll look at you. They'll all see how fucking gorgeous you are." He leans in, his mouth right above mine. "You want them to look at you, don't you?"

I crack my eyes open to find his icy gaze on mine, heat flaring in the blue depths. "I don't care about anyone else seeing me."

"Really." His voice is full of doubt, and I hate that.

"Only you." I touch his face. Streak my fingers down his cheek, my touch gentle.

He ducks his head away from my fingers and removes his hand from my pussy. I literally cry out at the loss, aching with need. With hurried movements, he undoes his belt, unsnaps and unzips his trousers and slips them along with his boxers down his legs, until they puddle around his ankles. I watch as he wraps his fingers around his shaft and begins to stroke.

"Come here," he demands and I go to him, falling to my knees on the floorboard of the car, suddenly greedy for him. Ravenous. I wrap my lips around the head of his cock and swallow as much of him as I can before I release him, sticking my tongue out so I can lick the veiny length. He doesn't look away as I suck and lick, tracing the flared head with my tongue, lapping at the precum leaking from the tip.

"Fuck me," he says, his fingers gripping my hair tightly, his gaze never straying from my mouth and what I can do with it. "Suck it."

I suck him deep. As deep as I can. He lifts his hips, the head bumping the back of my throat and still I take it. I push his hand away and wrap my fingers around the base, guiding him, keeping my rhythm as I bob up and down on his cock. His entire body quickly grows tense and I know it won't take long for him to come.

But he rips himself out of my mouth, our ragged breaths filling the steamy confines of the car as we stare at each other.

Without a word I climb on top of him, straddling his hips before I sink myself onto his thick cock.

Our moans mingle in the air as I begin to ride him. He slips his hands around me so they settle on my bare ass, guiding me, holding me. I lean into him, pressing my mouth to his, losing myself in his delicious kiss. Our tongues dance and lick, a whimper sounding low in my throat. This is what I've missed all day. Being with him. Having him inside me. I want him all the time.

Every single minute.

We don't last long. We're both too keyed up. I tumble first, headlong into my orgasm, the shudders taking me over, my inner walls milking the orgasm right out of him. He falls quickly after, his mouth on my neck, his hands still gripping my ass, kneading my flesh as he holds me to him and spills inside of me with a shudder.

I clutch him close as we catch our breaths, his face against my neck, his cock still inside me. Until finally, we pull away from each other, and I shift to the side so I'm sitting on the seat next to him.

"Keep me inside you," he says, grabbing my hand and pressing it against my pussy before he lets me go.

I can feel his semen drip onto my fingers and I lift my hips, trying to keep it inside me, but it's no use.

"That's...impossible," I say, watching as he tucks himself away and zips himself back up. He runs his fingers through his hair, sending me a look.

"Nothing is impossible if you want it bad enough," he whispers, ducking his head so his mouth brushes mine as he speaks. "I want to watch you walk around the party tonight and know that my cum is dripping down the inside of your thighs. I want people to smell it on you when you stop and talk to them. I want people to know you just got fucked and you belong to someone else. To *me*. Do you understand?"

Just like that I want him again. How does he do this? With just a few words?

His hand comes up to grip my chin, his fingers pressing as he forces me to look at him. "Do you?"

I nod, my heart heavy in my chest as I whisper, "Yes."

"Good." He kisses me, and it's soft and sweet and completely unlike our usual kisses. I want him to kiss me like this forever. "Get out of the car."

I do as he says, always the good girl for Whit. I climb out of the car, feeling the unmistakable sensation of his cum leaking out of my body, coating the inside of my thighs. I don't do anything about it. Instead, I walk up the steps, putting extra swish in my hips as I do, knowing Whit is right behind me, staring at me the entire time.

I hope he likes it. Even more? I hope he can smell himself on me.

He's marked me. Like I'm his territory.

And I don't mind. Not one bit.

THIRTY-SIX

WHIT

I'M FUCKED. I don't know when it happened, or even how exactly, but I am so far gone over this girl. I don't even know what to do with myself anymore. Or with her.

The party is a complete rager, the house packed with people, most of them I know, or at least know of. Everyone here tonight is around my age or a little bit older. Don't think there's one person in attendance that's over thirty.

Meaning there are drunk teenagers everywhere, openly doing drugs. Passing blunts, hovering over a mirror snorting coke—how eighties of them—and I swear to fucking God I saw a small group in the shadows, shooting up.

Stereotypes exist for a reason. We are definitely rich kids with too many fake friends, as Frank Ocean says in his epic song.

"Whit."

I turn to find Spencer approaching me, a giant smile on his face, his eyes glazed over. He's either drunk or high—or maybe a combination of both.

"What's up?" I ask him. "I thought you were in the city for the week."

"Found out about Leighton's party and had to show." Spence shrugs.

Leighton Michaels. Hottest girl from Newport. Graduated from Lancaster last year. Yes, I fucked her. Only once though. She keeps that pussy on lockdown most of the time, and honestly?

It's not that special.

"You got such a thing for Leighton you had to rush right over?" I ask, raising my brows. Who hasn't sometime in their life?

"Nah. I was bored. Knew you would all be here tonight," Spencer says, glancing around the giant drawing room we're currently standing in. "Have you spotted Dean yet?"

"I haven't seen him, but I only just arrived." After thoroughly fucking Summer in the back of the town car.

I can still smell her. Taste her. The feel of her pussy gripping my dick, Jesus. I can't get enough of her.

It's worrisome.

"Your sister around?" He does his best to keep his tone casual, but I know the truth.

Spencer has it bad for Sylvie, and I think she feels the same way about him. And while I'm not one hundred percent approving of this relationship, I can't stop her from going after who she wants.

I can threaten Spencer to treat her right, though, which I already have. He blows me off every time I bring it up, and he's about the only one who could get away with that.

So I leave the topic alone. Sylvie's a big girl. I've come to terms with the idea of her and Spencer together. But if that asshole breaks her heart?

I'll fucking destroy him and he knows it.

"She's here," I say drolly as I glance around, trying to spot her blonde head. "Not sure where though. She's probably with Summer."

"Savage?" He sends me a questioning look and I nod. "What the fuck is she doing here?"

"Sylvie brought Savage with her for Thanksgiving as her play-date," I answer.

"More like *your* playdate. Or plaything," Spencer says with a chuckle. It fades when I send him a dirty look. "What? It's true. We all know you're fucking her."

"I am," I admit, shocked that I said it out loud. "But it's nobody's business but ours."

"I don't care what you do with her. I'm not interested so have at it," Spence says.

"You better not be interested," I say, my threat only mild. "You saw what happened to Bryan."

"Right, and Elliot. He was a part of our friend group, man," Spence says. "He was about as close as he could get to you."

"He was a dickbag who jumped my ass," I remind Spence, who's smart enough to shut the fuck up. "Don't defend him."

"Hope that pussy is worth it." Spence shakes his head. "I need a drink. See ya later?"

"Sure." I watch him go, not caring that he left. My head is too full of thoughts of Summer, and what I've done for her. What she's done for me. What I still have on her.

Like that stupid fucking journal I don't give a rat's ass about anymore. I should give it back to her. What if it falls into the wrong hands? From what I've seen, her biggest secret is the relationship between her and Yates.

Which is all sorts of fucked, but I can't judge her for it. I've done some messed up things in my life, just as she has.

Maybe that's why we're so—perfect together. Because we are. I can admit this. I'm all sorts of fucked up and so is she. I'm mean to her and the girl likes it. She gets off on it. I call her a whore and she takes it as a compliment.

But she's my whore. No one else's.

I make my way around the cavernous room, stopping to talk to people I know, vaguely or otherwise. Girls smile and flirt but I keep moving. I'm not interested, my thoughts consumed with only one female who's here tonight.

Where the hell is she anyway?

I search the lower level of the house, where the party is. There are people spilling out of every single room. Lingering in the corridor that leads to the private wing. So much laughter and food and drink. I feel like I'm standing alone among the party-goers. An observer who can't participate.

My head is everywhere but here. I think of the earlier conversation between my father and me. It's not like I want to stay with Summer forever—hell, I don't know what I want—but being with her has made me realize that I don't want to end up like my parents either. Bored and unhappy, and in search of something else with someone else. Fuck that.

I'm just never getting married.

"Whittaker!" the hostess says when she spots me, pulling away from a group of women to come over to me, a big smile on her pretty face. "I didn't expect you to show up."

"You're having the hottest party over break," I tell her as she wraps me up in a quick hug. "Why wouldn't I be here?"

"I should've known." Leighton steps back to take me in. "I saw your sister a few minutes ago. She's looking...thin."

"She's had some health issues." I'm vague because it's none of Leighton's business and besides, Sylvie's issues are vague. I don't understand what's going on with her, and Sylvie doesn't talk about it much beyond telling me she's going to die.

"She told me she's staring at her last days, and I quote." Leighton appears amused. I'm sure she doesn't believe Sylvie.

I don't really either, though I suppose I should. But she's always been fascinated with death, ever since she was a little kid. Lately she's been saying she's going to live fast and die young.

Couldn't we all claim that? Every single person in this fucking estate is living fast and could die young.

"Don't listen to her," I say dismissively, not wanting to talk about my sister. "How are you?"

"I'm great. Harvard has been...amazing." She smiles. Her daddy donated a quarter of a million dollars to the famed institution so, of course, she got in. "Where did you apply?"

"A few colleges," I say and leave it at that. I'm not wanting to discuss my choices because I don't want to jinx myself. What if I don't get in?

What the hell am I saying? I will get in wherever I want to go. I'm a fucking Lancaster. And if my grades aren't good enough, then I'll buy my way in.

"A few colleges," she says lightly, mimicking me. "Whatever, Whit. I'm sure you'll end up at Harvard. With me."

"Who says I want to go to Harvard?" I'd prefer to go to a college somewhere on the west coast. Stanford is my first college of choice, with USC a close second.

"We could be the golden couple on campus." She takes a step closer, rubbing her body against mine. "We always did go well together."

What the hell is she talking about? We flirted for a year and fucked once. She was too much effort for very little payback. No thanks.

Glancing around to make sure no one sees us, I settle my hand on the small of her back and lean in to whisper, "I already have someone."

Leighton laughs, the sound tinkling and light. Like I'm a big ol' jokester. "If you're referring to Leticia, please. That girl will sit and wait for you in the wings for years. Her parents are dying for you to marry her. She'll do whatever it takes to make them happy."

"Do you actually know Leticia?" I ask, raising a brow.

Her smile is sly. "Darling, Leticia is here. Coked up in my bathroom upstairs."

I'm fucking floored. "Leticia does coke?"

Leighton laughs. "She does more than coke, if you want me to be honest. But you'd think you'd already know, considering she's your future bride."

"Not any longer," I admit, hating that I said it the moment the words leave me.

Leighton has a big mouth. She'll tell everyone.

"Oh really? And does Leticia know this?"

"No, and I'd appreciate it if you didn't tell her." I give her back a rub before I drop my hand. "Be a friend, would you?"

"A friend? I would never call us that, Whit. Lovers? Briefly, yes. But friends? No." She steps in closer. "I can keep a secret though. If you want to sneak off and...catch up."

I'm not even tempted. The last thing I want to do is find myself caught up in Leighton's web. The girl is gorgeous, but toxic.

"Gonna have to pass," I tell her.

"Oops. Not sure if I can keep your secret then." She gives me the doe-eyed look, her glossy lips formed in a pout. "Might have to go check on Leticia right now. I'm sure she'll need consoling, since her future has been suddenly snatched away from her."

She starts to walk away and I grab her arm, stopping her. "Help a friend out."

"*You* help a friend out," she tosses back at me, yanking her arm out of my grip. "Come on. For old time's sake."

"Like I said, Leighton. I have someone," I remind her, my gaze scanning the area yet again.

But Summer is nowhere to be found.

"When has that ever stopped you before, hmm?" She presses herself against me again, her hands landing on my shirt front, her fingers stroking my chest. "Let's go to my room. I remember you being exquisitely talented with your tongue."

"I'm not eating your pussy," I tell her flatly, which only makes her laugh harder.

"God, Whit. Have a little class." She stands straighter, reaching up and brushing her fingers along my jaw. "Fine. Maybe I don't want you to eat my pussy. Maybe I want you to fuck me against a wall. I also remember you always did like it a little rough."

Nothing is happening down below, despite her offers. I could take this girl into the nearest empty room with a lock and fuck the shit out of her. A year ago, I would've, no questions asked. Hell, six months ago, I would've done it.

I can't now though. I won't cheat on Summer.

Jesus, listen to me. We're not together, but I can't stand the thought of being with someone else. Worse?

I absolutely cannot bear the thought of Summer being with someone else. Just imagining her with another guy makes me want to tear something apart.

Namely the faceless guy she might be with.

Clearly I've got problems. All of them having to do with the beautiful, irresistible Summer.

"What do you say, Whit?" Leighton purrs, cozying herself up against me. "You in? It'll be our little secret."

I rest my hand on her waist, about to shift her away from me when something catches my eye. More like someone.

Summer. Standing only a few feet away. Watching me with sad eyes.

Just before she turns and runs.

THIRTY-SEVEN

SUMMER

I DON'T EVEN KNOW where I'm going in this gigantic, gaudy house, but I know I need to get far, far away from Whit, after what I just witnessed.

Whit wrapped up in a girl. Leighton Michaels, who just so happens to be the owner of said gaudy house. She's stunning. Goes to Harvard. Has a huge social media following and is seen at all the top fashion shows. She dresses impeccably and has a carefully cultivated image. She is better than me by leaps and bounds.

Like...I can't even compete.

I hurry up a back staircase, my heels clacking loudly against the marble steps, but I don't care. I'm sure he gave up chasing after me real quick. Why does it matter?

Why do I matter? I don't. I'm sure I don't.

I find a closed door and I test the handle, pushing my way inside with ease. I slide my hand on the wall until I find a light switch and turn it on to find I'm in a nondescript bedroom. There is literally a bed, a dresser and a single bedside table with a lamp. That's it. It looks like a freaking jail cell compared to the opulence I've seen in this house.

Probably a room for someone on staff. Rude of me to think, but most likely true. People as rich as Leighton Michaels' family have plenty of staff, and don't offer them much luxury.

I collapse on the edge of the bed and wipe the back of my hand against my eyes, sopping up my tears. Why am I even crying? I knew this would happen eventually. He always implied he couldn't be loyal. Oh, he expected me to not even look in another guy's direction but he could fuck whoever he wanted.

Looks like he finally found someone else.

Fresh tears start and I cover my face. After what happened last night. Earlier. I guess I expected more, which is foolish of me considering nothing really happened. There have been no declarations of love or even caring. Nothing like that because I don't matter to him. Not like that.

I'm an idiot. A fool to think I could fit in with these people.

Sniffing loudly, I drop my hands. Wipe at my tears before I rub my damp hands on the comforter I'm sitting on. I glance around the room, wishing I had my phone so I could text Sylvie or even better? Call an Uber and get myself out of here.

But where would I go? I don't want to go back to the Lancaster estate, but it's not like I have a choice.

I wish I could find Sylvie. Earlier when Spencer approached and I saw the look on her face when she saw him, I decided to give them a little privacy. I set off in search of Whit and boy, did I find him.

With a beautiful woman wrapped all around him, looking ready to devour him whole. He wasn't pushing her away either. He was looking at her with an almost pleading expression, and at the last second, he glanced up, his gaze meeting mine. I saw the shock there. And the guilt.

Busted.

He's the worst. Seriously, why did I think he could be faithful? He has no reason to be. I'm nothing to him. While he's become everything to me.

I hate myself for caring so much. I really, really do.

Sighing, I rise to my feet and make my way to the door, opening it slowly and peeking outside to see if anyone is in the hall. With the coast clear, I step out of the room and carefully shut the door, glancing to my right to find someone emerging from the room next to mine. I come to a complete stop, my heart racing at getting caught.

By a boy who looks about my age or a little older, with a curious expression on his face when he spots me. Dark, longish hair. Pouty lips. Fashionable black glasses. He's clad in dark rinse, stiff looking jeans and a tweed jacket slung over a black polo shirt. Terrible fashion. Only someone who doesn't give a damn and is ultra-rich would wear something that awful.

"Aw, aren't you sad, little beauty?" he croons when he spots me. "What's your name?"

I take a step back, pressing myself against the door. Wishing I could disappear. "Who are you?"

"I asked first," he says pleasantly as he approaches.

I watch him warily, completely untrusting. I only had one shot earlier, so I'm definitely not drunk. And I refuse to put myself in a situation like the one I experienced at Halloween. My defenses are completely up and sirens are going off in my head at being alone with a complete stranger.

"I'm lost," is what I say with a faint smile. "I think I got turned around. This house is so big."

"Easy to do if you're not familiar with it." He leans against the wall directly in front of me, his gaze raking over me from head to toe. "I don't recognize you, and I know everyone at these shitty parties my sister hosts."

Oh crap. I do know who this guy is. It's Montgomery Michaels the fourth. Monty Michaels is brilliant and goes to MIT. I think he's a senior in college now? A bit eccentric, from what I've heard.

Not that I personally know him.

"This is your house?" I ask, feeling like an idiot.

"Correction. This is my *parents'* house. I just happen to live here on occasion." He smiles, and it's friendly. Not menacing at all. "Tell me your name."

"Summer," I admit.

"Like the season?"

I nod and sniff, a wave of emotion cresting over me, weakening my defenses.

"Oh no. Don't start crying. I don't know what to do with emotional girls," he says, sounding panicked.

"Don't you have two sisters?" I ask, wiping at the errant tears streaking down my face.

"I do. And I avoid them at all costs," he says so seriously, I can't help but start to laugh, which in turn causes him to smile. "Please don't cry. Why are you sad?"

A laugh escapes me, though it sounds more like a cry. "What else? A boy."

He frowns. "Boys are the worst. But I love them. Don't you?"

"I suppose." An ally, I think to myself as I contemplate him, noting the sincerity in his gaze, how he's so focused on me. As if I matter to him, which is silly. We're practically strangers. "Why are you back here and not at the party?"

"I hate parties. I'm more of a one-on-one person," he admits.

My smile is weak. "Same."

"Tell me now. What boy upset you?" he asks softly.

I can tell he's genuinely curious. It's in the way he watches me, as if he wants to fix my problems. Or maybe I'm reading too much into this conversation, I don't know.

All I know is he's the first friendly face I've seen in a while, and I want to confess all of my deep, dark secrets to him.

"You might not know him..." My voice drifts.

"I know pretty much everyone in this house. And there are currently hundreds of people here. Though I suppose I don't know you." He mock scowls at me. "Tell me now. Who did you come with?"

"Sylvie Lancaster," I answer.

His entire face lights up. "Love her. Is her gorgeous brother here too? God, that boy is exquisite. Such fine bone structure."

I nod, my lower lip trembling.

"Please don't tell me he's the one who broke your heart." He frowns.

A single tear falls from the corner of my eye and I dash it away.

"You don't need to answer." He sighs. "Whit Lancaster is absolutely divine. But he's also the absolute worst."

"Terrible," I agree with a little hiccup.

"Gorgeous though. Those eyes. The cheekbones. The faintly sinister expression always on his face, as if he's plotting your death and you'll smile the entire time as he murders you. Why do I always like them when they look so mean?" he asks himself.

"I have the same problem," I admit, and we both laugh.

"Don't let him bother you. He's not worth your tears, baby doll." He stops directly in front of me and reaches out, wiping away the single tear that's making its slow descent down my cheek. "Want me to accompany you downstairs?"

The hopeful look on my face says it all, I'm sure. "You would do that for me? I thought you hated parties."

"Oh, I do. But I'm also a sucker for a damsel in distress." He gives me another look, then gestures toward the door he just came out of. "We need to clean you up first."

"Is this your room?" I ask as he reaches for the door handle.

He tips his head back and laughs. "No, darling. This is the servants' wing. It's where I meet my secret hook ups."

My mouth drops open. "You had a secret hook up? With who?"

"If I told you, then it wouldn't be a secret." The sly smile on Monty's face makes me smile in return. "Let's just say he's a testosterone-filled jock with a player reputation, yet he secretly loves sucking dick."

Oh dear. That is quite the secret. I can think of a few people at my school who would fit that jock description. "College or high school?"

"I don't kiss and tell, and I definitely don't mess around with high schoolers," he says with a tilt of his nose as he cracks open the door. "Teen boys come too fast anyway."

Hmm. Monty has never been with a teen like Whit Lancaster then.

He offers his arm and I hook mine through it, letting him lead me inside.

It's nice to find another friend.

———

TWENTY MINUTES later and I'm descending the stairs with Monty escorting me, his arm still looped in mine as we each survey the scene laid out before us. He helped clean me up and set me to rights, giving me a pep talk the entire time on how I'm going to handle Whit, and then demanded we go greet the subjects.

That's what he calls the guests in his home. The subjects.

I'm kind of in love with him already. He has so much confidence. He flat out doesn't give a shit what people think of him, though I suppose his name and his breeding has something to do with that. I wish I had even an ounce of his confidence within me.

Maybe if I hang around him long enough, his attitude will rub off.

Once we step off the staircase, everyone clamors around Monty, most of them casting me curious looks since they have no idea who I am. When they ask about me, he claims I'm his guest and that's all he says.

It makes them want to know more, I can tell. But he shuts them down if they ask about me. And I don't say a word. I just stand there with a mysterious smile on my face, my gaze everywhere, desperate to find Whit.

God, I'm so stupid. Why would I want to find him? He'll just destroy me anyway. He's probably with that girl. Monty's sister. Leighton. They're probably fucking right now, while he's telling me I need to walk around this party with his cum coating the inside of my thighs like he owns me.

I hate him. I do.

"Darling, your lip is curling, as if someone just shat their pants," Monty warns, his mouth close to my ear as he leans in to whisper to me. People are talking all around us, some are even speaking directly to him, but he doesn't seem to care. "Keep your composure. Whit has entered the room."

My legs want to give out and I lock my knees, clutching Monty's arm as I do my best to twist my lips into a faint smile.

"There you go. Chin up," Monty encourages. I glance over at him to find he's looking to his left, a pleased expression on his face. "Ah, he's headed this way. Act like a princess, love. You're above this. You're above *him*."

My chin goes up and I stare down my nose at the people surrounding us, my smile turning real. Mysterious. I duck my head toward Monty, my gaze fond as I look at him and he smiles at me in return. As if we're old, dear friends.

We're good, Monty and me. I feel like I've found a kindred spirit.

The air suddenly shifts, becoming charged. I feel his presence before I see him. Every hair on my body rises, goose bumps following swiftly.

"Montgomery." The voice is familiar. Dark.

Devastating.

"Whittaker," Monty says, amusement lacing his tone. "What's got your panties in a twist tonight, darling? You appear ready to breathe fire."

Whit literally bares his teeth at Monty before sliding his fiery gaze to me. "You're with my date, Monty. And you know I don't like to share."

The crowd surrounding us goes silent. My lips part in surprise, but no sound comes out.

Did Whit really just publicly claim me as his date?

Monty laughs, his arm squeezing around mine. "You were always selfish with your toys, Whit."

"I haven't changed. I'm still selfish. Give me back my toy," Whit demands, his deep voice wrapping all around me, leaving me feeling weak. "What you're currently holding onto, belongs to me."

"Don't you mean *who?*" Monty chides as he turns to look at me. "Don't mind him. He has the most boorish manners sometimes. It's almost as if he were raised by wolves."

"I was. Feral ones who'll slit your skinny throat with their teeth." Whit reaches for me, his fingers casually locking around my wrist and tugging me toward him. But Monty won't let me go. Not yet. "She's not your type, Monty."

"Oh I know, but she's a beauty." Monty's gaze is filled with longing as he studies me. "You're such a lucky girl. Does he ravish you every night?"

I don't answer him. I'm sure the look I send him is answer enough.

Monty lets go of me at the same time Whit pulls on my arm, and I go to Whit easily. He wraps his arm around my waist, his fingers spread wide across my butt as he holds me to him. It's a possessive gesture. I feel as if I've been claimed.

I don't mind.

"Thank you for taking care of her," Whit says to Monty, sounding sincere.

"I will watch over your precious toy whenever you need me. She's an absolute doll." Monty waves his fingers at me. "Enjoy him tonight, my sweet little season. I have a feeling he'll be extra feral. Watch the teeth though!"

Whit escorts me away from Monty and his group before I can respond, practically dragging me out of the cavernous room. We rush down a hall, neither of us speaking, my breaths coming faster and faster as worry consumes me.

He's angry. But I did nothing wrong. And if he accuses me of something—of anything—I'm not going to stand for it.

I'm not.

"Whit," I protest, but he ignores me. I try to slow down, but he's moving so fast, his momentum keeps me going, until I finally stumble into him, my entire body pressed against his side.

He turns, pulling me into his arms and roughly pushes me against the wall. I wait for him to kiss me. Grope me. Whatever it is he feels the need to do.

But he does none of that.

Instead, he slips two fingers beneath my chin, tilting my face up so I have no choice but to look at him.

"It isn't what you think."

I study his face, how calm he appears. A war wages inside of me. I could hurl insults and accuse him of terrible things. I could cry and carry on and act like a jealous lover.

I do none of those things.

"What happened then?" My voice is even. As if I'm completely unfazed.

"Leighton and I...we have history," he admits.

Now I am a jealous lover. I hate hearing that.

"And she's very persistent when she wants to be. I wasn't interested. She threw herself at me. Even vaguely threatened me." A storm stirs in his eyes. One moment dark and threatening, the next moment gone. "Leticia is here."

My heart goes into freefall at just hearing her name. "Your future wife."

"My future nothing," he reiterates through clenched teeth. "No one determines my future. Not anymore."

I blink at him, surprised by the vehemence in his tone.

"Leighton was all over you," I say.

"That's correct. She was all over me, not the other way around." He removes his fingers from my chin to smooth back a strand of my hair, tucking it behind my ear. I shudder at his gentle touch, confused. "It was nothing. I ran after you, but I lost you."

"I was fast, despite the shoes." My smile is faint.

"And you ran into Monty."

"Isn't he wonderful?" I ask with a dreamy smile. "My new best friend."

"Don't tell Sylvie that. She'll be jealous." The answering smile on Whit's face is a surprise.

"No one could replace Sylvie. But I adore Monty."

"He's ruthless."

My lips part in surprise. "He's sweet."

"If he likes you. Or respects you," Whit says. "We've had a tentative relationship since we were children. I've always been wary of him."

"He's enamored with you. Called you, and I quote, 'exquisite,'" I tell Whit, laughing when I see the scowl.

"He would say something like that," he murmurs, his expression thunderous.

"He's not wrong. He also mentioned you have beautiful bone structure." Feeling daring, I touch Whit's cheek. "And he's right. You do." My fingers drift down his face. Across his mouth. "An aristocratic face. I see why your parents are so insistent you marry well. You have to keep up the appearances with a beautiful wife. You two would need to make equally beautiful children who look the part."

"Fuck that." He grabs my wrist, keeping my fingers on his lips. "I don't care what they think."

It's all lies. He cares. Too much. It's his family name. His legacy. He doesn't want to disappoint them.

Whit parts his lips, his fingers loosening around my wrist as he draws my fingers into his mouth. "I don't like it when you run away from me," he admits.

I watch him, completely transfixed. The flicker of his tongue as he curls it around my finger, his eyes only for me. Something deep inside me catches fire and I let out a shaky breath as I keep my focus on his face. His mouth.

His beautiful, terrible, wonderful mouth.

"You want to leave?" he asks, his deep voice wrapping all around me. My breasts feel heavy and my core throbs at the promise in that question.

"What about Sylvie?"

"I'll text Spencer. Tell him to bring her home." He drops my hand and leans in, his mouth brushing against mine as he speaks. "Let's go, Savage."

THIRTY-EIGHT

SUMMER

OF COURSE, I agree to leave. I'm so caught up in him, there's no way the word no could pass my lips. I follow after him as we go in search of a door. We stumble upon Sylvie, who's cozied up next to Spence on an oversized chair, her legs draped over his, his hand low on her back, almost on her butt.

He shifts his hand upward when he spots us.

Whit stiffens and comes to a stop, watching them carefully. "Bring my sister home, will you?"

"Of course." Spence nods.

Sylvie smiles and stretches like a cat, blatantly rubbing her body against Spencer's. "Where are you two off to?"

"I'm going to fuck Summer in the back of the car, Syl, and we were hoping for a little privacy," Whit answers, his tone completely serious.

Sylvie laughs. "So naughty."

I say nothing. I just let Whit escort me through the house. Outside. To the car. He pulls me into the back seat, so violently, I crash into him and he pins me beneath his big body, his face in mine.

"I've already fucked you in the car," he murmurs as he runs his mouth down the length of my neck. "And what I have in mind can't happen back here."

Anticipation races through my veins, leaving me hot. Curious. "What do you want to do to me?"

"Claim you in the one place I haven't yet." He lifts away from my neck so he can kiss me, his tongue doing a thorough search of my mouth and leaving me a gasping mess when he finishes. "Or does the thought of me taking your ass scare you?"

My pussy clenches with need. He can have me any way he wants me. "I want it."

He grins, looking pleased. "Oh, you're going to get it."

As usual, his words are a threat. A promise. I sigh when he kisses me again. His lips are languid. As if we have all the time in the world. I drown in his taste. In the way he has me pinned to the seat, my thighs spread and his hips nestle between them. He shifts down, his knees falling to the floorboard with a soft thump; his hands move down my sides, slowly shoving my dress up, up.

Exposing me completely.

"Sit up," he commands and I shift my body so I'm half-propped up against the seat, my entire lower body completely exposed. He never takes his gaze from mine as he lowers his face to my pussy, his tongue darting out for a lick.

I feel that flick of his tongue all the way down to my soul.

My thighs tremble, my ass is perched on the edge of the seat as he thoroughly destroys me with his tongue. He licks and searches. Sucks my clit between his lips. Slides his finger inside me, thrusting in and out.

It feels so good. Too good.

He slips his hand beneath my ass, holding me to him. "Grind on me," he says. "You know you want to."

Oh fuck.

I do.

Bracing my feet on the floor, I tilt my hips and rub against his face shamelessly, the friction of the stubble on his chin driving me out of my mind with pleasure. He eats my pussy as if he's ravenous. Like he can't get enough of me and I spear my fingers into his hair, holding him to me.

Using him.

Getting off on his beautiful, exquisite face.

He removes his finger from my pussy, reaching behind me to tease at my asshole. He strokes me there, featherlight touches that have me moaning. Clenching. Releasing. He doesn't let up. His mouth and his finger are tormenters, pushing me further. He presses harder, his touch persistent, his eyes on mine as he laps at me and when I feel his finger break past the barrier, my entire body begins to spasm.

I whisper his name, my breathing frantic, the orgasm washing over me in wave after wave. Such a cliché, but god I feel like I've been flung out to sea as the unbearable pleasure shimmers over me. Again and again. Until I'm desperately trying to push him away from me. It's too intense.

Too much.

But he won't let go. His mouth softens. Slows. His finger is still in my ass as he licks delicately at my sensitive flesh. Teases my clit. Circles it. Again and again as his finger pushes deeper, before it starts to move.

"Fuck," I bite out as another, less intense but still overwhelming, orgasm pulses through me. I toss my head back, my entire body shaking as I ride it out against Whit's face. Tears leak from the corners of my eyes when I finally slump onto the seat and he shifts away from me.

He watches me carefully, rubbing the inside of his arm against his mouth. "I could watch you do that all night."

"I'd probably end up dead if you kept making me come like that," I admit, my throat scratchy.

"No better way to go, am I right?" His devilish grin lights me up inside and I nod in agreement.

This is what he does to me, I realize as we pull through the ominous gates of the Lancaster estate. He renders me helpless. He leaves me spent. Tingling with the anticipation for what's to come. I'm not scared at the possibility of him fucking me in the ass for the first time.

I'm more frightened of the day that comes when he's no longer interested in me anymore.

———

"Are you being so sweet to me because you want anal?"

He chuckles, his chest rumbling against my back, and I can't help but smile. "Maybe."

We're in his bathroom, sharing his giant soaking tub that's filled nearly to the brim with hot water, thin tendrils of steam floating from the surface. There's a fireplace nearby, the crackling sounds of the fire filling the quiet room. The only other sound is the lapping of the water against our skin when we move.

I could sit like this forever. Cradled in Whit's arms, nestled against his body, the hot water surrounding us. I feel loved. Cherished. Even though I know it's a crock and he doesn't really feel that way about me.

It doesn't matter. I can pretend. At least for one night.

"Would you ever let me touch you there?" I realize it's a lot easier to ask him this question since we're not facing each other.

"I don't want you ramming a dildo in my ass, but I wouldn't mind a finger. Just to try it out," he says conversationally.

A giggle escapes me and he presses his hand against my mouth, silencing me. "I'm serious, Savage. No dildos."

"I don't even own a dildo," I say, my voice muffled against his fingers.

He slips a finger inside my mouth and I flick my tongue against it. "Who needs a dildo when you have this?" He thrusts his hips against me, his erect cock nudging my backside.

Whit is playful tonight. Possessive. Almost...sweet? I don't understand his mood. But I'm not fighting it either. I wish he could always be like this.

But then again, I'd miss the dirty, dark Whit if he never showed that side again. The menacing tone and cruel words. They arouse me too.

Everything he does arouses me.

I suck his finger like it's his dick. Drawing it deeper into my mouth, circling my tongue around it before I suck on it hard. His other hand comes around me to grasp at my breast, his fingers toying with my nipple, his breaths accelerating.

"Do you really consider me your toy?" I ask once he pulls his finger from my mouth.

He's quiet for a moment, as if he has to consider his words and how to use them. He could be cruel or he could be kind. Is that half the thrill, never knowing what I'm going to get from him?

Yes. I think it is.

"You're more than that," he finally says. Both of his hands are on my breasts now. Kneading them. Squeezing them, rubbing his fingertips over my nipples, featherlight. Making everything inside of me ache for more.

I close my eyes, relaxing against him. "And you don't like to share?"

His hands stop moving. "I never share."

The firm tone of his voice tells me there's no arguing that point. As if I would.

"Not even with another boy?" I only ask to provoke him.

"Definitely not with another boy," he says, resuming his exploration of my chest again.

"How about another girl?"

His hands pause. "You go that way?"

I shrug. "I've watched girl on girl porn. It's a turn-on, I can admit that. A woman is more...delicate."

"I can be delicate."

I laugh. Loudly. "No, you cannot."

"I wasn't delicate earlier?" He pushes my wet hair away from my neck with his face to nuzzle me there. "In the car?"

"Delicate torture," I whisper, tilting my head back as he kisses me there, just under my jaw. "You're relentless."

"You like it."

"Maybe we have sex too much," I say, my voice small.

"I think we're perfectly normal."

Another laugh escapes me and he presses his hand over my lips again.

"Normal is probably the wrong word." He licks my neck, running his tongue down the length of it. "We fit, Savage. You and me."

"We're a mess," I murmur beneath his hand. He tightens his fingers around my mouth, making it hard to breathe. "Whit."

He slides his hand from my face downward, until his fingers are clamped around my throat, his thumb pressing. Reminding me of his strength. The hold he has over me, physically and emotionally. "Haven't done this in a while."

My heart races in fear. Anticipation. I shift my body, the water sloshing over the sides of the tub. "Don't hurt me."

"I would never. I only hurt you when I know you like it." The tightening is subtle. He doesn't move fast. His fingers exert the slightest amount of pressure, but I know he could do more. "And I think you like this."

I keep my eyes closed, concentrating on my thumping heart, the sensation of his body behind mine, surrounding me. His other hand drops from my breast to move between my legs, cupping me there for only a moment before he slides his fingers into my folds, his touch rough. Thrilling.

A claiming.

"Did you see how everyone was looking at you tonight? When you were with Monty?"

I nod, my eyes popping open. I stare at the fire, the flames dancing high, the wood cracking and splitting from the intense heat.

"You looked like a fucking queen," he murmurs, his voice full of pride. "That's why I claimed you, Savage. I didn't want anyone else taking what was mine. My queen. You belong to me."

His possessive words send a ribbon of heat twisting through my body. "What about Monty?"

His deep chuckle sounds in my ear. "He's not a threat. I can trust him with you."

"Because he likes boys?"

"Even if he was straight, he wouldn't touch you. Not once he found out who you belong to."

"I'm not an object, Whit. I'm a person. You can't just claim me," I say, deciding to stand up for myself a little bit. Even though his possession is a heady thing.

No one's ever publicly claimed me before—at least, no boy ever has. I'm usually a dirty little secret. Even Whit hid me away, though I wanted to keep what we were doing under wraps as well.

Not anymore. Everybody who was anybody in that room tonight knows I'm with Whit Lancaster. And I can't seem to muster up the energy to care.

"Mmm, that's where you're wrong." He nuzzles my face with his nose. Presses his thumb firmly against my clit as he tightens his fingers around my throat even more. "You've already been claimed. I've possessed you in just about every way I can."

His hand works my pussy, his arm stirring the water, making it slosh in the tub, spilling over the top and all over the floor. I spread my legs wider, as wide as they can go in the narrow tub, wanting more. Wanting his fingers inside me.

Wanting him inside me.

"I've owned you since you were fourteen," he whispers, his voice dark. Stirring up all the dark things buried deep inside of me. "You've been in my head ever since that night, you know. Haunting me. No one else could ever measure up."

My heart goes still at his confession, all the breath in my lungs drying up. "What?" I gasp out.

He doesn't even hesitate in his confession. "It's true. I saw it in you that night. Your soul matched mine," he admits as he lets go of my throat. "Move forward."

I lean away from him, glancing over my shoulder to send him a questioning look. "I don't understand."

"Grasp the edge of the tub." He gives me a gentle shove and I fall forward, my hands clasping the curved marble edge. In one swift move he rises up and slides his cock inside me, our positioning aiding in him filling me extra deep. A groan leaves me the moment he's fully-seated inside my body and we remain like that for a moment, the water churning, our bodies connected yet completely still. Him rising above me, commanding me, taking complete control over me.

My breaths leave me in short gasps, excitement fizzing in my veins as I wait for him to say something, to do anything.

"Sometimes I would think you weren't real. You couldn't be that perfect," he says as he slowly starts to move, pulling himself almost completely out of my body before pushing back in. "But you are real. It's as if you were made for me."

I feel the same way about him. As if he were made for only me.

There's a loud popping noise and then the gurgle of the drain. He somehow released the plug, and the water is slowly lowering in the tub. He rests his hands on my hips, positioning me carefully before he removes one hand to drift his fingers down the crack of my ass. Up and down, his pace slow and steady, lingering over the place he wants me the most.

"With you positioned like this, you're so open to me." He slowly slips his finger into my ass with ease, and I suck in a breath, my muscles tensing. "Relax."

I try to, but this is the farthest he's gotten since he started trying, and I feel so full. His cock inside of me, plus his finger. It's too much.

It's not enough.

"Your skin is glistening right now," he says, almost to himself. "All wet and smooth. God, look at you."

Turning my head, I study him from over my shoulder, and his molten gaze meets mine. His eyes are so dark. Like a storm. His mouth is red, his cheeks ruddy and he smiles, thrusting his hips upward at the same time.

Hitting a spot deep inside of me that has me seeing stars.

I face forward once again, gripping the edge of the tub with all my might, the water slowly lowering. Exposing me completely. I must look a sight, but I don't care. All I can focus on is the friction of Whit's cock as he slides in and out of my pussy. His finger soon following the same rhythm in my ass. I move against him, my knees slipping against the slick marble, my fingers cramping from how tight I cling to the tub's edge.

Whit fucks me hard, his grunts filling the room, our wet skin slapping together in rhythm. With my knees spread, his finger sinks deeper and I bite out a moan as I arch against him.

A string of curses leaves Whit's mouth, every single one of them filthy. My entire body is on fire, muscles taut with expectation, waiting for that delicious climax that hovers just on the edge.

And then he's gone. He pulls out of my body, both his cock and his finger, and I watch in shock as he hurriedly climbs out of the tub and goes to stand in front of me. Somewhere along the way, he found a towel and he holds it out toward me. "Come on. Get out."

I step out of the tub, nearly tripping since my body is so weak. Thank God he's there to take my hand and guide me out.

My pussy aches. My asshole burns. And still, I go to him, letting him wrap me up in the giant, thick towel. He cuddles me close, his hands roaming all over my body, rubbing the towel against my skin and drying me. He presses his mouth to my forehead, the gesture so sweet, so unexpected, I almost want to cry.

He's a contradiction tonight. One I don't understand.

"Let's go to the bedroom," he suggests once he's removed the towel from my body. I can only nod my reply, sleepiness threatening to take over. His taking care of me felt so good. It was just what I needed.

Whit grabs my hand, interlacing our fingers as he leads me out of the bathroom and toward his massive bed. There's another fireplace, the fire roaring, the flames licking high and I watch them, trembling when Whit comes behind me and wraps his arms around my waist.

"Get on the bed," he says, his voice low. Commanding. "On your hands and knees. Let me look at you."

I do as he says in a trance. Lost to the moment. The magic of the night. He goes to the bedside table and pulls open the drawer, revealing a bottle of lube.

My mouth goes dry as I watch him pop the cap and squeeze clear droplets onto his fingers. He rubs them together, the sticky liquid stringing between his fingers as he spreads them wide.

He moves behind me, his fingers delving between my cheeks without hesitation, stroking me there. His touch is achingly gentle and I close my eyes, willing myself to relax. Telling myself that it'll feel good.

That I can trust him.

"Spread your legs wider," he encourages and when I do as he commands, a groan leaves him. "God, I can see everything."

He strokes. Teases. His fingers press. Deep. Deeper. Until he slips just the tip of his index finger into my ass, leaving it there. "Does that hurt?"

"No," I whisper.

He plays with my ass for what feels like hours. Gets one finger inside. Then two. At one point, he slides beneath my body and licks at my pussy, sucks my clit, making me come. Gets three fingers inside me by then. He sucks my clit again, his fingers sliding in and out of my body and I climax once more within seconds, my asshole clenching tightly around his fingers as I come on his face.

"That is what I want to feel around my dick," he says, his voice strangled as he shifts his position so he's behind me once more. I hear a lid pop open and I can tell he's squirting out more lube. Slicking it onto his cock maybe?

A jolt moves through me when he covers my asshole with the cool liquid.

"Tell me to stop if it hurts," he says, notching the head of his cock right at my ass. He sounds eager. Excited. "You're already open to me."

He rubs his cock against me, and I moan softly at the delicious sensation. Oh God, he feels so big. Bigger than three fingers. I don't know if he'll fit. I don't know if I want him to fit.

But he's persistent. And oh so patient. This is what he wants, so he's going to take his time. He rubs and teases, pushing just the head of his cock inside me before withdrawing completely. My mouth goes dry as I wait for the inevitable invasion, but he takes it so slowly, he's halfway in before I realize what he's doing.

"Fuuuuuuuuuck." He draws the word out into at least five syllables as he slowly pushes inside. I hang my head, breathing hard, my body, my mind in shock.

He's in my ass. And oh God, when he starts to move?

It hurts. But it's a pleasurable sting. He has trouble finding his rhythm at first, and I can only assume it's because it's such a snug fit. I try to remain in position, but my arms are tired and they start to shake. Whit pauses and bends over me, his voice rough as he says, "Lift up."

"Wa-wait—what?" I glance back at him as he reaches forward, his hands finding mine as he effortlessly pulls my body into an upright position.

I thought for sure that might bend his dick at a weird angle, but if anything, it sends him deeper inside my body, easing some of the stinging pain. My back is plastered to his front and he reaches around me, his fingers finding my pussy and rubbing it in circles.

"Holy shit, Summer," he says, his voice in agony. In pleasure. "You're so fucking wet. And you feel so damn good."

I can barely move. Can only take his punishment as he thrusts into me again and again as he holds me to him. His soft grunts fill the quiet room, the slap of our skin, my panting breaths. It's too much. Not enough.

"Such a good girl," he croons as he plays with me with his fingers, strumming my clit so hard I cry out in agony, the orgasm slamming into me, stealing my breath, my thoughts, my everything. I go completely still before my body is consumed with shudders, my asshole clenching tightly around his cock over and over.

He comes with a strangled shout. I think my orgasm surprised him, and made him come too. I feel the hot flood of liquid, so foreign in my asshole, and he pulls out quickly, his semen dripping out of me and all over the bed.

"Jesus. You are a sight." He touches me. Scoops up his cum with his fingers and spreads it all around my ass. "Messy. Sexy. Fuck, I'm still hard."

I collapse onto the mattress, rolling away from the wet spot, my entire body weak with exhaustion. "I can't do anymore," I whisper as I close my eyes and snuggle my face into the mattress. My bones are weary. My mind, blank.

He climbs off the bed and I can sense him watching me quietly. I don't move. Don't say a word and neither does he.

Minutes later I can hear him moving about the bathroom. The toilet flushing. The faucet running. And then he's back, his body causing the mattress to dip as he reaches for me, his hands at my waist, tugging me close to him.

"I'm going to clean you up," he murmurs, just before placing a warm, damp washcloth against my ass. He washes my body, cleaning every last bit of semen from me before rubbing me gently with a thick, dry towel. I lay there and take it without a word, like a baby who needs to be coddled and cared for.

He moves away from the bed again, no doubt getting rid of the washcloth and towel, and then he's back. Wordless as he shifts me around and pulls the covers over my limp body before he climbs into the bed, joining me.

Holding my breath, I wait for him to touch me. Or to just say goodnight. His body is so still, I wonder if he's even breathing.

"Did I hurt you?" he finally asks, his voice rough. A rasp in the air.

"No."

Whit rolls over so he's facing me. I can make out his beautiful face from the firelight. "Don't lie to me, Summer."

I much prefer it when he calls me by my first name. The moment becomes more charged. More intimate. "I'm not lying. I liked it. You made me come, didn't you?"

"Still. I think I hurt you. No, I *know* I hurt you." He reaches for me, pulling me into his arms so I'm pressed against his long, hard body. I nestle my head against his chest, savoring the sound of his steady heartbeat. "I've never done that before."

"Done what?" I ask sleepily.

"Anal. You're my first. The only girl I've ever wanted to be with like that." He tightens his arms around me. "I didn't want to fuck it up."

His admission does something to me—makes me feel lighter than air. Floating. Weightless. I tip my head back, my lips pursed. Eager for his kiss. "You didn't fuck it up."

He kisses me, as if he knows I need it. Maybe he needs it too. "We should go to sleep."

"Can I—"

"Stay," he says, cutting me off. "Sleep with me."

This is the second time we've done this. And it throws me. *He* throws me. I don't know what's happening between us. Why he's being so agreeable. Thoughtful. It's exhilarating.

It's scary.

But I do realize one thing.

I'm completely defenseless. Weak to him and his wants. His needs. He knows it. He has complete command of me. Body and soul.

And it is a terrifying position to find myself in.

THIRTY-NINE

WHIT

I WAKE up with Summer's naked body sprawled across mine. I'm hard as usual in the morning, but it feels more intense, thanks to having her in my bed. On top of me. Her soft pussy pressed against my thigh.

I refuse to fuck her. Or even touch her in a sexual manner. Last night I pushed her to her absolute limits. I used her body in almost every single way I possibly could.

In a way, I pushed myself to my limits too.

Carefully I disentangle her from me and climb out of bed, going straight to the bathroom to piss. My erect dick makes this almost impossible and I try to think of other things. Boring things. School. The drive here. My parents' endless disappointment in me.

My dick deflates a little.

I turn on the shower and jump in, the icy cold water brisk against my skin. It eventually warms up, and I wash myself quickly. Hop out and dry off. Brush my teeth. Study my reflection in the mirror, annoyed with myself, and how I treated Summer last night. She gets under my skin. Burrows herself in there until I'm consumed with her, and I can't shove her out. No, I made everything fucking worse after last night.

Chasing after her. Fighting over her with Monty as if she's a prized possession that I won. Publicly claiming her at the party. I'm sure they're talking about us. Me. Wondering who she is. It won't take much digging to figure it out.

And then there will be hell to pay. I'm sure of it.

Right now, last night's behavior feels worth the trouble. For whatever reason, I couldn't resist her. I wanted her every which way. Fucking her every chance I got. I came three times last night? Four? She came more.

She's a drug and I'm hopelessly addicted.

I exit the bathroom to find her sitting up in the middle of the bed, clutching the comforter to her, her dark hair in complete disarray. She's beautiful on this cold, gray morning. A spot of vibrant color in the drab. When is she not? Smooth shoulders on display, her pink mouth swollen, her eyes puffy from sleep— or lack of it. I can see the exhaustion on her face, it's obvious. Yet I still find her stunning.

My dick stirs. I glance down, remembering I'm naked.

"Someone's glad to see me."

Her response makes me smile before I remember I'm not supposed to do that much and I turn it into a scowl.

But she saw the smile, and her eyes widen, dancing with delight. She holds her hand out, beckoning me. "Come back to bed."

"My parents will want me downstairs for breakfast." It's a weak excuse. I can almost guarantee my parents aren't at the table. It's already past nine. They rise with the sun; the both of them similar, yet not wanting to deal with each other.

She pouts. "Please?"

Giving in, I go to her. Wrap her up in my arms. Kiss her senseless. What the hell am I doing? Girls mean nothing to me. People mean nothing to me. I'm treating her like a precious and fragile thing, when I usually call her a horrible name and demand that she suck my dick.

I decide to try it out.

I curl my fingers into her hair at her nape, pulling her mouth from mine. "I want your mouth on me."

Her smile is saucy. "My mouth is on you."

"On my cock," I correct, not letting her go as I press my back against the ornate headboard, a pillow tucked behind me. "I want to come in your mouth."

Her chest rises and falls rapidly as her breath quickens. "Is this a normal morning request?"

"When I'm with you—" I clamp my lips shut, not about to complete that sentence. "Do it."

My tone is hard. Rude. After the last couple of nights of sweet talk and tender gestures, I need to remember who I am. Who she is. And she remembers. I see it in her response. How agreeable she becomes.

She shifts down the bed, my fingers loosening in her hair, allowing the movement. Her mouth hovers above my cock, her gaze meeting mine. "Did you shower?"

I nod. Run my tongue over my lips. She hasn't showered yet, though I did clean her up. But I had my cock in her asshole last night, so I get why she asked.

Summer lowers her head, her hair falling forward, cutting off my view. Her lips touch the tip of my dick. A fleeting kiss. Her tongue laps. Catches the precum.

A groan leaves me. She is an expert with that mouth.

Her slender fingers squeeze the base, jacking me slowly as she works her mouth on my cock's head. I reach forward, catching her hair, pulling back the curtain so I can watch. It's a sight to see. My cock filling her mouth as she swallows me down, her naked body swaying over mine. I could start my day like this every morning and have no complaints. I'd be a cheerful fucker for once in my life.

All thanks to her.

It doesn't take much for her to draw me closer to the edge. The familiar tightening begins within minutes. My entire body tenses, especially at the base of my spine. Deep in my balls.

"Spread your legs," she whispers and I do as she says, curious. Watching.

Summer shifts so she's in between my thighs, her hand still wrapped around my dick as she dips her head and licks at my balls, leaving fiery heat everywhere her tongue touches. She moves lower, licking beneath them. Licking a place so forbidden, I suck in a sharp breath at her daring move.

I tilt my torso forward automatically, giving her better access. She licks around my ass, that ridge of skin between my asshole and balls lights on fire every time she touches me.

I groan, wanting to close my eyes and lose myself to the sensation of her mouth, but not willing to miss the show she's putting on for me. What she's doing right now feels wicked. Filthy.

Fucking hot.

With her free hand, she touches me there, stroking my ass. Pressing firmly against my asshole. Just like I did to her last night. Her fingers squeeze tightly around my shaft, my cock almost an angry purple color thanks to her aggressive touch. My breath stalls. My entire body goes still, anticipation licking at my veins as her mouth draws closer.

She makes direct contact, her tongue covering every inch of my asshole and I come with a shout, semen spurting high, like I'm a fucking geyser. It's endless, the cum. Streams of it landing all over the bed. All over me. She pulls away from my ass, her smile faint, her fingers still strangling my cock as I try my best to come down from what she did to me.

That wasn't just an orgasm. It was a goddamned religious experience.

Her smile is arrogant as she studies me. She's most definitely the queen in this moment, and I'm her lowly, quivering servant. Vulnerable. Shaking. "You made a mess of yourself."

My own words tossed back at me. I can only look at her, unable to find my voice.

"And you came so easily." She laughs, like a siren. Like my own personal torment. "Someone enjoys having their ass licked."

"I know a filthy little whore who enjoys licking my ass," I toss back at her, knowing she'll take it as a compliment.

She practically glows at my words. "I need to take a shower."

"I'll join you."

"Didn't you just take one?" She raises a brow.

"Look at me." I spread my arms out wide, a grunt leaving me when she finally lets go of my softening dick. "I'm a mess, like you said."

"Oh, you definitely are. Then join me." She slides off the bed, her long, elegant limbs reminding me of art in motion. "I'll wash you, and you can wash me."

"I'll wash you first." I follow after her as she darts into the bathroom, my hand going to her perfect ass and giving one rounded cheek a slap, the sound echoing off the tile. She yelps.

I growl.

What the fuck am I doing?

FORTY

SUMMER

WHEN THINGS FEEL TOO good to be true, that usually means they are. And what is unfolding between Whit and I is absolutely a lie waiting to be revealed. We spend the week together at the Lancaster estate, sneaking off where we can, messing around in every room, on every available surface. It's not easy. There are so many rooms. So many places to sneak away. But he's persistent. He fucks me everywhere. In every way he can. My thigh muscles ache from being spread so wide all the time. My mouth is sore from all the kissing and the blow jobs.

But I'm not complaining.

Our sneaking around is difficult, considering there are so many people in this house. Servants, everywhere. Staff. Assistants. Parents. Sylvie. Spencer.

He came to the Michaels' party, brought Sylvie home and never left. Their parents didn't bat an eyelash at Spencer's arrival. It was all explained under the guise of, "Sylvie brought a friend so Whit did too," which is absolute garbage.

I am here for Whit. And Spence is here for Sylvie.

Guilt swamps me every time I think about how I abandoned my friend, but she never gives me a chance to talk to her about it. She avoids me. Every time we're around each other, she ignores me, focusing all of her attention on Whit, or Spence, or whoever else is nearby.

Never me.

Until Thursday morning. Thanksgiving Day. I find Sylvie downstairs in a sitting room that looks out over the enormous back yard, sipping on a latte someone made for her.

The true princess. The future queen. Ah, to be a Lancaster. To have everything done for you, mapped out for you, so you don't have to lift a finger or even so much as think.

"There you are," I say cheerily as I enter the room. "I've been looking for you."

"Oh?" Her tone is guarded, making me halt. "I figured you were in search of my brother. Or have you two finally grown sick of each other after the constant fucking all week?"

Her words feel like a slap. I go to her, sitting in the chair across from hers. "You're mad at me."

"Of course, I'm mad at you. You were my guest first." She shrugs one shoulder. "I told you I needed you. That I didn't want you to leave my side, and you did. I know why you came with me—to spend time with Whit."

The guilt is like a heavy, wet blanket. Settling over me, making me weary. "I'm sorry. That wasn't my true intention. Whit and I had sort of split—"

"I don't care what you and Whit have done. Or haven't done. Though I'm assuming from all the gossip I hear from the servants, you two have done everything." She sends me a look, her upper lip curling in disgust. "They all talk about you, you know. I suppose changing cum-stained sheets every day builds resentment."

I refuse to let her embarrass me. Instead of going into defensive mode, I remain quiet. She contemplates me, reminding me of her brother as she studies me, until she finally sighs.

"Since your swift abandonment left me completely alone in this hell hole, I had to re-strategize. It's why I convinced Spence to stay with us. Not like he was doing anything for the holiday. Probably would've snorted too much coke and fucked too many wannabe models if he'd remained in the city," Sylvie says bitterly.

Still, I say nothing, wondering if they've had sex yet.

I'm guessing no.

"Whit is overwhelming, I get it. And from what I hear, he's *completely* enamored with you," Sylvie says, her tone haughty.

I frown. "What did you hear?"

"At Leighton's party, the gossip was rampant. Everyone witnessed that peculiar discussion between Monty and Whit," Sylvie says, looking down her nose at me. "How in the world did you get Monty on your side so quickly?"

"He found me crying after he had a tryst with some unknown jock who enjoys sucking his dick," I tell her truthfully.

Sylvie bursts out laughing, and hearing it gives me hope. "I can hear Monty say that. I'm sure it was Ty Peters. He's so over the top with his maleness, it wouldn't surprise me at all that he enjoys a dick in his mouth on occasion."

I have no idea who he is, and it doesn't matter. I can't get past how I hurt Sylvie's feelings, and how badly I need her forgiveness. She's only ever been kind to me. One of the only people at the entirety of Lancaster Prep who has.

"I hate that I disappointed you," I tell her, my voice soft. "I didn't mean to hurt you, Sylvie. It's just—"

"Boys. They're infuriating and wonderful, all at once. Aren't they? And please, I need no details when it comes to you and my brother," she says. "I've heard enough already."

"How are you and Spence this week? Enjoying each other's company?" I ask, changing the subject.

"I wish we were having as much fun as you two are having," she says drolly, just before I see a flicker of disappointment in her gaze. "He's terrified of me."

"What? How?"

"Scared I'll break. I'm fragile, don't you know."

"You're the one who always talks about dying," I remind her.

A sigh leaves her and she sips from her latte. "I suppose I can't win."

I watch her continue sipping from the delicate cup, then turn my gaze to the window. It's a sunny morning, but the wind is whipping the trees, making them sway wildly. I see two male figures standing out in the distance. Similar heights. Their heads bent close together. At first, I think it's Whit and Spence.

But no, it's Whit and his father.

Frowning, I tear my gaze away from them, trying to ignore the sudden lump in my stomach. We sit in silence, Sylvie scrolling on her phone and drinking her coffee. Me chewing on my thumbnail as I watch Whit talk to his father. I can't see their faces from this distance, but they both seem tense. It scares me.

I can't look away, filled with worry. His father has great influence over him. Of course, he does. Augustus Lancaster is a powerful man, and Whit is heir to the Lancaster name. He will do whatever his father asks, no question.

"He doesn't approve," Sylvie says out of nowhere.

Whit takes a step back, and even from this distance, I can tell he's angry. His body is rigid, his mouth open. As if he can't stop talking. Or he might even be yelling. "Who doesn't approve?"

"My father. He doesn't approve of you. And he definitely doesn't approve of you and Whit together." I glance over at Sylvie to find her watching me, her lips pursed, her eyes wide. "Not sure if he approves of you as a friend of mine either."

Unease slips over me. "What are you saying, Sylvie?"

She sets the cup onto the tiny table beside her chair, regarding me with a look of pity in her eyes. "My parents gave me a little lecture this morning at breakfast."

"What about?" I ask carefully.

She shrugs. "You. And Whit. And how they don't want you here, ruining everything."

"What exactly am I ruining?" I ask, my voice faint. I've been waiting for this moment, but as time went on and we got deeper into the week, I figured I'd dodged it. Their disapproval.

Silly me. I was wrong.

"Whit's plans. His life. You're not supposed to be a part of it," Sylvie says, as if it's as simple as that.

But life isn't simple. She of all people should realize this.

"Aren't you tired of having your parents telling you what to do? They control your every move. You're sixteen, Sylvie. Don't you plan on leaving the nest? Going to college? Or does your mother have a say in your future plans too?" I ask, my tone snotty.

Sylvie's eyes narrow as she contemplates me, and this is the moment where I realize I made a mistake.

I took it too far.

"You have no idea what you're talking about, or what it's like, being a part of this family. One of the most important families in this country, if not the world. Our place in society is firmly rooted, and we can't afford to let it be ruined by some stupid, whorish girl who's set her sights on us. You're just on the fringe. Always on the outskirts, the sad little girl staring longingly in the window." Sylvie sneers. "Just like your mother, I hear."

I gape at her. "Sylvie..."

"Stop." She holds up a hand. "You don't care about me. I don't think you ever really did."

"That's not true. You were the only one kind enough to reach out to me at Lancaster," I remind her. "No one else wanted to be my friend. Whit convinced everyone—"

"Right. He had everyone hating you, while I was thinking of how I could become your friend just to piss him off." Her smile is cruel, and I feel like it's a lie. She truly wanted to be my friend, right? I watch as she grabs her cup and takes another dainty sip. "I think it's best if you go back to campus a little early. Say...first thing tomorrow morning?"

"Why?" I ask incredulously, wishing Whit were here. With us. He'd defend me, right? Tell Sylvie to stop being such a bitch?

Would he?

Sylvie slams her cup onto the nearby table and leans forward in her chair, her narrowed gaze aimed at me. "Listen. You just used me to get to spend a week alone with Whit. So you can fuck him into thinking you're the perfect woman for him. I always thought Whit was smarter than that, but clearly you have a magical vagina because it's all he can think about. And now, somehow you've convinced him to go against everything our family stands for."

My mouth pops open, ready to defend myself, but she keeps talking.

"Mother hates you. Calls you the daughter of the slut who broke our family apart, and when she says it like that, when I see what you're doing with Whit. To Whit. To all of us..." She clamps her lips together, studying me with complete disdain. "I have to agree with her."

I rise to my feet on shaky legs, praying I don't collapse. "Sylvie. Please. You're my only friend. I swear I didn't use you to get closer to Whit."

"Could've fooled me," she says, her voice filled with disgust. She averts her head, staring out the window. "They're plotting how to get rid of you right now, I hope you know. Mother doesn't want to see you at the table for dinner. A meal where we're supposed to discuss what we're thankful for. She forbids it."

Forbids it. I suppose I have to agree with her demands, since this is her house.

"You really didn't believe the two of you could be in an actual relationship, did you?" Sylvie faces me once more, her gaze searching. "Oh, look at you. You did. You probably believe him fucking you constantly is a sign of—*love*."

Tears threaten and I will them from my eyes. I can't do this. I can't cry. I can't.

I won't.

"It's not," she says flatly. "He's done this before. You're not the first. And you certainly won't be the last."

We stare at each other, Sylvie's expression oh so cold.

"You know who you remind me of right now?" I ask her, my tone deceptively soft.

Sylvie raises her brows. "Who?"

"Your bitch of a mother. You're exactly like her, Sylvie." I turn on my heel and leave the room, hurrying blindly down the corridor, tears blurring my vision. I don't know why Sylvie had to be so cold. Her words cut like a knife, destroying me.

Was it all a façade? Her friendship, my relationship with Whit. Was it all fake?

It had to be.

I see the staircase that leads to the guest wing and I hurry toward it, running up the stairs, about to turn toward my bedroom when I hear a voice call out.

"Summer. I'd like to speak with you. Do you have a moment?"

Ice-cold dread slides down my spine and I turn to find Sylvia Lancaster standing in front of me, impeccable in wide leg black trousers and a soft cream-colored sweater with a glittery flowered broach pinned to her right shoulder. A Chanel piece, I'm sure. Her blonde hair is sleek and smooth, tucked behind both ears and her lips are coated in red.

The color of blood.

"I was just going to my room—" I start, pausing when she smiles.

It's not friendly. Not at all.

"I'll only take a few minutes of your time. I promise. Please." She inclines her head. "Would you care to see my salon?"

I've seen it. Whit sprawled me out across the massive desk only yesterday, pulling down my panties with eager fingers, pressing my thighs apart and licking me until I came with a sigh. A moan.

"Yes. Please," I say with a weary smile. Only I would say please to the woman who's probably going to destroy me with a few choice words right now. Sylvie already did her damage. I'm barely holding it together as it is.

Sylvia leads me toward the double doors of her salon, swinging one open and striding inside. I follow after her, noting that she doesn't bother closing the door. Giving us no privacy.

I guess she doesn't care who hears what she's about to say.

"Please. Sit." She indicates a delicately wrought chair and I settle in, watching as she stands behind her desk, that pleasant smile still on her face. "Have you enjoyed your time here this week?"

"I have," I say with a nod, unsure of where she's going with this.

"Wonderful. I'm sure the tour Whit has taken you on has been most satisfying." Her smile never falters.

"He's shown me some of the estate, yes."

"I'm meaning the special little tour. The one where he fucks you everywhere he can, no?" Her thin eyebrows rise as she points at the top of her desk. "Including here? What did he do to you yesterday, hmm? Fuck you? Go down on you? Or perhaps you sucked his cock."

Horror rises, stealing my breath. I gape at her, unable to answer.

"You think no one sees what you're doing? There are people all over this house, and the majority of them work for me. You don't think they don't tell me what's going on? What they see? Hear? *Smell?* We're not blind, Summer. We see you. It's quite obvious, what you're doing," Sylvia says.

I blink at her, my brain scrambling. It's exactly what Sylvie said to me only minutes ago. The servants. They're talking. They see everything. How do I excuse my behavior to this woman? She's right. We've been all over this house, fucking. Kissing in dark corners. Touching each other. Laughing. It's been wonderful.

Knowing Whit's mother is aware of every single thing we've done is...devastating.

Their knowledge of our times together taints everything.

"The manipulation of my son ends now." Sylvia leans forward, opening a desk drawer and reaches inside for something. "I found this."

My journal lands with a loud slap in the middle of her desk. I stare at it, horrified, before my gaze jerks to hers. "Wh-where did you get that?"

"It was in Whit's bag. It's your journal. Don't bother denying it." She cracks it open, riffling through the pages, going straight to the back. The section where my darkest secrets lie. "It's rather interesting, all the details you shared. Care to hear it?"

"No," I say, but she ignores me and starts reading it instead.

It's my fault they're dead. I tipped over the candle when I left Yates' room. I did it on purpose, after what he did to me. He was especially brutal tonight. Saying horrible things. Holding me down as he fucked me. I hated every minute of it, but I took it. The anger rising inside of me with his every thrust. Crying in frustration when my body betrayed me and I came. Oh, how he loved that. God, I hate him.

Once he was finished with me, I said I would tell his father what he's been doing to me, and he laughed.

Laughed.

So I lay there quietly, knowing he would soon fall asleep. And he did. He's so predictable. The moment I heard him begin to snore, I slipped out of bed. I slipped on my underwear, grateful I still had my shirt on. He doesn't bother with any sort of foreplay or undressing me anymore, he just goes straight to fucking. Once I was dressed, and collected anything that belonged to me, I left the room.

And purposely knocked over the candle on the dresser.

I figured he would wake up when he smelled the smoke. It would've taken nothing to put the fire out. He had a giant water bottle sitting on his bedside table. He could've doused it out with that.

He never woke up. The fire grew while we all slept. Even I fell asleep, my anger leaving me exhausted. Spent. I was awoken by my mother frantically shaking me. She grabbed my hand and practically dragged me outside. Yates and Jonas were still in the house. We left them in there. They both died in their beds. Smoke inhalation, the police told us later. They most likely never woke up, never knew what happened.

But I knew.

I killed them.

Sylvia slaps the journal shut with one hand, her smile menacing as she studies me. "I was fully prepared to pay you off, you know. I even wrote you a check for a most generous sum."

"I would've never taken it," I tell her with conviction.

"It doesn't matter anymore, because I no longer need to give it to you. This is enough." She holds the journal up. "You leave this house right now, and you will never talk to my son again. Understood?"

My heart races and I struggle to breathe. "And if I don't do what you want?"

"Then I will turn this journal over to the police department. Or better yet, the arson investigator who was originally assigned to the case. I'm sure he'd *love* to read this."

"You wouldn't." I'm testing her, but I already know her answer.

"I would," she says firmly, opening the drawer once more and dropping my journal inside. "Your mother would lose everything. The house, the money she inherited, her friends, her social status, whatever's left of it. Everything. She'd be broke, just like before. And so would you. I can destroy your entire life with one phone call. Do you really want to risk it?"

I say nothing. There's nothing I can say. Everything is true, what I wrote in that journal. How did she get it? And worse, why did Whit bring it with him here? Why would he do that? Was he in on this all along? Did he do this to ruin me too?

"It was never going to last," she practically croons, her voice soft, her gaze hard. "Just because you fucked my son doesn't mean you get a piece of the Lancaster fortune. It didn't work for your mother. It won't work for you either."

A tear streaks down my cheek and I dash it away with trembling fingers, angry at myself for showing emotion.

"You have thirty minutes. I'll have a car waiting for you. I want you gone before the guests arrive. Go pack your pitiful little bag. Now."

I jump to my feet and hurry for the open double doors.

"Don't bother looking for Whit either. He already knows you're leaving," she calls after me.

Her words make me flinch but I don't turn around. I don't say anything at all. I enter the corridor to find Sylvie there, spying on our conversation.

"I'm sure you're happy," I tell her as I turn on my heel and head for the guest wing.

"I didn't know she had anything on you. I swear," she says, trailing after me.

I turn on her, making her stop short. "Don't lie. You're all in this together. Are you all so twisted that you love nothing more than destroying someone completely? What the fuck is wrong with you?"

Sylvie parts her lips, but says nothing. I think I stunned her silent.

"Never been called out for your shit before, have you? Little miss, 'oh, I'm dying'. Looking for attention. The middle child. The forgotten child. You're pitiful," I say, all the anger I'd been holding on to while her mother spoke to me spilling out. "I hope you're happy with your mom dragging you around to every doctor for the rest of your short, miserable life."

I stride away from her, noting the unmistakable sight of tears streaming down her face. Seeing them makes me feel bad, but I also don't care. I'm hurting too much. I feel used. Beat up.

By all of them.

It doesn't take me long to pack up all of my belongings. I didn't bring much. And anything Sylvie bought me when we went shopping—and there were a few items—I leave them all on the unmade bed in a pile. I don't want any of her so-called gifts. I sling my duffel bag strap over my shoulder and march out of that stupid, ridiculously huge house with my head held high.

The same driver who brought us here waits for me, standing by the town car. He opens the back passenger side door for me and I slip inside, keeping my duffel with me even though he offers to put it in the trunk.

I trust no one handling my things. I'm sure he ratted me out to Sylvia Lancaster. About my interludes with Whit in the back seat of this very car. Why didn't we ever take Whit's car? We were so stupid.

Careless.

We drive along the winding driveway, and I study the landscape as we pass by. It's beautiful. Perfect. Cold. Lifeless.

That's how I feel. Dead inside.

We approach the gates, and they automatically open, revealing a car waiting on the other side. A sleek Rolls with a handsome man driving. A beautiful woman seated beside him. As we pass by, I spot the blonde head in the back seat, our gazes connecting for the briefest moment.

Leticia. Her family is coming to Thanksgiving dinner.

Of course.

"Excuse me," I say to the driver, who lifts his gaze to mine in the rearview mirror. "Can you take me to the train station?"

"I was given explicit orders to take you straight to Lancaster Prep," he says.

"I'd rather you take me to the train station. I need to go see my mother. She's in Manhattan," I tell him, my voice firm. "Please."

He drives for a while, his hands gripping the steering wheel perfectly, at ten and two. I have my permit, but I haven't gotten my license yet. When you live in the city, what's the point? I never needed it.

I wish I had it now.

"I will take you to the train station," he finally says.

Relief makes me slump into the seat. "Thank you," I murmur as I pull out my phone to check if I have any messages from Whit.

Of course, I have none.

FORTY-ONE

WHIT

I ENTER THE HOUSE, immediately in search of Summer. I look for her downstairs, in her newfound haunts. The library, where I found her curled up in an overstuffed chair reading a book from my family's collection. Or our favorite guest room upstairs, the one with the humongous bed, where I've fucked her endless times already.

But she's in neither of those places.

I wander the guest wing, peeking into every open doorway, prepared to find her lying in wait. A smile on her beautiful face as she comes for me, whispering, "Gotcha," before I sink into her willing kiss.

She's nowhere to be found.

Her bedroom door is shut, and I sense she's gone before it's even confirmed. I suddenly feel hollow. It's as if my heart stops beating as I wrap my fingers around the door handle, counting to three before I enter the room.

Her things are gone. There's a pile of clothing in the center of the messy, unmade bed. The very bed which I fucked her in last night. There's a piece of paper folded neatly on the bedside table with my name written in block letters on the front of it.

WHIT

Frowning, I open the letter to find it typed. Fucking strange.

I HAVE TO GO. *I realized this morning I don't want to be with you after all. I know your life is mapped out completely, and there's no room for me in it. And while I've enjoyed our time together, I know it won't last. So I'm leaving now, before we hurt each other too much. You belong with Leticia anyway. She is your destiny.*

I'm sorry I typed the letter, but my hands were shaking too much to write it. I found a printer in your father's study and wrote this letter in my notes app.

Take care,

Savage

I CRUMPLE the note into a ball and clutch it in my fist as I exit the room. I don't stop until I reach my mother's salon, where I can smell her before I actually enter. How I knew she'd be in there, I'm not sure. But I certainly knew she wouldn't be in the kitchen, preparing today's family meal.

She can't even cook.

I don't bother knocking on the partially opened double doors. I just stride right in, tossing the balled-up paper directly at her head. She glances up at the last second, her mouth dropping open before the paper ball nails her right in the nose before dropping to the desk.

"*Whit.*" She sounds furious.

Good. We're on an even playing field. Our emotions match.

"What did you do to her?" I demand.

Mother doesn't even bother looking at the crumpled paper. "Which *her* are you referring to?"

"You know who," I say between clenched teeth.

Mother sighs. Pushes the paper ball out of her way so she can rest her arms on top of her desk. "Darling. It was bound to happen."

"What was bound to happen?"

"That your—whatever you want to call her would abandon you for someone else."

"What the fuck are you talking about? What did you do to her? What did you tell her?" My voice is barely contained rage.

"She came to me." I watch my mother sit up straighter, elegant as always. Completely put together, not a hair out of place. Nothing ruffles her. Not even after discovering her husband was cheating on her for the last ten years of their marriage with a variety of women, I never once saw her lose her damn mind or yell.

When she's calm like this, it's infuriating.

"Who came to you? Summer?"

"Yes. I didn't want to tell you this, but she demanded money from me, or she said she'd go to the police and tell them you raped her." She drops this bomb with utter calm.

I see red. Would Summer actually do that? "*Raped* her? Are you fucking kidding me? Let her go tell the police then! She was always willing."

"Oh, I know. Trust me, everyone has informed me of your— dalliances around the house."

I start pacing the salon, thrusting my hands in my hair, my mind awhirl with everything my mother just told me. I find it hard to believe. Only earlier this morning Summer and I woke up together, snug in her bed. Her head resting on my chest as I ran my fingers through her silky soft hair. We talked about things we were grateful for, thanks to the holiday, never actually mentioning each other, though I wanted to tell her so badly how thankful I am she came into my life.

I'm an idiot.

"She really threatened to report me to the police?" I pause in my pacing and stare at my beautiful, emotionless mother.

"Yes. Of course, she did. She asked for money and I gave it to her. Then she left." Her gaze barely drops to the crumpled paper ball at her elbow. "I assume that's from her."

Realization dawns. I don't believe Summer would ever do that to me. Not after everything we've shared. "I assumed the letter was from you."

My mother is an excellent actress, I'll give her that. She doesn't even flinch at my accusation. "Why in the world would you think the letter is from me?"

I go to her desk and snatch the paper, smoothing it out so I can read it to her. "'She is your destiny.'" I send her a look. "You're the only one who says that sort of shit."

"Who exactly is she referring to? Leticia?" Mother asks calmly.

"Oh, what a lucky fucking guess. Yes, Leticia. And she signed the note Savage. She would never do that."

"Isn't that her last name? Isn't that what you call her?"

Not anymore. Not like that. She doesn't refer to herself by her last name. Ever. That's my thing. She's Summer. My Summer. "You wrote this."

"I did not."

"She didn't try to bribe you."

"She did. I gave her one hundred thousand dollars to walk away from you. That's it. That's all you're worth to her," Mother says, keeping her voice, her expression even.

"I don't believe you." I crumple the note and toss it at her again, but she dodges it this time, and it lands on the floor. "I'm going to look for her."

"Don't you dare."

"I am. Fuck your little Thanksgiving dinner. I'm out." I turn away from her, but she's quick. She chases me all the way to the doors, inserting herself in front of me as she pulls them shut behind her. "Move."

"No. You're going nowhere. Dinner is in a couple of hours. Leticia and her family have just arrived."

"You invited Leticia and her family to Thanksgiving dinner?" I ask incredulously.

"Of course I did. It was your father's idea, truly. He thought it would be a show of good faith that you two are still committed to each other," she explains.

"I'm not marrying her."

"You are."

"I'm not!" The two words burst from my throat, making it raw and I finally see a reaction from my mother. She presses herself against the doors, cowering. "I won't marry her. I made that very clear to my father earlier. He said that was fine. It's my life. My choice."

"He was humoring you, darling. He knew what was going on between me and your little slut, and he was trying to distract you so we could get her out of the house without your interference. Trust me, you're better off without her in your life."

"How the hell would he know if Summer came to you and threatened you?" I ask. What she's saying is completely illogical. And she knows it. I got her. The expression on her face tells me so.

"You bribed her," I say as everything comes together in my brain. "You paid her off to get her to leave."

"And she took it." Mother lifts her chin, haughty as ever. "Didn't even hesitate. What does that say about her character?"

"Move out of the way," I tell her, my voice low.

She glares at me, but doesn't budge.

"Mother." I crowd her, putting my hands on her suddenly quivering, bony body. "Move." I shove her aside and throw open the doors to find Sylvie standing there, spying on us, as usual.

"You have anything to do with this too?" I throw at her as I walk past.

She scurries along beside me, surprisingly able to keep up despite her supposed weakened condition. "Don't make a fool of yourself over that girl, Whit. She's not worth it."

"I see Mother already got into your head," I say, sneering as I start down the stairs.

Sylvie keeps pace with me. "She used me to get to you. Don't you see it? She just wants our money."

"Our money." I come to a stop in the middle of the staircase, Sylvie stopping on the step above me. "Yes, she's so fucking eager for my money, she was asking for gifts all the time. I never spent a dime on her, Sylvie. Not a single dime."

"She wasn't looking for it from you. Why do you think she came here with me? And what she must've realized when she did?" Sylvie waves her arms around, indicating the massive foyer we're currently standing in. "Look at this place through her eyes. *Look at it.* It's all we know, yet it's wealth beyond what she could ever imagine. She wants a piece of that. A piece of us."

"You shit all over her, didn't you?" I ask, my voice low. Deadly. I love my sister, but I know how she can operate. She is a Lancaster, after all. "You were jealous when she chose me over you, and now look at you. Butt hurt and wanting to strike back. Not giving a shit if she has actual feelings. She's a human being, Sylvie. You were her friend."

"What, like you're her boyfriend?" Sylvie arches a brow.

Breathing deep, I feel my nostrils flare as I exhale. "What Summer and I have, there's no definition."

"Uh huh. How convenient." She thrusts her finger in my face. "She used me. And she used you, too. You just don't want to admit it."

I watch her practically skip down the rest of the stairs, calling Spencer's name once she lands on the floor. I hear his answering call, the telltale sounds of laughter and glasses clinking, and she dashes off toward the sound. I'm sure they're all socializing with our newly arrived guests.

Mother chooses that moment to come down the stairs, her narrowed gaze on me. "Touch me and I'll tell your father."

I roll my eyes at her but say nothing.

"And join us. Dinner will be served soon. You need to come visit with Leticia and the rest of her family before we eat." She says the words like a command. As if I'm supposed to readily agree with her.

Once she's on the bottom step, she turns to look up, her gaze raking over me from head to toe. "Do go change. You look like you're ready to go for a jog."

"Fuck off," I mutter under my breath, but she doesn't hear me.

Turning, I head up the stairs, but I don't go to my room.

I return to my mother's salon.

The doors are locked, and I shake the handles in frustration. One of the maids happens to exit Summer's room at that exact moment, walking down the hall straight toward me. When our gazes meet, she stops in her tracks, her dark eyes wide.

"Do you have the keys?" I ask with a friendly smile. "I need to get in here."

She approaches me carefully, as if she's afraid of me. "That is your mother's study."

"I left my wallet in there," I tell her, leaning against the door jamb and trying my damnedest to appear carefree. "She won't care. I'd ask her to come open the door, but guests have already started to arrive."

The maid chews on her lower lip, reaching into her pocket at the same time and pulling out a ring of keys. She's been at the estate for a couple of years. I recognize her face. She's nice. Quiet. Doesn't cause any problems. The perfect employee, according to my mother's standards. "Here you go," she says as she unlocks the door.

"Thank you," I tell her sincerely. "I appreciate your help."

I step into the room, turn, and pull the double doors shut as quietly as possible. I scan the room, my gaze zeroing in on the desk. Remembering how I had Summer spread out on top of it yesterday afternoon, the sun's beams shining upon her, bathing her naked skin in golden light. My mouth on her pussy, watching her writhe beneath me.

God, she was beautiful.

And now she's gone.

The longer I stare at the desk, the more I realize...

There's something in there.

I can feel it.

I settle into her desk chair and start rummaging through the drawers. I come up empty, finding nothing of interest at first. I'm about to give up when I open the bottom drawer on the left side, seeing nothing but hanging files.

Something tells me I should look between those files. In them. I thumb through them, one after the other, stumbling upon a thick, black book. A journal.

Summer's journal.

My heart hammering, I pull it out and flip it open to find the familiar writing. The pages I've already read. I brought it with me as safekeeping. I didn't want to leave it in my room back at the school, thinking it was smarter to travel with it.

That was my mistake. Of course, my mother went through my things. Of course, she found this. I'm sure she read every goddamn word and then used those words against Summer.

My mother is a conniving bitch. My sister is one in training.

Keeping the journal with me, I put everything back in place on my mother's desk. Looking exactly as I found it. I slip out of the salon, locking the doors behind me, and make my way to my bedroom, where I hide the journal before I change clothes. Go to the bathroom and comb my hair. Wash my face. Splash on some cologne and smile at myself in the mirror.

It looks more like a grimace, but it'll do. I can fake this so-called family dinner, and the minute it's over, I'm out.

I need to find Summer.

If she even wants to be found.

FORTY-TWO

SUMMER

I ARRIVE at my mother's apartment late in the evening, exhausted from today's emotional events, the long train ride, all of it. I enter the darkened living room, thankful I kept my keyring on me so I can get in here in the first place.

I realize fast I'm not alone. I can hear other voices, coming from down the hall. In the bedroom. A male and a female's. My mother and...whoever.

She's back from the Caribbean, and she didn't bother telling me. Didn't wish me a happy Thanksgiving either.

Typical.

Dropping my duffel on the floor in the living room, I start for the hall, calling out as a warning, "Mother! I'm home!"

The voices go silent. And then, "Summer, is that you?"

"Yeah." I go to my closed bedroom door and open it, flicking on the lights. It's the same as I left it, though the air is stale. As if no one has been in the room for months, which I'm sure is the case. I flop onto the edge of the mattress and chew on my thumb, glancing up when my mother appears in the doorway, clad in a white silk robe and nothing else.

"What are you doing here?" she asks, breathless, pushing her hair away from her face, her cheeks pink.

I frown. "You aren't happy to see me?"

"I didn't expect to see you." She smiles, but it's fake. "I'm so glad you've come home, but don't you have school Monday?"

"I'm not going back." I'd made that decision on the train ride home, after my phone died and I realized I left my charger behind in the guest room. I've had a lot of time to think. And I realized there was no way I could go back there and face everyone. Sylvie.

Whit. Especially Whit.

"What do you mean, you're not going back?" Mother frowns, her hands tugging absently at the belt cinched around her waist.

"Too much has happened—I want to graduate early. I have enough credits, so I think I can," I tell her, flopping backwards atop my bed. "I can't do this anymore."

"Do what?" She sounds confused.

"Go to school. Pretend I'm normal. I'm not. I'm messed up. I can't deal with the repercussions of what I've done. I need therapy," I tell the ceiling, my throat aching with unshed tears. "I feel so much guilt over the fire. What happened. What I did."

She glances over her shoulder before fully stepping into my room and pulling the door shut behind her. "You promised we would never discuss that again."

"It's eating me up inside," I practically wail to the ceiling, closing my eyes to try and stop the memories, but it's no use. "I can't stop thinking about it."

I had kind of stopped, but thanks to Sylvia Lancaster's oh so lovely reminder, it hasn't left my mind since. Knowing that she knows what happened is terrifying. I could go to jail. And I would deserve to go. What I did is...horrible. I took a man's life. Two of them. One I hated, and one who meant the world to me.

I've made so many mistakes already. I deserve to be punished for them.

The tears stream from my eyes, sliding down my face as I think of Jonas and all the things he'd done for me. I never got a chance to tell him thank you for changing my life.

Though he changed my life in different, dark ways too, by bringing Yates into it.

"Darling." She comes to the bed and settles on the edge of it, sitting close enough that she can reach out and cup my cheek, forcing me to look at her. "You didn't *do* anything."

"But I did. I started the fire. I knocked the candle over. You know this," I tell her, my face crumpling as the tears really start to fall.

She holds me close as I cry, pulling me into her arms. I press my face against her neck, letting it all out. Crying not just for what I've done, but for all that I lost, especially these last few months, even the last couple of hours. How I had Whit in my life, only to lose him completely, thanks to what I did in my past. I loved him.

I still love him.

And I lost him.

The fire and the secrets I keep will affect me for the rest of my life. Maybe it's time I come clean.

"It wasn't your fault," she murmurs against my hair, her voice so low, it's almost as if I don't hear her at all. "It was never your fault. The one candle you knocked over didn't start that fire."

I go stiff in her arms, pulling away slightly so I can look at her. "What are you talking about?"

She strokes the hair away from my face, her expression dead serious. "I was furious that night, you know. Jonas and I had another raging argument. He told me he wanted a divorce. He was through with me. He couldn't forgive me for what I did with Augie, even after everything we'd been through."

That she would even bring up Augustus Lancaster right now makes my stomach cramp.

"I saw you leave Yates' room," she says, averting her gaze, staring off into the distance as if she's lost in her memories. "I had a suspicion about you two, and I didn't want to believe it. Deep down, I knew. I *knew*, but I didn't know how to stop it. I thought, perhaps, that you wanted—to be in a relationship with him."

Tears well in my eyes and I want to scream at her. That was the last thing I wanted. And if she suspected, why didn't she try and stop it? Stop him? Why didn't she say something to me? To Yates? To Jonas?

Because she's selfish. Thoughtless.

Too wrapped up in her own bullshit.

"When I saw you leave his room, I went in and confronted him. He was asleep, and I noticed the candle had fallen over, the flame sputtering in the spilled wax. It wasn't going to start a fire, Summer. There was no way that could happen."

"Then how did it start?" I whispered, scared yet eager to hear her explanation.

"I fixed the candle, set it back in its holder, and it knocked into the one next to it, making a clanking noise. Loud enough that it woke Yates up. He became very defensive when he realized I was in the room with him. Asking where you were, what did I know. And I told him I knew *everything*, even though I truly didn't. I was only making assumptions." Her eyes narrow as I can only assume she recalls the memories of that night.

"You said that?"

Mother nods. "He accused you of being a slut. That you asked for it. Begged for it. He said because you were so beautiful, how could he resist? As if it's your fault. Men can be that way sometimes. Never wanting to take responsibility for their actions."

I let her words sink in. It's so true. Of course, Yates would blame me and say that I asked for it. Heaven forbid he be responsible.

"Then he started in on me. Saying he was going to tell his father I snuck into his room. As if I wanted to, I don't know, *molest* him? Please. When I laughed, he got angry. Said I was nothing but a slut who used his father for his money," Mother explains, her eyes falling shut for the briefest moment. "That's when I grabbed one of the empty iron candle sticks and struck him in the head with it."

I suck in a gasp, shocked by her confession. "*What?*"

"I killed him." She nods, her gaze sliding to mine. "I thought I did. There was so much blood, baby. So much blood. I panicked. I didn't know what to do. I went and washed up. Changed into clean clothes. Then I went back to his room and I tipped over a couple of the candles, making sure they caught the drapes on fire. But that happened so fast. Too fast. The fire climbed up the wall, eating the drapes until they were nothing but ash, and I knew. I needed to get us out of there. I ran from the room, went and got you, and you know the rest of the story."

I stare at her, a whirlwind of emotions twisting inside of me as I absorb her words, and the meaning behind them. All this time, she let me believe I killed them. She let me believe *I* started the fire, when she did it all along.

My mother caused it. The fire. Their deaths.

And she was willing to let me bear the weight of all that guilt and fear.

"Why did you let me believe I was the one responsible?" I ask her.

"I couldn't tell you what I did to Yates. You would've freaked out. Gone to the police. I'd be in prison right now if you did that. I couldn't risk it," she explains.

"But I could've ended up in prison too," I remind her.

"From your perspective, it was an accident. You didn't mean to do any of it. You would've never been convicted," she says, dismissing my protest. "Thank God his body was burned beyond recognition. His autopsy results were inconclusive."

"You told me he died of smoke inhalation." My mind is racing, searching for all the details from that night and the aftermath. Some things I remember. Some memories are faded, or damaged by shock.

Others I'd rather forget completely.

"There was smoke in his lungs, which showed he was still alive during the fire. But he would've never survived what I did to him. Or he would've ended up brain damaged and hooked up to machines for the rest of his life." Her expression turns bitter. "I did that little fucker a favor. How dare he force himself on you, and for so long."

Just saying those last words tells me she knew all along. She knew and she never did a damn thing to stop it.

The disappointment that crashes over me is overwhelming and I rest a hand over my stomach, praying I won't get sick. She didn't care enough to stop it. She didn't do enough to protect me. I've been on my own for so long. Longer than I've even realized.

"After a while, he didn't have to force himself," I admit, hanging my head in shame. "It was easier to just—take it."

She rubs my back. "It's a cruel world, darling. Men use us. I hope that doesn't happen to you ever again."

Her advice rings hollow. I've been traumatized and molested by my stepbrother, and that's all she has to say to me?

Unbelievable.

I think of Whit and how he used me too. He used me up, and I let him. Worse, I enjoyed it. I could tell her about our relationship, but I'm scared of what she might do.

I don't trust her. How can I? That hurts to admit, even to myself, but I've known this for a while. I just wasn't as aware of the lengths she'd gone to in order to protect me—and herself.

I frown. More herself than anything else—this was never about me. She could say she did it because of what Yates did to me, but I know the truth.

She was on the brink of losing Jonas. Her social status. The money. The travel. Her entire life. She couldn't stand the thought. So she killed them both.

And became the sole heir to Jonas' fortune.

"Why don't you want to go back to Lancaster?" she asks.

Just hearing the Lancaster name makes my heart ache. "I can't, Mother. I hate that school and everyone in it."

Except for one. And he's just as bad as all the rest. He used me. As did his mother. And even Sylvie.

God, Sylvie. The venom in her voice. The cruel words she said. I adored her, but she hates me.

They all hate me.

"I can't go back," I say firmly. "I won't. You can't make me. I'll go to public school here. I'll take the GED test. I'll do anything. Just—please don't convince me to go back. It's a waste of your breath."

"Of course not," she says, her hand running up and down my back. "I agree with your earlier suggestion. I'm sure you have enough credits to graduate early. Maybe take a gap year before you start college."

"You'd really let me?" I send her a hopeful look, realizing that if I play my cards right, she can help me escape.

"You could travel," she says, lost in her thoughts. "Europe in the springtime. See the sights. See the world. College is wonderful, but life experience is just as important, if not more so."

"I want that," I tell her, leaning against her. She wraps her arms around me and holds me close. We haven't done this in years. I can't remember the last time she hugged me. And while I don't fully trust her, I need this. The comfort.

"I'll give it to you."

A muffled voice comes from down the hall. Deep and male, calling my mother's name.

"Janine? Where are you?"

I pull away from her, instantly wary. "Who is that?"

She smiles. "Howard. I went to the Caribbean with him. But don't say anything—his wife is down in Florida with the kids. She thinks he's in the city working."

"Oh Mother." I'm sure he's some rich asshole who bought his way into her panties, and she fell for his cheesy lines. This is how it always starts. She can't help herself. This is how she believes relationships are supposed to begin.

"It's different this time." I remember her saying that about Jonas too. In the early days, when I was little and she asked me if I wanted a big brother. I'd been so excited, so desperate for more family, I'd readily agreed that it would be the best thing to ever happen to me.

Instead, Yates turned into my nightmare.

There's a knock on my bedroom door. "Janine? What are you doing?"

"Coming!" she calls. "Give me a minute."

He shuffles away and I hear her bedroom door close.

"Is he staying the night?" I ask once he's gone.

"Of course he is. Why wouldn't he?" She smiles. Hugs me one last time before she stands. "We'll talk in the morning, okay? And I'll contact the school first thing Monday."

"You really won't make me go?" I ask hopefully.

She shakes her head. "I will give you whatever you want. It's the least I can do after..."

Her voice drifts, and I don't say anything either. She owes this to me, and she knows it. There's so much more she owes me too, but I can't collect on that debt right now.

I probably never will.

It hurts, to realize your mother is human. Flawed. She's made countless mistakes, many of them at my expense. I can either let those mistakes hold me back and make me hate her, or I can let everything go and pray she learns from the damage she's done.

I'd much rather let it all go.

I watch her walk across my bedroom and go to the door, pausing as she turns to study me. "Just—keep what I said to you between us, okay? Don't ever mention it again. Not even to me."

I nod, fully aware of why she's letting me drop out of Lancaster.

She's buying my silence.

My compliance.

And I'm going to let her.

FORTY-THREE

SUMMER

SIXTEEN MONTHS *later*

I EXIT THE UBER, taking a deep breath of the fresh, damp morning air before I start across the square, toward my destination. I've been in Europe, specifically Paris, for the last year. I attend school, studying art history, immersing myself completely in learning the different art periods, the meanings behind the paintings. Studying the artists themselves. It's been grueling. Fascinating.

I've enjoyed every minute of it.

I used to surround myself with beautiful people. Dazzled by their wealth and what they were able to do with it. Now I surround myself with meaningful art instead. Beautiful people will hurt you. It's just their way. Beautiful art?

It allows you to study it. Absorb it. It makes you feel. And it rarely hurts.

I make my way across the square, taking in the stately buildings surrounding me. The designer stores that are still closed. The hotel in the distance, subtle. You'd never guess a famous landmark was only a few feet away.

Of course, he would stay there. It makes perfect sense.

I haven't spent much time exploring the 1st arrondissement beyond visiting the Louvre, and even then, I don't venture much beyond the museum and the gardens that surround it. I'm not one to visit the shops much anymore. Though I never really was. I don't need to shop, to buy the latest designer clothing or handbags.

I leave that sort of thing up to my mother.

Place Vendome is quiet in the morning. The elegant buildings remind me of another time. The massive column in the center, with the statue of Napoleon on top. I stop and gaze up at it, absorbing the history, the cool breeze, the chatter of French women as they walk behind me.

Leaving everyone behind, leaving the US, has been the balm my damaged soul needed. What the Lancasters did to me still hurts, even after all of this time. Especially Whit, who never reached out to me once I left. He never called, never texted, and I haven't seen him since. Did he believe the lies his mother told? I'm sure Sylvie spun an intricate tale as well.

After everything Whit and I had been through, it still bothers me that he believed them over me. But of course, they're family. I'm nothing. He discarded me easily, and never looked back. What we shared ended up a vicious dirty little secret after all. He's a monster. A villain.

And I'm his stupid little plaything.

Yet despite it all, my feelings haven't faded. I miss him.

Sometimes, I'm afraid my feelings toward him have only gotten stronger, which is terrifying.

After everything that happened at the Lancaster home, the day after Thanksgiving, Mother took me to a store and purchased me a new phone, and changed my number. I shut down all of my social media, never bothering to check any of my comments or private messages before I did. I started an Instagram account, but don't really post. I'm on TikTok. I see what's going on with the people that I went to high school with. Most of them have public accounts, broadcasting all of their exploits for the world to see. I study their posts, watch their stories, and sometimes, when I'm feeling especially lonely, yearning will rise within me. Reminding me of everything I've lost.

But being here, I've gained so much more.

I've made a lot of mistakes in my life. I will continue to make them, but I feel more in control now. More mature. I know I still have a lot of growing to do, but I was on the track to nowhere back in the States. At Lancaster. With my mother. If I'd stayed in the city, God knows what would've happened to me. I am without a doubt my mother's daughter, though I don't plan on following in her footsteps.

I see her mistakes. And how she continues to make them.

Using men, depending on them in order to survive, I refuse to do that. I want to fall in love with a man despite his wealth. I don't care whether he has money or not—I already know it doesn't buy happiness. I want to create my own career, my own life, so I'm solely dependent on myself.

And no one else.

Ironically enough, right after I graduated early from high school, and before I left for Europe, Mother admitted she kept something from me—Jonas had left me a small inheritance. An account that I could use for college—or whatever I wished. I think of the money as a gift. A blessing from Jonas. I'm sorry we lost him. I know Mother panicked, and believed we would've lost everything, which she was probably right. I hate that he died because of it. I loved him as if he were my own father, though I'm not sure how my mother felt about him near the end.

I have no regrets over Yates though. I hope he burns in hell.

My gaze catches on the Van Cleef and Arpels shop nearby and I wander over to study the window display, my gaze lingering on the glittering jewels. Part of a special Romeo and Juliet themed collection, which reminds me of senior year honors English with Whit. Star-crossed lovers who are forbidden to see each other because of their rival families.

Sounds familiar.

The jewelry glitters and shines under the lights. Van Cleef is one of the most expensive, coveted brands. Jonas gave Mother one of their Alhambra necklaces for her birthday when I was fourteen. There was a time she wore that necklace every single day, showing off to everyone she encountered that she was wealthy enough to own one.

Turning away from the window, I go to the Ritz, entering the hotel and trying my best not to look like a country bumpkin who can't stop staring at the opulence surrounding me. The lobby is absolutely gorgeous, as if I'm stepping into another time. The air, fragrant. The people, elegant. Bountiful spring flower arrangements are everywhere, glittering chandeliers hanging above my head, casting fragmented light into the room.

"My favorite season!"

I glance over to see Monty approaching as he glides down a flight of elegantly curved stairs, a smile on his friendly face. I go to him, his arms coming around me and holding me close. I cling to him, giving him a squeeze, so thankful we have remained friends. He somehow found my obscure new Instagram profile and reached out via DMs. We've stayed in contact ever since. When he messaged me recently saying he would be in Paris and wanted to get together, I couldn't agree fast enough.

"It's so good to see you," he says as he pulls away, his hands still clutching my shoulders. He blatantly checks me out in his typical way. "You look marvelous. Paris is good to you."

"You look wonderful too," I tell him. It is so nice to see a friendly face. "Why are you in Paris?"

"Oh darling, let's save that for when we sit down. Now come, let's go have some tea and discussion."

Monty escorts me to a lovely restaurant that's straight out of a Parisian dream. Beautiful gilt trim frames the massive windows, the ceiling painted the color of the sky, the paneled walls painted a milky white. All of the furniture is cream and pale pink and the lightest gold, the tablecloths a stark, pure white with thin glass vases filled with delicate fresh flower arrangements.

We sit on the dainty chairs, and I quietly admire Monty, who seems completely in his element. Wearing a brown checkered suit and a pastel yellow button up, sans tie, his longish hair flopping over his forehead, his eyes dancing with mischief as they meet mine.

"You dressed...impeccably." He smiles, his gaze scanning my attire.

I'm wearing a simple floral print dress I found in a little shop last summer. My hair is loose, diamond studs that Jonas gave me on my sixteenth birthday in my ears. I carry one of my mother's old black Chanel bags, bringing it out only because I'm in the Ritz and I hope I look the part.

Always desperate to fit in. A habit that's still proving hard to break.

"I was just thinking the same thing about you," I tell him with a smile.

"This old thing?" He glances down at his chest before returning his gaze to mine. "I was going for the dandy look."

"I think you succeeded."

The server approaches and Monty orders tea for us. "It's still early," he says once the server is gone. "They'll humor us while we sit here for a few hours and gossip, until it's finally lunch and we can order from the menu. Unless you have other plans?"

"My day is completely cleared, just for you."

He props his elbow on the table, resting his chin on his fist as he bats his eyelashes at me. "Tell me what you're doing. How many pretty boys have you met? Why haven't you gained fifty pounds because of the pastries and butter? Swear to God you're thinner than ever, darling."

"Tell me first why you're here." I haven't changed my ways when it comes to talking about myself.

I still don't like to do it.

"Oh, a man. Of course." He makes a dismissive gesture with his hand. "I came for the dick. Unfortunately, he turned into a giant dick, kicked me out of his shitty little flat and now here I am at the Ritz for the next week, not sure what to do next. Change my flight and return home early? Or enjoy my time here in the city of love?"

"You have to stay." I reach across the table to gently touch his arm. "Explore Paris. Eat lots of croissants with butter."

"By myself?" He frowns. "I'd rather spend time in that shitty little flat with that shitty guy and his giant dick. Unless *you* want to show me the sights."

"Haven't you been here before? You could probably show me around better than I ever could," I remind him.

"True. I'm sure you've been on a bus tour and went up the Eiffel Tower since your arrival and that's about it, am I right?" He raises a brow.

I roll my eyes. "Of course that was one of the first things I did. It was my first time here. But now I'm over that. I only hang out in the Louvre when I'm in class. Otherwise, I hate it around there. Too many tourists."

"Ah, soon you'll be smoking cigarettes, sitting outside of a small café, full of disdain." He laughs, sounding thrilled. "Paris has been very, very good to you."

"I'm sorry that it didn't work out with your boy," I say softly, once his laughter has died. "Are you sad about the breakup?"

"Darling, I am most definitely not sad. It wasn't what I would call a breakup. I came here for the sex. That's it. It wasn't a grand love. Not like what you suffered through." Monty makes a tsking noise.

He's the only one I told about Whit and what happened between us. I didn't go into all the details, but he knows enough. And now, even a year later, he thinks we're star-crossed lovers who were meant to be, until Whit's family interfered and messed everything up. In Monty's eyes, we are a modern-day retelling of Romeo and Juliet.

If only it were that simple.

For the next hour, we gossip and laugh and I hang on Monty's every word as he shares stories from over the past year. He graduated from MIT in December and he's now taking a gap year between college and real life.

"Is that a thing?" I ask, frowning.

"No. Probably not. But I made it a thing. Who wants to get right to work and toil their life away?" He waves a hand. "Not me."

"Do you even need to work?" I ask, taking a sip of my milky tea.

"Of course not. My children's children won't need to work, not that I plan on having any. But I'd get bored. A man can travel around and fall into one relationship after another for only so long. Oh, and shop."

"Do you like to shop?" I ask, sounding hopeful. I suddenly have the itch to check out a few stores. Something high end and beautiful. Little commercial works of art.

"I am gay and I'm into fashion. Of course, I love to shop," he says drolly, rolling his eyes. "Let's have lunch and I'll take you somewhere."

We order salads and split a sandwich, and the food is delicious. As is the company. Monty tells so many stories, about people I've heard of but don't really know. Of people whose younger siblings I went to school with. He even mentions Sylvie.

"She was admitted to the hospital just before Christmas," he says, his voice lowering. "She almost died."

"What?" I may hate what she did to me, but I will always care about her. Even if she despises me.

"Yes." He nods, his expression solemn. "The family kept it very hush hush. She's out now. I believe she was released on New Year's, but they still don't know exactly what's wrong with her. She's never returned to Lancaster Prep. I hear Spence is beside himself."

"That's awful," I say, gazing at the tablecloth, my mind filled with memories of Sylvie. She was so good to me—until she wasn't. "And what about—Whit?"

"What about him?"

Monty's voice is filled with so much barely restrained humor, I glance up at him sharply, my eyes narrowing. "What do you know that I don't?"

"So. Much," he says, his smile devilish. "Where shall I start?"

"Tell me the juiciest thing first." I lean forward, anxious for any news. Good and bad.

"He ended everything with Leticia."

"*What?*" I suck in a harsh breath, my mind awhirl with the news, turning it over and over. He may have said that's what he wanted, but I thought that was just talk. That he didn't mean it. That his parents would never allow it.

"Here's the deal." Monty's voice lowers to a whisper, as if he could know someone in this room who would hear him gossip. And he just might. "She's a *huge* coke addict. It got really bad. The Christmas before you left? She was in a bad way. Flunking school, barely functioning on a day-to-day basis. Her parents sent her to rehab at the beginning of the year. Whit came up with some nonsense about how they signed a contract, and that she broke a clause because of her drug use. I mean, I can't blame the guy. Who wants to marry a coke fiend?"

"Is that true though?" I ask, trying to wrap my mind around the idea that they actually brokered a bona fide deal. "They had a contract for their impending marriage?"

"Something like that. I'm sure they did. Old money families are weird. They want everything in writing." Monty shrugs. "Anyway, he ended things with her. He also tested out like you did, and graduated early. Didn't go away to college either, much to his parents' shock and horror. He decided to do what every respectable young man of means does and travel the continent."

I frown. "The continent?"

"Mostly Europe, darling. The Virgin Islands for a while, where he picked up a deep tan. Australia for a very short period. I heard he thought the people were too nice there."

I want to laugh. I also want to cry. It sounds just like something Whit would say—that the friendly Australians were too nice.

"He's been all over. Don't you follow his Instagram?" Monty asks.

I wouldn't allow myself. I blocked him immediately after everything that happened and I didn't check up on him. No matter how badly I wanted to. "Where is he now?"

"I don't know." Monty shrugs, but there's something in the tone of his voice, the way his eyes twinkle.

I think he might know, but he's not telling.

Once we're finished, Monty pays for the tab—he wouldn't let me split it, calling me his guest—and we leave the hotel, walking past the Van Cleef and Arpels window display slowly.

"God, their jewelry is exquisite," he says, darting over to one of the windows. "Like little works of art."

"It's beautiful," I agree once I stop to stand next to him.

He stares at it for a while, and something changes in his expression. As if he suddenly came up with the best idea. His gaze never leaving the window, he says, "If you could have any piece of fine jewelry, say a giant diamond ring or huge emerald earrings, what would you choose? What would be your most coveted piece?"

"A necklace," I say without hesitation.

"A necklace?" He frowns as his gaze meets mine, seemingly disappointed.

"Yes. If the sky is the limit, I'd want it to be thick with diamonds, and it would clasp tightly around my neck, almost like a collar." My mind wanders toward Whit, as it's so wont to do. Still. Even after all this time. "I want it to be heavy, so I can feel the weight of the stones and the metal on my skin. And I want the person who gives it to me to see the necklace as almost...a claiming. As if they own me." I clamp my lips shut, embarrassment quickly following.

I got a little lost in my fantasy there for a moment.

"Well, well," Monty drawls. "That sounds downright kinky."

My cheeks catch fire. "I told you before I like that sort of thing."

And he's the only one who knows about it—with the exception of Whit.

"Noted. So when your fantasy man comes to me one day asking what he should buy for you, I know what to tell him," Monty says.

"I doubt my fantasy man will want to buy a diamond necklace for me," I say.

Monty purses his lips, offended. "And why not?"

"My ultimate fantasy man most likely won't want to be seen with me. I'm probably banished for life from New York society," I tell him. My mother is more on the fringe, sneaking around with her lover, Howard. Always the mistress. Very rarely the bride.

Am I destined for that life?

No.

I won't let it happen.

"Darling," Monty drawls. "With me by your side? You will be the queen of New York society. And don't you ever forget it."

FORTY-FOUR

SUMMER

THE NOTE—IT'S more like a missive, like an old-fashioned calling card—is left tucked between my door and the frame. I notice it as I approach the door of my flat, my steps slowing, curiosity filling me. I tug at the piece of paper, impressed by its sturdiness. Thick, cream colored cardstock with elegant black embossed typeface.

An invitation.

You have been cordially invited to dinner
By
Montgomery Michaels the IV
At
Guy Savoy
Friday, April 22nd
Eight o'clock
Please RSVP

SMILING, I walk inside my flat, shutting the door and leaning against it as I type out a quick text to Monty.

Me: **Got your invitation. RSVPing.**

He answers quickly.

Monty: **Perfect. This is by far the most delicious and expensive place you'll ever eat.**

Me: **Of course it is. Who all is coming?**

Monty: **People.**

That's all he says. People.

Me: **How many?**

Monty: **Enough to make it interesting.**

Me: **How should I dress?**

Monty: **Sexy elegance. I suppose I should've put that on the card.**

Me: **I can't believe you went to so much trouble just for a dinner invite.**

Monty: **I don't do anything half-assed. You should know that about me by now.**

I send him a string of laughing face emojis.

Monty: **You'll need a new dress.**

Me: **I will?**

Monty: **Whatever you have in that tiny closet in that tiny flat of yours, won't do.**

I had Monty over yesterday for drinks before we went out to dinner. He hated every minute of it. Said my small apartment made him feel claustrophobic. I just laughed and let him whine for a while before we went and had dinner at one of the outdoor restaurants on the Seine. It was such a beautiful night, and we were surrounded by couples. Lovers.

It made me miss having a man in my life. Though I have no idea what it's like, to be in a normal relationship. Something long-term and full of love. I'm young, almost twenty, I still have plenty of time.

But I long for that. For a man to look at me with hunger in his gaze. To reach for me as if he can't help himself. I want to be adored. Ravished. Loved. I want it to be big and wonderful and messy and overwhelming.

I want what I had with Whit.

My phone dings with another text from my friend.

Monty: **We'll shop tomorrow. Do you have class?**

Me: **In the morning.**

Monty: **In the afternoon then. I'll make an appointment. They'll pull dresses for you and give us champagne and a giant dressing room for you to try them on in.**

Me: **That sounds wonderful. And expensive.**

Monty: **Money is no object.**

Me: **For you.**

Monty: **Tomorrow at this shop? For you too. Arrangements will be made.**

I frown, staring at the phone. What could he be talking about?

Me: **What sort of arrangements?**

Monty: **Don't you worry your pretty little head about it. I'll send more details in the morning via text. You shall meet me there. And you will try on every single thing I bring you. No complaints. Understood?**

Me: **Yes Mother.**

He sends me two rows of the middle finger emoji, making me laugh.

What is he talking about, arrangements have been made? I don't understand.

But now I'm dying to know.

I ARRIVE at the shop on the Rue Cambon at two o'clock on the dot. Three gorgeous, statuesque women dressed in severe black await me inside, all of them greeting, "Bon jour," in the sweetest of voices.

"Bon jour," I return, coming to a stop in the middle of the shop. It's sleek and white, with very little clothing on display.

"Are you Mademoiselle Savage?" one of them asks me.

I nod, glancing around the store in search of Monty. "Is Mr. Michaels here yet?"

"Monsieur Michaels shall be here very soon. But we have plenty of dresses pulled aside just for you to start trying on. Would you like me to take you to your dressing room?"

"Please," I tell her, following after her as she heads for the back of the shop.

The other women nod and smile as I pass by, and I can't help but feel underdressed. I'm in jeans and a sweater, since I was in class all morning, and I didn't have a chance to change into something a little more, I don't know, proper?

But what's proper to wear when shopping? I feel silly, having to get all gussied up just to shop, even if it is in a designer area.

In Paris, they take their shopping very, very seriously.

The woman pulls back a heavy, shimmery gray curtain to reveal a spacious dressing room with two chairs and a rack filled with dresses in a variety of shapes and colors. Long and short. Black, white and every color in between. I go to the dresses and thumb through them, my breath stalled in my throat as I take them all in.

Not a one of them has a price tag on them. I cannot afford this place.

Turning toward her, I ask, "Who picked these dresses out?"

She smiles politely, clasping her hands behind her back. "My staff and I did, mademoiselle. I hope they are of your taste."

"They're beautiful, *merci*." I hesitate, not quite sure how I should word this. "Who...put this together?"

She frowns. "Your friend did. Monsieur Michaels."

"No one else?" I don't know why I'd think anyone else is involved. This is just...so strange.

Yes, I know Monty loves to shop. He's taken me on a few excursions since arriving in Paris. But I don't understand why he's having me choose a gorgeous designer dress that probably costs thousands of euros for me to wear once? At an ultra-expensive restaurant to...what? Show me off?

I don't get it.

"No one else," she says, her expression brightening. "Would you care for some champagne?"

"That would be lovely," I tell her with a faint smile.

I watch her go before I start to look through the dresses once more. They're beautiful. Most of them aren't much. Skimpy. Strapless. Deep Vs in the front. Backless. Short, showing off plenty of leg.

I think of the dress I wore for Whit before Thanksgiving, oh so long ago. When he fucked me in the back of the town car.

My skin warms at the memory.

"Darling."

I glance up to find Monty peeking around the curtain, his hand over his eyes. "Are you decent?"

I laugh. "I'm stark naked."

He drops his hand, disappointment written all over his face. "Damn it, you liar."

My laughter grows. "You actually want to see me naked?"

"You're a gorgeous little creature. Of course I want to see you naked. But I don't want to fuck you, so you're safe with me." He's already clutching a champagne flute between his fingers as he comes up beside me to thumb through the clothes on the rack. "I see they've pulled some quality pieces for you."

"All of them are very beautiful. And very revealing," I say.

He smirks. "The more skin, the better."

"For who? I'll freeze." It may be springtime, but April in Paris is still very cold.

"You have the smoothest skin. Show it off," he says, leaning in close. "There are so many rich men at Guy Savoy. You could probably find a new lover Friday night."

"I don't want a new lover," I immediately protest.

"Why not? Aren't you lonely? I can never hold out for too long. I always end up missing dick." He pouts.

"I haven't had dick in a long time," I admit.

"How long?"

"Since Whit."

Monty stops, his mouth dropping open in disbelief for a second or two before he swigs from his champagne flute, draining it. "You're kidding me."

"I'm serious."

"God, aren't you starved for it? I would die. Absolutely fall apart," he says gravely.

"I've been focusing on me," I admit.

"Are your fingers tired from all the masturbating?" He raises his brows.

"I don't masturbate all the time," I murmur.

"Liar." He laughs at my shocked face. "I'm just kidding. Hurry and try something on. Here, I'll choose the first dress."

It's long and strapless and when I take off my clothes, Monty waves his fingers at me. "Get rid of the bra."

"But—"

"It's strapless. Besides, you won't be wearing undergarments Friday night. Trust me," he says knowingly.

I frown. "I won't?"

"You want your clothes to lay nicely. Not show panty lines or bra lace. Ew." He mock shivers.

He's right. I know this. So I rid myself of my bra and slip the dress on, Monty immediately dismissing it. He dismisses all of the long gowns, and most of the short ones too. Until the only dresses remaining on the rack are extremely short and revealing.

I pluck one from where it's hanging, contemplating it. It's heavy, made of a lightweight silver and black mesh, and it's so short, I'm sure my vagina will hang out of it. "This looks dangerous."

"More like marvelous," he drawls. "Put it on."

I slip it over my head, and it falls into place perfectly. One side of the dress is silver, the other side black, the pieces crossing in the front across my right thigh, revealing it completely, almost to my hip bone. The neckline dips low, far past my breasts and nearly to my navel, and it's held up by two thin straps. That's it.

I feel completely exposed.

"Turn around," Monty demands and I do so, glancing over my shoulder to stare at myself in the mirror.

My entire back is on display too, the mesh fabric dipping in the middle of my lower back, almost exposing my butt. The dress's hem flirts at the top of my thighs. The mesh is sheer enough that I can see my black panties, and when I turn to face the mirror once more I can also see my nipples.

"I can't wear this," I say, my tone firm. "I look like a prostitute."

Monty comes to stand behind me, his hands settling lightly on my bare shoulders. "You must wear it. And you don't look like a prostitute. Trust me. You will fucking stun every single man who lays eyes on you."

"I don't want to stun them. I don't even want them to see me." I turn to the side, the material sliding against my body, making my skin prickle with awareness. The dress is sensuous. Revealing. Sexy beyond belief. I've never worn anything like it before in my life. "How much is this anyway?"

"Not exactly sure. I'd guess at least two thousand euros," he says nonchalantly.

I practically choke on my own saliva. "What the *fuck?* Are you serious, Montgomery? It's made of—nothing." I run my hand over the mesh, my nipples hardening. I may as well be touching my bare skin, it's so thin.

"It's designer," he corrects. "And I think it's perfect. You are gorgeous."

"If I were a paid escort," I retort.

He laughs, sounding delighted. "Oh darling, in your dreams."

"More like in some man's wet dream." I glare at him in the mirror, which only makes him laugh harder. I can't help but start to laugh too.

"You need silver shoes," he says, still chuckling. "Stilettos so you'll be impossibly tall. Like an Amazon. Thin straps, barely there. They shouldn't overwhelm. I don't want people to see anything but this dress and your body."

"Why?" I ask him, my voice, my gaze sincere. "Who exactly am I trying to impress?"

His barely contained smile is unnerving, filling me with wariness. "Only one of the most powerful men in the world."

FORTY-FIVE

SUMMER

I ARRIVE at the restaurant at exactly eight o'clock, letting the wind in with me as I push through the heavy doors. It's a chilly night, and I'm clad in a thick black faux fur coat Monty found for me on our shopping excursion. It's short, but just enough to cover my minidress, my legs still completely exposed. They glow from the exfoliation treatment I gave them in the shower earlier. I paid special attention to my entire body for tonight, Monty instructing me to do so. He wanted me to prepare myself as if I were going to have sex with the King of Sultan, direct quote.

I don't know where he gets his silly ideas, but I went along with it, enjoying the pampering. Since I've been in Paris, I haven't indulged in much self-care. I've been too busy, trying to keep my mind and body active so I won't sink back into the memories that haunt me.

This last week with Monty has felt like a high fantasy moment. Giving me a glimmer of my old life, when I naively believed Whit would gladly relinquish everything to be with me. That week leading up to Thanksgiving were some of my favorite moments with him. When he chased me all over the Lancaster estate, finding me in dark corners where he would then ravish me with his beautiful mouth and hands as my prize.

I miss that mouth and those hands. I even miss the dark, disturbing things he would say to me. No one made me feel like Whit Lancaster.

No one.

An imposing set of marble stairs rises before me, draped in blood red carpet. I carefully walk up them, my ankles wobbly thanks to the five-inch heels of my stilettos. They're whisper thin, as are the silver straps that cross my feet, and I know it would take nothing to topple me completely over, planting me on my face.

Reaching out, I grab the balustrade, holding onto it for dear life as I reach the top of the stairs. The floor is covered in black and white marble tiles, my heels clicking as I walk across them, toward the single open doorway with the restaurant's subtle sign to the left of it. The room within beckons, dark and mysterious, and I frown, surprised I don't hear the low murmurs of conversation, the delicate clink of silverware hitting fine china.

I hear nothing at all.

Still not quite sure of Monty's motives, or what he's all about in regards to tonight's dinner. I feel like I'm his doll and he's playing dress up with me. He wants me to look a certain way, to be this sort of—sex bomb to drop men to their knees or whatever. I kept questioning him about tonight's dinner guests, but he remained frustratingly mum. It's annoying.

I'm sure he's doing it on purpose, wanting to be mysterious. It's working.

Too well.

Once I enter the overly warm restaurant, my hands go to the front of my coat, and I wish I could rid myself of it. A man in an elegant gray suit materializes out of nowhere, stepping toward me with a polite smile as he helps me out of it. I smile at him, murmuring, "Merci," as he takes my coat for me.

His gaze remains trained on my face the entire time, never once looking at my body, and I wonder if someone warned him of what I could be possibly wearing.

Though the idea is ridiculous. Why would anyone need to do that?

"Right this way, mademoiselle," he says, his French accent heavy as he holds his hand out, indicating where I need to go. The restaurant is small. Dark. Intimate. There's no one else in the room, which is strange. It's Friday night. It should be bustling with business, every table full of people eating and drinking and talking.

We pass through many connected rooms, every single one of them empty, before we stop in the last room. There's a singular round table in the center with only two chairs and place settings in front of them. Frowning, I glance over at the man but he merely smiles and nods before he leaves me completely alone.

Our dinner party is really only for two? Me and Monty? That's it?

Disappointment floods me, and I revel in it for a while. I'd hoped to meet someone new. Other people that are Monty's friends who I could laugh and drink with. Instead, it's just the two of us, and for a moment, I allow myself to be sad.

But that only last for a few minutes. I've wallowed enough about things almost my entire life. Time to move on and be strong.

I walk around the room, trailing my fingers along the dark gray-paneled wall, until I stop in front of the window, staring outside at the busy Paris night. There is an endless stream of cars on the street below, and people walking along the sidewalks. The trees are starting to bloom, lovely and hopeful in the dreary, windy weather, those blossoms clinging to the branches for dear life. I touch the cool glass with my fingertips, my nipples tightening from the outside chill.

It's when I feel the presence of someone entering the room that my body stiffens, and I keep my back to him. It's a man. I can smell his cologne. Rich and distinct, I inhale discreetly, not recognizing the scent. Did Monty change his signature cologne? Highly doubtful, since he bought a vat of it at Hermes when I was with him, and it smells nothing like this.

Seconds pass, gaining quickly on a minute, and still the man says nothing. I avert my head, about to glance over my shoulder, when he barks at me:

"Don't turn around."

My heart thumping wildly in my chest, I do as he says, vaguely recognizing the voice. It's purposely deeper, as if he's trying to disguise it, and I wonder who he is.

In the darkest, deepest recesses of my soul, I recognize him. I know him. He draws closer, my entire body lighting up, and I close my eyes, hope against hope filling me. I'm trembling, a mixture of fear and excitement swirling within me. He pauses directly behind me and I dip my head, glancing down at my feet. I can see his dark dress shoes, the hem of his black trousers. My breath lodges in my throat as I wait for something, any sort of acknowledgment.

A shaky exhale leaves me when I feel it. A single finger drifting down my back, featherlight, goose bumps rising in its wake as he goes down. Down. Until he's touching the base of my spine, his finger tugging on the mesh fabric pooled there, his knuckle brushing against my flesh.

His finger is gone, filling me with disappointment, but seconds later, he settles his hands on my shoulders, gripping me surely. I breathe a sigh of relief, my body responding immediately to his touch.

"Whit," I breathe.

His grip tightens on my flesh, keeping me in place. I open my eyes to see my face reflected in the window, and his too, right behind me. I drink him in greedily. He's just as beautiful as I remember, maybe even more so now. He looks older. More like a man. His jaw is just as sharp, as are his cheekbones, set-off by that plush, delectable mouth. I study him unashamedly in the reflection, realizing that he's doing the same to me, though his gaze is elsewhere.

Traveling all over my body.

"What the fuck are you wearing?" he asks, his deep voice full of wonder. "Did Monty choose this dress on purpose to drive me out of my damn mind? Because it's working."

I stiffen beneath his touch, trying to jerk away from him, but he won't let me go. "You planned this with Monty?"

"How else do you think I found you?" He steps closer, so close I can feel his body heat. The brush of his clothes against my mostly bare skin. "Are you happy to see me, Savage? It's been a long time."

I want to both smack him and jump him. "Why are you here, Whit?"

"We have the restaurant to ourselves. I bought it for the night," he informs me, his voice smug.

I frown. "Monty said it was a dinner party."

"For two."

"I thought there would be more people," I tell him hating how confused I sound. "Like Monty. He said he would be here."

"Your precious friend lied to you." Whit drifts his fingers down the length of my arm, leaving me shaky. "Have you missed me?"

I thought the first time I would finally see Whit after all of these months—well over a year—I would be happy. Thrilled. But I'm not.

I'm mad. Infuriated. I feel tricked. Used.

What else is new?

"No," I bite out.

"Really. Your body is telling me otherwise." He blatantly touches my breast, his thumb slowly brushing against my nipple, the mesh giving me little protection from his seeking fingers. My nipple hardens in an instant, and he flicks it again, making me ache. "This dress should be fucking criminal. I can see everything."

I swallow hard, fighting the shame that wants to wash over me. Wearing this dress, coming tonight was a huge mistake. I willingly walked into a trap, like the stupid girl I've always been. I'm just like my mother. "Why did you do this? How?"

"I missed you," he says simply, as if that's enough. "I wanted to give you some time on your own before I made my approach."

"That sounds like complete bullshit," I spit out.

"It's the truth," he says, his voice firm. "I've known you were in Paris pretty much from the first day you arrived here."

I'm fuming. Monty is the only one I kept in contact with out of anyone Whit would know. So basically he ratted me out to Whit from the very beginning. But why?

And why is Whit here?

"Yet you didn't reach out to me." If he really wanted me, he would've done something about it by now. Not keep away from me for so long.

"You didn't want to be found." He lets go of my shoulders completely and reaches around my front, his hands settling directly over my breasts, tugging gently on the mesh fabric. "You may as well be naked."

"Don't touch me," I say between clenched teeth.

He laughs, the sound vibrating against my ear, just before he lightly sinks his teeth into my earlobe. "You're shaking, Savage. You want this so fucking bad. Just as bad as I do."

Whit thrusts his hips against my ass, his cock nudging me. I close my eyes, powerless to him, but not willing to give in to him yet.

"You need to talk to me first," I tell him, hating how weak I sound. He hates weakness too. I know he does. "Tell me why you're here, and what you want from me."

"First, I want this." He releases my breast, his hand drifting down my side, slipping beneath the hem of my dress to settle that big hand in front of my pussy, cupping me between my legs. "I'm reclaiming it."

"You don't own me," I whisper, biting my bottom lip when he exerts the slightest pressure against my sensitive flesh, thinly covered by my nude thong.

"I own this. It's always been mine," he says arrogantly. "Since we were fourteen, Savage. Remember that night?"

How could I forget?

"It's burned on my brain," he admits. "And all the other nights we've shared, too. So many. We couldn't get enough of each other." He shifts his fingers, pressing harder, his index finger sliding between my pussy lips.

I lean my head against his chest, a sigh leaving me as he begins to stroke. What is he doing to me? I'm ashamed of my instant reaction to his touch. How my knees wobble, threatening to give out. My core tightens, eager for more. My head swims with memories at the sound of his voice. And my lips.

They ache for his.

"I've bided my time. Waited for you while I've gotten my affairs in order," he says, his fingers toying with me, streaking across the front of my thong. I feel it grow damper with his every stroke. "And when the opportunity arose, I took my chance. Now here we are. Together once again."

I tear myself out of his hold completely, immediately missing his warmth. His touch. I turn to face him, drinking him in, hating how elegantly handsome he looks in the black suit, his hair trimmed neatly, and his face.

Oh God, his devastating face.

He's looking at me as if there's no other woman in the world for him.

Just me.

Only me.

"I have something for you," he says, his gaze never straying from mine as he reaches for the table behind him, picking something up. "It doesn't belong to me."

He stretches his hand toward me and I glance down to see my journal, clutched in his long fingers. My stomach pitches and roils at first seeing it, my mouth going dry. I hate that stupid journal. It's what got me in trouble in the first place.

I lift my head, my gaze meeting his, those icy blue eyes seeming to penetrate me to my very soul. "The last time I saw my journal, it was in your mother's possession."

A flicker of irritation crosses his face and then it's gone. "She said and did some things to you I'm still not happy about."

"She *threatened* me, Whit. Said she would call the police and tell them the fire was my fault. That I killed my stepfather and Yates," I throw at him.

He flinches when I say Yates' name, and I wonder at that. "Idle threats. She's not a worry to you. Not any longer."

"Yeah, right." I snort, unable to keep it in. "I don't trust you. I don't trust *any* of you," I say. I start to walk past him but he grabs hold of my arm, his fingers loose, but not so much that I could escape him. "Let me go."

"Listen to me first."

"No."

"Summer." His voice turns faintly pleading, which is a shock. "At least sit and have dinner with me. Let me explain myself."

I twist my mouth up into a pout, still glaring. "I hate you and Monty for tricking me into this."

"You don't hate Monty." He makes this statement with complete confidence.

"I definitely hate you," I spit at him.

Whit actually grins, and the sight of it takes my breath away.

"That's what I was counting on."

"Why couldn't you have just asked if I wanted to see you?"

"Would you have said yes?"

"No," I immediately answer.

"That's why," he says drolly.

He lets me go, his words lingering in my brain as he pulls the chair out for me so I can sit at the table. The moment we settle in, a server appears. An older gentleman in a crisp white jacket, who serves us each a glass of wine before Whit speaks to him in fluent French.

I stare at him, wondering who this man is, who has he become? I don't know him anymore. Not really. It's been a year and a half since I've seen him last, and we've changed so much in that time. At least, I have.

I'm sure he has too.

Once the server is gone, I lean across the table, glaring at him when his gaze drops to the front of my mostly nonexistent bodice. "You need to start explaining."

He reaches for the wineglass, taking a sip. Staring into it as he swirls the pale liquid within. "What do you want to know?"

"What happened with you and Leticia?"

Whit sighs, setting the glass on the table. "You would ask that first."

"She was your future bride after all," I say tightly.

"I ended things with her not too long after you ran away. She broke stipulations that were part of our contract thanks to her very nasty, very secret drug habit," he says. "She's been clean for over a year."

"Goody for her," I say, sounding like a jealous shrew. "You still talk to her?"

"I do." He tilts his head toward me. "You have a problem with that?"

"Not at all," I say haughtily before I sample the wine. It's crisp, cold and delicious.

"Good. Her girlfriend doesn't have any issues with us communicating either."

I set my glass down with a heavy thud. "She's a lesbian?"

He arches a brow. "You say lesbian like it's a bad thing."

"No, of course not," I say defensively. It's just that Leticia seemed so into Whit at that stupid birthday dinner...

"She's bisexual, not that I should air her private business to you, but I'm sure she won't mind," he says. "That's part of the reason she became so reliant on drugs. She couldn't be who she really was. Her parents wouldn't allow it."

"And your parents are now allowing you to be who *you* really are?" I ask pointedly.

"Not particularly. I just don't give a fuck anymore what they say," he says as he drags his fingers across the pristine white tablecloth. Up and down, up and down, I watch those fingers move.

Imagining those fingers on me. Inside of me.

"Why did you run away, Summer?" he asks, his voice soft.

The words don't come to me at first. All I can do is stare at him, hating how accurately he describes me. How I used to be. A runaway. A scared, meek little girl.

I lift my chin, refusing to let old memories and insecurities hold me back any longer. I decide to be completely truthful with Whit. "I didn't run away. Your mother threatened me, Whit. She somehow had the journal and read sections aloud to me. She said I had thirty minutes to pack and she wanted me out of the house. She gave me no choice."

His lips thin. "She told me she paid you off."

"She lied," I throw at him, anger suffusing me, making my voice rise. I wasn't a runaway. I was forced to leave. What else could I do? "I figured you gave her the journal."

"As if I would," he retorts.

"Then why did she have it?"

His expression turns contrite. "I brought it with me to keep it—safe. I assumed she went through my things."

"Lucky her, she found my journal and used it against me." I slowly shake my head. " I was afraid your mother would turn me into the authorities and I'd be arrested for murder. That's why I didn't return to Lancaster Prep. I came into a little bit of money, I got a new phone, shut off all of my social media and stopped communicating with basically...everyone."

"People who run are usually trying to escape something they did." He stares at me, his expression hard. I don't bother correcting him about the running bit. "Did you start that fire?"

"Didn't you read the journal?" I ask pointedly. He nods. "My confession is in there."

I don't bother bringing my mother up. I'm not about to tell Whit the truth. God knows what he would do with that information.

"I read it," he bites out. "I also know you and Yates were...involved."

I grimace, hating how that sounds. "Let's call it what it really was. Yates forced me to have sex with him. Multiple times. And rather than cause a scene and upset our parents, I gave in to him and let it happen."

Over and over and over again.

"You were a child." Whit's expression is filled with disgust.

With me?

"When we fucked, we were children," I point out, just to annoy him.

"Not quite," he says, his voice full of irritation. "We were practically eighteen. And I didn't force you to do dick."

"Please." I scoff, grabbing my glass and draining its contents. I need more liquor to get through this conversation.

"Are you really putting me in the same category as your lecherous, dead stepbrother who would beat off in the bathroom while watching you take a shower? The one who *forced* himself on you?" He raises a brow. "If that's the case, I may as well leave now. There's no point in continuing this conversation."

God, he's infuriating.

"What do you want from me, Whit?" I ask, pounding my fist lightly on the table, making everything rattle. "Are you here for another go around with me, for old time's sake? I don't know if I could handle the likes of you. Not anymore."

"So you're weaker than you were when you were seventeen? Because you were pretty fucking strong back then, Savage. You took no shit from me, and definitely not from anyone else," he says, his tone admiring.

That's not true. I took all the shit from him, and then some. He was rude and degrading. He called me names and treated me like garbage, yet I kept coming back to him. There's something about the way he looks at me. The words he says. His commanding touch and persuasive kisses that always had me at his mercy.

Maybe I don't want that anymore. Despite the undercurrent of desire trembling through me at this very moment at his nearness, I'm starting to think Whit Lancaster isn't good for me.

Not at all.

The server reappears with our first course, setting the tiny plates in front of us. I have no idea what it is, but I smile at the waiter as he nods and bows before leaving the room.

"I refuse to let myself get pulled in again," I say once the server is gone.

"Pulled into what?"

"Your orbit." I glance down at my plate. "What is this?"

"Foie gras, you peasant," he says cheerfully as he digs into it with his fork.

We eat in silence until our plates are clean and the server reappears, whisking them away after pouring each of us another glass of wine. I sip from it, needing the liquid courage, hating how shaky I feel. I don't want to be here with Whit.

Yet I do. I'm so glad he's in the room with me, watching me with his careful gaze, taking note of my every movement. I've missed him. He was so abruptly ripped out of my life, and now he's just as abruptly thrust himself back into it. I don't know what to think.

I don't know how to feel.

"Have your parents found another breeding cow—oh excuse me—another *heiress* for you to marry?" I ask.

Whit leans back in his chair. "Jealousy isn't a good look for you, Summer."

I clench my hands into fists. "I'm not jealous of anyone. I felt sorry for Leticia. As if her sole purpose in life was to marry you and give you sons to carry on the Lancaster name. This isn't the Middle Ages."

"That wasn't her sole purpose in life, though I doubt I could convince you otherwise. You'll believe what you want to believe. And no, I haven't found another heiress to marry. I don't plan on ever getting married, if you must know," he says insolently, reminding me of a spoiled prince.

"Just going to travel for the rest of your life and spend all your money?" I arch a brow.

"I couldn't spend it all for the next three generations at least," he says, fully bragging. "And what the fuck is wrong with that anyway? I didn't come here tonight to fight with you, Savage."

"You can't just walk back into my life as if you never left it, Lancaster," I toss back at him, annoyed.

"I just did," he says, seeming very pleased with himself.

The server returns, and the night quickly turns into one course after another, each one better than the last. A delicious artichoke soup with black truffle. A variety of baked bread with fresh, rich butter that tastes like sin. More and more wine, until my vision gets blurry and I have no problem whatsoever shoving a forkful of lamb in my mouth, immediately wanting to cry afterward when I think of the poor furry creature who was slaughtered in order for me to enjoy this meal.

"You're acting like a baby," Whit chastises after I push my plate away, disgusted with myself.

"Lambs are so adorable." My lips quiver. I'm this close to crying.

Whit can only shake his head at me, his lips curling.

I don't understand what's happening between us, but I don't want to question it. Worse, I don't know what's happening to me, or why I'm so emotional. It's confusing, being with Whit once again. Eating an extravagant meal with him, basking in his presence. I should be furious with him. I also should be stronger. Letting him back into my life is most likely a mistake.

He'll just use me. I know he will.

Once our dinner plates are taken away, Whit leans back in his chair, contemplating me, his demeanor one of pure, lazy insolence. Oh, to be so confident, so commanding of your surroundings. Money gives him power, though I'm sure his parents told him he could have whatever he wanted.

All he had to do was buy it.

"Come back to my hotel with me," he says, his voice dark.

The word yes is on the tip of my tongue, but I refrain. "Why? So you can fuck me?"

He grins. "I'm game."

"I'm not." I toss my napkin on top of the table and rise to my feet, ignoring my shaky ankles.

Stupid shoes.

Taking a deep breath, I stalk toward the window, keeping my back to Whit, staring outside. The traffic has died down. There are hardly any people on the street. The wind still blows, and when I reach out to touch the glass, it's ice cold.

Staff enters the room, and I can hear them clearing the table, their low murmurs of French, Whit conversing with them as well. I've picked up quite a bit since moving here, but I'm not fluent like Whit. His voice is melodic as he speaks, his accent precise. Perfect. It's sexy.

Everything about him is sexy, damn it, when it absolutely shouldn't be.

Frowning, I press my entire hand to the glass, needing the cold to shock my system. The frigid air seeps into my palm, awakening me from my wine and rich food-laden stupor. I am the one who ran away from him in the first place. He couldn't control his mother, or his father. They were controlling him, and I was a distraction. They needed to get rid of me, and I fell right into their trap.

Like the idiotic, naïve girl I was.

Once the server and staff have left, I hear Whit move. His footsteps draw closer, until he's once again directly behind me, his heat stretching toward me, trying to lure me in.

I close my eyes briefly, reminding myself I need to stay strong.

"When you left the house," he starts, then immediately stops. As he's trying to find the right words. "It was almost a year and a half ago, and that day is still so vivid in my mind. I figured out what my mother did to you, but you were already gone. I tried texting you. Calling you. But you didn't respond. You never responded. It was like you ran away and completely disappeared. I figured you didn't want to be found."

"I didn't," I admit, my voice soft.

"And then everything happened with my sister." He sighs, and my heart aches for him, hearing all of the emotion in that one sound. "Leticia was a problem as well. All of it distracted me, and I needed to be there for my family. Sylvie is still not well.

She accuses our mother of making her sick on purpose, and I don't know what to believe."

I whirl around at his last sentence, my mouth dropping open in shock. "Are you serious? About Sylvie?"

He nods, his expression pained. "I don't believe her though. Our mother would never do that. She loves Sylvie more than anything. She just wants her well."

I remember all of the things Sylvie said to me. All of the little clues. It makes perfect sense, hearing the accusation. I believe her. But I can't say that now, not in front of Whit.

"Early last year, I tried to search for you myself. But when I came up with nothing, I hired a private investigator, and he found you here. In Paris. I ran into Monty a few weeks after that, and he confessed he'd been talking to you," Whit further explains.

"Why come to see me now? Why not back then?" I ask, needing to know.

"Time heals all wounds?" His smile is weak and it immediately disappears when I glare at him in return. "I don't know, Summer. I knew you wouldn't want to see me."

The problem is, I would've loved to see him, but not like this. Not when he conspires with Monty and tricks me into coming to a restaurant under the guise of a fabulous dinner party with other guests.

"You tricked me into seeing you. As if that's so much better," I retort, crossing my arms. The movement only causes Whit's gaze to drop to my chest, his eyes flaring with heat. "Luring me here under the guise of a dinner party. Did you really think I would be okay with that?"

"It was Monty's idea," he punctuates with a frustrated exhale. "I should've known you'd be angry."

"Why did you search for me, Whit?" I ask, my voice soft. I need to know.

"I wanted to make sure you were all right," he admits. "I felt— guilty. As if I were responsible for making you leave."

"I was scared," I admit, my gaze going to the now clean table. Only my journal sits on top of it. God, I hate that thing. "Your mother is someone I don't want to cross."

"She's all bark, no bite," he says, though I don't believe him. Maybe she's that way with him, but certainly never me. "I'll never let her hurt you."

"I won't be back in her life to give her the chance," I tell him.

"If you're with me, she'll be in your life," he says.

FORTY-SIX

WHIT

I WAIT for Summer's reply, everything inside of me seizing up in anticipation. She'll most likely tell me to fuck off. I'd deserve it. After everything I've put her through when we did spend time together, and then tricking her to see me tonight, she should tell me to fuck off once and for all and that will be the end of it.

I'd deserve it.

Fucking Monty and that dress. He played fairy godmother with my money and dressed Summer in something so fucking sexy I can barely see straight, let alone think rationally. My hands itch to touch her. Drag the mesh up her mostly naked body and run my mouth all over her soft skin. Lick that delicious little pussy of hers. Drive her wild with my tongue until she's coming all over my face.

My cock twitches at the thought. At the memories. Her scent all over my face and fingers. Watching her lick my fingers after she came. Shoving my cock into her welcoming mouth. We were fucked up in the worst possible way, but we understood each other. It came naturally for us, the darkness. The fucked-up thoughts and words. I originally wanted to punish her for what her mother did to my family, and instead I did the fucking craziest thing.

I went and fell in love with her.

Not that I can say those words. She'd laugh in my face. And maybe she'd be right to do that. I have no idea what love is. My parents never acted like a loving couple. They merely tolerated each other throughout most of their marriage. If they were ever free and happy and in love, it was during a time I wasn't there yet, or I don't remember it.

Summer drove me out of my mind with lust, but she also...softened me. Made me smile. Made me happy, damn it. An emotion I didn't believe I was capable of feeling.

Only she did that for me. And I haven't felt that way since she walked out of my life.

Not once.

"Are we not having dessert?" Summer asks out of nowhere, completely ignoring what I just said.

Her gaze is on the empty table, her journal lying there, mocking the both of us. This all started because of that stupid journal. If I could, I'd burn it. But maybe she wants it. She might feel safer with it in her possession, and I'll give her that safety. I'll give her whatever she wants, as long as she'll agree to continue seeing me.

All she has to do is ask.

"I thought you could be dessert," I say, my tone light, my thoughts dark.

Her dark eyes light up as she studies me, her expression wary. "What do you mean?"

Like she doesn't know.

"Let me show you." I take a step toward her and she presses her back against the window, wincing from the cold glass. I can hear the wind blow outside. "Do you not trust me?"

"No," she responds immediately.

I take another step closer, discreetly inhaling her fragrance. "I won't hurt you. Unless you want me to."

Her eyes widen at that last bit and I can't help but smile.

"Do you want me to?" I reach for her, drifting my fingers down the front of her dress, deliberately touching her warm, smooth skin. "Or do you want me to make you come?"

"Do you think you still can?" she asks, her voice shaky.

"Is that a challenge?" I raise a brow. She doesn't respond. "Let me show you what I can do for you."

I shift her away from the window and press her against the wall with my body, crowding her, pinning her in place. She's taller with the heels on, practically at eye level and I keep my gaze locked with hers as I reach for the hem of her dress. Slowly I lift it, past her hips, until it's bunched at the waist, the lower half of her body completely exposed.

Pulling away slightly so I can look at her, I take note of her long, glowing legs, the flesh- colored thong she's wearing. She's thinner than I remember her, her hip bones jutting, her stomach so flat, it's almost concave. I touch her there, feel the slight tremble of her skin.

"Do you never eat? You're skin and bones," I whisper, my fingers traveling to her left hip, stroking her there.

"I'm busy," she admits. "I don't have time."

"If you were with me, I'd make sure you'd eat," I tell her, skimming my fingers back and forth across her stomach, my finger dipping into her navel. "I'd feed you breakfast in bed. All the fresh croissants and butter you could ever want."

"I'd be fat."

"Fat and beautiful." I lean my face in closer to hers, our lips almost touching. "I would do whatever you wanted as long as it pleased you."

"Really." Her voice is flat. Clearly, she doesn't believe me.

"Yes." I barely kiss her lips and pull away, her mouth following after mine, making me smile. "Come with me."

I take her hand and lead her over to the table, plucking the journal off and tossing it onto the floor. It lands with a loud thwap, making Summer jump.

"Get on the table," I tell her, my voice low.

She frowns. "What do you mean?"

"I want you spread out, on the table." I go to her, wrapping my hands around her waist and lifting her so she's sitting on the edge. "Go on," I tell her after I let her go. "Lie back."

She glances behind her before returning her gaze to mine. "Why?"

"I told you why," I say, impatient. "You're dessert."

"Whit, I don't know—"

"Oh, for fuck's sake." I grab the back of her head and lower my mouth to hers, delivering a punishing kiss to her welcoming lips. She opens to me immediately, a low moan sounding from deep in her throat, her tongue dancing with mine. She wants this. Wants me. All the protesting and complaining is a front. A ruse.

She can pretend all she wants, but we were made for this.

Made for each other.

We kiss for long minutes. Tongues tangling, teeth nipping, lips eager and hungry. I push her farther back on the table, so she's sitting almost in the middle of it, her legs dangling off the edge. I break the kiss, the both of us breathing heavily, watching each other, our chests rising and falling in time.

"Lie back," I demand roughly and this time she doesn't hesitate or argue. She leans back, resting on her elbows, her gaze still connected with mine.

"Like this?" she asks, spreading her thighs a little wider, offering me a teasing glimpse of her thong just beneath the mesh.

"Exactly like that." I reach for the hem of her dress once more, shoving it up, over her waist, her breasts. "Take it off."

She sits up and rids herself of the dress, sitting before me in just her panties. I want them off too, but I'll take care of it soon enough.

"Beautiful," I murmur as I reach for her breasts, weighing them in my palms, brushing my thumbs across her hardened nipples.

A sigh leaves her as she thrusts her chest toward me, and I stroke her sensitive skin. Dip my head to snake my tongue out and lick. One nipple. Then the other. She trembles, the table legs rattling beneath her and I hope to fuck we don't send the table crashing down.

Talk about ruining the mood.

Her breasts, her pretty pink nipples beckoning, glistening from my mouth. I suck one in deep, tonguing it, pulling on it with my lips, drinking from her. She grasps the back of my head with one hand, holding me to her as I suck. Lick and tease. We've barely started and I can't get enough of her.

Will I ever?

I lavish the same attention on her other breast before I start a journey down the length of her body. Running my mouth across her stomach, her hip bones. The flat plane beneath her belly button. I can smell her cunt, the rich, musky scent reaching my nostrils and making my mouth water for a taste of her.

God, it's been too long since I've had her. My cock is so hard it fucking hurts, but I'm not going to do anything about it.

This moment, right now, is all about her.

"Whit," she whispers as I trace my tongue along the top of her panties.

I glance up to find her watching me. "Yes?"

"Take them off," she demands, her voice quivering.

I smile. Run my tongue across the front of her drenched panties, making her whimper. "You're not the one in control of this situation right now, are you?"

"Please," she whispers as I continue to lick and nip at her. The thong's fabric is whisper-thin, almost as if I'm actually touching her skin, but not quite. The barrier adds something to the moment, and I'm not ready to be rid of it yet.

"You're not enjoying this?" I ask before I lap at her, my tongue flat against her throbbing flesh.

She hisses out a breath, her eyes falling closed as I continue to eat at her. I remember why I wanted to be in this room in the first place and I pull away from her, glancing up to see the mirror hanging above us. Her sprawled on the table, her legs wide, her beautiful body on display. Her head is cut off. I can't see that gorgeous face, or all the frustrated fury on it, and I wish I could.

"Look up," I whisper and she does as I ask, her eyes going wide when she notices. "Watch me."

FORTY-SEVEN

SUMMER

MY ENTIRE BODY breaks out in goose bumps when I see our reflection. Whit between my spread legs, tilting his head back to watch me in the reflection. I'm cut off at the shoulders; I can't see my face, but there's something sexy about it. Almost as if I can detach from the moment and watch myself. As if it's not even happening to me.

But it so is. I can feel his hands on me. Big and warm and possessive. Claiming me as if I've always belonged to him.

I suppose I have.

He gets rid of my panties, tossing them on the floor after he disentangles them from my shoes. "Bend your knees and brace your feet on the table," he commands.

I do what he says automatically, as if I can't help myself. Breathless, I watch as he descends closer, his hands going to the inside of my thighs, spreading me open. Pink, glistening flesh on complete display.

I think of the employees at the restaurant. What if they walk in? What if they catch us? I'll be so embarrassed.

But then I remember Whit paid for the entire restaurant for the night. He probably told them we needed some alone time, and not to walk in on us.

He puts his mouth on me and I moan for so long, it's almost embarrassing. I force my eyes open, watching his head move between my thighs, his hands holding me. I run my fingers through his soft hair, unable to look away as I experience his busy tongue and sucking lips driving me out of my mind.

All the while, I watch. My own personal porn movie, come to life.

I lift my hips, smashing my pussy against the lower half of his face and he slips his hands beneath me, holding me to him as he licks and eats at my quivering flesh. He doesn't let up. Not once, and I close my eyes only for a brief moment, trying to gather myself. Compose myself. What he's doing to me is torture. Exquisite, almost painful torture, but I know it's going to be worth it in the end.

Watching him go down on me makes it that much easier for me to orgasm. I'm already going to come. I can feel it building inside of me. Big. Bigger. Little cries fall from my lips as he continues lapping at me, the tip of his tongue flickering against my clit. His mouth completely covers my pussy and I want to die when he starts tongue fucking me. In and out. In and out. I can't stop whimpering. Moaning. Moving. He holds me to him, his fingers teasing along the crack of my ass, probing deeper, finding my asshole. He presses one finger against the tight rose-bud, stroking me there, and that's all it takes.

I come with a shout, drenching his face with my juices as I rub against him unashamedly, my body heaving, my clit on fire as he keeps sucking on it, his probing fingers driving me wild. He moves over me, his fingers still on my ass, his mouth finding mine and I kiss him with complete abandon, sucking on his tongue, tasting myself. I reach for him as well, my fingers finding his cock, stroking him over the fabric, wishing he were inside me already.

"I can't fuck you here," he tells me, panting against my mouth.

I find the snap on his trousers and undo it. "Why not?"

"This wasn't part of my plan," he admits, pressing his forehead to mine.

I slide down the zipper, delving my hand inside, my fingers shifting beneath his boxers and finding velvety smooth, hard flesh. He drips onto my palm as I begin to stroke him. "I want you inside of me."

He groans, thrusting his hard cock into my palm. "Not like this."

"Fuck me, Whit," I demand, letting go of him so I can awkwardly shove at his trousers, too eager to have him inside me to worry about anything else.

He bats my hand away, grabbing hold of my hips and pulling me down the table so I'm hovering right on the edge. He shoves at his clothes, freeing his cock and then he thrusts inside me, to the very hilt, filling me completely.

We remain still, the only thing moving is his cock as it throbs inside of my body. We study each other, our breaths harsh, and I squeeze my inner walls around him as tightly as I can.

He moans. "Fuck."

Tilting his head back, he stares at the mirror. At our connected bodies. I watch too, biting my lower lip as he slowly withdraws, his cock pulling almost all the way out, coated with my juices, before he shoves his way back in.

It's the sexiest thing I've ever seen.

His pace is lazy as he fucks me, easing in and out of me as if he has all the time in the world. I enjoy the slowness, savoring the way he completely fills me, possesses me with his every thrust. Reminding me that I belong to him.

Because I do. I belong to him so completely, but I don't want to say it out loud. To admit it means I have to admit other things, and I'm not ready to go there yet.

I concentrate instead on the way he fucks me. Almost reverently, as if he wants to savor the moment too. He has so much self-control, it's admirable. Is all that self-control just for me?

Sometimes I wonder if the stars aligned that night at his parents' apartment in Manhattan. As if we were meant to meet. To kiss. To touch.

We kissed. We touched—each other's souls. We marked each other. Connected.

Forever.

"Look at how beautiful you are," he whispers harshly, his gaze locked on the mirror.

I glance up, my entire body in the reflection. We stare at each other as he continues to push inside me. My skin is flushed pink, my nipples hard, my pussy so wet I can hear his every thrust.

"I've missed you," he admits. "I've missed everything about you."

My heart cracks at his words, the emotion in his voice. "I've missed you too," I whisper.

He tears his gaze from the mirror and kisses me, our mouths locked, our tongues in battle. He increases his pace, fucking me hard, the promise of another orgasm building inside of me. Growing. I'm at an awkward angle, my back hurts as he shoves me against the table with the force of his body, but I don't mind. Not when another epic orgasm is just within reach.

Without warning, Whit slips his hand between us, his fingers finding my clit. He rubs it in maddening circles, making me breathless, my entire body going still for a few mindless seconds before the orgasm washes over me, making me shudder over and over again.

My pussy milks his cock, squeezing and releasing, and he groans, jabbing inside of me before he calls out my name. I clutch him to me as he trembles and quakes, his semen filling me completely.

He hangs over me for a few moments once the shaking subsides, and I stroke his back, wishing he was naked. Without a word, he withdraws, pulling his softening cock from my body, his cum leaking out of me, coating the inside of my thighs, my ass. Most likely dripping onto the tablecloth.

"Messy girl," he says, reminding me of seventeen-year-old Whit. The boy I fell for so hard. "Look at you."

I reach between my legs, coating my fingers in his cum before I bring them to my lips and suck, my gaze never straying from his.

His eyes light up as he shoves his cock beneath his boxers, zipping himself up and putting everything back together. "Dirty little whore."

"You like it," I say, not taking offense to his name-calling.

He says and means it with affection. I'm no one's dirty little whore.

Just Whit's.

———

AFTER HE HELPS me get dressed, he retrieves my coat from whoever took it and slips it over my body, tucking me close to his side as we exit the building, my stupid journal clutched in his hand. The cold wind slams into us and I'm grateful his car approaches within seconds of us going outside. He opens the back door for me and I climb inside, giddy as he climbs in after me, his fingers diving beneath my skirt to stroke my ass.

The moment the car pulls away from the curb, he lunges toward me, pulling me into his arms, kissing me as if this is the last time we'll ever be together. I return the kiss with equal, enthusiastic fervor, drinking from his perfect lips, my hands reaching for whatever part of him I can touch. He's just as eager, just as greedy as he tugs the front of my dress down, his mouth finding my nipple yet again.

"You're coming back to my hotel with me," he growls against my skin, just before he bites it.

I squeal, immediately wishing he'd do it again. "Okay," I say breathlessly.

"I'm going to fuck you all night." He reaches between my legs, fingers delving beneath my panties and finding nothing but wet flesh. "Fuck you raw. Fuck you until you beg me to stop."

Warmth pools low in my belly at the thought and I bring his mouth to mine once more, kissing him with all the pent-up emotion I've saved for him the last year and a half.

"I'd fuck you in the back of this car, but we're not too far from the hotel and traffic's light," he says, sounding amused once he shifts away from my seeking mouth. "So greedy, Savage."

"You're just as greedy, Lancaster," I remind him, stroking my hand over the unmistakable ridge of his erection.

He grins, and it is a sight to see. The boy he once was only grinned for me like this near the end, when we spent the week at his family's estate. Before everything was ruined.

Frowning, I drop my hand away from his trousers, the memories coming back, one after another. Dousing me in sadness.

Wariness.

His grin is gone, replaced by a questioning look. "What's wrong?"

I look away from him, staring out the car window as the city lights rush by us. "Nothing."

He slides across the seat, his hands settling on my shoulders, featherlight. Almost as if he's afraid to touch me. "You're lying."

I dip my head, sucking in a breath when I feel his mouth brush against my nape. So gentle. So sweet. And Whit is never gentle or sweet. "This feels like a lie."

He goes still. "What does?"

"This. Everything between us. The moment earlier, in the restaurant. How you and Monty set me up. Yet I don't know what you want from me."

His hands remain on my shoulders, keeping me in place. Not like I can escape him, considering we're in a moving car. "I just want—you."

"For the night?" I glance over my shoulder, startled by how close his face is to mine. "One last fuck before you move on to your future bride?"

He scowls. "I don't have a future bride. I told you, it's over between Leticia and me. There's no one else."

"I'm sure your mother found someone for you." I look away, resuming my study of the city at night. Looking into his ice blue eyes is disconcerting. I should be mad at him. And Monty. They both deceived me, and I don't like it. I trusted Monty with my entire life, and he still put this together, despite his knowing how I felt about Whit and our relationship. How fucked up it was.

How fucked up it *still* is. I see him after more than a year, after his complete betrayal, and here I am, a willing participant in our sexual games.

I'm addicted to him, and I suppose I can find solace in the fact that he's addicted to me as well, but I don't. All it does is confirm to me that we're both a complete mess. Together, we don't make any sense.

I'm tempted to say it out loud, but I keep my mouth shut.

"My mother stays completely out of my personal life," Whit says, interrupting my thoughts.

"Really." I sound full of doubt, because I am.

"Yes." He leans in, his mouth brushing against the shell of my ear. "I can be with whoever I want. Neither of them can tell me what to do."

My heart hammers in my chest, threatening to burst from my skin. I want to ask if he wants to be with me, but I'm too scared. It's been so long since I've seen him last, and I'm not about to look like a needy little thing, begging him to take me back. As if I ever had him in the first place.

"You're not going to ask me what I want, are you." He drifts his lips along my ear, tickling me. "Afraid?"

"I'm mad at you."

"You're mad at me, hmmm." He doesn't sound like he believes me. I suck in a breath when he slips his hand inside the front of my dress, palming my breast. "Your body doesn't feel like it's mad at me."

"My body is a liar, just like you." I close my eyes when he circles his finger around my nipple again and again. Back and forth.

"Look at me, Summer."

I keep my head bent, concentrating on keeping my breathing even, but it's no use.

"Look at me," he demands.

I turn to face him, fully expecting him to be angry. Full of hatred, all of those furious emotions aimed straight at me.

But he's watching me with—tenderness in his gaze. As if I'm the best thing he's ever seen. "Come back to my hotel room with me. Let me explain."

"Explain what? What else do you need to explain? Haven't we talked enough?" I cry, frustration rippling through me, making me curl my hands into fists where they rest on top of my knees.

Whit reaches for me, gently prying my fingers apart so he can interlock his fingers with mine. His touch is a comfort when it absolutely shouldn't be. "You're going to make me say this in the car, aren't you?"

"Please don't say anything," I whisper as I study him, all the blood roaring in my ears, making me feel dizzy. My gaze drops to his mouth, staring, entranced with how red his lips are. They're swollen too. From our kisses. From everything he does to me. Unable to stop myself, I reach for him, settling my hand over the front of his trousers. His cock is huge. Hard and thick. I stroke him and he hisses in a breath. Thrusts his hips up as I continue to rub him.

"You want to make me come in my trousers?" He lifts a brow.

"Yes," I murmur without hesitation.

"This suit is worth over fifteen thousand dollars," he informs me.

I smile. I can't help myself. This is better, us communicating sexually. I don't want to hear a bunch of nonsense. A bunch of meaningless words that he won't stand by. He lies. He changes his mind quickly, leaving me helpless. Defenseless. I shouldn't do this. I shouldn't have let him have me at the restaurant, and I shouldn't be toying with him now in the back of this car, but it's like I can't help myself.

That's no excuse, but it's the truth.

"More reason to make you come in them." I say with a light laugh.

"God, you're beautiful," he says, reverence filling his tone as he studies me.

My laughter dies, pure joy coursing through my veins. My gaze never leaves his, my fingers still curved around his dick. We're lost in each other, the air growing heavier between us with every second that ticks by.

The car stops and the driver speaks in French, letting us know we've arrived at the hotel. Whit pulls away from me gently, my hand falling away and the next thing I know, we're leaving the car, Whit escorting me into the hotel lobby, my fur draped over my shoulders once more, covering me completely.

The building is gorgeous, numerous glittering chandeliers hanging above us, large flower arrangements filling the space with their sweet fragrance. It's not as elegant as The Ritz, but it's spectacular, though I expect nothing less for a Lancaster.

We enter the elevator alone, Whit hitting the button for the very top floor.

"Penthouse suite?" I ask.

"Close enough," he drawls, his gaze trailing the length of my body, where my coat gapes open. "That dress is indecent."

"I told Monty that. He insisted I get it," I say.

"He did that for me." His gaze sears into me. "I told him to find the dress that would show off your body the best."

I glare at him. "Prostituting me still?"

"Never. I wanted to see you. All of you. Just for me. I wanted you to tease me without saying a word or sending me a look. That dress is a work of art, but it is nothing compared to you. Your body is perfection."

I gape at him, shocked by the lavish compliments. This is not like the Whit I knew back at Lancaster Prep.

Not even close.

The elevator comes to a stop, the doors sliding open with a quiet swoosh and Whit settles his hand on the small of my back as he steers me out into the short hallway, stopping in front of a pair of imposing double doors. He pulls a key card out, opening the door with a wave of his hand and I hear the distinct sound of a lock turning.

We're inside the room in seconds, the hushed quietness of it deceptively calm. I'm not even close to calm. I'm a riotous mess, inside and out. My heart rattles. My breaths are coming rapid fire, catching in my throat and my hands visibly shake.

The door slams shut, shrouding us in darkness and he grabs one of my shaking hands, leading me deeper into the room.

"Come see the view," he says, his deep voice washing over me, reminding me that yes, I'm really here, and yes, we're actually together. In this hotel room in the middle of Paris on a cold early spring night.

This isn't a dream. Or a nightmare.

He brings me to the window and shoves it open with a simple push of his hand, a rush of cold air hitting me, making my already hard nipples ache. I follow him, sticking my head out the window, noting the stellar view. The city spread out before us like a blanket, the Eiffel Tower looming in the distance, still putting on its glittery light show. I watch in fascination, letting myself get caught up in the romanticism of the moment. Whit behind me, his hands drifting. Drifting. Pushing the coat away from my neck, down my arms, until it falls in a soft heap at my feet. He presses his firm, warm body behind me, holding me up, and I can't stop shaking. Because of the cold.

Because of him.

"This doesn't feel real," I murmur.

"It is real," he says against my neck, winding his arms around my center, resting his hands on my stomach. "I've finally found you, Savage. And I'm not going to let you go."

His words, the way he says them, haven't changed. They sound like a promise.

A threat.

I'm happy with both.

With him.

Despite everything that's happened and what he's doing to me, I'm happy.

So happy.

FORTY-EIGHT

SUMMER

I WAKE UP IN A DAZE, confusion swarming my brain at first as I try to bring the room into focus. I push my hair out of my face, squinting into the darkness, barely able to see anything, even with my vision adjusting. I can hear the traffic coming from somewhere down below, heavy and insistent, with the occasional frantic siren. The impatient honking of a horn.

A shift in the bed, the mattress dipping. A warm body rolling toward me, strong arms clamping around me from behind. His large body nestled close, muscled arms holding me tightly, his hot mouth on my neck, his seeking fingers testing me between my legs.

I moan when he touches me there, but it's not the kind of moan he wants to hear. "No more," I whisper in agony, and he laughs, the sadistic bastard.

"I wore you out." It's a statement, not a question.

"I don't think I could take another orgasm," I tell him truthfully. I lost count of how many times I came last night. Too many to mention. Until I was pushing him away, my clit on fire, my body and my mind completely exhausted.

"I told you I'd fuck that pretty little pussy raw." He kisses the side of my neck hungrily, thrusting his hips. His erection slips between my ass cheeks, heavy and insistent, and I close my eyes, bracing myself.

If he fucks me back there again, I don't know if I can take it.

"Go back to sleep my sweet little whore," he croons in my ear, his fingers drifting across my cheek. "Get some rest. You'll need it."

I fall back into a deep sleep within minutes, and don't wake up for a long time.

I don't dream either.

It's blissful.

The next time I wake up, the curtains are pulled back, letting in plenty of warm light. I see an elegantly set table at the foot of the bed, two dishes covered in silver domes. Cutlery and glassware, a basket overflowing with a variety of breads, a dish full of creamy pats of butter. There's a bottle on ice in a stand next to the table, and I can only assume it's champagne.

A celebratory meal? My hopes are too high. There's nothing to celebrate between us, unless he views us slipping back into our old roles a cause for celebration.

"You're awake."

I turn toward the sound of his voice to see him standing in the doorway of the bathroom, leaning against the frame. He's got his hands in his pockets, his pale blue button down completely open, revealing his smooth, muscular chest. His hair is damp, as if he just got out of the shower and oh my God, I don't think I've ever seen him look so delicious. So relaxed.

So heartbreakingly handsome.

"Good morning," I say, my voice scratchy.

"Closer to afternoon." He pushes away from the door and strides toward the bed, stopping on my side to bend down and drop a kiss on my surprised mouth. "Good morning, beautiful."

I blink up at him, clutching the snowy white duvet to my chest, speechless.

"Hungry?" He glances toward the table. "Room service came just a few minutes ago."

Oh God, did they see me sprawled out naked in bed? I woke with the covers mostly over me, one leg falling out. How embarrassing.

Whit must sense my embarrassment because the look on his face softens. "I pushed the table and stand closer to the bed. They left it right inside the room. Come on." He holds his hand out for me. "Let's eat."

"Um, I'm naked." I tuck the duvet closer to me, oddly uncomfortable. I'm not used to kind Whit. It's...disconcerting.

"I'll bring your food to you then." He goes to the table and whisks the silver domes off each plate, revealing a sumptuous meal of fluffy scrambled eggs and crisp strips of bacon, accompanied by small bowls of a colorful variety of fruit.

My stomach growls and I lift my gaze to his. "Bacon?"

"They serve American breakfast at this hotel," he explains. "Want a croissant?"

"Please."

Watching him complete domestic tasks, taking care of me, is mind blowing.

"Coffee?" he asks, his gaze locked with mine.

"With cream, yes, please."

"Champagne?"

Tempting, but I don't need any alcohol right now. "In a little bit."

He brings me the plate, laden with so much food I know I can't eat it all, and hands it to me, along with the cloth napkin and silverware. He sets a very full cup of coffee on the nightstand and then does the same thing for himself, settling on the bed beside me, his back propped up by pillows.

We eat in companionable silence, the tension between us growing thicker and thicker as we get closer to finishing. I can't stop nibbling on the croissant, tearing it into tiny shreds, and I've already ate all of my fruit, most of my eggs and of course, the bacon is long gone.

"You're nervous," he says after far too many minutes of silence. "I can sense it."

I set the plate on the table next to me, wipe my hands and mouth on the cloth napkin and then turn to look at him. "Of course, I'm nervous. I still don't understand what's going on. Or why you're here. Why exactly you were in cahoots with Monty and put together last night's dinner. I don't get it, Whit."

"I knew you'd never agree to see me if I just—asked. I had to use some element of surprise to get you into the same room as me again," he explains.

"And now here I am, like an idiot, naked in your bed. Your perfect little whore." I mutter that last sentence under my breath, shame washing over me, making me regret I just ate so much.

"Don't call yourself that." His voice is firm.

"Why not? It's true. It's what you've always called me, ever since we first met. That's what you wanted from me from the start. You wanted my body. You wanted to destroy my self-esteem and completely control me. You wanted me at your every whim, to play with and fuck and torture. Haven't you had enough?"

He drops his plate on the nightstand with a loud clatter, reaching for me, but I scoot away from him, needing the distance. "It's not like that. You make what we've shared sound so...sordid."

"That's because it *is* sordid." The duvet falls and I cross my arms, covering my breasts, not wanting him to look at them.

But of course, he's looking at them. Staring at them. Staring at me, as if he can't get enough of me.

"You want the truth? I'm obsessed with you," he whispers, his voice hoarse, his gaze...pleading. "At first, I hated you, and what you represented. Then I was drawn to you, despite it all. Eventually, I had to have you, and once I did, I couldn't get enough."

I stare at him, my entire body trembling with some unknown emotion. God, when he's so close, I become completely confused. He's too much.

"Do you know how strong you are? How fucking beautiful you are? You walked around campus like you owned the fucking place, despite me trying to destroy your reputation every chance I could get. I admired your strength. I respected it too," he admits.

"Respected me? Please. You got the biggest thrill out of degrading me every chance you got," I retort, dropping my arms. Fuck it. Let him see. He had his hands and mouth and cock all over my body last night. What does it matter anymore?

He continues on as if I didn't say anything. "And then you show up at my birthday dinner, sitting with my family as if you belonged there, while I show up with that joke of a girl who I was supposed to marry. I fucked you in the bathroom only because I was so fucking desperate to get inside you. I couldn't control myself."

"You were trying to humiliate me," I interrupt.

"Absolutely not."

"You touched Leticia with my—juices on your hand," I remind him, closing my eyes at the humiliating memory of that moment.

He comes closer to me, and I can feel his body heat. Smell his delicious, expensive cologne. "You marked me. Reminding me that I was yours. Didn't you see that? You fucking imprinted on me the entire week at my family's house. I couldn't get enough of you. I went to my father and begged him to let me out of the arrangement with Leticia."

I crack open my eyes to find his face directly in mine. "Why? So you could be with me?"

He doesn't say a word. Doesn't look away either. He won't say it, but I see the answer in his eyes.

Yes.

"We would never work," I whisper.

He touches my face. Grasps my chin lightly with his fingers, tilting my head back. "We will always work, Summer. Look at me." I meet his gaze, noting the intensity in his light blue eyes. "We were made for each other."

His mouth settles on mine before I can say anything, and I open for him. Of course, I do. It's like a bad habit I can't kick no matter how hard I try. The moment his tongue curls around mine I whimper, reaching for him, my hands finding the bare skin of his chest. I stroke him, grasp at him, overcome. Needy.

A groan sounds low in his throat and his hands are everywhere, but it's not enough. It's never enough when it comes to him. And me. I fall back onto the bed and he undoes the front of his trousers, shucking them and his boxer briefs down, exposing his erect cock. I climb on top of him, straddling him, reaching for the base so I can guide him inside of me.

The moment I slide down the length of him, we're both moaning in agony. His pants are still around his ankles, his shirt still on and I start to fuck him in earnest, chasing after the bliss I know will wash over me in mere minutes.

He wraps his hands around my waist, controlling the pace. He's so thick, filling me completely every time I slide down. I ride him, my pussy clenching with need, tightening around him and he nuzzles my chest. Draws a nipple into his mouth and sucks. Bites. Sucks some more.

I hold him to me, my knees at his hips, bouncing on top of him, my face buried in his soft, fragrant hair. The orgasm lingers just on the peripheral, so close I can taste it and I take him deep. As deep as he can get.

A strangled groan leaves him, muffled by my breasts, and then he's coming. Filling me with his semen, triggering my own orgasm. We writhe against each other, clinging, moaning and gasping until finally, finally, it's over.

I hold him to my chest, not wanting to hear any more of his words or look him in the face. Not yet. I want to savor this moment. The closeness. We're as close as any two people can get. I don't know if anyone could ever make me feel like Whit does.

I don't know if I want anyone else but Whit.

And that's a terrifying realization.

"Come home with me," he murmurs against my skin, his lips tickling.

"What do you mean?" I stroke his hair. Kiss his temple. If I could, I'd stroke and kiss him all day. I'd never want to stop.

"Come back to the States with me. Live with me. Be with me." He licks at my other nipple, the one he ignored the entire time we were having sex just now, and I close my eyes, my womb clenching with every pull of his mouth.

"As your mistress?" That's all I could ever be, remember? Whit's pretty little whore.

"As my equal. As my partner. Perhaps...eventually....as my wife."

His words send a bolt of terror running through me. This is the same man who said he'd never get married.

Ever.

I scramble off of him, rolling right off the bed so I can stand beside it. His cum coats the inside of my thighs and my hair is an absolute disaster that I have to push it away from my face. I'm sure I look a sight.

He stares at me as if I'm the most beautiful thing he's ever seen.

"You don't mean it."

"I do."

I start to laugh. "We're too young."

"We've been connected for the last six years at least," he says, his voice calm. Logical. "That's long enough, Summer."

"You don't know what you're saying. Your mother won't allow it. Neither will your father."

"Fuck my parents. I'm independently wealthy. They can't tell me what to do. They don't control my life." He swings his legs over the side of the bed, tugging his boxers and trousers up before he stands and pulls them completely on, doing the zipper and closing the snap. "You should take a shower."

How can he be so normal, doing such mundane tasks when we're having such a life-changing discussion? "Whit..."

His gaze meets mine, his lips curled up with faint amusement. "What?"

"What are you doing?" I wave a hand at him.

"Getting dressed. I suggest you do the same. Though you definitely need to shower first." He approaches me, stopping directly in front of me and reaching for the inside of my thighs. He draws his fingers through his own cum and brings them to my lips. "You're messy."

I suck the semen from his lips, just as I always do. "And then what?"

"I want to explore Paris with you."

"Explore it how?" My eyes grow wide and I take a step back. "I'm missing class."

"Fuck class. You're with me." He snags my hand and pulls me close once more. "Let's find secret spots in the city where I can fuck you. We'll leave our mark everywhere."

"That's...we shouldn't do that." I tamper down the wave of arousal that takes over me at the thought of doing exactly that.

"Don't lie, Summer. It's unbecoming." He kisses me. Drinks from my lips. Dips his fingers between my legs to gather more of his cum so he can slip those cum coated fingers into my mouth yet again. I lick and suck, his eyes flaring with heat until he pulls away, leaving me feeling empty.

"Get in the shower." He reaches behind me and smacks my ass. Hard. I yelp, jumping away from him. "Or there's more where that came from."

"Promise?" I tease, batting my eyelashes at him.

He smacks me again, even harder this time, and it's like a jolt straight to my core. "Yes. We'll do more of that later, if that's what you like. Now go wash yourself. So I can dirty you up again."

FORTY-NINE
SUMMER

IT FEELS LIKE A TRICK, being with Whit again, as if he never left. Even more so, actually being happy with him, amongst other people, in public. He holds my hand as we walk through the streets of Paris, as if he's afraid he'll lose me forever if he lets me go.

And maybe he does actually feel that way, I don't know. One minute we were together, and the next I was gone.

Never to be seen again.

Monty sends me endless text messages throughout the afternoon, but I ignore them all. I'm mad at him. He knew what he was doing the entire time, putting together a scheme with Whit behind my back, and while I can't necessarily complain that I'm in Whit's company, I can be hurt by the one friend from my old world who deceived me.

Proving he's just like everyone else. Easily influenced by money and power, the two things Whit uses as his arsenal.

Throughout the afternoon, Whit steals me into dark corners or hidden behind walls. A thick grove of trees. Anywhere, everywhere, he pulls me into the darkness, his mouth finding mine, his hands searching for my aching parts. Between my legs. My breasts. Smoothing over my back, my ass. He fucks me against a brick wall deep in the heart of Paris, tucked away in a little alcove that feels private but definitely isn't. He makes me get on my knees in front of him in a darkened, forbidden corner of the Louvre. That felt wrong, as if we were desecrating a sacred place, but he didn't care. He was insistent.

He made me come every single time.

We end up at a beautiful café right on the Seine late in the afternoon, drinking and noshing on a light snack in the waning sunlight. It grows chillier, and I'm grateful for the black cardigan and dress Whit had brought up to the room from the hotel boutique while I showered, along with a delicate lace and silk bra and panty set. I had nothing to wear beyond the scandalous dress, not even a pair of panties, and I'm impressed Whit thought of everything. Even the sweater.

Whit's phone buzzes and he smiles as he reads the text before he sends a reply.

"You're ignoring Montgomery and he doesn't like it. He claims he's jealous of my dick," Whit says. "Since you're giving it all of your attention instead of him."

"He probably wants it for himself," I mumble under my breath, feeling petty. Immediately feeling regret for my words, I sigh. I shouldn't have said that. I don't mean it.

"I told him earlier that you're mad at him. That's why you're not responding," Whit says.

"It's true. I am mad at him." I take a sip of my wine, wishing it were stronger. "I don't like that he tricked me."

"He did it for you." Whit reaches across the table, settling his big, warm hand over mine. "He knew you missed me."

"He did it for you." I send him a look through my lashes. "I never once said I missed you to Monty."

Whit rests his other hand against his chest. "I'm offended."

"I never talked about you at all." I shrug, slipping my hand from beneath his. "It hurt too much to think of you."

He stares at me, the sunlight cutting across his face, enhancing his stupid male beauty. Why did I have to fall for a boy who's so achingly gorgeous? Just looking at him makes my heart hurt. Knowing what he's capable of, the power he has over me, also makes me cautious.

Something I don't want to share with him.

"I'm here. I want to be in your life. I don't care what you did in your past, or what happened between you and your stepbrother." He leans closer yet I don't move. I'm too shocked by his declaration. We've never spoken of my past, nor has he mentioned what he read in my goddamn journal that is currently sitting in his hotel room. If I could burn that thing, I would. "I want you to come home with me."

His tone is so earnest, his expression so raw and open, my heart cracks. "I can't."

"Why not?" His voice changes, just like that. Becomes deep and commanding, as if he won't accept any answer but the one he expects. "It makes sense, Summer. Come home with me. Live with me in New York. You can study art history there. You can do whatever you want. You won't have to work. You can sit on your knees all day and suck my cock continuously. I won't complain."

He grins.

I scowl.

His smile falls and he leans forward, tucking a wayward strand of hair behind my ear. "I didn't come all this way for you to reject me, Savage. I expect you to come home with me."

"You can't just waltz into another country and demand I do what you tell me to," I say wryly. "I have my own place with a lease I can't break. I go to school. I have a job. Friends. Things I do every day that I enjoy. A routine I've made. I like it here."

"Have you met someone? Is that it?" His expression turns fierce, and he tries to control it, but it's no use. I see jealousy and fury war in his gaze.

"No," I admit softly. "I've been too busy. And I...didn't know if I could ever find someone to replace you and what we shared."

I close my eyes the moment the words leave me, hating that I just confessed so much. Too much. I should never give him the advantage. He knows how to use it against me.

"Share," he corrects, and I open my eyes when he slides his hand along my cheek, tilting my head back so I have no choice but to accept his soft kiss. "We still share it," he whispers against my lips. "And I will do whatever it takes to make you forget anyone else has ever touched you."

A shiver slips down my spine at the possessive gleam in his eyes. He pulls away from me, his hand dropping from my face, his fingers curling around the stem of his glass and bringing it to his lips. "It's settled then," he says once he's swallowed.

"What?" I ask him.

"You're coming back to the States with me." His smile returns, triumphant now. "We'll be married."

I gape at him. "Married? Whit, we're still young. I don't want to marry you."

"Why the fuck not?" He sounds offended.

"Because—marriage is so legally binding. It's just a piece of paper. I don't want it. Or need it."

He watches me, just before he throws his head back and laughs. "Any other woman would die to marry me. They'd want that lock on my money. And here you sit, calling it a piece of paper we don't need. You don't want it."

"I don't," I stress. "Marriage isn't for us. Not yet."

"There's no one else for me," he says, his blue eyes glowing. "No one else. Only you."

I can't find any words to say. To protest. No way to convince him otherwise, so I do the first thing that comes to my mind.

I settle my hand on his thigh and kiss his stubble roughened cheek, breathe in his familiar, unique scent. Despite every-thing, despite my wariness still, I want to believe Whit. I want him in my life, caring for me. Protecting me. We'd protect each other.

But he didn't say the words I longed to hear, like declaring his undying love for me. I suppose it's not about that with us. It's about something else. Something different. Edgier. Darker.

Love shouldn't be dark. All-consuming. That's passion.

Obsession.

And won't we eventually get tired of that?

Grow tired of each other?

"I SHOULD GO HOME," I tell him as he practically drags me into the lobby of his hotel after a late dinner at a very cozy, very expensive restaurant. I'd felt sorely underdressed in my flowery dress and cardigan, my bare face and messy hair thanks to Whit's endlessly seeking hands. I saw the looks we received when we first arrived, the people at the tables staring down their noses at us.

They had no idea one of the richest men in the world was in the restaurant, and once the waitstaff realized exactly who Whit was, our service was impeccable. We sat at a table directly in the middle of the restaurant, the wine continuous, the food, endless. Rich and delicious, to the point that I couldn't make myself eat another bite. Eventually, people figured out Whit was important, and by the time we left the restaurant, paparazzi was there, taking our photo.

It was shocking, finding them outside of the restaurant, waiting for us. Despite Whit throwing his hand up to block the photographers and me tugging my cardigan over my head, someone got a photo of me. With Whit. They'll eventually put together who I am, and our past family connection.

And it could possibly turn into a frenzy with the tabloids all over again.

"No. We need to talk first," Whit tells me as we walk across the lobby, every employee in the hotel nodding in his direction when he makes eye contact with them. An endless stream of, "Bon soir, Monsieur Lancaster," follows his every step.

The beauty of the hotel, the man beside me, the dream-like quality of it all, can't go on forever. Not for me. I couldn't be so lucky. I need normalcy. Crave it. I want to sit in my small flat and sleep in my narrow little bed and go to class in the morning. I want to be reassured that my life won't change just because he re-entered it.

This won't last. I know him. I know myself. We want each other, but it becomes too much. It's all-consuming. We will destroy each other.

Just like last time.

"Whit, please." I clutch his arm as he guides me into the elevator and the moment the doors slide shut, he's upon me, his mouth on my neck, his hands beneath the hem of my dress, hot fingers teasing my thighs.

"I'm never letting you go, Summer. Can't you see?" He pushes me hard against the wall, grunting with the force, and I blink my eyes open, staring at his face, shocked to see so much emotion there. It's as if it's permanently etched into his skin, and I remember the Whit of old. The boy who would stare at me with blank eyes. Who looked at me as if I didn't matter. Who would actually tell me to my face that I didn't matter to him at all.

He's gone. Replaced by a seemingly overly passionate man whose entire focus is on me and no one else.

"We can't have this conversation right now," Whit says.

I frown. "What do you mean?"

"I'm not prepared."

"Whit, you're making no sense."

"That's all your fault, then."

The doors slide open moments later and we're out, Whit's fingers curled around mine as he practically drags me to the suite's double doors, he's so fast.

"I'm never letting you out of my sight again," he says once we're inside the suite, the both of us panting from the exertion. "Take your sweater off."

I remove it with trembling hands, my entire body shaking. He's scaring me, he's so intense.

"The dress," he says once the cardigan is gone, his voice short. "All of it. I want you naked."

I do as he says, his urgency frightening, until I'm standing in front of him without a stitch of clothing on. The hotel's heating system chooses that moment to click on, and the rush of warm air over my bare skin sets gooseflesh rising, my nipples hardening into aching points. My knees are practically liquid and I lock them, sucking in a breath when Whit brushes past me, walking deeper into the room.

I start to turn but pause at his sharp voice.

"Don't look. Face the door."

I inhale, paying attention to my breathing, desperate to keep it measured. In and out. In. out.

In.

Out.

He's rustling around in a suitcase or a dresser, I can't quite tell. I don't know what he's looking for. A strap to smack my ass? In his eyes, I probably deserve it for wanting to get away from him.

He pulls something out of a bag. Or a box. I'm not quite sure. I hear his soft footsteps approach, his rich, masculine scent surrounding me, until he's right there, directly behind me, his breath touching my bare shoulder.

"I have a present for you," he says, his voice low and full of promise.

"What is it?"

"Open it and see." He reaches around, his hand in front of me, clutching a pale gray velvet box. I stare, afraid to open it, though I couldn't explain why. "Summer."

He sounds exasperated with me and so I take the box, opening it with trembling fingers. I flip back the velvet layers, revealing a necklace that takes my breath away.

The diamonds glitter despite the dim light. Delicate flowers form a thick diamond chain, fanciful and gorgeous and terribly expensive, I can tell.

"I absolutely cannot take this," I whisper.

"You can and you will." He reaches for the box, plucking it from my fingers and gently pulling the necklace from it, undoing the clasp. He winds it around my neck carefully, the weight of the stones heavy on my skin and I close my eyes when his fingers brush against my nape, connecting the clasp. "It's white gold. Twenty-four carats worth of diamonds in a flower design. I saw it and knew immediately that it belonged to you."

"I don't want to know how much this cost," I whisper, reaching up to lightly touch the heavy diamonds.

"You're worth every penny." He kisses the side of my neck and my eyes pop open, my gaze catching on our reflection in the mirror on the wall across from where we stand. "What do you think?"

I stare at the two of us, my gaze going to the diamonds circling my neck. It's exactly what I described to Monty, when I said I wanted a heavy necklace, like a collar, so I could feel the weight of it and know that I'm owned. That I belong to someone. This necklace isn't just a gift.

It's a claiming. Whit Lancaster owns me.

I belong to him.

"I wanted to wait. I wanted to give you this necklace and say these words to you later. I wanted to spend the next week lavishing you with my undivided attention and take you all over Paris. I wanted to buy you whatever you wanted and eat with you and drink with you and fuck you everywhere I could, but you keep trying to pull away from me. And I can't let you go," he says, his voice full of agony as he presses his cheek against mine, turning his face toward me so he can breathe in the scent of my hair.

I'm breathless with anticipation, unable to say anything for fear I could ruin the moment. I can tell he wants to say more and I wait, dying to hear his next words.

"I'm in love with you, Summer," he whispers, his mouth right at my ear, brushing the sensitive skin. "I have been since I first laid eyes on you all those years ago."

"You have a funny way of showing it," I say, my lips curling into the faintest smile as I try to contain the joy that's rising within me.

Whit loves me.

He's in love with me.

"I was an idiot. I still am. But I will do my damnedest to prove to you that I love you. Every single day for the rest of your life, as long as you let me." He rests his hands on my shoulders, squeezing them gently, and my gaze finds his in the mirror once more. "Look at you. You're so beautiful. I've missed you so much. I searched for you everywhere, when all along Monty knew you were here. I only asked him about six months ago if he remained in contact with you. Did you know that? He wouldn't reveal shit to me at first, either. Said he didn't trust my motives."

It's reassuring that Monty didn't just blab to Whit where I was the first time he asked. "I wouldn't trust your motives either."

"We arranged all of this, and while you may feel tricked, and you're angry at both of us for not being truthful, I had to do it this way. You would've run if you knew I was here. You would've never agreed to see me." His hands slip down my arms, his light touch making me tremble. "Say something. Tell me you want to be with me. Tell me you forgive me for being such an asshole. Just...anything, Summer. Please."

I don't believe I've ever heard this man say the word please before in my life.

And he just did. For me.

I turn to face him, tilting my head back so our gazes can meet. "I love you too."

He inhales so deeply, his chest brushes against my naked skin and he leans in, pressing his forehead to mine. "Thank Christ."

I frown. "Did you think I would tell you no?"

"I didn't know what to think." He closes his eyes, shielding the vulnerability in his gaze. Too late, I already saw it, and I'm clutching it close to my heart. "You love me."

"I love you." I reach up, press my mouth to his. "I'm in love with you. And I don't want to marry you, Whit. Not yet. Let's just...be together first. We can do that later. Or maybe never. I just want to enjoy my time with you without all of the responsibilities the Lancaster name brings with it."

Such as heirs and duties. Like he's part of the royal family. It's ridiculous, but there are expectations set upon him from birth that he won't be able to dodge forever. If we got married, they would want babies right away.

And I don't want babies.

Not yet, at least. We are far too young. And I'm not about to trap him either.

"What about school? I know it's important to you," he says.

"I only said that because you weren't saying what I needed to hear." When he opens his eyes and frowns at me, I continue, "you declared your love for me. That's all I ever wanted."

"It's real. My feelings for you. They overwhelm me. I don't know what to do with them," he whispers, his hands finding my breasts, cupping them. "I love you so fucking much."

"Show me how much you love me, Whit." I touch his face. Slide my hand along the front of his chest. "Show me."

He takes me to bed. He loves me with his mouth and his hands. He makes me come over and over, and when he finally enters me, his throbbing cock touching the deepest part of me, his gaze locked with mine, he traces his fingers along the diamond necklace, his light yet possessive touch making me tremble.

"Mine," he whispers. "You're mine, Summer."

"Always," I tell him as he begins to thrust.

Always.

FIFTY

WHIT

ONE MONTH *later*

I show up at my lawyer's office precisely at ten. I left my apartment early, not taking any chances with the Manhattan traffic, and still my parents managed to beat me here.

Irritation fills me as I'm escorted to Madison's office by his assistant and I spot them sitting inside with matching annoyed expressions on their faces. My lawyer Ben Madison is a skinny little man who looks like he couldn't squash a bug, but he's as ruthless as they come.

It's why I hired him. I need a vicious shark on my side when I'm going into battle with my family.

"Mr. Lancaster. Good to see you." Madison rises to his feet and walks over to me, shaking my hand. "Have a seat."

I walk over to the one empty chair closest to Madison's desk, unbuttoning my suit jacket before I sit. I am all business this morning, because I'm not about to let my parents fuck with what's mine. I'm here to play.

I'm here for war.

"I don't understand why we're meeting this morning. I've already expressed my concerns. My son is with a woman who isn't good enough for him. She will spend all of the family's money and most likely leave my children destitute," Mother says to my lawyer, her icy expression one that is long familiar. She doesn't like being put in a corner, or bossed around. She's had control over my life for a long time, but once I became an adult, I told her to fuck off.

With relish.

She's been fighting me tooth and nail ever since. Trying to take control of the trust fund I received from her side of the family when I turned eighteen—didn't happen. She's busily working to limit the amount of the trust fund I'm about to inherit when I turn twenty-one. That's not going to happen either.

My father doesn't fight me. He's currently in this office as a formality, and hopefully, as a united front with me.

But we shall see. Mother is persuasive. And while I love my father, I also know he's weak.

Especially when it comes to women.

I think of the one woman who has complete and total control of me, and my heart immediately softens. Perhaps she's a weakness, but together, Summer and I are strong. It was difficult leaving her alone in my bed earlier this morning. Naked and warm, her hair a mess from last night's activities. I'd kissed her and she wound her arms around my neck, begging me to stay.

"One last meeting, love," is what I told her, my voice firm and full of determination. "And then they can't control me any longer."

Getting Summer to come back to the States with me took some convincing. She was reluctant. Scared. My mother doesn't like her, and Summer feels the same. They will most likely never get along, and I'm okay with that. I will choose Summer over my mother any day.

Every day.

"I don't want to argue with you," I tell my mother. "But your assumption of Summer is ridiculous. She doesn't even care about my money."

She barks out a laugh. "I find that hard to believe."

"It's true," I say, baring my teeth in a feral smile.

My father says nothing, which is best. One wrong word and Mother will latch onto it.

"It is true," Madison says, opening a slim folder and pulling out a document. He hands it to my mother. "This is the prenuptial agreement Miss Savage signed in regards to marrying your son."

Mother's mouth pops open as she takes the document, not even bothering to look at it. "You two are getting *married?*"

"Not yet," I say, hating how Summer keeps denying my proposals, but I have to agree to her wishes. Though I'm positive I'll wear her down. Eventually. "But she wanted a prenup drawn up immediately upon her moving into my apartment. Said she didn't want anyone to think she was a gold digger."

"She *is* a gold digger—" Mother says, and I sit forward, cutting her off with a look.

"Watch what you say about her," I say, my voice sharp. I'll carve her up with words and have zero regrets over it too. "She's the mother of my future children."

"Please do not tell me that girl is preg—"

"Sylvia." My father's voice booms, startling her. "Shut up."

She clamps her lips shut, her gaze dropping to the document I had Madison draw up earlier in the week. "So what?" she says when she's finished reading, dropping the paper on the edge of my lawyer's desk. "I'm sure she'll figure out a way to spend your money somehow. Our money."

"My money is my money," I tell her vehemently. "She won't have access to yours. Or Father's, or Sylvie's or Carolina's. We all have our own trust funds and bank accounts. You know this. You helped set up our inheritance when we were babies. Why are you so damned determined to steal it away from me?"

"Because of her!" She jumps to her feet, her face red, her eyes bulging. Sylvia Lancaster doesn't lose control. She's disturbingly calm in almost every situation—with one exception.

"You did this." She rounds on my father, who rears back at the vehemence in her tone. "It's all your fault. First you fuck that little slut for all those years and destroy our marriage once and for all, and now our own flesh and blood is having a torrid affair with the slut's daughter. I won't have it!"

My father stands, looming over his ex-wife with a faint sneer on his face. "You take everything so damn personal, Syl. Acting like Whit is trying to hurt you by being with

Summer." He glances over at me, his expression full of understanding. "Sometimes we can't help who we fall in love with."

She whips her head in my direction, blue eyes blazing. "I know I haven't always been the most—nurturing mother to you, but—"

"This has nothing to do with you," I say, my voice deceptively soft. "And everything to do with me. And what I want. You've never given me a choice. My entire life, up until the moment I turned eighteen, I let you call the shots. I even believed you were looking out for my best interests."

"I was," she says. Father makes a dismissive noise and she turns her attention toward him. "What? It's true!"

"You're forgetting my parents didn't always approve of you, especially not at first," he reminds her.

She laughs nervously. "Please. They chose me over everyone else. Your father handpicked me from a swarm of debutantes who were all vying for your attention."

"And then they met you," he says, cutting her right to the bone. I can tell by the way her gaze dims. "My mother worried you were too controlling. I always wished I could tell her she was right."

I say nothing. I worried over what he could say, but looks like Dad is turning out to be an asset after all.

"I just want what's best for my children," she says, her eyes suddenly shining bright.

Here come the phony tears.

"Sometimes even at the expense of our children's health." He thrusts a finger in her direction. "Don't even get me started about Sylvie."

The tears fall now, silently rolling down her face. She looks away as if she's ashamed. Mother and Sylvie haven't spoken to each other in almost a year. Sylvie recently ran away. Well, she's calling it a gap year. Last I heard, she's spending time in Fiji.

"You need to let our son live his own life," Dad continues, his voice gentle. "He's old enough to make his own decisions, and he chooses to be with Summer. There's nothing you can do about it, Syl. Let him be. Stop harassing him over the trust fund. Call off your lawyers and be done with it."

Her gaze finds mine, and I just look at her, not able to smile. Not able to feel anything at all. This woman might be my mother, but she didn't have much of a hand in raising me. That was thanks to nannies and private schools. She was never nurturing. Cared too much about appearances and social status.

I refuse to ever let that happen to me. To my future. I want to raise my children. Love my wife. I don't want to cheat. I don't want to control.

Well. I do like control. But privately is where I get the most joy out of it.

"Fine. I'll stop the legal proceedings." She lifts her chin, haughty as ever.

I don't bother saying thank you. Why should I? She's the one who started this mess. She should be apologizing to me.

"You'll realize someday, that I was trying to do you a favor." She approaches me and I gaze up at her from where I sit. She might be standing over me, but we both know who's in control of this situation. "You'll come to me and say that I was right. This girl is just using you. Mark my words."

"Whatever you need to believe, go ahead and believe it. I know the truth," I say, my voice calm.

She scans the room, realizing quickly she has no one left on her side. With a huff, she walks out of the office, slamming the door behind her.

"I'll reach out to her lawyer this afternoon." Madison reaches across his desk and grabs the prenup Summer insisted on. "I'm hopeful she'll let this matter go."

"Don't even know how she believed she'd have a legal leg to stand on anyway," Father mutters. "Got anything to drink in here, Madison?"

I watch as my lawyer pours my father a glass of scotch. He asks if I want any but I refuse. It's not even noon yet. Instead, I pull my phone out of my pocket and send a quick text.

Me: It's done.

She responds almost immediately.

Summer: Come home.

I rise to my feet, shaking my lawyer's hand before I give my father a brief hug. "Wish I could celebrate with the two of you, but I need to get going."

"Where to?" My father asks, sounding suspicious.

I just offer him a quick smile. "Duty calls."

———

I FIND her in my bedroom. Still in bed. Still naked and mussed and sleepy. The moment I enter the room, I start shedding my clothes, watching her watch me, a tiny smile playing upon her lips as I tear out of my button-down shirt so violently, I pop a button. It lands on the hardwood floor with a soft ping, making her giggle.

"Lazy," I murmur, my cock straining the front of my trousers when she sits up, letting the covers fall and exposing her bare breasts.

She flips her hair over her shoulder, letting me see even more. "You left and I couldn't help but drift off back to sleep. I think I still have jet lag."

"You've been on New York time for over a week, Savage. That excuse is getting old," I tease, toeing off my shoes before shucking my trousers and boxers off in one go, kicking them onto the floor. Last are my socks, and I sit on the edge of the mattress, yanking them off before I crawl up the bed. Until I'm lying on top of Summer, her legs falling open to accommodate my hips as I settle myself in between her thighs. I stare at her, my gaze never straying from hers as I push a few wild strands of silky soft hair away from her face.

So beautiful. And all mine. Since finding her again, I can barely stand to keep her out of my sight. She's still my Summer, but older. More mature. More thoughtful and not as impulsive as she used to be.

I'm not either.

"It went well then?" she asks, her brows drawing together in concern.

Nodding, I lean in and drop a kiss on her perfect lips. "Mother threw a fit."

"Of course she did."

"My father was supportive."

"He's not so bad."

"He's really not. I think he sees himself in me, and how he didn't get a choice at my age." I kiss her cheek. Her jaw. Her ear, and the soft spot just behind it.

"And what's your choice?" she asks, breathless.

"You." I lift away slightly so I can look into her eyes. "Always you, Summer."

Her smile is slow, her eyes glowing. "I don't want your money."

"You're a fool for saying that, according to my mother."

"I suppose I'm not as greedy as her. Though I do feel greedy." She reaches up, her fingers drifting across my lips. "For you."

I part my lips and nip at her finger, making her yelp. She drops her hand and I kiss her, my lips on hers as I murmur, "I love you."

"I love you too," she says, just before I take the kiss deeper.

Words are pretty, but most of the time they're meaningless. That's why I show her that I love her.

By worshipping her body for the rest of the day.

FIFTY-ONE

SUMMER

"DARLING!"

I rush toward Monty the second I spot him, letting him embrace me fully. I try to restrain myself, but give in quickly, hugging him back with all of my might. I even give him a sloppy kiss on the cheek, which makes him squirm and pull away from me.

I can't help but laugh evilly.

"You're still angry at me. I can tell," he says the moment we sit down at the table across from each other.

He texted last night, informing me he was back in New York and was desperate to see me so he could apologize.

"Put the poor man out of his misery and go meet him for lunch," Whit told me after I let him read the text. "He adores you."

"He hurt me," I said, my voice small.

"Are you complaining? Look at us." Whit waved a hand around, indicating his bedroom. We were already in bed, though it was early. It's as if we couldn't get enough of each other. "I don't hear you griping when I'm balls deep inside of you every damn night."

No, I suppose he doesn't hear me complain at all. Why would I?

I'm with the man I love, all thanks to him plotting with Monty.

"I'll get over it eventually," I say with a sigh, shaking my head.

Monty pouts. "Please. I was off traipsing across the continent all by my lonesome while you celebrated your triumphant return to Manhattan by getting thoroughly fucked by that exquisite boyfriend of yours, day and night. Don't bother denying it," he immediately says when I pop my mouth open to protest. "You love birds are all over the gossip sites. They can't stop talking about the two of you."

"Only because of my mother and his father," I say.

The headlines scream of history repeating itself. It's downright embarrassing. To avoid photographers, Monty chose a small café not too far from his place, and I showed up with a wide-brimmed hat on my head and giant sunglasses covering most of my face. It worked too. No one is paying us any attention, and it helps we met during such a random time. The lunch crowd is long gone.

"Right? So scandalous. I love it. I'm sure it makes Sylvia scream into a pillow at least three times a day." Monty throws his head back and laughs.

"She'll get over it," I say with a pleasant smile, though really, I'm not so sure. She's so angry with me. With us. Whit didn't fall in line, and I know she's disappointed.

Doesn't help that she hates me and my mother.

He sobers immediately. "I've spoken to Sylvie recently."

"You have?" My heart pangs at just hearing her name. I still miss her. Despite everything that happened between us, she was my only friend at Lancaster, and there's a void inside of me that she used to fill. We said such cruel things to each other the last time we spoke, and I hate that. All of those outside influences conspiring against us.

"Yes. She's doing wonderfully. Soaking up the sun, clearing her head. Finding herself, she said. Poor little lost rich girl in search of the meaning of life," he explains.

"I know the feeling, though I wouldn't call myself rich," I say, my tone wistful. I miss Paris, where I found myself, but I'm grateful for my life here too. With Whit. I didn't realize how much I needed him until I saw him again. And now we live together. He wants to marry me.

I keep refusing him. It makes him so angry. I tell him to channel all of that energy into our sex life and he does exactly that.

It certainly makes for some interesting experiences together.

"You're rich now," Monty says with a grin.

"I don't care about his money."

"Half the appeal of Whit Lancaster is his money. I'd roll around naked in one hundred-dollar bills with that man if he'd let me." Monty fans himself.

I laugh, knowing he's full of it. He just likes to say those sorts of things. He's not interested in Whit, though he does respect him as a friend. He did so much for him. Finding me. Arranging for us to see each other after being apart for so long.

His seeming betrayal still stings a little, but I can see now that he did it for the both of us. We were hurting without each other. Monty was just trying to help.

"Do you think you'll ever forgive Sylvie?" Monty asks, pulling me from my thoughts. "She might end up being your sister-in-law someday, you know."

I don't like thinking about marrying Whit. Not yet. We're still so young, and a marriage is meaningless if you're not ready for it. I just want to be with him. Learn more about him. Grow with him.

That's enough for me. For now.

"I'm sure I will forgive her eventually. After all, I've forgiven you," I tell him, making him smile.

He rests his hand against his chest, and I examine him closely. He looks tan and fit. Got rid of his eclectic wardrobe and is clad in a simple black T-shirt and very expensive looking jeans. He even looks like he might've lost a little weight. He did complain to me in the past that college life left him pale and pudgy since he sat on a computer all day. "You have? Really?"

I nod. "Of course. You're one of my only friends. Same with Sylvie. I just hope she can forgive me as well."

There is still much work to be done between Sylvie and I. And even with Whit and I. None of us are perfect.

But we're doing the best that we can.

Monty and I chat and eat, sipping on fizzy cocktails, and I listen to Monty's gossipy stories, which are fascinating. He knows so many people, and somehow knows plenty of their secrets too.

Makes me extra glad he doesn't know mine.

By the time our server has taken away our empty plates, Monty's phone won't stop buzzing, and he discreetly checks it, pushing the phone away each time.

"Who is it?" I ask curiously.

"No one." He grimaces. "A boy."

"Someone special?"

"Someone with a big dick and a bigger ego." Monty rolls his eyes. "I pick the worst sort of men."

"I happen to like big dicks and big egos," I say with a laugh.

"You would, considering who you're with."

"He might not be so bad," I tease, waving my fingers at his phone. "Answer him."

"He wants to meet me for drinks," Monty says.

"You should," I urge.

"Right now." He sends me a look. "I don't want to just bail on you to go hang out with my boo. That's rude."

"Oh, he's your boo now?" I raise a brow, sipping the last of my drink.

"I'm just calling him that. I don't know what he is," Monty says dismissively.

"You should go," I say, my voice soft. "Have fun tonight. See where your boo might take you."

"You won't be mad?" He sounds truly worried.

"No." I shake my head. "I can't ever stay mad at you for long."

We pay for our meal and exit the restaurant, hugging each other for a long time in front before we finally part.

"Don't be a stranger," he tells me, just as his Town Car pulls up in front of the curb.

Of course he has his own car service. I'm sure I could have one too if I mentioned to Whit that I wanted one. But I'm perfectly content taking an Uber or a Lyft.

"Bye!" I wave at him.

Monty opens the door, pausing to turn toward me. "Want a ride?"

I shake my head. "I'm good. Thank you."

I watch the car leave, just before I pull my phone out of my bag and start tapping at the screen to order a car.

"Summer?"

I go completely still at the familiar male voice, and slowly turn around to find...

Augustus Lancaster standing in front of me, with a pretty woman under his arm. She doesn't look much older than me, which is a little scandalous.

But not necessarily surprising.

"I thought that was you," he says when he sees my face. "What are you doing around here?"

"Meeting a friend for lunch." I try to smile, but it's hard. I never felt as if he liked me much, though Whit swears he does. "How are you?"

"Great. Wonderful. Uh, this is my friend, Janna." The dark-haired woman waves and smiles, revealing blindingly white teeth. She's beautiful. Dressed impeccably and with a red Chanel bag on her arm.

I immediately wonder if Augustus bought it for her.

"Nice to meet you," I tell Janna, my gaze going to Augustus's.

"Where's Whit?" he asks me.

"Back at the apartment."

"Tell him to answer his old man once in a while. I would love to take you two out to dinner sometime soon. After all the—noise dies down of course," he says.

I'm sure he's referring to the photographers and gossip sites.

"Sounds good. I'll be sure to let him know."

They start to walk away and I watch them. They actually make a stunning couple. Augustus murmurs something to Janna before he pulls away and comes back over to where I'm standing, stopping directly in front of me, a hopeful expression on his face.

He reminds me so much of Whit in the way he holds himself, his voice, his looks. He looks like the older version of the man I love.

"I want to thank you, Summer. For making my son happy," he says, his voice sincere. "He was so angry after the divorce. He completely withdrew from all of us, and I didn't know how to get through to him. He's changed since the two of you have been together. And that's all thanks to you."

My cheeks warm and I duck my head. "Thank you. I—he makes me happy too."

"I know." He pats my shoulder in a very fatherly way, and I remember what Sylvie told me. How she warned me away from him. I don't get those sorts of vibes from him now, and I lift my head, smiling at him. "How are you getting home?"

"Oh, I was just about to call an Uber—"

"Absolutely not," he interrupts. "I'll drive you home."

"What? No, that won't be necessary."

"Yes," he says firmly. "Come on. My car isn't too far. Plus, it'll give us an excuse to drive it. It's brand new."

He grins like a little boy as I follow him over to where Janna stands, waiting for us.

Hmm. Maybe it won't be so bad being a Lancaster after all.

EPILOGUE

FIVE YEARS LATER...

I STAND on the dais in the middle of the studio, staring at the many versions of my reflection in the multiple mirrors surrounding me. I slowly turn to the left, then to the right, examining each side with a critical gaze, vaguely displeased. I gather the mounds of fabric that make up my skirt and let it drop heavily with a pout and stomp of my foot, careful not to step on the hem.

"I'm fat." I'm acting like a baby, but I hate how round my face is becoming, and how we've had to let out the waist on this dress yet again. I'm also incredibly emotional, and overwhelmed with everything that's happening. Hence the pouting and behaving like a baby.

I'm ridiculous, I know this. But at least I'm self-aware, right? Thank God I'm getting married this weekend, or else I wouldn't be able to wear this dress at all.

"You are not," my mother says indignantly from where she's perched on an elegant pink velvet tufted chair, watching me. "You're pregnant."

I smile at myself in the mirror, my hand automatically going to my belly, rubbing across it gently. "True. But it's all happened so fast."

"More the reason for you to hurry and get married once and for all." Mother rises to her feet and comes to stand beside the dais, her gaze meeting mine in the mirror. "You look stunning."

I smile. "Thank you."

"Let them pin you where they need to and then you can change out of your gown and I can get you home." Mother checks her phone when it buzzes, frowning at the screen. "He won't stop texting me."

My smile stays firmly in place as the seamstresses both step forward, eager to complete the fitting. "He can't stand being away from me. He's so needy."

"I've never seen a man so enamored before. And after all these years too." I can tell she's pleased. "You're a very lucky woman, Summer."

I am so lucky. She doesn't know the half of it.

Once the fitting is finished, we exit the atelier together and climb into the back of the Town Car that's waiting for us, the driver's gaze meeting mine in the rearview mirror. I give him a little nod and a smile and off we go, zipping through the streets of Manhattan, headed home. My mother lives in the same neighborhood, since she and Howard got married last year.

She has quite the reputation among society for breaking up marriages, but she doesn't give a damn. And for once, I believe she is truly happy. Howard doesn't set any expectations on her. He appreciates who she is and lets her be herself. Her happiness with Howard—and his firm encouragement—has allowed our relationship to flourish once more. We've never been closer.

We still have our secrets though. I never told Whit what really happened the night of the fire. He doesn't know about the confrontation between my mother and Yates. I will take that secret to the grave.

Some things are best never to be discussed again.

We drop my mother off first at her building before we travel the next few blocks to mine. The moment he pulls up to the curb, the driver leaps out of the car and comes to my door, opening it for me and offering a hand.

"You feeling all right, miss?" he asks me, concern lighting his eyes.

"Just a little tired, Lou," I say with a soft smile. We've become friends, Lou and me. He drives me everywhere. He's seen me at my best, and my worst.

Like the time last week when I demanded he pull over so I could throw up on the side of the road. Not one of my finer moments. Luckily enough, Lou doesn't judge.

Within minutes I'm at our apartment, which takes up the entirety of the twenty-first floor. Over six thousand feet belong to us, which sounds like a lot, but truly? It's as if we fill every inch of space.

I open the door to a little burst of energy running toward me, his golden hair flying, ice blue eyes just like his daddy's sparkling with delight at seeing me.

"Mama!" August Whittaker Lancaster wraps his chubby arms around my knees and squeezes me tight, just before dropping a kiss to my denim covered leg. "I missed you."

"I missed you too." I swing him up into my arms and smother his delicious face with endless kisses, making him squirm and giggle. He's such a beautiful baby, though he's nearly three and about to become a big brother thanks to me being pregnant with his sibling.

We are the Lancaster scandal. Babies out of wedlock. Doing whatever we want, living however we want, the establishment be damned. The only thing Whit was a stickler about was the tradition in keeping the names passed down to the Lancaster sons. I got him to compromise, shortening our son's name to August.

My own little Augie, that's what my mother calls him. I just roll my eyes and humor her. She's rather possessive of Augie, but so am I.

I love this little boy with all of my heart.

"Where's your daddy?" I ask him as I walk deeper into the apartment. There's a fire currently in the fireplace, and I glance toward the wall of windows, taking in the impressive city skyline. The sun has started to go down, shining off the windows of the skyscrapers that surround us, and I have one of those surreal moments I seem to experience every few months or so, still. A moment where I realize this is actually my life, and I'm so incredibly happy, it's hard for me to believe I deserve it.

Happiness.

Whit does his best to convince me I deserve all the happiness in the world. And I adore him for that.

I adore him for so many things. This damaged, seemingly deranged boy who scared me just as much as he intrigued me. I'm so lucky he came into my life. He's given me so much. A home. His heart. His love. Our children.

Still can't believe I'm going to have another one. I suppose this is what happens when two people who can't keep their hands off each other fall in love.

I find Whit in the kitchen, snapping the lid on one of Augie's sippy cups. "There you are," he says when he spots us, his mouth stretching into a smile. Only to be replaced with a frown within seconds. "You shouldn't be carrying him."

He takes Augie out of my arms and sets him on the floor, handing the cup to our son who takes it and sips from the cup loudly before making a loud "aah" sound. "Delicious," he says with an adorable little lisp.

I send Whit a look. "What did you give him?"

"Water," he says with a shrug. "How was the fitting?"

"Exhausting." I go to Whit and rest my hands on his chest at the exact moment he leans down and drops a kiss on my upturned lips. "I want a nap."

"It's nearly dinner time," he says.

"For old people," I tease. It's as if we've become old people lately—or more like, I have—eating early and going to bed early too. I'm tired all the time from being pregnant and I'm barely out of my first trimester. "Come nap with me."

Our nanny Mari chooses that exact moment to walk into the kitchen, grabbing hold of Augie's hand. "Want to go to the playroom?"

"Yeah!" he shouts, grinning up at her.

"Thank you, Mari," I say, grateful for some alone time with my husband.

"Of course," Mari says with a smile. "Are you eating dinner together this evening?"

"I think we'll eat a little later tonight," Whit says, grabbing hold of my hand. "If you don't mind feeding Augie at his usual time, we'd appreciate it."

"Not a problem," Mari says.

The moment the nanny and our son are gone, I turn on Whit. "Eating later? We always eat with Augie."

"Not tonight." Whit grabs my hand and whisks me out of the kitchen and down the hall. "You deserve a break."

"Taking care of our child isn't a job," I protest, which only makes him laugh.

"Augie is a full-time job all by himself, and we're going to have two before the end of the year." He smiles at me from over his shoulder. "Besides, Daddy wants to get Mommy alone for a little while."

Only Whit could make that sentence sound positively filthy.

By the time we're in our bedroom with the door firmly locked, our mouths are fused, Whit's busy hands everywhere. He strips me to my underwear before we collapse together on the bed,

Whit lying beside me, his hand moving over the gentle swell of my stomach.

"It's a girl," he says reverently, his fingers drifting back and forth across my skin. "I just know it."

"She'll have you wrapped around her finger from birth," I tease.

"Just like her mother." Whit's glittering blue eyes meet mine and he dips his head, his mouth finding mine once more. The kiss turns instantly carnal, his tongue thrusting, making me moan. He breaks the kiss before we get too carried away. "I have something for you."

"Whit," I protest as he jumps up from the bed and goes to his dresser, pulling open the top drawer. "You do too much for me already."

He never stops giving me gifts. Expensive ones, too. I don't need all that. I'm happy with him and our little life, which isn't little at all considering who he is and what he has. He's an important man who comes from an important family, and he's recently started devoting his time to philanthropy, wanting to help organizations that are dear to his heart raise money. Right now, his favorite charities involve children, thanks to our sweet little boy.

Whit returns to the bed with a small, black velvet box clutched in his hand. He thrusts it towards me. "Open it," he demands.

I take the box from him and pop the lid open, a soft exhalation escaping me when I see what's inside.

A glittering yellow diamond ring, surrounded by tiny white diamonds. The thin band is also covered in white diamonds, and it glitters and flashes in the light.

"What do you think?" he asks, joining me once more on the bed. He slips his arms around me from behind, his chin resting on my bare shoulder. "I saw it and thought of you."

"You need to stop buying me gifts," I gently scold as I withdraw the ring from the box and slip it on my ring finger on my right hand. It's a perfect fit. "It's beautiful."

"Almost as beautiful as you," he whispers, his mouth finding my neck, delivering soft, wet kisses along the length. "Should I fuck you? Or am I going to do permanent damage to my daughter?"

"What are you talking about? She's about as big as a grape right now," I tease him, turning so I can kiss him fully.

He touches my cheek, deepening the kiss, pulling me into him. "This is where I admit I'm dying to treat you terribly. Call you names. Spank your pretty ass."

I laugh. Our passion for each other is as strong as ever, but Whit isn't quite as cruel as he used to be. I miss it sometimes. And sometimes, we fall back into those roles because we enjoy it.

"You can spank my ass," I tell him softly, a faint smile curling my lips.

"It's no fun when you tell me I can do it," he teases, growling when I lean forward and nip at his lower lip. "You'll get punished for that."

"I can't wait." I scoot away from him and go on all fours, wagging my lace covered ass at him like a taunt. "Go ahead. Spank it."

He doesn't spank me. Instead, he tugs the lace out of the way and spears his tongue inside of me, lapping at my folds, driving me out of my mind with need within seconds. He licks and sucks and teases and touches until I'm gasping his name and coming with an intensity that hasn't happened in a while.

"You're always so horny when you're pregnant," he says after I've come down from my orgasm. "You were the same way with Augie."

"You're the one who got off on fucking me endlessly when I was eight months pregnant," I remind him, rolling over on my back and kicking off my panties at same time. He studies me, his gaze settled on the spot between my legs. Such a typical man. "Only a few more days until we're married."

He lifts his gaze to mine. "Are you excited?"

I nod, fighting the nerves that want to attack. "There are going to be so many people at our wedding. It's a little—scary."

"You're going to be beautiful. Finally making you my bride." He crawls over me, his face in mine. "I would've married you at nineteen."

"Ridiculous." I roll my eyes.

"No, you're ridiculous. You're also the only girl I've ever met who wasn't impressed by my money," he says, and I see the sincerity there. How much he appreciates that.

When we were younger, he was always shocked when I would turn him down and tell him no. He wasn't used to it. He definitely wasn't used to me not being interested in his family fortune. He eventually came to realize it was because nothing mattered to me but him.

I find the fortune that comes with his family name a nuisance, really. I only like some of the Lancasters. Sylvie and I talk, but it hasn't been the same after our falling out. Whit's father comes over often. He's completely enamored with his grandson.

Sylvia and I don't get along whatsoever. I barely let her spend time with Augie. I don't trust her at all, and I have my reasons.

So does Whit. He feels the same way I do.

The massive fortune doesn't matter either because the money doesn't make the man. Whit is special all on his own. He is my lover. My protector. My fighter. The father of my children. The man I adore more than anyone else in the world.

I can say this from a very privileged place. I'm lucky we have enough money that myself and my children never have to worry for the rest of their lives. But even if we were to lose every penny, I know Whit and I could survive, because we have each other.

"Did Monty show up for your fitting this afternoon?" Whit asks me.

I burst out laughing. "I banned him from it. I knew he would call me out for getting fat."

The frown on Whit's face is fierce. "You're not fat. You're pregnant. I should kick Monty's ass for saying that."

"He never said it, but I know how he thinks. Besides, to him, I'm fat. And that just wouldn't do for the wedding day, darling." I imitate Monty's voice, but Whit is still scowling.

"I think you're beautiful." He kisses me, and it's not as passionate this time. It's softer. Sweeter. Just as intoxicating because these gestures are full of love. I know he mentioned spankings and wanting to be wicked with me, but lately we can't manage it.

We fall into a lovey dovey pattern, as I call it, which secretly drives Whit crazy.

"So sweet," I murmur against his lips as I run my fingers through his thick hair. "You can't resist me."

"I should growl and demand you suck my cock," he says, his voice stern.

"Go ahead," I tell him. "I'll do it."

"Call you a—" He winces. Presses his forehead against mine for a moment, a soft laugh escaping him. "It's hard for me to call the mother of my children a pretty little whore."

"But I am your pretty little whore, Whit," I whisper running my hands down his back, settling them beneath the waistband of his jeans so I can grip his ass. "You can call me that. I won't be offended."

"You'll be my wife in mere days."

"And your whore forever," I say with a laugh, which doesn't seem to lighten his brooding whatsoever. "Go ahead. Tell me what you want."

"I want you completely naked. On your knees with your mouth stuffed full of my cock," he murmurs, his gaze darkening as he imagines exactly that.

I scoot off the bed, taking off my bra so my breasts pop free. I kneel on the carpet, resting my hands on my knees like an obedient servant. "Whatever you want."

He strips himself of his clothes eagerly, until he's sitting on the edge of the bed completely naked, his thick cock curving upward, toward the flat expanse of his belly. I reach for him, but he rests his hand over mine on his thigh, stopping me.

I frown. "What's wrong?"

"Nothing. I just..." He smiles, and it's sheepish. Almost bashful. "I love you so fucking much, Summer. How'd I get so lucky to find you?"

"It's what you've always said." He removes his hand from mine and I grab his erection, curling my fingers around the base of his shaft, squeezing him tightly. "We were made to be together. The stars aligned that night oh so long ago, allowing us to find each other."

"You truly believe that?" He leans back, his hands propped on the mattress behind him as I rise up on my knees and take him into my mouth, sucking him deep. He leaks onto my tongue, the musky, slightly sour taste lingering there and I release him from between my lips, swirling my tongue around the flared head.

"I believe it with all my heart," I tell him. "Which you own, by the way. I belong to you."

He touches my face. Strokes my hair. Presses on the back of my head until my mouth is once more aligned with his dick. "That's nice," he says, his tone smug and I can't help the soft laugh that escapes me. "Now suck."

I do as he asks, drawing his impressive cock into my mouth. Bringing him to the brink of orgasm in mere minutes. Smiling in my knowledge that no one understands this man like I do. No one.

He's mine.

Just like I'm his.

ACKNOWLEDGEMENTS

THIS BOOK, you guys! It's a monster. A beast. The never ending story. The book that never stopped. The longest one I've ever written! This is also the book that made Devney Perry say I might need an intervention if I couldn't wrap it up soon. Ha! It never wanted to end!

What I'm saying is this story could've gone on forever like one of those sweeping sagas that were so popular in the '80s. Whit grabbed hold of me back in December and didn't want to let me go. This book just flowed from my fingers but also drove me bonkers because the story is...bonkers. I hope you enjoyed it. I hope you loved Whit and Summer as much as I did. I might write a book for Sylvie. Her story is very much unfinished, don't you think?

Thank you for reading TIWTS. I hope you enjoyed it. This book was dark, darker than my usual stuff, but I occasionally like to visit the dark side...

As usual, I want to thank everyone at Valentine PR for all that you do to make my job easier. To Brittany and Serena for the EPIC beta read notes. Hang Le for the amazing cover and Kevin Roldan for the gorgeous photo of model Zach Cox. To Rebecca and Sarah for their hard work on this book as well.

And as always, thank you to the readers, bloggers, reviewers, etc. who read my books and share them everywhere. I appreciate all the thought and care you put into your posts and reviews! It means a lot to me.

Dearest reader, if you enjoyed this book, I would greatly appreciate it if you left a review on the retailer site you bought it from, or on Goodreads. Thank you so much!

Enjoyed what you just read?

Check out *I'll Always Be With You*, Monica Murphy's swoon-worthy and brilliantly addictive book in the Lancaster Prep series.

First chapter on the next page . . .

WHICH BOOK WILL YOU READ NEXT?

ONE

WEST

Summer

Mɪᴅ-Jᴜʟʏ ɪɴ Pᴀʀɪs is when I first saw her in the flesh—it was hot as balls, thanks to the heatwave that swept over most of Europe. Everyone was sweating on the crowded dance floor at this random nightclub, with the exception of one.

Carolina Lancaster.

I knew who she was. Of course, I did. Her last name is on practically every building at the private school I attend back home, though she doesn't even go there. Then there's the fact that her family moves within the same social circles as mine, not that she's ever around. She's lived outside of the U.S. for years.

It was almost as if she didn't exist. She's more a myth or an apparition: much discussed, yet never seen.

She's a principal dancer at the London Dance Company, or some such shit. A prima ballerina at an extraordinarily young age—or so the media says. What she's doing in Paris, I don't know. But she's sexy as fuck out there twirling on the dance floor, moving to the music.

Clad in a pair of skimpy black shorts that show off her long, long legs and the tiniest tank top I've ever seen.

White. Cropped. See-through. Hard nipples poking against the thin fabric. She dances effortlessly. Without thought and total abandon. Her slender arms wave above her head, her lips curved into a dreamy smile, eyes unfocused as if she's in a trance. She's not very tall, but her legs are endless. She's fascinating. Everyone is watching her.

She doesn't even notice.

Staring at her for so long, I find myself licking my lips like I'm fucking starving. For her. It's like I can't take my eyes off of her. My skin feels electrified just watching her, so without thinking, I take a step forward. Then another. Until I'm out on the dance floor, surrounded by writhing bodies, not moving a muscle, yet sweating profusely while she completely ignores me as I stand just to the side of her.

She sees me, though. I can tell by the way her gaze flicks in my direction, quick as lightning, a flash of interest before she turns her back to me. Pretending I'm not there.

No one pretends I don't exist. Most people—especially girls—can't ignore me. I sound like an asshole, but I'm just stating facts. Everyone knows my family. My last name.

Even me.

The song ends, the DJ announcing the next song in French, and I take my opportunity.

"Hey."

She whirls around at the sound of my voice, and I blink at her, mesmerized by her stunning face. The perfect symmetry of her features. Blue eyes, elegant nose, rose pink lips formed into a pout. Her expression flips to bored in an instant, and she says something in French as her gaze roams over me from head to toe.

I tilt my head, frowning. "What was that?"

She laughs, and I can't help but smile, even though I'm positive she's laughing *at* me.

She repeats the phrase, her blue eyes going wide.

"*Fous le camp de moi.*"

Get away from me.

Playing the cool Parisian to the dumb American, who just so happens to speak French, and I'm totally down for this game.

"You're playing me."

"*Non.*" She shakes her head, her eyes wide—innocent, though I call bullshit on that. Not a single blonde hair falls out of place. It's slicked back into the tightest ponytail I've ever seen, and I don't think there's a lick of makeup on her face.

She's fucking gorgeous.

I stare at her. Hard. She stares back. Just as hard.

"I know you can speak English," I finally say to her.

The music finally starts once more, a slow and jazzy beat, and the majority of the dance floor clears. The remaining couples cling to each other, shuffling around us as they dance, yet neither of us move.

Until finally, she takes a step closer, her cool scent wrapping around me, making me fucking dizzy. This girl is giving off some sort of vibe that has me in a goddamn trance.

"Who are you?" Her voice is thick with a fake French accent.

"That doesn't matter." It's my turn to shift closer, dipping my head so my mouth is at her ear. I inhale sharply, taking in her delectable scent, and it hits me like a drug sliding into my veins. "I know exactly who you are." I hesitate. "Carolina."

She lurches away from me, disgust written all over her face. "Paparazzi, eh? Well, go on."

"Wha—"

Carolina throws her arms out wide, her tank riding up until it rests just beneath her almost non-existent breasts. "Take your photos. Sell them to the rags. Then everyone can gossip about me dancing at a Paris nightclub with my tits out."

I like that she said *tits* in that haughty little voice of hers. She sounds like a princess.

A spoiled, little princess who gets whatever she wants, whenever she wants it.

"I'm not a pap."

She frowns, her slender arms falling back to her sides. "Then who are you?"

"I went to your school." Now she appears even more confused. "Lancaster Prep."

"Oh fuck." She rolls her eyes.

Right before she turns and walks away.

Without hesitation, I chase after her, making my way through the crowd, calling out her name, but she ignores me. She's fast as hell, slipping through the clusters of people filling the nightclub, and at one point, I lose sight of her buttery blonde head.

She appears again seconds later, directly in front of the entrance, pushing her way out of the club.

I speed up, hurrying after her, busting through the door to find her standing on the sidewalk facing the street. A man stands next to her, thin and freakishly tall, and he whips a lighter out of his pocket. That's when I realize she's holding a cigarette and she places it in between her bee-stung lips, leaning toward the guy when he flicks the lighter, the tip of her cig glowing red before she blows out a breath laced with smoke.

Smoking isn't sexy. Not one bit. It's a fucking killer, and it stinks.

But watching Carolina Lancaster puff away on a cigarette makes my dick hard.

She catches sight of me, a look of pure disdain on her face, and she withdraws the cigarette from her lips, murmuring out of the side of her mouth to her skinny friend.

He laughs. Most likely at me.

"You followed me." Her gaze is on me, her tone an accusation.

I approach them slowly, wanting to get near her again, so I can catch another whiff of her scent. Soft and wet like the ocean. Salty and...violent.

Again, like the ocean.

"You ran away before I could explain," I tell her, slipping my hands in my pockets, going for nonchalant. Like she has no effect on me.

"Explain what? I don't care what you have to say."

Damn, this bitch is mean.

I kind of like it.

"You didn't even ask my name." I pause only for a moment, ready to tell her who I am, but she interrupts me.

"Like I said. I. Don't. Care." She sucks on the cig, blowing the smoke directly at me. I grimace and she smiles, pleased with herself.

"I want to know," her friend pipes up. I turn my attention to him, which is fucking difficult, because all I want to do is stare at Carolina all damn night. "What is it?"

"West."

"West. That's a direction, not a name," Carolina mutters, flicking ash on the sidewalk.

"What kind of name is that?" The guy frowns.

I open my mouth, ready to explain, when Carolina interrupts me yet again.

"Probably a family name that goes back generations. Might be short for something. Most likely an old surname that belonged to his mother or his grandmama." She arches a brow.

"Nailed it." I incline my head toward her.

Her friend laughs. She doesn't even crack a smile.

"Well, it's nice to meet you, West. I'm Gideon." He steps forward, offering his hand, and I shake it, smiling at him.

At least he's friendly, though he's not the one I'm interested in.

"I'm bored," she whines, turning to Gideon. "Let's go somewhere else."

"More like you're rude," I tell her, a faint smile still planted on my face.

She glances over her shoulder, her eyes narrowing as she contemplates me, the cigarette still hanging from her lips. She removes it before she says, "Well, look at you, calling me out for my shit."

I shrug. "Someone has to."

"I like him," Gideon says with a nod.

"Thanks."

"I don't," Carolina says, turning to face me fully. It's jarring, how beautiful she is. I try my best not to react as her gaze races over me, taking in every single detail. My skin tingles like she just touched me all over. "The last thing I want to do is spend the evening with an American."

"You're an American," I point out.

"I haven't lived there in almost six years." Her smile is serene, just before she takes another puff on her cigarette. "If I want to fuck a nice, rich American boy, I can go home and find a long list of them."

I'm slightly taken aback by her saying the word *fuck* so easily. She's so dainty and elegant, not what I would consider the usual type to drop f-bombs so casually. "I never said anything about fucking you."

"You want to, though." She sniffs. "I can tell."

Damn it, she's not wrong.

"Let's find another club." She turns to her friend, the suggestion obviously just for him. "I want out of here."

"Okay." Gideon looks beyond her, his gaze locking with mine, a mischievous smile on his face. "West, you should come with us."

"No—" Carolina starts.

"I'd love to." It's my turn to interrupt her, and she doesn't like it. At all.

She viciously takes another drag off the cigarette, exhaling the smoke with a sexy purse of her lips. I watch her unabashedly, drinking in everything about her that I can visibly see as she continues to ignore me, chattering away with Gideon in fluent French.

The melodic sound of her voice puts me in a trance as she complains about me accompanying them on their night out, and my gaze drifts to her tits. The tiny nipples that are still hard, rubbing against the fabric of her tank. She doesn't have much, but it's enough for me to wrap my hand around one and draw that pretty little nipple into my mouth—

"Stupid American."

I glance up at the sound of her voice, ignoring the insult.

"Come on. Let's get out of here," Gideon says to her, waving his hand, his gaze on mine once more. "Are you going with us?"

Pausing, I think about my friends still inside. Last I saw them, Brent was still at the bar hitting on the bartender. TJ and the others were dancing/grinding on girls.

They won't care where I went. They might not even notice I'm gone.

Fuck it. I'll text them later.

Gideon flags down a cab—why not take an Uber?—and next thing I know, I'm crammed in the back seat of a tiny car, with Carolina in the middle of us. She's pressed so close to me, it's as if I can feel every single inch of her.

Electricity sparks the moment our skin makes contact and she studies me, the cigarette long gone, a mint in her mouth. Between her lips.

On her tongue.

"You wear the uniform of every American teenage boy who comes to Europe for the summer," she accuses me. "Trying to fit in when you do nothing but stand out."

I glance down at my khaki shorts and white button-up shirt. It's untucked, with the sleeves rolled up, and I recall how every single one of my friends is wearing a similar outfit. Some of them are even wearing a hat on backwards.

"Brooks Brothers shirt. Ralph Lauren shorts," she continues, her gaze landing on my lap. My crotch.

"Loafers on your feet." Her voice is tinged with amusement when her gaze meets mine once more. "I can't tell any of you apart."

"You sound like a snobby European."

She shrugs one bare, smooth shoulder, and it rubs against my arm. Sparks fly due to the friction. "I am one."

"You're American."

"As you seem to love to remind me. But like I said, I don't live there anymore. I don't like it." She leans her head toward mine and I inhale as discreetly as I can, taking another hit of her intoxicating scent. "And I normally don't like boys such as you."

"Then why am I sitting with you in a cab?"

Carolina jerks her thumb in Gideon's direction. "It's his fault."

I lean forward, so I can make eye contact with him. "Hey, man. I owe you one."

"I'll collect too," he says with a laugh, going silent when she glances over her shoulder, sending him a look. "What's your problem tonight?" he asks her.

She says nothing, turning so she's facing forward once again, and I unabashedly stare at her profile. Her mouth is formed in a perpetual pout and she works her jaw, her lips parted, her gaze sliding to mine to find I'm already watching her.

The taxi speeds down the road, taking us to another nightclub, and we continue to stare at each other. Gideon is tapping away on his phone, the screen illuminating his sharply-angled face with a silver glow, the only other light coming from outside.

"You're rude," she barely whispers, her voice hardly making any sound.

"You're fucking beautiful," I whisper back, shocking myself. I don't tell girls they're beautiful, especially ones who so obviously know it. I don't need to feed their egos. I prefer they feed mine.

Shitty but true.

Her eyes widen the slightest bit, but that's her only outward reaction. The mask drops into place just as fast, her gaze narrowing, her teeth sinking into her lower lip, like she's thinking about feasting on me. "You're a flirt."

"So are you."

She laughs. "If you think me being mean to you is flirting...then you have problems."

"Yeah." I lean in closer, invading her space. "I do."

My gaze fixes on her mouth, the way she plays with the mint. Swirling it around, teasing it with her pink tongue. I stifle the groan that wants to escape, readjusting myself. Wishing I could get away from her, yet also dying to haul her into my arms.

"Would you care for a mint?" she asks after I stare at her—we stare at each other—for about a million beats too long.

"Yeah." My voice is gravelly, like I just woke up, and I swear I saw something flash in her eyes.

"West." She shakes her head, her lips curling up in the faintest smile. "Such a silly name."

"You should hear my actual name." It's really not that strange. I'm just playing it up.

"I don't want to know," she whispers. Her hand rests on my chest, gently pushing me away before I can tell her what it is.

Frowning, I contemplate her, confused. She's giving me serious whiplash, and fuck, it's torture.

"Come here." She reaches for me, her long, elegant arm sliding up my chest as she tucks her hand around the nape of my neck, pulling me close, her lips brushing mine when she says, "take my mint."

Her hand is a gentle tug, a hint of encouragement, and I dip my head, my mouth hovering above hers. We share the same air, the same fucking breath. I suck in her minty exhale, my forehead pressing against hers. My skin prickles with awareness when I hear the catch in her throat and I lift my chin.

Angling myself just right.

Until my mouth is resting on hers.

Her warm, soft lips part beneath mine, somehow pushing the mint toward me and I lightly suck on her tongue, the mint sliding into my mouth. Every single hair on my body stands on end when I relax my lips, loosening my hold on her tongue. She laps at my top lip like a cat, right in the dead center. The flicker of her wet tongue, the sharp sting of her teeth upon my lower lip making me hiss.

Slowly I pull away, the mint resting on my tongue, my entire mouth tingling, but not because of the winter-fresh flavor flooding my mouth.

No, she's responsible for that feeling. Swear to God I'm shaking, and I note the tremble in her body too. She's watching me with wide blue eyes, her chest rising and falling rapidly.

I offer her a smile, showing that the mint is clenched between my teeth, and she laughs.

"Fine," she says, as haughty as a queen. "You can dance with me."

"What, like it's an honor?"

"One of the highest." Gideon leans over, getting in on our conversation. "She usually dances alone at the clubs."

"It's true." She nods her confirmation.

The air is electric in the cab, and by the time we're slipping out of it, I don't hesitate to reach for her hand, tangling my fingers with hers. She doesn't pull out of my grip, the both of us falling into step behind Gideon. He doesn't say a word until we're in front of the doorman, and Gideon points at Carolina, letting him know her last name.

Apparently, if it's Lancaster, that can open a lot of doors. I don't bother mentioning my last name. It opens a lot of doors too, especially in France.

But she doesn't know that.

Within minutes, we're inside the giant club, Gideon getting us drinks at the bar while Carolina leads me onto the dance floor. This place is somehow even more crowded than the club we left. The air is hotter. Heavier. The music louder, the bass thumping in my body, rattling my bones. When she turns to face me, she begins to dance to the beat, her hips swaying, her arms above her head, while I stand there like an idiot and just watch her as if I'm hypnotized.

"You don't dance?" she shouts at me.

I shake my head, unable to speak. Too captivated with the way she moves her body. The clothes she's wearing don't cover much, and my imagination kicks into overdrive, envisioning her naked.

Spread out for me on my bed like an offering.

Her smile is wicked. Like she knows what she's doing to me. What I'm thinking. "That's a shame. What if you have rhythm?"

"I don't."

She places her hands on my chest, dragging them down. Slowly. Her fingers skim across my stomach, making the muscles tighten and clench beneath her touch. "I bet you do where it counts."

My dick stands at attention at her words, at the suggestion in them.

"You're very fit," she observes, her gaze full of amusement.

"I'm an athlete."

She rolls her eyes. "Of course, you are. Lacrosse?"

I make a dismissive noise. "Track."

Her brows lift. "You throw things? Jump over things?"

"I run." I give in to my need and rest my hand on the spot where her waist dips in, pulling her closer. "I'm fast."

Her hands are still on my stomach, pressing. Burning. "Is that a good trait to have, or a bad one?"

"Depends on how you look at it."

Someone bumps into Carolina from behind, sending her nearly falling into me, and I grab hold of her firmly, my hands on her hips, yanking her closer.

"I don't like fast boys." She rises up on tiptoe when the music gets louder, her mouth right at my ear so I can hear her. "I usually like to take things nice and slow."

I run my right hand over her ass and she takes a step away from me, shaking her head. My hands fall away from her. "Too fast, American."

I stare at her, watching as she digs into the tiny pocket of her even tinier shorts and whips out a crumpled cigarette. "Do you have a light?"

"No."

Without a word, she abandons me once again on the dance floor.

A frustrated growl leaves me as I chase after her, keeping track of her bright blonde head so I don't lose her. Until we're both at the crowded bar, where she's standing next to a dark-haired guy dressed all in black with a thin mustache, a devilish smile on his face as he offers her a light. She leans in close, the flame igniting the tip of her cigarette, and with a laugh she pulls away, shaking her head when he says something to her.

Jealousy consumes me and I march over to where she stands, grabbing the crook of her arm and jerking her around to face me.

"What did he say to you?"

Her smile is small, a gleam in her eyes as she yells, "He wants to take me away somewhere and fuck me."

White hot fury floods my veins. "What did you tell him?"

"I said I came with someone." She pats my chest, like I'm a pet. "Calm down. I won't fuck him."

The fury is still there but not as strong. "Good to know."

"I don't like it when people touch me. Men." She contemplates me for a moment, her blue eyes narrowed, her upper lip curled in an almost-snarl. "They say I'm cold."

"Who?"

"The boys who want to touch me."

"You let me touch you." When she doesn't say anything, I continue, "In the cab. When you gave me the mint."

Her lips curl in a faint smile. "That was different."

"How?"

She shrugs. "I don't know. There's something about you that's approachable. Like a cuddly teddy bear."

I can't help it, I laugh. "No one would *ever* describe me in that way."

"Brooding, scary American boy? I'm sure you ruled the school, am I right? I know the type. You're probably just like my brother." She shakes her head, as if her older brother is a complete disappointment.

Her brother is a fucking legend. Whit Lancaster is an insufferable asshole, who ran Lancaster Prep with an iron fist back in the day when he attended the school. The heir to the oldest Lancaster's empire, Whit is wealthy beyond measure and gives zero fucks about anyone else but his wife and child.

I *aspire* to be as ruthless as Whit, and lucky me, no Lancasters have attended Lancaster Prep since I was a sophomore, when Crew Lancaster graduated. They're always the ones who are automatically in charge. The ones everyone follows with undying loyalty. And now I'm prepared to have that kind of allegiance my senior year.

"I hear your brother is a complete prick."

She laughs and the sound nearly sends me to my knees. "He is. He's terrible." She hesitates. "I get the feeling that you're terrible too."

I shift closer to her, bending my head so my mouth is close to her ear yet again. "Wouldn't you like to know."

Carolina doesn't even hesitate.

"I would very much like to know." She grounds out her fresh cigarette in the ashtray on the bar before taking a step closer. Her hand sneaks beneath my shirt so fast, I suck in a breath when her cool fingers land on my stomach. "Want to be my secret?"

Before I can answer, she's curling her fingers around the waistband of my khakis, tugging me forward. I go willingly, her hand falling away as she turns and heads toward the farthest side of the club. I follow her, my heart racing, my skin still tingling from where she touched me. Her knuckles brushed my abdomen when she curled her fist around my waistband, leaving me with a throbbing hard-on.

Her words didn't help either.

Want to be my secret?

Fuck yeah, I do.

But I'm no one's secret. More like they're always my secret.

Not this girl. This girl has me chasing her. Willingly.

She doesn't stop moving until we're in a darkened hallway, the music nothing but a dull throb. A blast of arctic air conditioning brushes my sweat-covered skin, offering instant relief, and when she turns to face me, my gaze automatically drops to her chest.

"You know how to kiss, American boy?"

"I know how to do a lot of things," I tell her. There have been plenty of girls, but nothing too serious. I've had sex. I can make a girl come easily with my fingers.

With Carolina Lancaster, I can imagine us getting pretty damn creative.

"Then show me what you can do." She plasters herself against the wall, her arms slightly spread, palms flat, legs braced.

Slowly, I approach her, remembering what she said. How she doesn't want to go too fast. How she doesn't like to be touched.

The longer I take, the quicker her chest rises and falls. Tempting me. I want to touch her so fucking bad. But will she just shove me away?

Taking my chances, I lightly place my hand on her hip, the sharp edge of bone startling. She's thin. And from the looks of it, nothing but muscle.

I'd guess she works out more than I do.

An impatient noise leaves her, making me smile, and when my gaze meets hers, I find her glaring at me, her expression murderous. Like she wants to hold a knife to my throat and watch me slowly bleed out.

Leaning in, I pause only when my mouth hovers directly above hers, my tongue darting out for the quickest lick. She leans forward with parted lips, as if seeking more from me, and I smile as I tilt my head, retreating.

"You're mean," she whispers.

"So are you," I remind her, using every ounce of self-restraint I've got to keep still. I squeeze her hip, my touch gentle. "If I move too fast, will you run?"

She nods, lifting her chin, her lids lowering, gaze focused on my mouth. "Yes."

"What if I move slow?" I slide my hand upward along her side. Over the dip of her waist, along her ribs. "Will you run then?"

"I always run," she admits, sounding breathless.

I focus my gaze on her chest, watching it rise and fall rapidly. My fingers tease the hem of her cropped tank, slipping just my fingertips beneath the thin fabric and brushing the underside of her tits. She sucks in a sharp breath and I lift my gaze to hers. "Too fast?"

Carolina shakes her head. "What are you doing?"

"I want to see you." I slip my fingers farther up, over the gentle curve of her breast, my thumb teasing her hard nipple. "Feel you."

She glances around, as if she's afraid we'll get caught. "Someone could spot us back here."

"Let them." With only two fingers, I tug the fabric up, exposing her to my hungry gaze. Her nipples are tiny and pink, and my mouth waters. "Fuck, you're gorgeous."

"Stop." She brushes my hand away, and I step back, the fabric falling back into place, covering her. She's visibly trembling. "You're naughty."

I can't help but chuckle. "I think you like it."

"Are you always so forward?"

"No," I say truthfully, letting the word sink in before I say, "Let's get out of here."

Her frown is so deep, a little crease forms between her eyebrows. "What do you mean, let's get out of here?"

"I mean, I want to leave this place." I crowd her once again, resting my hands on her waist, my fingers burning into her cool, smooth skin. "Take me somewhere that's special to you, fake Parisian girl."

Carolina tilts her head back, her gaze assessing. "You're very bold, you know."

"I could say the same about you." I streak my thumb beneath the cropped hem of her tank yet again, like a dare.

I'm pushing her limits, but she still doesn't run, and I take that as a good sign.

Her eyes darken to the color of the Italian coastal waters—the Sardinia is the deepest, darkest blue I've ever seen, and it's the same exact shade as Carolina Lancaster's eyes, swear to God. "You're also a tease."

"Again, so are you."

The music stops, shifting into a slower tune, and she pushes away from the wall, slipping away from me, glancing over her shoulder as she keeps walking.

"Come on," she calls, and without hesitation, I fall into step behind her.

Pretty sure I'd follow her anywhere.